PRAISE FOR THE NOVELS OF CLAIRE HARRISON

*A MOTHER'S SONG**

"[A] vivid portrait of real life—with all its pain, complexity and banality . . . Expertly captures the fossilized compromises, savage silences, familiar comforts and chilling distances that are part of any long-term relationship . . . Rings with authenticity."

—*Ottawa Citizen*

"This poignant novel is a vivid portrait . . . a sharply observed picture of a very special mother-daughter relationship."   —*Artnews*

*AVAILABLE FROM POCKET BOOKS

SOMEBODY'S BABY

"A down-to-earth story . . . firmly rooted in reality— the reality that comes *after* romance. [Harrison's writing has] warmth and wit."   —*Toronto Globe & Mail*

"The beauty of this novel is the frighteningly brutal honesty with which the author writes. . . . A well-rounded look at a multi-leveled problem . . . This is a daring novel of our times."   —*West Coast Review of Books*

"Sensitively offering pro-choice and pro-life views . . . Harrison also probes the strengths and weaknesses of love within marriage."   —*Publishers Weekly*

"The author's portrayal of parental frustration is vivid and maddening. *Somebody's Baby* succeeds beautifully as an evenhanded discussion of the abortion issue. It is the drama of *Roe* v. *Wade* played out on a family stage."   —*The New York Times Book Review*

Books by Claire Harrison

In a Mother's Heart
A Mother's Song

Published by POCKET BOOKS

In a Mother's Heart

CLAIRE HARRISON

POCKET BOOKS

New York   London   Toronto   Sydney   Tokyo   Singapore

This book is a work of fiction. Names, characters, places and incidents are products of the author's imagination or are used fictitiously. Any resemblance to actual events or locales or persons, living or dead, is entirely coincidental.

An *Original* Publication of POCKET BOOKS

POCKET BOOKS, a division of Simon & Schuster Inc.
1230 Avenue of the Americas, New York, NY 10020

Copyright © 1995 by Claire Harrison

All rights reserved, including the right to reproduce
this book or portions thereof in any form whatsoever.
For information address Pocket Books, 1230 Avenue
of the Americas, New York, NY 10020

ISBN: 0-671-75898-5

First Pocket Books printing May 1995

10 9 8 7 6 5 4 3 2 1

POCKET and colophon are registered trademarks of
Simon & Schuster Inc.

Cover design by Cathy Saksa

Printed in the U.S.A.

To my friends
whose lives have so enriched mine

PROLOGUE

T HE LAKE IS A DARK, GRAY-GREEN BLANKET, CONCEALING WHAT lies beneath. Items have dropped off boats and disappeared. Secrets spoken by lovers have fallen to its surface and sunk without trace. In the winter of 1932, a child broke through the ice while trying to cross to the end of the lake on a dare, and his body was never recovered. The townspeople say that the lake is almost sixty feet deep in some spots. One year scuba divers went down and reported that the bottom is shaped like an upside-down hat with a sloping brim that drops off precipitously to the center.

The lake has no knowledge of what it hides and what it reveals. The nature of water is simply to seek its own level. During spring the lake rises, the shores narrow, and the river that bounds the town of Cassandra swells and runs fast. By August the water has receded, and the shoreline includes what was once stony bottom. Small pools of water caught in rocks get separated from the body of the lake, and minnows swim in ever-decreasing circles as the pools slowly dry up. Throughout the summer swimmers report shifting warm spots as if the lake were being heated by an erratic burner.

The lake cools in the fall, and fishermen say the mist in the early morning is so thick they can't see where their lines

3

enter the water. In 1963, a child won a literary prize in a Syracuse newspaper for a story about a monster fish that lived in the depths of the lake and exhaled white smoke all night to confuse any fisherman who was trying to find where it was sleeping. The published version of the story was framed and still hangs near the mayor's office at the town hall. The original got lost when the child's family left Cassandra.

The lake has its history, but the townspeople only remark on it now and then. Eventually the items, secrets, and bodies the lake conceals disappear not only from sight but also from memory, for the nature of the townspeople is to forget and get on with their busy lives.

PART I

FRIENDS

Chapter
1

THE REGISTERED LETTER, WHICH I HAVE TO SIGN FOR, ARRIVES in a creamy vellum envelope with her name and address printed in royal blue script across the back flap. *Marla Hudson*. I run my fingers over the letters, feeling the raised, engraved curves and simultaneously the stir of old emotions as if they too were raised and engraved on my psyche.

"Is that the Marla Hudson who wrote all those books?" Caroline asks.

"Yes," I say.

"And she lives—where?" She looks at the back flap. "Malibu. Wow, she must be rich and stuff."

"I guess so."

"That's what I want to be," Caroline says. "A writer."

"A novelist?"

"A journalist. You know, like have assignments around the world and travel everywhere."

"That would be exciting," I say.

"I know," she says. "I can't wait."

Caroline Deacon, who works part-time as a postal clerk after school and on Saturdays, is in the same class as my son, Joel, and is the oldest daughter of a former boyfriend of mine. She has turned from a cute little girl into the prettiest teenager in town, with the kind of infectious smile that makes you want to smile back. She resembles Brian, who took me to the senior prom. In those days, he was tall, slender, red-haired, and had an appealing shyness. But that Brian doesn't exist anymore. He got heavy, his hair dulled and retreated, and over the years, his shy charm disappeared and he turned into one of those grinning, jovial backslappers. Caroline, it seems to me, is the result of the best of Brian as he was at seventeen and some mysterious gene pool, since she looks nothing like her mother, Molly, who is short and dark. In the last year, I've noticed that she's becoming beautiful in a dazzling way. Light seems to shimmer off the coppery glint in her hair, the smooth, creamy skin and the big, turquoise eyes. I used to think Joel had a crush on her, but she started going out with Benjamin Phillips, my friend Frances's son, and that seemed to end that.

"Marla Hudson grew up here," I say. "We went to high school together."

"Here?" Caroline says. "I didn't know that. That's amazing."

I turn the envelope over and study the handwriting on the front. Marla used to make her letters so round they were the shape of bubbles. Now her handwriting is slanted and angular. She uses a fountain pen with a wide tip so that the letters are formed of broad strokes and sharply curved points. It's the same type of pen she wrote with when she autographed my copy of her first novel. *Friends forever, Love, Marla.* She sent me this copy in the mail, and I thought about that autograph for months. I hadn't seen Marla for seven years then, although I received a Christmas card every year. Also, the last time we'd been together she was called Martha—Martha Hudson, who was named after her grandmother and who decided in our senior year that she sounded like a scullery maid in a Jane Austen novel and would change her name just as soon as she was of legal age to do so.

The trouble was that while I knew everything about Martha—the ferocity of her dreams, the depths of her fears, all the intense loves and hates—I knew nothing about Marla beyond the surface details of her life—the two husbands, the daughter, the success of her novels, the house in California. "Visit anytime," she wrote each Christmas. "Just drop me a note and I'll pick you up at the airport." But, of course, a trip like that wasn't practical—not with graduating from university and getting married right away, buying a house within the year and taking on a mortgage, Joel's birth, my job and Dan's work, the car that needed to be bought when Dan's clunker died, the new roof, the cost of landscaping and the cedar deck, the years flowing by so quickly it hardly seems possible I'm now forty-three years old and haven't seen Marla for twenty-five years.

"We were best friends," I say to Caroline, and remember how Marla had been my bulwark against the outside world, surrounding me with a wall of secrets shared, vulnerabilities exchanged, sensitivities protected, and loyalty given without question.

"Wow, and now she's rich and famous." Caroline leans forward. "I'd love to be in *People* magazine or on *Oprah*. That would be fantastic."

When I see one of those talk shows, I'm horrified by the eagerness of people to expose the rawness of their lives as if they were so many sides of beef. "Not me," I say. "I'm happy right here."

Here is the town of Cassandra, New York, population 8,927, named after a daughter of Priam and Hecuba of Troy, who tricked Apollo and was tricked in turn. She promised to fulfill his passion if he gave her the gift of prophecy, but when he did so she refused him. Poor, naive Cassandra thought she could defy the gods. But Apollo wet her lips with his tongue, a curse that ensured no one would ever believe what she said. "No! Don't bring it in!" she cried about the wooden horse that stood outside the gates of Troy. "There are Greeks inside, armed with spears!" But the Trojans didn't listen, because they'd decided she was insane. Of course, most of the inhabitants of Cassandra, N.Y., don't know or care about the long-dead-if-she-ever-existed Trojan princess. They're farmers and businesspeople with a lot of other things on their minds. Besides, most of our civic pride rests on our location. We're south of Syracuse, east of Rochester, west of Albany, and north of the Pennsylvania state line. When you enter Cassandra on Route 240 from the south or north, you'll find a sign that says "Welcome to Cassandra, the Navel of Central New York."

"How are the folks?" I say as I take a pen out of my purse.

"Mom and Dad just had their twentieth anniversary."

"I hope they lived it up."

"Well, they went out to dinner."

"That's nice," I say.

"I guess so."

I hear the small note of doubt in her voice. "But it's not exactly your idea of living it up."

"I guess it's because I'm a little younger."

I'm amused by her tactfulness. "Just a little," I tease her.

She laughs and wrinkles her nose, and I think how nice it would've been if Joel had tried a little harder. "And it's kind of dead here, too," she says, "if you know what I mean."

I follow her glance out the glass window of the post office to the street. If you're looking for action, there isn't much to see on this corner other than Ashley's Drugs, the Exxon station, and Grieber's Deli. There's the occasional shopper, a car pulling in beside a gas pump, a couple of kids racing down the street. If you're not looking for action, however, you might notice items of beauty or interest like the huge old elm with its intricate whorls and gnarls that stands behind the gas station, or the prints Edgar Ashley, the pharmacist, put in his store window. Edgar told me several months ago he would like to build a small gallery onto the side of the drugstore, but he wasn't sure Cassandra was ready for it.

"It's deplorable," he said, fussing with his pale brown mustache, which is as small and thin as he is. "This town's a barren wasteland when it comes to art."

Edgar often talks this way to me. He believes that, because of my position as librarian and presumably keeper of the literary flame, I am au courant with art trends and desirous, as he is, of making Cassandra a more literate and cultural town.

"You'd have to get people interested first," I said.

"Small scale," he said. "That's how I'm going to start."

In keeping with the spirit of the beauty care business, he chose three prints of women in the process of bathing and placed them next to displays of Lancôme skin creams, Max Factor eye shadow, and Bonne Bell lipsticks. His choices ranged from the classic—a nude of the Romantic period scrubbing the back of her neck while squatting over a tub—to the abstract—lines suggesting eyes, curves, and a pool of water. In between was a more graphic painting of a thin woman staring out brazenly at the watcher. Her breasts were perky, the nipples hard, and, although she held a cloth in front of her genitals, her bright red pubic hair peeked out on either side. This middle print caused an excited flurry of attacks and counterattacks when our leading conservative light, Arlene McPherson, brought it to the attention of the town council, arguing that the sight of this bare woman, however gracefully sketched, would upset the youth of Cassandra.

Edgar buzzed angrily, defending the stature of the painter and the importance of exposing youth to art. "And that painting's in a museum in Paris, if you don't mind," he would say to anyone who came into the store.

Rumor had it that when Arlene heard this, she just snorted and said, "Paris," in a disdainful, belittling way.

At which point, Edgar fussed with his mustache even harder and said to me with despair, "I'm wasting art on yahoos."

"There are a number of us staunchly behind you," I said.

He perked up. "How many?"

"The Phillipses, the Fellers, the Brenners, Margaret Lontis, Jerry Hearndon," I paused, searching for more names. "The Silvers."

His face fell. "It's hopeless," he said. "Doomed."

Art inspired art. Several local artists, unidentified, used the glass window over the prints as canvases. They drew mustaches on Edgar's nudes, and one daringly extended the red pubic hairs into long tendrils. Art also inspired literature. Letters pro and con flew into our weekly, the *Cassan-*

dra Gazette, and to the town councillors, who finally, in a narrow vote, decided Edgar could keep the Romantic nude and the abstract in his window, but not the lady in the middle. While I couldn't say the issue exactly pitted neighbor against neighbor, it certainly, as I pointed out to Edgar, recharged our cultural batteries.

"You'll be out of here soon," I say to Caroline. "One more year and then it's college."

"It's never going to happen," she says.

"It will," I say.

"My mom says I'm too impatient."

"That year will be gone before you know it."

She heaves a huge sigh, but very little can make Caroline look less beautiful than she is. The extra oxygen only serves to make her skin more luminescent. "I hope so," she says.

"Now, where do I sign for this letter?"

She pulls out the ledger and opens it. "Over here. On the dotted line."

I don't have stationery with my name engraved on rich paper. I buy recycled paper at Edgar's store when he's having a sale. I don't own a fountain pen that makes my signature look like calligraphy. I use whatever ballpoint pen I can find in the kitchen drawer, which isn't often, because such pens have a way of traveling in our house from room to room and disappearing for months at a time. And I haven't changed my name. I just added on a new last name when I got married.

I lean forward and pull the register to me. *Barbara Gardiner Breymann,* I write next to the red X.

"So I've put Miller in charge of that part of programming, because he's good at pulling the team together and pushing things through. More cucumber, hon?"

I assess Dan's handiwork: chopped lettuce and half a cucumber sliced. "It's enough," I say. "Put in some green pepper."

He picks up the pepper and begins slicing. "We've got to get that solved before we can go on to testing, and then Brownlee called me in and said marketing wanted to know when they could start package design and I told him that . . ."

I listen as I peel the potatoes, but the letter from Marla forces me to disengage and step outside of myself. How would this scene look to her? What would she see if she stood in the doorway about to step into my life? I survey my kitchen, which we enlarged and renovated last year, adding a bay window that looks out on the garden, replacing the dark cabinet doors with light formica, and putting down cushioned flooring in a shade of terra-cotta. I survey Dan, busily chopping a green pepper and wearing an apron over his white shirt and suit pants. I could say that he too has been enlarged and renovated, unrecognizable from the boy we graduated from high school with. I survey my life, with its serene round of home, work, and friends, and engage in an imaginary conversation that is half apologetic, half proud. *It's not exciting,* I explain to Marla, *but it's mine.* Then I examine myself, Barbara Breymann, twenty pounds heavier than I was at seventeen, my dark hair tinted to hide the gray that started to come in during my late thirties. She will be thinner, I think, and she was always prettier.

". . . so they're setting up a meeting in San Diego after the fair, which means I'll be gone five days instead of three, but I prefer the face-to-face meetings rather than the never-ending conference calls."

Dan? I say to Marla as I put the peeled potatoes into a pot of water and then onto the stove. *Oh, he's doing very well. And he's happy—that's what counts.* Dan works for LogoDraw, a software company with headquarters in the nearby city of Laurel Grove. Since the time he joined the company in the late seventies as a computer programmer, it has grown tenfold, its success based on a graphics package that is ranked one of the best in the world. Now he's a vice president in charge of research and design, a job that he loves. I don't know precisely what he does, only that he's responsible for each new version of LogoDraw, and that no sooner do they issue one version than he's begun work on the next.

Oh, I know—if someone had told me at seventeen I was

going to marry Dan Breymann, I'd have cracked up entirely.
I give an imaginary little laugh, a pale reflection of the
hilarity that would have had both of us doubled over back
then, and try to look at Dan through the eyes of a woman
who does not love him. He's a tall, big-boned man with
blond hair, thick and straight, and eyes that are pale blue
and wide apart under blond eyebrows. He could have been
handsome, but his features are too coarse, as if he has lived
outdoors all his life and the wind and sun have eroded them.
Dan's family moved into Cassandra when I was in grade
three. He was, from my eight-year-old perspective, an
entirely forgettable little boy except that he was the only one
in our class who had to wear glasses, and he had an
enormous chemistry set that he brought to school one day.
Our paths bumped and intersected for the next ten years. In
grade five, we had to do a project together on China. In
grade eight, I was paired with him by a sadistic teacher
during a dancing class when I was still a head taller than he
was. In high school, he was one of the boys with bad skin
and cowlicks who grew so fast their knees and elbows jutted
out at odd angles and got such good grades in math and
physics we dismissed them as "brains." Dan was in many of
my classes, but he was invisible to me. When I saw him back
then, circa 1962, I looked right through him. My eyes only
registered certain types of boys whose dark good looks and
inaccessibility made my longing for them that much
stronger.

After our high school graduation, I didn't see Dan until
three years later at a Christmas party when he was home
from college. I barely recognized him. Where was the boy
with the black-rimmed glasses and the too-short crew cut?
Who was only interested in obscure scientific facts? Who
had absolutely no cool and less sex appeal? Dan still wore
glasses and loved arcane science, but gone were the pimples,
cowlick, and bumpy elbows. He'd grown several inches
taller and wider, his face had become interesting in a rugged
sort of way, and the Christmas lights gleamed in his silvery
blond hair. Besides, my criteria had expanded since I'd gone

to university. I still liked dark men but no longer yearned after aloofness. At sixteen, I'd only wanted the pleasure of the chase; what came after was too scary to contemplate. Now I wanted the prey: in my mind, my heart, and my bed.

Over the punch bowl, Dan and I talked about university. I was majoring in English, he was studying computer languages. He tried to explain exactly what these were, and while I didn't understand what he was talking about, I found his enthusiasm appealing. We discussed acquaintances: who had gone to what college, who was working, who was married. Then I said how sorry I was about his father, who had died the previous spring, and asked how his mother was doing.

"I mean, she seems to be okay, but it must be hard with your dad not there and everything." I was making a horrible mess of this and took a large swallow of punch to hide my embarrassment.

"She's kind of depressed."

"Oh," I said.

"She gets headaches."

"I didn't know," I said.

"She spends a lot of time in bed."

"Oh, I—"

"It's like I come home and nobody's there."

His lips trembled, and I fell in love. That's how it happens when you're twenty-one years old. You fall, not for the man, but for some small action that seems to epitomize the whole. It doesn't cross your mind that he may never repeat the action again, that it may be an aberration or, even worse, nothing more than a muscular twitch. The tremble that began at the corner of Dan's mouth and traveled across his lower lip—that tiny show of emotion—spoke volumes to me. I wanted to comfort him in my arms, I wanted to suck at that bottom lip, I wanted to make love to him.

When? That night. No, I'm perfectly serious. The backseat of his car. A Beetle, what else? Marla throws back her head and laughs, her deep, loud, and thorough laughter. I remember how she had to stifle that laugh when we slept over at my house or hers. We'd obediently turn off the lights as our parents requested, but then we talked for hours, sotto voce, so we wouldn't wake anyone up. We both smoked, and the only light in the room would be the flare of a match and the red-hot tips of our cigarettes. Under the cover of darkness, we explored every inch of our world: boys, parents, siblings, friends, teachers, dreams, pasts. We talked about subjects that couldn't be discussed in the light of day, speculating intensely on what it felt like to have a penis inside, whether it would really hurt the first time, how long intercourse would take.

Sometimes Marla would get her parents' flashlight, and we'd study the way the beam of light caused shadows to appear in the corner of the room, in the closet, and on ourselves. We'd put it under our chins to appear haunting and diabolical. When we were fifteen, Marla began a game we could play only in the smallest hours of the morning when we were sure everyone else in the house was asleep. She would make-believe the flashlight beam was the spotlight on a runway and that we were fashion models. The game started innocently enough. We draped sheets around ourselves or put on Marla's dresses, although this was difficult for me because Marla was taller and thinner. One of us would focus the flashlight on the other, who would mince along the narrow path between the mattresses we had put on the floor. We usually had our hair up in rollers and looked ridiculous. We often laughed so hard playing this game that we had to bury our heads under pillows. Marla then made the game more exciting by stealing some of her mother's dresses during the day so we could wear them at night. I still remember with great clarity a black cocktail dress of Mrs. Hudson's that left one shoulder bare and covered the other with a puff of tulle decorated with tiny rhinestones. I loved that dress and the silken feel of the taffeta against my skin.

Then, when the fun of illicitly wearing adult clothes paled, Marla changed the rules of the game without telling me. One night, she went into the closet to change while I sat on top of her dresser so I could train the flashlight beam down on her.

Actually, by this time, we had two flashlights so we could have double spots or spots that joined to form a figure eight.

"I'm ready," she whispered.

I flicked on the flashlights and she stepped out of the closet. She was dressed only in scarves tied together to criss-cross over her breasts and hang in folds over her hips. The scarves were gauzy, and I could see her breasts and pubic hair through them.

"Martha!" I said.

"Sssh!"

"Jesus." I was starting to giggle.

"Shut up!"

I quickly flicked off the flashlights and we listened intensely to the silence in the house. Then I turned the flashlights back on, training them on Marla's chest and hips. She pivoted and swiveled, thrust her pelvis forward and arched her back. Laughter bubbled up in my throat and the flashlights trembled in my effort to hold it in. Marla ignored me. Her eyes were closed and her expression intent as if she were listening to some internal music. Then she began to strip, pulling the gauze down from one breast and then the other. Her breasts were fuller than mine and those of most of the girls in our class. In the yellow illumination, the aureoles and nipples were red-brown and as glossy as polished mahogany.

This was 1962. *Playboy* had not yet been published. On television and in the movies, grown-ups slept in twin beds and love scenes never went beyond a kiss. The words *erotica* and *pornography* were not part of my vocabulary, but it didn't matter. As always, Marla's daring revealed new possibilities to me, that slow striptease opening secret doors to dark vistas of sexuality and unexpected powers. Beneath my hilarity, something stirred, something disturbing and intensely pleasurable.

"That's it for the pepper. You want me to put in the tomato?" Dan asked.

"Joel doesn't like tomato that much," I say.

"Where is he, by the way?"

"Baseball practice."

"You think they'll finally let him play?"

I open the oven door and check on the chicken I've been roasting. The hot, rich smell of it fills the kitchen. "He tried so hard to make that team," I say. "He's so proud."

Joel, my son. What can I say beyond those three words? Joel, my seventeen-year-old son, has possession of my heart in a way that Dan does not. That tremble of Dan's lips, that moment of pure vulnerability, never occurred again. Dan is an easygoing man, successful in what he does and content with his life. I love his steadiness, his dry sense of humor and his devotion to me and Joel. I love the way he makes love to me, with full attention to my needs and uncritical of my aging body. But Dan has not made my heart run the full gamut of reactions and clichés. For Joel, my heart has swelled with pride, raced with fear, softened with pity, and ached with pain and love. Not that he is different from any other boy. He crawled, walked, talked, toilet-trained, ran, and biked at the appropriate ages. His grades are average, his interests typical, and lately he's begun to have the standard teenage sulks and minor rebellions. But the thing is—Joel is mine, and his presence is a glow that illuminates my life. That doesn't mean I brag about him. I'm not superstitious, I walk under ladders and ignore black cats that cross my path, but a sixth sense tells me that to brag about Joel might be dangerous.

So I explain to Marla how desperate Joel is to be a sports hero. In the fall, it's football, in the winter, hockey, in the spring, baseball and swimming. He usually makes the teams, but he often sits on the bench or is an alternate. When this happens, when Dan and I go to a game and watch Joel spend most of his time off the field or coming in close to last, my heart feels painful and heavy as if the failure is all mine. Joel keeps right on trying, overcoming each loss with an equanimity of spirit I find awesome.

"I was a little off, Mom," he said at the last swim meet last winter where he was eliminated after the first heat in the 200-yard butterfly.

"I thought you looked great," I said.

"Yeah, well, my kick needs more work."

"Really?"

"It's tricky," he said, and carefully explained to me the problems of coordinating the butterfly arms and the butterfly legs. All the while, he flexed his shoulder muscles, which had started, only recently, to coat his bones. I recognized that he's going to be as big as Dan, but the same slow physical starter. Some of his friends are already as thickly muscled as men and have dark beards shadowing their skin. Joel is lanky and awkward with blond fuzz on his cheeks and above his lip. When he lifts his arms, his ribs corrugate his abdomen and his armpits reveal tiny tufts of pale hair.

"I got a letter from Marla Hudson today," I say to Dan as I take the chicken out of the oven. "She's coming to Cassandra."

"For how long?"

"To live, believe it or not."

Dan raises his eyebrows. "I suppose I'd get tired of Malibu, too. Too much waterfront."

"She says she's exhausted and needs to get back to her roots."

"The town's changed." Dan tosses the salad. "She won't recognize it."

"I wonder if she'll recognize me," I say slowly.

Dan pulls me into the circle of his arm. "You don't look a day over eighteen."

"Oh, right," I say.

"Not to me you don't."

"That's why I married you," I say.

"For my gallantry."

"For your blindness."

We are smiling at each other when the front door bangs open and there's the thud of baseball equipment hitting the floor.

"I'm home," Joel says as he appears in the kitchen doorway. "Don't everyone applaud at once."

Lately I've noticed that, as he gets older, Joel resembles

Dan more and more. He has my mouth, softer and fuller, and my nose, which is narrower, but the rest of his face is pure Breymann: blond, blue-eyed, and wide-browed.

"How was practice?" Dan asks.

"Great." Joel investigates the pots on the stove, taking off the lids and peering inside. "We're going to beat the shit—oh, sorry, Mom—out of Laurel Grove. Are you going to mash the potatoes?"

"While you set the table," I say. "And school?"

"The math test was real hard." He takes knives and forks out of the drawer and brings them over to the table where the letter from Marla is sitting. He picks it up. "Is this from that writer friend of yours?"

"She's moving here."

"Cool. You'll have someone to talk to."

"Joel," I say, protesting. "I have lots of people to talk to."

"I just meant you'd have somebody to talk to about the old days," Joel says, going over to the cupboard that holds the plates and glasses.

"I can talk to your father about the *old* days. He's ancient, too. Right, Dan?"

"Decrepit," Dan says.

"Girls talk different," Joel says.

"Really? How?" I ask. I know Joel has a healthy interest in sex; I've found *Playboy* and *Penthouse* magazines beneath his bed. But he doesn't seem to be interested in actual and accessible girls. His friends are a group of boys whose activities keep them constantly on the move. They play tennis, go swimming, watch movies, and hang out at one another's houses where they eat and watch television. I imagine that girls are a main topic of conversation, but not when I'm around. When they're at our house, they talk sports, play Ping-Pong, joke around, and ask me politely if they can use the phone to call their mothers.

"Girls are always laughing and telling secrets," Joel says.

"That's the way your mother was," Dan says as he begins to carve the chicken. "She and Martha Hudson used to stand in front of their lockers whispering as I walked by."

"Not about you," I say.

"I knew that," Dan says. "I was beneath your notice."

Joel loves it when we talk about our high school experiences. "Dad was a nerd, wasn't he, Mom?" he asks with a grin.

"One of the worst," I say. The truth was that Dan never agonized about his place in the high school pecking order. He was too distracted by his science projects and tinkering with machinery to care. My theory is that this innocence is why Dan's such a happy man today. He emerged from adolescence with few shadows and no demons.

"Your mother and Martha Hudson were popular," Dan says.

"Martha was. I wasn't."

"I worshiped your mother from afar," Dan says to Joel.

"He did not," I say. "He wasn't interested in me at all. He took Mary Alice Dobson to the senior prom."

Dan shakes a drumstick at me. "Mary Alice lived next door to me. My mother made me take her."

"Who'd you go with, Mom?"

"Brian Deacon."

"Mr. Deacon? Who owns the hardware store? You went out with *him?*"

"That's right."

"You mean Mr. Deacon could've been my father?" Joel says. "Wow, that's weird."

The three of us are smiling, and the kitchen is redolent with the scents of dinner. *So this is it,* I say to Marla. *The story of my life—my husband, my son, my home, my friends, my work, and the accumulation of many small events and tiny moments over twenty-odd years.* I add that there've been ups and down—the deaths of parents, my two miscarriages, the time Joel fell down the back steps and needed five stitches in his leg—but these are ordinary life events experienced by many others, and we've weathered them to the best of our abilities. I realize too that our lives are blessed by the luck of our births and genes. We are middle-class and untouched by poverty, Anglo-Saxon and untouched by racism, and Presbyterian, untouched by religious discrimination. We are protected by our skins, our education, our health, and our income. Around us the world swells and bellows with tumult and change, but we exist like a pond hidden by a copse of thickly leaved trees, our surface smooth and still, rippled only now and then by the occasional breeze.

This, I say to Marla, *is not the stuff of fiction.*

Chapter 2

MARLA'S INABILITY TO APPRECIATE THE FOOD HAS NOTHING TO do with the quality of the restaurant. Casper's is beautifully decorated in shades of taupe and rose, the pale pink linen is heavy and monogrammed with large *C*s, the food and service are excellent and the prices outrageous—in short, the ideal restaurant for the senior editor of a major publishing house to take one of his best-selling authors to lunch. Marla knows—she has spies—that Harold Sibley has a list of five restaurants, maintained by his executive assistant; the names begin with Casper's and descend in order of importance to the Thai House. Where Harold entertains his authors depends entirely on their commercial success. He takes new, about-to-be-published writers and published authors with limited profit potential to the Thai House. "The best ethnic food in New York," he tells them with that bubbly enthusiasm of which only Harold is capable. Marla imagines those unwitting, anxious writers hanging on Harold's every word, unable to appreciate the food because they can taste only the thin, distant flavor of success. She imagines Harold beaming paternally on them, his round face split by that broad, toothy smile. How benign Harold appears! How friendly! How understanding!

Marla was deceived once, but no longer. Behind those bushy, graying eyebrows and seemingly tender, brown eyes is a shark swimming through the waters of New York publishing. She knows—those helpful spies again—that literature interests him little, he's risen through the ranks by crushing weaker opponents, and he'd think nothing of taking a failing author to a lesser restaurant to let her know her sales were down. Marla takes heart from being in Casper's, but she senses from his effusive compliments that Harold has made the choice reluctantly.

"My dear," he says, "you look wonderful. Absolutely wonderful."

Lies, all lies. She looks terrible, the mirror doesn't lie. *Mirror, mirror, on the wall, who's the best-selling author of them all?* Not Marla Hudson, who is too sallow and too drawn, and whose latest book teetered and fell off the edge of the *New York Times* Best Sellers list.

"Thanks, Harold," she says. "And you've lost some weight."

"You think so?" Harold gives his midriff a delighted pat. He's a man prone to vanity and insecurity, a difficult combination. He has nervous, self-stroking mannerisms: caressing his tie, fingering his mustache, patting the hair over his ears where the dark curls are turning silver. "I've joined a new club," he says. "I swim every afternoon."

"And how is Dolores?" Marla asks. Dolores is Harold's wife.

"Exhausted. Of course, she ran herself ragged trying to put everything in place. Photographers, caterers, florists, dressmakers, hairdressers—" Harold waves a hand in the air to indicate the cast of thousands that attended his daughter's wedding.

"The full catastrophe," Marla says with a smile.

"Now, let's talk about you. I want to hear everything. About California, Didi, the move, your next book."

Marla picks at her salad: radicchio, walnuts, apples, julienned carrots, and parsnips. "I sold the house," she says.

"Oh." It's a groan more than a word. "That wonderful house."

Her Malibu house was designed so that every room faced the ocean. She loved that house: the skylights that illuminated every nook and cranny, the interesting angles of the rooms, the pale oak staircase that curved to the first floor in a gracious sweep, the expanse of sandy white carpet that seemed to merge with the beach so that, on certain days, the inside and outside were one and the same. When did her delight in the house start to sour? When David left? When the troubles with Didi began? When she felt her writing weaken and soften like a fighter out of practice? There was no drawing the exact line between her affinity for the house, her sense of it as a living, connected entity, and the day she realized it held nothing for her, as if the air in it were dead, the walls no longer breathed, and the view from the windows was artificial, a painting of an ocean by a bad artist with a brush full of clichés. The water was too green, the whitecaps too pointed, the sunsets too orange.

"That house inspired some of your best writing," Harold says.

"Did it?" Marla takes a sip of her wine.

"Some of those passages from *Fly the Night Away* and *Silver Crescents* seemed to come from a unity you felt with that house." When she doesn't respond, pragmatism overwhelms his small supply of sentimentality. "Well," he continues, "I'm sure you got a good price."

The waiter stops by their table and fills up the wine glasses. "Everything all right, Mr. Sibley?" he asks.

"Delicious," Harold says, and as the waiter walks away, he leans forward and whispers, "He's writing a collection of short stories."

"The waiter?" Marla glances at the waiter's profile as he leans over another table of diners. He's clean-cut with dirty-blond hair and several studs in his ear.

"We signed him last month," Harold says. "The collection isn't finished, but it shows a lot of promise. Richard Lowe," he names an associate editor, "is working with him."

"Let me guess," Marla says. "Stories about waiters?"

"And very gay," Harold says. "AIDS, dying, the whole

safe-sex shtick, which is very in right now. Those AIDS books move like hotcakes even in Boise or Peoria. Maybe death is a universal thing, that's what some of our marketing people think, but you know what I think those sales are? Gloating. All those women readers having their revenge for the way faggots have dominated the fashion industry and designed clothes most women can't wear."

Marla takes a sip of her wine. "That's an interesting theory, Harold."

"Now, tell me. How's Didi?"

"She's fine." Marla lies about Didi with surprising facility, although she's always found it easier to lie than to tell the truth. As a small child, she recognized that the truth was often flat and drab. Lies, on the other hand, formed interesting shapes on her tongue and developed textures, colors, and tastes.

("Did you brush your teeth, Marla?"

"Yes": a pale mauve lozenge.

"Have you done your homework?"

"Yes": a minty, crunchy ball.

"What did you get on that math test?"

"Ninety-one": the cool, liquid sweetness of lime sherbet.)

Harold sips his wine. "Didi's such a lovely girl," he says. "How old is she now?"

"Seventeen."

"Is she looking forward to moving?"

"No, she's staying in California with friends. She didn't want to leave her school. You know how kids are at that age. And she has a job working as a camp counselor this summer—a place in the Rockies."

"But she'll visit."

"Of course," Marla says. "Frequently."

And this is the only part that's true, if not in the sense that Harold understands it. Didi is a frequent visitor, unwanted but persistent, arriving when Marla's guard is down—when she's writing, in the middle of conversations with friends, on the highway in the midst of heavy traffic, and at that most vulnerable moment, when sleep is ending and wakefulness begins. How often has Marla woken to discover that Didi has arrived, complete, whole, and angry? How often have those early morning visits turned immediately into full-blown battles, the voices raging through her skull, her head rocking with the sounds, the pain clawing at her temples? And how often has she forced herself out of bed and into a shower, because the only way she can seem to get away from the voices, the screaming, and the heavy burden of loss, is to drown them in the hottest water she can take without burning?

If Marla looks at Didi's life from conception to her seventeenth birthday, she sees a tiny, sweet bud, opening to a tiny, sweet flower that grew in unpredictable, difficult ways. Long and leggy as if seeking a different sun. Unruly with foliage that could not be trimmed. Spreading until it could not even be contained. What had begun with a few broken curfews when Didi was thirteen turned into overnight disappearances that had Marla frantically calling the police. Didi's passing marks slumped into failures no matter how many teachers Marla talked to or how many tutors she hired. Didi gave up neighborhood and school friends and hung out with kids she met in shopping malls and convenience stores. It was no surprise to Marla when Didi dropped out of school, screamed that she couldn't stand having Marla on her case anymore, and insisted she live on her own.

Although she's not a gardener—in fact she's hired gardeners to keep the grounds at the house in Malibu—Marla understands that delicate flowers need proper care, good soil, and a hospitable environment. She knows that her three-year marriage to Sean, a would-be actor, was a time of aridity when her own thirst for love was never quenched. Sean was so self-centered that mirrors reflected back only his image even if she was standing beside him. Didi was two when they divorced and already rebellious, a toddler who would not accept the word no. Three years later she married David, a lawyer with such an air of competence she believed he could take the pieces of her life and put them neatly back together. She didn't foresee that the hot winds of passion could change so quickly or how frigid such competence could be. David didn't like the way she managed her business, her agent, or her publisher. He objected to the way she handled Didi. Cold winds blew through that marriage, chilling her to the very bone. Didi's rebellious streak widened. She had behavior problems at school, at camp, and with friends. By the time Marla separated from David, Didi was thirteen and looked eighteen. She was tall, with Marla's dark, lustrous hair and Sean's beautiful bone structure; a broad brow, high cheekbones, and a small square chin with a cleft, and she was into sex, drugs, and full-scale defiance.

Marla tried—how she struggled and cried and argued—but nothing worked, not the beautifully decorated bedroom and lovely clothes, not the expensive riding, ballet, and art lessons, not the elaborate birthday parties, not the world-renowned child psychiatrist and prestigious family counselor. It was as if the soil Didi had grown in contained an imbalance that couldn't be corrected, or the climate was such that no one could control the rampant proliferation of foliage. In the last days before Didi left, Marla had been barely able to breathe. There didn't seem to be enough air in the house, and what there was made her choke and gasp until tears flowed down her cheeks. And then Didi was gone, and although she could breathe again, Marla discovered that the roots of such plants are embedded so deeply in the heart they can't be removed. The plant breaks off only at the base of the stem, and the severed roots tremble with exquisite pain.

"Now, the move," Harold says. "Are you sure it's the right thing?"

"I couldn't live in California anymore."

"But upstate New York? There are more exciting places—Paris, London, here for that matter."

"I couldn't live here," Marla says. "I need some green space. And I don't know anyone in Paris or London."

"Those cities have been rich fodder for writers. Think of Dickens, Thackeray, Hemingway."

Marla shakes her head.

"Your parents still live there?" Harold asks.

"No, they moved away after I finished high school."

"How long has it been?"

"Twenty-five years."

"Things will have changed in—what's that town called again?" Harold says.

"Cassandra."

"Wasn't she a Greek princess?"

"A Trojan. No one would believe her prophecies."

"The point is that very little will be as you remember it in Cassandra after twenty-five years."

"A lot of the people I went to school with are still there."

"But you, darling, have moved on."

"I don't think you ever move very far from your adolescence. It has a long reach."

"Ah," he says, "I believe I hear the makings of a novel. Music to my ears."

Cassandra: an appropriate first entry to this journal, because that's where it all started, that's where I started, conceived (I've come to believe) in the backseat of a '46 Chev parked by Misty Lake on an April night when it was too cold for my bachelor father and spinster mother to screw under the pines.

I've patched my beginnings together from hints dropped by my mother over the years. I began, in spirit, at a Valentine's Day dance held by the Women's Auxiliary to the Cassandra Fire Department to raise funds for the new school library. My mother was a hometown girl, my father an ex-GI who came from the next town. Their love affair heated up in the beginning of March when my father's persistence—phone calls, flowers, flattery—wore down my mother's resistance, and she agreed to go out with him. By April they were at it hot and heavy, as I am their witness, by July married, and by December parents. It was all downhill from there; the slippery slope of incompatability began right after my mother told my father that she was pregnant. He went on a five-day bender, shades of things to come.

I'm going back to Cassandra to get to the bottom of

things. *The bottom of things.* Why the bottom? Why not the top? Or the middle? Because I believe the truth lies in layers, one truth on top of the next, obscuring what exists beneath. And I need the truth to write, because without the truth, I can't create the lies.

Marla's first success was a thinly disguised autobiographical novel about Didi's birth, the death of her marriage to Sean, and her own coming to terms with the feminist movement. The critics adored it, the public bought large quantities. Her other successful novels reflected what she saw and heard in California. They weren't about stars and celebrities but about those wannabes and failures like Sean who stood at the periphery of fame, unable to step into the charmed circle. According to critics, she wrote the "quintessential California novel," and "delicate dissections of frustrated ambition and lost love" with "sharp insights into the pathological underbelly of the film industry." But somewhere between her divorce from David and her problems with Didi, she lost her touch. The critics had panned her last two books as "repetitious" and "mechanical." So she decided it was time to go back to Cassandra, to traverse old paths, both joyous and painful, to seek the solace of old friendships, to find the answers to old questions never asked, and to allow the old wounds, long hidden, to emerge into the light.

Christian: How can I describe him? He had that special beauty seen only in some young men when they stand between the innocent realm of the boy and the complex terrain of the man. It was a dark, gleaming beauty, built of strong bones and finely honed angles, but it didn't sit on him lightly. He was restless with it, caught between vulnerability and arrogance.

He made me helpless. The line of his shoulders cut across my heart, and his smile caused me to become breathless and giddy as if the floor were falling away from my feet. I sat beside him in English and behind him in American History. I used to write his name in the margins of my notebooks: Christian French, Mr. French, Christian Robert French, and more daringly, Mrs. Christian French.

They've reached the end of the meal. The waiter has taken away their plates and is serving coffee.

"Cream, Mr. Sibley? Sugar?" Marla notes the servile dip of the waiter's head as he pours the cream into Harold's cup and wonders where Harold took *him* to lunch.

"Thank you, Peter," Harold says, and briefly touches the waiter's arm. "We'll talk soon."

The thrill of Harold's attention, which shows clearly in the waiter's face, does not distract him from his duties. "Cream?" he asks Marla. "Sugar?"

"No, thank you."

He slides soundlessly away, and Harold says, "And he's a good waiter, too. Such luck." He clears his throat. "Now, my dear, we have a slight problem to discuss."

Marla knows Harold will not use words like "sales." Such commercial terms would contaminate the conversation and pollute the subject of literature. Instead, he talks about themes, plots, and character development. He talks about the expectations of her readers and the demands of the book market. The unpleasant topic of money, of lesser advances and other penalties of failure—these issues he'll discuss with her agent, Brian Lamm, who, in turn, will relay them to her, putting the unhappy facts in the best light possible. Dear Brian—not even his highly developed sense of tact will be able to conceal the reality of critical disapproval, a diminishing audience, and editorial displeasure.

"And we're in difficult times," Harold concludes. "The recession has forced people to pull back. It's my humble opinion that we're going to see the end of the hardcover novel. Well, not entirely, there'll still be library sales, but most people prefer to buy paperbacks. But theory aside, Marla, my dear, you've strayed off the path and your audience is confused. They used to know the kind of punch a Marla Hudson novel delivered. Now they're not sure."

"I can't write the California novel anymore," Marla says.

"It ran its course. I can't keep producing them as if they were widgets."

Harold's hand with its manicured nails touches his chest as if she has mortally wounded him. "Darling Marla," he says. "Not widgets. No one wants you to produce widgets. I just want to see you happily back on track, writing the kind of novel your readers love. Now, tell me, is there a particular story in Cassandra? Is that the reason for this move?"

Marla sips at her coffee and then puts it down. "I couldn't write it before. I needed distance from it."

He lay in the hospital bed. I didn't know what the sheets were hiding: what was broken, what was gashed, what had been lacerated. His hands lay palms up, the fingers slightly curled. Every now and then, his right wrist would twitch as if life's spark had found its only niche nestled among those intricate bones.

I've carried this image of Christian for twenty-five years like a snapshot with its colors intact—hospital-white walls, chrome bed rails, pale flesh tones, black hair, a bright blue pitcher holding water he would never drink. In this snapshot, there are no smells, the sheet lies perfectly still, and he doesn't take those raspy, shuddery breaths. This image isn't my truth. I never actually saw him dead. But that doesn't mean it didn't happen. Only that it's a truth that belongs to others.

"At the time," Marla says, "I thought I was responsible for a tragedy."

"Ah," Harold says. "Would you like to tell me about it?"

"It's not ready yet. It's not quite clear in my head."

"You haven't started writing about it then."

"Only in a journal."

"My dear, I want you to take all the time you need." He pauses. "May I hope that we'll have some sex, violence, and mayhem?"

He says this as if he's making a joke—*all that commercial*

nonsense, my dear, wink, wink—but Marla senses his greedy anticipation and plays to it. "A little bit of everything," she says. *Wink, wink.*

"How nice," Harold says, caressing his tie with one hand and stroking his mustache with the other. "It sounds delightful."

Chapter

3

I HAVE THREE FRIENDS IN CASSANDRA—DAPHNE, VIRGINIA, and Frances—who are as necessary to me as the air I breathe. I've known them all for at least fifteen years, and we met indirectly through our children. We've passed through many stages together, as wives and the mothers of infants, toddlers, prepubescents, and teenagers. We've shared births, illnesses, accidents, deaths, infidelities, and divorces. When I look back over the years I see our lives weaving together in a huge web. This web is not neat and geometrical like that of a spider's but chaotic, as life is chaotic, with the strands forming loops, turns, coils, twists, kinks, and knots.

For the past thirteen years we've played bridge together on Wednesday nights to ensure that we all see one another at least once a week and catch up on the news. These games have been ritualized over time. We begin at 7:30 and end at 10:30, we rotate location from house to house, we serve low-cal foods like fruit and diet sodas, and we always play with the same partners. If one of us is sick, we cancel until the next week. We don't invite outsiders to substitute, because the bridge game is not really the point.

On this Wednesday night, we are at my house. It is 9:15, and I've closed the curtains in the living room, where the card table is set up. The circles of light from the lamps overlap and cast a warm, generous yellow glow upon us. We need such generosity, because time is beginning to inflict small wounds. We range in age from forty-three to forty-six, and we are all going gray and our skins are softening and creasing. What I see in the mirror is reflected back to me around the table. There are the same radiating lines at the eyes, deeper brackets at the mouth, minute wrinkles above the lips. I've noticed in the past year that we talk more about our transformations: exchanging anecdotes, confessing to the changes hidden by our clothes, prescribing remedies and making jokes about middle age. We know the talk will not stop the inevitable, but it has the momentary power of lifting, very slightly, the weight of the future from our shoulders. On these evenings, when we are separate from work, family, and our daily selves, we are able to look at our lives as if they were rooms and we were voyeurs at the windows.

"Then I said to him, 'So it isn't a brain tumor.' And he said, 'No, Mrs. Feller, you're just getting short-sighted.'" We laugh and Daphne shrugs. "I guess my wandering cancerous tumor will have to come to rest somewhere else."

I've finished dealing out the hand, and we take a moment to rearrange our cards. Mine always go in the same order: spades to the extreme left, followed by hearts, clubs, and diamonds. I count quickly. "One club," I say.

"Then," Daphne continues, "I took one look at myself in the mirror, saw those gray hairs, and realized I couldn't bear to have those lines at the bottom of my glasses the way my mother did. So these are invisible bifocals."

We study her glasses, and Virginia says, "I would never have guessed."

"Of course, they're harder to get used to," Daphne says. "The world has a way of swaying."

"What was your bid?" Frances asks me.

"One club."

Daphne, who's my partner, makes a face. "A biggie. A real show of strength."

Of the three women, I'm closest to Daphne. She and I

were in high school together, although we weren't friends at the time. She went away to college in Maryland and moved back to Cassandra in the early seventies when her husband, Matt, got a job as a reporter with the *Laurel Grove Leader*. I bumped into her at a children's store in the Baymont Mall when I was pregnant with Joel. Actually, I bumped into Celia, her two-year-old, who was racing around the store and ran into my legs. Celia fell down, Daphne picked her up, and we eyed one another with sudden recognition. Our exclamations of surprise turned into an exchange of phone numbers, which turned into meetings over morning coffee. I hadn't liked Daphne when we were in school. She'd hung around with a loud group of girls who were on the basketball team. They were rowdy in the locker room and liked to throw one another into the shower, the aggressors laughing hysterically while the victims squealed with outrage and pleasure. Ten years later, Daphne had changed from tall and almost emaciated to plump, curvaceous, and more attractive than she'd been in high school. Her loudness was transformed into a love of the dramatic and a tart sense of humor that made me laugh, no easy task during the last trimester of my pregnancy, when I felt heavy, awkward, tired, and apprehensive.

"One diamond," Frances says.

"My partner is bidding," Virginia announces, and studies her cards.

"One spade," Daphne says.

"I have news," Frances says. "I've started having hot flashes."

There is a shocked silence—we haven't seen this in our respective mirrors—and we put down our cards. "You're too young," Virginia says. "Forty-four is too young."

"I went to a talk at the Y, and the speaker said hot drinks could trigger hot flashes. And that's when I realized it wasn't just the coffee."

"But you're still having periods," I say. Frances's painful, heavy periods have been the subject of many bridge evenings.

"She said menopause doesn't happen overnight. It's a long process."

We contemplate the word *menopause,* taste it and roll it around in our mouths.

"It makes sense," Virginia says. "Puberty didn't happen overnight either."

"The big M," Daphne says. "I'll welcome it with open arms. Come and get me, baby."

"You wouldn't," Virginia says. "Not really."

"Are you kidding? Matt and I fight over birth control all the time. In the past, I've had to do it all. I took the pill and screwed up my hormones. Then I got a loop and had the cramps from hell. Then there was the diaphragm with all the associated mess. So I told him, 'We've been married twenty years. Now it's your turn.' Of course, he hates rubbers. He says it's like making love with his raincoat on."

Virginia leans forward. "But menopause isn't just about birth control," she says in her quiet voice. "It's about an ending. It's about loss."

Her face is earnest, a crease appearing between her brows. That crease takes me back seventeen years to Joel's birth and the maternity ward of Laurel Grove Hospital, where I met Virginia after she had Sarah. We'd given birth within minutes of one another and were roommates in a semiprivate room. At the time, I was amazed that Sarah, who weighed more than Joel, had emerged from such delicacy. Virginia was tiny, barely five feet tall, and there was something wispy about her. She had thin, pale hair, which flew about her face, and extremely fine features; a nose that came to a point and lips whose middle and ends formed a small, perfect triangle. Sarah, on the other hand, was nine pounds of screaming infant with a shock of coarse, black hair and an Amazonian appetite. While I fretted when Joel couldn't seem to figure out what my nipples were all about, Sarah latched onto Virginia's almost nonexistent breasts with a lusty ferocity. Virginia would nurse her, all the while staring down at her baby's head with a bemused frown, a tiny line creasing the skin between her pale eyebrows.

"Would someone review the bidding for me?" Daphne says.

"A club, a diamond, a spade," I say.

"Virginia, it's your bid," Daphne says.

"Oh, I pass," Virginia says.

"Menopause isn't about loss," Frances says. "I refuse to think about it that way. It's another healthy stage in a woman's life."

I sit a little straighter in my chair, and I notice that Daphne and Virginia do the same. We all have special roles in this foursome. Daphne presents us with drama and humor, Virginia forces us to reach deeply into our psyches, and Frances makes us attend to our feminist p's and q's. Virginia and I met Frances when our children were enrolled in the same preschool pool program at the YMCA. Her son, Benjamin, was willing to wear his water wings and get into the pool, but he was the only child in the program who could not be cajoled to put his head in the water and blow bubbles. I knew I was going to like Frances when she stopped the instructor—a young teenager—from pressuring Benjamin and said she'd blow bubbles for him. Frances also has the distinction of being truly beautiful. She has thick, dark hair and extraordinary light brown eyes, surrounded by long, dark lashes. Her skin color is high and her bone structure elegant. Daphne has observed to me that while the rest of us hope to age gracefully, only Frances will age beautifully. This is already noticeable. She's not going scatter-shot gray like the rest of us. A white streak has appeared in her hair near the right temple, forming a lovely accent as it sweeps backward.

"And I don't like what I'm reading," Frances continues. "I don't like the term 'ovarian failure.' Why is it a failure when the ovaries are doing just what they're supposed to be doing?"

"It's the male medical establishment screwing us again," Daphne says.

"Precisely," Frances says. "Now, whose bid is it?"

My four of spades is no support for Daphne's bid. "Two hearts," I say.

Frances studies her cards and then sighs. "Well, Virginia," she says, "I think we're out of the picture. Pass."

"Two spades," Daphne says.

"Pass," Virginia says.

"You really have a yen for those spades," I say, and Daphne shrugs. "I need a moment to think."

They put their cards down and nibble grapes. "They're in trouble," Virginia says to Frances.

"She's trying to decide whether to go for a small or grand slam," Daphne says.

"Dreamer," Frances says.

And where do I fit in this foursome? What is my role? I am neither so irreverent as Daphne, serious as Virginia, nor politically committed as Frances. I think of myself as the glue that holds us together. Although all of us and our families have taken part in many activities together—picnics, dinner parties, New Year's Eves—I'm the only one of the four who calls and sees all the others on an individual basis. Daphne and I frequently drop over at one another's houses. Virginia and I go together to the Laurel Grove Film Society, have coffee after the films, and dissect plots and characters. And I lunch with Frances, who teaches literature and composition at the local community college. We spend these lunches discussing books—our favorite authors are Anne Tyler, Fay Weldon, and Margaret Atwood—and deploring the literacy and reading levels of nineteen-year-olds.

I close the fan of cards in my hand, the others stop talking, and Daphne says, "Hallelujah, she's going to bid."

"Actually," I say, "I have news, too. My best friend from high school is moving back here from California."

"Martha Hudson?" Daphne asks, and I nod. "Well, well."

"Her name isn't really Martha anymore," I say. "It's Marla. Marla Hudson. She's a novelist."

"She wrote *Fly the Night Away*," Frances says. "That was a good book."

"Martha Hudson," Daphne says, "was one of our class celebrities. She got leads in all the plays and had a poem published in the local newspaper. I remember an awful assembly when we had to sit for an hour while she read that epic."

"Have you been in touch all these years?" Virginia asks me.

"Only Christmas cards," I say.

"You must wonder if she'll fit in or not."

Dear Virginia, with her instinct for going right to the heart of the matter. "I'm sure she will," I say. "I think you'll like her."

"But will *you* like her?" Virginia says. "You're not the same person anymore."

"The question is," Frances says, "why would she move here? I can't imagine what the appeal of Cassandra would be. She must make enough money from her books to live anywhere she wants."

"She says she wants to find her roots," I say.

"Is she married now?" Daphne asks.

"Divorced twice," I say. "Her daughter's staying in California."

"There's an old saying," Frances says. " 'You can't go home again.' "

"I would think," Virginia says, "that going back home might be very important for a writer."

"I know why she's coming back," Daphne says. She pauses for dramatic effect and takes a sip of her drink. "To rake up old ashes."

"Come on, Daphne," I say.

"Her boyfriend was killed," Daphne says, "the night of the Honor Society barbecue. He smashed his car into a tree. What was his name, Barbara?"

"Christian French," I say, and fan open my cards.

"Imagine my forgetting his name," Daphne says. "I had such a crush on him my panties used to get wet every time he passed me in the hall. He didn't even know I was alive."

"Maybe it's better that way," Frances says. "I had a crush like that on Paul, and you know how that turned out."

Frances's divorce from Paul, eight years ago, wasn't one of those events where one day a couple are together, the next day they separate and their friends are stunned by the news.

The marriage had been a war zone of his sleeping around, her recriminations, his drinking, and her smashing dishes. Our bridge games became episodes of their soap opera in which Frances played out the traumas of the week before us, and the final three months before their separation we hardly managed a rubber of bridge. Frances has never remarried, and although there have been a few men she's dated, none of her relationships have been serious. She says Paul turned her off men as permanent commitments for life, but what I think is that she never trusted another man to be Ben's father.

"There were a million rumors going around," Daphne says, "because Christian left the barbecue before it was over and Martha wasn't with him. People said she broke up with him and jilted him for someone else. Some people said she was pregnant and told him that night. It scared him so much he took off and couldn't drive straight."

"She wasn't pregnant," I say.

"Was it drinking?" Frances asks.

"He wasn't drunk," I say. "Three clubs."

They pick up their cards, and Daphne asks, "So what was the story?"

"They had a fight," I say. "She never wanted to talk about it."

"All the leads in those plays really helped," Daphne adds. "She was like Medea. She covered herself in black. She'd break down in class and have to go to the nurse's office. Didn't she manage to get out of finals?"

"She got some sort of special exemption," I say. "How do you feel about my clubs?"

"Miserable," Daphne says.

Virginia says, "I can't remember what's been bid."

"One club," I say. "One diamond, one spade, two hearts, two spades, three clubs."

"Pass," Frances says.

"We're a total mismatch," Daphne announces. "We're a fiasco. Three spades."

"What can I do?" I say. "I pass."

"Double," Frances responds.

"We're the *Titanic,*" Daphne says. "We're a catastrophe."

Sometimes I wonder why Dan and Joel aren't enough for me, why I need these friends to round out my life. They don't always make me happy. We're subject to disagreements, jealousies, and bad feelings. For example, when Virginia went through yet another bad patch in her marriage, she spent one bridge game tearing her husband, Raymond, apart. Daphne tactlessly said she'd never understood why Virginia had married Raymond in the first place, he was so rigid. Later, when Virginia and Raymond were back on an even keel, Virginia told me that Daphne had no right to talk about Raymond that way, that she didn't live with him and she didn't know the first thing about their relationship. A frostiness hung over our bridge games for about a month.

"Well, isn't he rigid?" Daphne complained to me in private. "He's got those kids so regimented, it's a wonder they don't salute."

"Virginia loves him," I said.

"Love," Daphne said with disgust. "I love Matt, but I'm not blind to his faults."

"Virginia isn't blind either. She's loyal."

Then there was the time I was trying to be helpful and suggested that Frances take Benjamin to the new ophthalmologist in Laurel Grove to have his eye checked. I was beginning to extol the virtues of this doctor when Frances coldly cut me off, saying there was nothing wrong with Benjamin and that his vision was perfect. I was so upset I couldn't sleep that night and kept Dan up as well.

"Isn't there something wrong with Benjamin's eye?" I asked him.

"It wanders a bit," he said.

"So why did she say that?"

"How do I know?" Dan said.

"She was so cold."

"Barbara, please. Count sheep or something."

The next morning I called Virginia, who said, "She's in denial."

"But Frances is so logical and precise."

"Not when it comes to Benjamin."

"I feel terrible," I said. "I feel just awful."

"We all have these sensitive spots," Virginia said. "The thing is, they're not always visible."

And when I called Daphne, she said, "It's all right. Frances will take him to a doctor, get his eye fixed, and act like nothing happened."

"I hope so."

"Barbara, you're not guilty. Stop killing yourself."

And, in fact, it turned out just as Daphne predicted. Frances did take Ben to a doctor, and Ben wore a patch for about a year. It took Frances several months even to mention the patch to any of us, and she never once acknowledged denying Ben's eye problem. Ben's eye corrected itself just fine, and he's become a very handsome boy, but I never see him without wondering if he'd still be slightly cross-eyed if I hadn't said something to Frances in the first place.

As I lay out my cards, I don't forget these problems of the past, but they pale in comparison with fifteen years of compassion, support, laughter, and understanding. I think of Frances, who came in the middle of the night to drive me to the hospital when I had my second miscarriage and Dan was out of town. I think of the hours I spent with Virginia when her second child, Melissa, was only six weeks old and she discovered Raymond was having an affair with his secretary. I think of the parties Daphne has thrown for all of us during the years to celebrate important events: birthdays, anniversaries, promotions, and the publication of the first child's book that Virginia illustrated.

As Daphne, Virginia, and Frances play out the hand, nodding and smiling to one another, I notice the play of yellow light on their faces. It softens their faces, their idiosyncrasies, their prickly, sensitive edges. I notice their beauty, not just Frances's obvious symmetry of face, but the more subtle hooks by which they hold me—the depths and shadows in Virginia's gray-blue eyes; Daphne's eyebrows, which angle like startled, feathered wings; the crease below Frances's bottom lip that defines the perfect circle of her chin. I think of Marla standing at the edge of our foursome. I've said she'll fit in, but I really have no idea. She may step easily over the lines we've drawn, or she may find herself stalled at the periphery, unable to enter the square.

Chapter
4

ON THE DAY MARLA ARRIVES IN CASSANDRA, CAROLINE DEA-
con disappears. I'm getting ready to leave for the airport
when Daphne phones to tell me. Daphne is privy to all kinds
of information earlier than the rest of us, partly because
Matt works for the *Laurel Grove Leader* and partly because
she's in charge of administration at our town hall where all
the town offices are located, including that of the police.

"Caroline Deacon is missing. She left for school this
morning but didn't show up."

Our junior and senior high schools are combined together
in a low-slung brick building located on twenty acres of
wooded property at the edge of Cassandra. Some children
are bused in, others ride their bikes or walk. The Deacons
live close enough that Caroline could walk.

"Are the police searching for her?"

"Not yet. Reg says if he had a nickel for every kid that
skipped school, he'd have retired to Miami Beach years
ago."

"But Caroline isn't that kind of kid." In addition to being
the prettiest teenager in Cassandra, Caroline won the class
prize in English and French last year. She also plays the oboe

in the school band and is on the girl's basketball team, which won the intrastate trophy last year.

"I have a bad feeling about this," Daphne says.

Sometimes I find Daphne's yen for the dramatic irritating. "Maybe she and Ben had a fight and she needed a walk in the woods."

"Frances says not. She says he and Caroline were supposed to meet at school early and study French for an exam today."

"Then maybe she went to the mall," I say. "She needed a day off."

"Brian and Molly are looking there now."

"Oh," I say. The thought of the Deacons searching through Baymont Mall suddenly frightens me. "Listen, I'll call when I get back from the airport. I'm picking up Marla."

"Did you know the *Leader* is planning to do a feature on her return?" Daphne says.

"And the *Gazette,* and WCNR and Channel Five news."

"It didn't take long for word to get out, did it?" Daphne says.

"I think Virginia told Edgar," I say.

"Well, Edgar," Daphne says. "That explains it. Do you know I'm afraid to let him fill really personal prescriptions? I get those filled in Laurel Grove. After all, do I want the whole town to know I've got a rash in an unmentionable location?"

"Oh, do you?" I ask. "Where?"

Daphne laughs. "Go pick up the celebrity," she says. "Have fun."

The drive to the airport takes me into my past. When I was growing up, Cassandra didn't have a high school. We attended Cassandra Elementary School, which went up to grade nine, and then were bused fifteen miles away to Walt Whitman High School in Laurel Grove's east end. This was in the early sixties, when Cassandra was changing from a small farming community to a satellite town of Laurel Grove, which was home to a state university, an industrial base of leather and china manufacturers, and a growing postwar population that spread into surrounding towns like Cassandra where the land was cheaper and the taxes lower. Route 240 between Cassandra and Laurel Grove was the road we took twice a day, when it was only two lanes instead of four. At that time, I considered the trip boring in the extreme—too many hills, trees, and rocky cuts. I was more interested in the social events within the bus, such as who was sitting with whom and who was gossiping about what. Now I have a different view of the trip. I ignore the businesses that have taken root on Route 240—car dealerships, lumberyards, landscaping, miniature golf— and note the sloping beauty of the hills beyond, where the color of the trees ranges from a pale green almost the shade of moonlight to a deep emerald. Several years ago I attended a lecture on the geology of central New York and learned that our valley, shaped by receding glaciers, had once been the silty bottom of a huge lake, several hundred feet below the surface. That night I dreamed of water flowing into our house and that each room had its own whirlpool, circular funnels that voraciously sucked sofas, chairs, carpets, and pictures into their vortexes.

I've lived in Cassandra all my life. Both my parents grew up on dairy farms, each within ten miles of the house I live in now. My father joined the air force during World War II, but he didn't have the eyesight for piloting. Instead, he discovered an ability for mathematics and taught bombardiering at an air force base in Big Springs, Texas. My mother, his high school sweetheart, traveled there to marry him. They had a great war. They lived in married quarters and spent the war years in one long round of parties, interrupted by his teaching duties and their amusing skirmishes with scorpions and other Texas wildlife. I was conceived in Big Springs but was born at Laurel Grove's Grace Hospital several months after my father's discharge. Until I was thirty-two, when Dan and I took a tour to Italy and France, that voyage *in utero* was the longest trip I'd ever taken.

My roots in the Cassandra soil go deep and strong, and that's the way I like it. My father, who never wanted to be a farmer, went to college on the G.I. bill, got a degree in accounting at Syracuse University, and came back to Cassandra to work for the First National Bank, where he reached the level of manager before retiring. My mother stayed home, as women did in those days, although she was active in a duplicate bridge club, the Women's Auxiliary for the Fire Department, the Women's Committee for the Cassandra Fall Fair, and Republican Women for Democracy. Unlike my brother, Rob, who left Cassandra as soon as he could and now lives in Denver, I've never envied those who've left or wished I lived in some bigger and more exciting city. I don't yearn for far-off places, new acquaintances, and different experiences. I like knowing every inch of my town, to traverse daily the landscapes of my childhood, and to be able to trace the genealogy of families, houses, and events. And I'm never bored but rather, constantly intrigued by the changing face of the familiar: marriages that wax and wane, babies that grow to teenagers, friends who make unexpected changes.

The airport, which was built on the site of a dairy farm and was once considered outside town, is now preceded by a huge shopping complex that includes a mall, a multiscreen cinema, and many fast-food outlets. As I pass by, I see a few teenagers hanging out in front of The Donut Hole, and I think of the Deacons searching through the Baymont Mall and remember the time Joel ran away from home. He was four years old and angry with me for reasons I can no longer remember. He went out the back door into the yard and disappeared. I didn't notice he was gone until an hour had passed. I called his name out the front and back doors, and when there was no answer called several neighbors, only to find he wasn't playing at the houses of his friends. I walked out onto the street and called again. It was fall, and the leaves on the trees had already turned to shades of ocher, orange, and flaming red. A breeze played in those leaves, tugging them off now and then, teasing them into the cool, blue air and then sending them in slow downward spirals to land on clipped hedges and carefully mowed lawns. It didn't seem right to stand on that picture-perfect street on that picture-perfect day and feel the dark spread of panic rising in my chest to my throat. I called Dan, who came home from work, and we decided to drive around, each in our separate cars, exploring streets well beyond ours. Dan took off, I opened my car door, and there was Joel, lying on the front seat fast asleep. The interior of the car was warm from sitting closed in the sun, and his cheeks were flushed pink and his blond curls dark from sweat. I remember clearly the dark fear draining from me, and light pouring back in and bringing with it all the glorious colors and clarity of that beautiful autumn day.

The airport is busy, and it takes me so long to find a parking space that I enter the building just as Marla's plane is landing and the announcement of its arrival is being made over the loudspeaker. I reach the doors in the Arrivals gate just as she walks through them, a slender woman with dark hair, dressed in turquoise slacks, a pale blue silk jacket, and a scarf colored with pink, mauve, and blue. I recognize her immediately. Or rather I recognize her mother, because that is what Marla has become, a dark-haired version of her blond mother. I haven't seen Mrs. Hudson in twenty-five years, and she is frozen in time for me, a pretty woman of forty-five years of age with a strong nose and sharply defined mouth, bracketed by deep lines. As Marla turns, looking for me, I see the same nose and mouth, cut by the same parallel lines.

"Martha!" I wave and then correct myself. "Marla!"

"Bobbie!"

When we embrace, I feel her thinness and smell the expensive perfume in her hair. We separate and look at one another.

"You look the same," she says. "I recognized you right away."

"No one's called me Bobbie for twenty-five years," I say.

"Twenty-five years," she says. "Do you believe it? I can't. Look at this place. Was it even here twenty-five years ago?"

"A much smaller version."

"I don't remember an airport. Oh, I bet I don't remember a lot of things." She smiles at me. "But I do remember you. Let me look at you."

I'm in beige slacks, a white cotton sweater, and makeup carefully applied. "Heavier and grayer," I say.

"Still wholesome and pretty," she says. "You always had the most appealing face."

"Me?"

She tilts her head. "Just looking at you made people happy. It's the roundness of your eyes, I think, and of course the smile. I always wanted to look like you."

"You didn't," I say with surprise. "Besides *I* wanted to look like *you.*"

She laughs, and it's the laugh I remember so well—deep, throaty, and rich. It makes my lips curve into a smile and then I'm laughing, too. In the years since I've seen her, I've forgotten Marla's ability to bestow compliments with a directness that makes them seem guileless and genuine. When we were in high school, I had difficulty understanding why some girls were popular and others were not. I knew it was important to have a pretty face, a good figure, and the right clothes, but the parts didn't always add up to a whole. There were pretty girls who didn't have boyfriends, girls with big breasts whom the boys ignored, girls with great clothes who sat home on Saturday nights. I always believed Marla's popularity arose from a combination of flair, looks, and shapeliness, but now I see she also has an unexpected and attractive charm. I feel the tug of it, pulling me toward her, making me like her all over again.

Marla tucks her arm through mine, and we begin to walk to the baggage claim area. "Oh, Bobbie, this is going to be fun, isn't it? Now, I want to hear everything—about your husband, son, house, job."

"Well, there's Dan, of course."

"I remember him. Blond and a math whiz."

I nod. "He's a vice president with a computer firm in Laurel Grove."

"What was it like marrying someone you've known almost your whole life?"

I'd also forgotten her insatiable curiosity. "We have a lot in common. It made things . . . easier."

"Was he sexy? I don't remember."

"Not when you knew him. He grew into it."

"Did you love him madly when you got married?"

"Yes," I say.

"Do you still?"

"Not exactly madly."

She squeezes my arm and laughs again. "Now tell me about Joel."

"What can I say? Very seventeen."

"Who does he look like?"

"Dan and a little bit of me. He's blond and tall and skinny. He's still growing."

"Any girlfriends?"

"Not yet. He's a late bloomer."

"And you're a librarian."

"At the Cassandra Public Library."

"Remember when we snuck out *Peyton Place* and read the dirty parts to each other?" She laughs. "Tell me about your house."

"A ranch built on an extension of Steeplechase Lane."

"Steeplechase Lane," she says. "Where was that?"

"Past the post office. A right turn off Meadow."

"I remember," she says with delight. "I remember it perfectly."

We pick up Marla's luggage, put it into the trunk of the car, and begin the drive back to Cassandra. We discuss practicalities. Marla has turned down my invitation to stay with us—"No, I wouldn't impose on you. Absolutely not." She's going to stay at the Cassandra Motor Hotel and buy a car. She's already got plans with a realtor to see several houses and a condominium in the new building on Preston Street.

"You're planning to buy a house?" I ask. I envisioned Marla renting an apartment or maybe a small house.

"I sold mine in California."

"It's such a permanent thing to do, buying a house."

She smiles. "You can always sell it again."

"I know, but—"

"I'm committed to doing this, Bobbie. That's the point. And you know which house I'm most excited about? The Hiller house. I understand it's vacant."

This house had been built by Dr. and Mrs. Hiller when they moved to Cassandra during the 1920s and thought they would have many children. It sits in isolation on a twenty-acre piece of land at the extreme edge of town and is notable for three things: its beautiful and panoramic view of Cassandra, the section of river that runs like white water through the property, and the fact that it's the only mansion in Cassandra. It has three stories of brick with oak floors, high coved ceilings, bay windows, a turret, and a grand staircase that curves up to the second floor. The Hillers lived until their nineties, dying within months of one another in 1985. They had no heirs except for a grandnephew who lives in Colorado. The house, which requires extensive renovation, had been on the market ever since, growing more dilapidated with the passing years.

"It's not in good shape," I say.

"It was so grand. The rooms were magnificent, weren't they?"

"The kitchen and bathrooms date back to the thirties. Nothing's been done with them."

"I had the realtor get an engineer's report on it. It's basically sound."

"You've already made up your mind," I say with surprise.

"When I was a kid, I used to hang around the house because it was so different than everyone else's. Mrs. Hiller took pity on me and invited me in a couple of times for a dish of ice cream. I remember the cool airiness of it and the lace curtains and the gleaming floors."

"It probably needs new electrical, plumbing, and heating systems," I say. "It'll cost a fortune."

"I have a fortune, Bobbie," she says.

She touches my arm lightly as if to bridge the gap between our differences, but she can't take the sting out of her words. I've wondered if my friends will include Marla in my circle, but now I wonder how Cassandra will take to the arrival of so much money. We're a middle-class town. The real wealth in our part of the country usually settles in Elverton, which is north of us and sits between two lakes so that the residents can live on waterfront property.

"Anyway, I think it's the view I'm really after," Marla says. "The front windows looked across the hills and down onto the river. Bobbie! Can we stop?"

Startled, I ease my pressure on the accelerator and glance around. "Here?" We're halfway to Cassandra on a bend in Route 240. On one side of the road is a farmer's field, on the other an impenetrable thicket of trees.

"The turnoff to Misty Lake is near here, isn't it?"

"A mile ahead," I say.

"I want to see it," she says.

"Now?"

"Do you mind?"

I feel a heavy, dragging reluctance. "I thought you'd want to get settled first."

"I didn't come here to get settled." She says this fiercely, staring through the windshield, presenting her profile to me. Her hair is thick and curly, cut in expert angles at the temples, ears, and nape of the neck, but there is something primitive and predatory about the high arch of her nose, the jut of her chin, the strongly curved lips.

I feel my reluctance give way. "All right," I say. "I haven't been to Misty Lake in years."

"Does it still get used for Honor Society barbecues?"

"No, not anymore."

We've reached the turnoff, and I make a right turn off the pavement and onto a bumpy dirt track. It hasn't rained for several days so the track is dry, and the tires of the car raise dust clouds behind us. Ahead is a tunnel of green formed by brush and conifer trees so thick that the rays of the late afternoon sun barely break through the foliage. We don't talk for several minutes, and branches scrape against the sides and roof of the car, punctuating our silence.

Marla finally says, "What do you remember about that night?"

"Not much," I say. "I was drinking."

"I met Derek Stone about ten years ago in San Diego at a cocktail party when I was there on a book tour. Remember Derek? He's a lawyer now."

"Dark? Heavy-set? He played soccer?"

"Miss Wapshupski practically raped him that night."

I give a little screech. Miss Wapshupski was the new Home Economics teacher during our senior year, right out of teacher's college. She had a twenties' flapper face—round and pretty with tightly curled blond hair, bow lips outlined in a rich red, and big, limpid green eyes. The boys thought she was sexy; the girls speculated on her love life. We paired her with Mr. Allen, the Latin teacher and perpetual bachelor whose nails gleamed with clear polish, with Jimmy Spiro's father whose wife had, in one of the town's biggest scandals, run off with Mr. Brush, the furnace-and-duct repairman, and even with old man Boileau, who owned the gas station and was missing several teeth on the upper right side of his mouth.

"And they slept together for the rest of the term and all that summer until he left for Penn State."

"She left, too," I say. "She moved to Michigan or somewhere like that."

"It was funny Derek telling me that," Marla says. "It was like he'd been holding it in for all those years and couldn't wait to tell someone who would understand just how significant it was. I asked him if he'd been in love with her, and he said, 'You want to know the truth? I was ecstatic and scared shitless the whole time.'"

"Poor Miss Wapshupski," I say. "Imagine being so desperate she'd sleep with Derek Stone."

"I thought about that," Marla says, "but Derek was the most developed of all the boys in our class. Remember his beard was so thick and dark he had to shave twice a day? Remember how hairy he was?"

"Didn't he have a wart on his thumb?"

"God, Bobbie, you remember the worst."

Before us, the woods open to a clearing that lies at the northern edge of the lake. Misty Lake, which is seventeen miles long and five miles wide, is shaped like a smile.

Cottages line the eastern and southern shores where the land slopes gently to the water, but the north shore is too rocky and hilly, and the shoreline falls off dramatically so there's only a narrow, pebbly beach and then deep water. I know from the geology lecture that the lakes in our area were gouges cut out of the earth by glaciers during the thousands of years that they advanced and receded, carrying rock and pebble in their icy grip. The lecturer told us that if we looked hard enough we could find striations on the rocks that surround such lakes, deep scratches caused by stone rasping on stone, the imprint of the past on the present.

I turn the car off and open the door. There's the shrill sound of a crow as it whirls overhead and the lapping of water against the rocky shore.

"It's beautiful here," Marla says. "I'd forgotten that." She steps out of the car and into the clearing, the turquoise of her shoes a sudden intrusion of color against the black, gray, and brown stones. She kneels down, picks up a rock, and turns it over in her hand. "A skipping stone," she says, and throws, her hand angled, so that the stone hits the water on its flat side, slapping the surface and then leaping into an arc to slap the water again. *Slap, slap, slap*—and each slap leaves a tiny fluid circle of reverberations. She turns to me and smiles. "That's one of those things you never forget how to do—like bicycle riding."

I stand by the car and watch as she picks her way to a boulder at the edge of the woods. Beyond the boulder and up the hillside are hidden nooks and crannies, spots concealed by tree and rock where the ground is soft with dead leaves, and where young couples used to spread old woollen, plaid blankets and sink into hungry sexual explorations.

"I dream about this place," Marla says. She sits on the edge of the boulder and looks across the gray-green lake. There is a splash on the water's surface as a fish jumps and then the bright droplets cascade back, pursuing the fish's fall. I've followed her now and sit on another stone after brushing the surface with my hand to make sure I won't leave any marks on my beige slacks. She continues, "In my dreams, it's evil. I couldn't tell you how it's evil, just that it is. I'm so frightened that I start to run, but I can't get away. The water's darker, almost black, and there's something in the air." She glances around and sniffs. "But that's just dreams, because it's innocent, isn't it?"

"It's just a place."

"Do you remember Sandy Arbut jumping off that rock?" She points to a jut of gray stone that hangs out over the water. "He was so drunk he didn't even take his clothes off."

I search my memory, but there's so little of that night that remains, except for a darkness, shifting shadows, the tones of a guitar, the flicker of the bonfire. "No, I don't remember any of that."

"But I saw you watching. The firelight lit up your face so that it was like a second moon."

"There was no moon that night. It was really dark."

We don't speak for a moment, but there's no true silence at a lake. There are cracklings and scurrying sounds in the underbrush, flies that buzz past, frogs emitting hoarse croaks, birds sending notes from the trees, the choppy sound of water lifted by a restless breeze. In the distance, a plane rises from the airport we've left behind, silver cutting through the sky, which heals itself immediately with a clear blue gauze.

"I wonder whose memories are the truest?" Marla asks.

"Why can't they both be true?"

"Then what is real? Both versions? No versions?"

"I got a C minus in Philosophy," I say. " 'I think, therefore I am.' That's all I remember."

"I remember, therefore I was," she says, and then catches sight of something in a nest of leaves on the boulder's far side. She leans over and picks it up. "Aha!" she says. I can't see what it is, only that it catches the sun in a pinpoint of gold. "This must still be a good make-out place." She stretches out her hand to me and I see an earring resting on her palm. It's a small gold circlet made for a pierced ear, and twisted slightly so that the catch won't stay in the metal loop.

"I hope she had fun," I say, "whoever she was."

"Today," Marla says, "that earring could've belonged to a boy."

I laugh. "You're right."

"And kids don't make out anymore. They fuck." Suddenly she stands on the topmost part of the boulder and cups her hands at the corners of her mouth. "Christian!" she yells. "Christian French! *Christian Robert French!*" There's no echo, only a reverberation in the air as if his name, like the skipping stone, had slapped the surface of the space around us. Above us, the crow circles again, making its grating call.

I find myself shivering and stand up. "Let's go," I say.

"He's not here," she says. "Not even his spirit."

"Marla, it's time to go."

She gives me a curious look. "You hate it here," she says, "even more than I do."

"I don't hate it. I just want to forget the bad parts of the past."

She steps down from the boulder. "We're different then," she says. "I want to step right back into it, muck around in it, get my feet and hands filthy with it."

I feel suddenly exhausted. "I have to get home," I say, and turn to leave.

Her hand, predatory as an eagle's claw, grabs my arm and stops me. "I want to know if there's one memory we have in common," she says fiercely. "Was he beautiful or is that only a figment of my imagination?"

The lid of my inner eye can barely rise, as if it's held down by weights and pulleys, but I glimpse a flashing smile, green eyes outlined by thick lashes, a curl of dark hair. "He was beautiful," I say slowly. "He was the most beautiful boy I've ever seen."

When I get home, the light on our telephone answering machine is blinking wildly. Wearily, I put down my purse and press the replay button. The machine whirrs, clicks, and beeps.

"Hi, hon, this is your husband calling to ask you to pick

up my blue suit from the cleaner's. I have a meeting scheduled at four-thirty and there's no way I can get there before the cleaner closes. Thanks, hon, and I'll be home at six-thirty."

Whirr, click.

"Barbara, it's Mona. I forgot to tell you that I have a dentist appointment tomorrow morning so I won't be in to work until ten. Frieda said she'd come in for me so you won't be alone. See you tomorrow. 'Bye."

Click, beep.

"Hi, Mom, it's me, Joel. I won't be home for supper. I'm going over to Andy's house to eat and to study for the History test. I'll be home at nine."

Click, beep, click.

"Barbara, it's Daphne. Caroline wasn't at the mall, and the police have sent out an APB and are now searching the woods between the Deacons' house and the school. Phil Potter's been notified and he's going to hold a school assembly tomorrow with the police there to talk to the kids no matter what's happened, but I have a feeling the news will be all over town before that. Frances and I are thinking of making a brief visit to Brian and Molly to show our support and just be there for them, but I don't know if it's appropriate. Would you give me a call as soon as you get in?"

I put my hand on the telephone, but my fingers slide on the hard plastic. My wedding band catches the light the way the earring did at Misty Lake, the sun caught in pinpoints of gold. I move my hand from side to side so that the pinpoints move across the band's curved surface. It's just a plain, narrow ring; we couldn't afford very much in those days and promised ourselves we'd replace it with something more expensive when we had the money. It's funny how promises like that, made with such fervor and commitment, diminish over time like sails losing their wind or balloons deflating. I think of the concerns I woke up with this morning: Joel's try-outs for the baseball team, when we'd get the bathroom painted, whether the library budget would be enough to cover the books that should be ordered, if it had been such a good idea to put Dan's bonus pay into those municipals the broker recommended. It's funny that what can be so important can become so trivial. I think of Marla's arrival and Caroline's disappearance, the earring, my ring, circles of gold. I think of the magician's trick where hoops connect and come apart although there are no openings in the metal surfaces. Are there patterns that we can't see? Cosmic connections? Huge, invisible hands arranging and rearranging our lives?

I shake off the thought. I'm not superstitious; I think life is a mixture of the consequences of our actions and random events. "Get a hold of yourself, Barbara," I say, and pick up the receiver.

Chapter

5

THE HILLER HOUSE. MARLA FALLS IN LOVE WITH IT ALL OVER again as she drives up the back road and it becomes visible through the trees. First the redness of the brick appears, then the gray roof whose edges are trimmed with ornate, white fretwork, and finally the glitter of many small window panes reflecting the morning sun into her eyes. When she reaches the top of the driveway, which forms a parabola with the house at its apex, she discovers that the house is now also embraced by trees, elms, and oaks with thick trunks and sturdy branches. They have grown and stretched since her childhood, brown arms reaching toward the roof of the turret, eaves, and chimney. When she steps out of the car, she hears the whispered *shh shh* of their caress as green fingers, excited by the wind, brush the brick and glass. She can also hear, in the background, the roar of the river released from its winter lethargy and swollen with rushing water.

Marla's been afraid the house has grown in size and stature in her imagination while reality would prove it to be shrunken and ordinary. But her memory has held the house's image accurately and she's not disappointed. Its

60

lines are as gracious as she remembers, the grounds expansive, and the turret still as romantic and mysterious as it ever was. As a little girl, she imagined herself sleeping in the room at the top of the turret, her dreams enclosed by white, smooth, curving walls.

"Yes." She says the word out loud as she gets out of the car. "Yes." What is her money worth if it can't recapture and make real the fantasies and wishes of her childhood? Her parents' house, that common bungalow with its L-shaped living/dining room, three square bedrooms, and basement rec room, couldn't contain the soaring flights of her imagination. She used to lie in bed at night, her physical self surrounded by the cherry headboard, the cherry desk and set of drawers (Sear's Best Girl's Room), her bedside lamp with the white tasseled shade, and the bulletin board pinned with photographs of family and friends, while her mental self flew to the Hiller house. There she was the queen standing regally on the second-floor balcony as carriages swept up the arched drive, the princess entertaining a suitor, the humble-but-beautiful servant polishing the dark wood of the staircase, the young girl dangerously disguised as a page boy, the chatelaine—a word she'd recently discovered in a novel about the Middle Ages—sweeping through the rooms in her long, pale blue gown, her dark hair enclosed in a white wimple (another wonderful word) and a circle of keys making music at her hips.

But Marla's not so blinded by her memories and fantasies that she doesn't notice the problems: the sagging front porch with peeling paint, a broken railing on the second-floor balcony, crumbling brick at the right-hand corner of the house, and the criss-crosses of tape that seal the cracks in several windows. During the phone call with the real estate agent to set up the viewing appointment, Marla was told that the grandnephew provided for upkeep of the house and grounds, but in recent years the funds haven't been sufficient for repairs, and the exterior of the house has been deteriorating.

"Also, it's"—the real estate agent carefully sought words

to describe the interior that wouldn't discourage Marla but would still fall on the right side of accuracy—"a bit antiquated."

"I expect renovations," Marla said.

"It's a one-of-a-kind, that's for sure." The agent's voice mixed eagerness with relief. "You won't see yourself coming or going in it, if you know what I mean."

Marla knows what she means. The Hiller house is unique, a white elephant by Cassandra standards. Marla re-acquainted herself with the town the day after she arrived. She bought a car, paying cash and delighting a salesman at Marvin's Honda on Route 240, and drove the streets of Cassandra. The center of the town still has some of the stores she remembers: Deacon's Hardware, the post office, Bilby's Opticians, the drug store, the Exxon station, the First National Bank. There are new buildings: Grieber's Deli, Sarah's Quilting Shop, medical offices, and Monty's Movie Rentals and Arcade Games. The old dusty A & P has turned into a Grand Union. But gone is Polly's Dress Shoppe, the appliance and shoe repair shop, and Walker's Five and Dime, where she used to spend many pleasurable hours with Bobbie. They'd spray themselves with perfume (the store had samples in cut-glass bottles with atomizers), pick through the scarf bin, and study the costume jewelry and cosmetics in depth. As she drove by, Marla remembered the importance of a circle pin worn strategically on a Peter Pan collar and the excitement she felt over a lipstick called Tangerine Dream, a lurid orange that she adored and her mother hated, saying it didn't suit her. Not that Marla listened or noticed that the bright orange gashes turned her skin sallow. She wore that lipstick until there was nothing left to it but a nub in a metal tube.

Cassandra, the Navel of Central New York. The sign had been put up sometime in the thirties, and the epitaph had stuck. She and her friends laughed about it. "Cassandra, the Armpit of New York," they said. Some boys were more daring: "The Asshole of New York is more like it." There were sniggers to that, embarrassed laughter and sideways looks, but then *asshole* was not a word in easy circulation back in the late fifties, not the way it is today. Didi spoke it with the same facility as she breathed.

About a teacher: "He's such an asshole." About a girl she didn't like: "She's the asshole of all time."

"I don't like that language."

"That's the way kids talk now."

"That doesn't mean I have to like it."

"It's just a word."

"Words are important. I make my living out of words."

"It's no big deal. Why are you making such a big deal?"

"I don't care what you say when you talk to your friends, but I don't want to listen to words like that here, in the house."

"Fuck."

"What was that?"

"Nothing."

Beep! Beep!

The blare of a horn snapped Marla back to reality. She'd been drifting into the opposite lane of traffic. Without her knowledge, when she wasn't looking, it had happened again. The door in her mind had opened a crack, only a sliver, but just enough to let Didi slip through. In real life, she took up more space than anyone Marla knew. She filled up the rooms of the house with her friends, her things, her sounds, her laughter, her rages, her likes, her dislikes. "Mom! I'm home!" she would yell, the door would slam hard and her footsteps would thud on the staircase. But in Marla's mind, she begins by taking up no more space than a shadow, sliding around corners, seeping under sills, and slipping past thoughts with the ease of quicksilver. Then she expands, growing monstrously, until she blocks out everything in Marla's mind and there's no room for anything else.

Marla slowed down and drove carefully down Main Street, focusing on the stores, the people, the activities. Four teenagers on bikes congregated in the Grand Union's parking lot. Several women pushed strollers down the sidewalk. A mother argued with a crying child in front of the post office. Three old men sat on the steps of the First National, smoking, talking, making wide, emphatic gestures with their hands. They could be the same old men who sat there in the early sixties, farmers chewing over politics the way their cows chewed cud. Except they might not be farmers now. An article in last week's *Cassandra Gazette,* which she'd found in the motel, bemoaned the takeover of the small dairy farm by huge conglomerates: FAMILY FARMS ON THE WANE was the headline.

But even if Cassandra has become primarily a town of commuters to Laurel Grove, it still has the sleepy air of a place where business is an act between acquaintances, and the transfer of money is almost an embarrassment. Marla remembered her mother in Polly's Dress Shoppe handing over a ten-dollar bill, while she and Polly fervently discussed peonies. It was as if her mother was not relinquishing a critical part of the family's cash flow, ten dollars that had caused a fight between her parents, which she'd overheard through the duct system that connected her bedroom to theirs.

"Another bill. Jesus Christ."

"I haven't bought a dress since last year."

"You think I work to fill your closet?"

"You barely give me enough money to feed the kids."

"That's a goddamned lie, Ruth. You spend that money on stuff like this."

"If you'd gotten that promotion—"

"Well, I didn't get it, did I?"

"Because you drink like a fish."

"Shut the fuck up!"

No, her mother discussed the planting and cultivation of peonies and gave Polly advice about not burying the tubers too deep, making sure the plants got enough sun, and clipping the deadheads before the petals fell, and Polly, who was fat and had the tallest platinum beehive in Cassandra, nodded her three chins and said she was going to replant that sorry old peony plant of hers just as Ruth suggested. Marla, who was not interested in peonies but feeling the frightening loss of that ten dollars (would she and her brother Billy starve now?), seemed to be the only one in the store who noticed the transaction of commerce. Under the barrage of horticultural jargon: *thinning, acidic soil, southern exposure,* Polly wrote out a receipt for the ten-dollar bill and put that small rectangle of dull green paper in her cash drawer.

"I know you don't have time now, Ruth," Polly said, closing the drawer with a neat tap of her pointed red fingernails, "but next time you're in, you must give me some advice about those roses I've got behind the house."

"It's been a hard winter for roses," Marla's mother said. "Mine are real droopy."

"They need lots of protection."

"You a gardener, too, Martha? You take after your Mom? No? Well, she looks just like you, Ruth. The spitting image. And she's going to be a beauty, aren't you, honey?"

Marla drove to the north section of town where her old house is located, several acres of bungalows built after the war on a grid of streets with names like Maple, Chestnut, and Oak. She parked across the street from 68 Willow, a low-roofed house made of brick and stucco. The door and shutters were no longer white but a pale green, and the roses and peonies that Marla's mother so lovingly cultivated in the front garden have been replaced with yew and juniper bushes. But the changes didn't alter her feelings about the house. Even as a small child, Marla knew there was something wrong with 68 Willow. There was a crack the shape of lightning in the basement wall behind the washing machine, and the floor of her parents' bedroom sloped so that pencils and marbles rolled into the closet. The stove had a defective burner that no one could fix; it went on the blink again as soon as the repairman's truck left the driveway. The walls of Billy's room were cold to the touch even on the hottest day, and Marla, whose bed stood above a hot-air vent, noticed that the breathy ducts held the sounds of anger long after the family's voices had died down. The taste of dislike, a copperish, grating taste, came to her as she sat in her car and overwhelmed the other, happier memories of hopscotch and jumping rope, of sleds dragged out of the garage to the hill on the other side of Elm, and of dusky summer evenings when she and Billy ran among the trees and caught fireflies.

"Mrs. Hudson?"

Marla's been so engrossed in her memories that she hasn't heard the sound of the car on the driveway or the closing of a car door. "Yes?" she says.

A handsome man in a dark suit walks toward her, holding out a business card, which she takes. "Tony Molino," he says. "From Gale Real Estate. Mrs. Deacon couldn't make it today. Perhaps you read about it in the paper?"

"I'm sorry, I—"

"Her daughter disappeared."

"Oh, I didn't know. How awful."

"Yeah, it's got everyone upset. Anyway, I'm taking over her clients for a while."

He smiles, and Marla feels the air stir around her. "I knew a Molino family when I used to live here," she says. "Four brothers."

"Wait a minute," he says slowly. "You're Martha Hudson."

"Weren't you a year ahead of me in school?"

"That was my brother, Guido. I was three years behind you." He shakes his head. "Jesus, Martha Hudson."

"Marla. I changed my name."

"Hey," he says, smiling again, "you never looked like a Martha in the first place."

It's not unpleasant, that small frisson of air. It's connected to the white teeth, his swarthy good looks, the bulky width of his shoulders, and the attractive sprinkling of gray in the dark waves of his hair. It's connected to the way his dark eyes are appraising her, frankly, with sexual intent. Marla thinks back to her last act of intercourse, an unsatisfactory meeting of minds and bodies with a screenwriter she met at a party a year ago. She'd ignored one of her cardinal rules: don't get involved with other writers. The screenwriter, who'd written a dozen proposals but had no production credits, toured her den before coming to bed, grunting as he noted her titles and the advertising posters for her books, *grunt*, the shelves of foreign-language editions, *grunt*, and the framed *New York Times* review, *grunt, grunt*. When he

66

finally made love to her, he made the same grunting sounds, and Marla realized he wasn't really entering her but coming as close as he could to fucking her success.

"You know what I remember best about you?" Tony is saying. "When you played the princess in *Once Upon a Mattress.* You were great. You were fantastic."

"I couldn't sing."

"Yeah? I never noticed." He smiles again. "And now you're moving back. That's really something. Your husband interested in this house, too?"

"I'm divorced."

"Me, too. Well, not actually divorced. Separated." He makes a fist and shows Marla the faint circle left by a wedding band. "You have kids?"

"A daughter. She's back in L.A."

"I've got two daughters. Ten and twelve. They're with their mother."

The white smile doesn't waver, but Marla catches a slight slump of his shoulders. "You miss them," she says.

"Yeah, well, that's the name of the game, isn't it?" His shoulders straighten. "Marla Hudson. I had a crush on you."

"You didn't." She starts walking toward the house.

Tony falls in beside her. "You were way above me. It was one of those at-a-distance, older-woman kind of things."

"I'm sorry. I never knew."

"You wouldn't have noticed me anyway. I was a real greaser. Duck's tail. Pegged pants. Besides, you were going out with that guy the girls were so nuts over. The one that got killed? Chris French."

The diminuitive of Christian's name catches Marla's attention. "Were you friends with him?"

"Me? Nah. He and Guido sometimes hung out together."

This is where the trail to Christian starts, Marla thinks, with faint, almost imperceptible, markings in the sand. "Does Guido still live here?"

"Nope. New Jersey. Five kids."

"Oh."

They reach the front door. Tony pulls out a ring of keys and begins to search for the right one. "And my brother Nicky has four kids, and get this, Romeo has six."

Marla watches his hands on the keys. They're the hands of a workman who does not work with his hands: muscular, square, with clean nails, trimmed blunt. His skin is white, the hairs on the back of his fingers are black. "So where did you go wrong?" Marla asks lightly, flirtatiously.

"Hey, it wasn't for lack of trying."

He's smiling but as he glances at her, Marla realizes he's thought about her since he was fifteen years old, that she's been fodder for his sexual fantasies for years. As she looks into his eyes, she wonders what those fantasies have been. She absorbs the frisson of air, and it strengthens to a rush of warmth in her veins, her groin. Then she breaks their locked glance and the moment of silence.

"Well," she says, "are you going to sell me this house?"

Tony blinks and his languorous smile tightens. "I hope so," he says briskly. "It's a one-of-a-kind, you know."

A house and a man: It's hard to tell which is the more intriguing investment. They both have potential, although the house promises a longevity that lust does not. Lust has a predictable rise and fall, a bell curve of sexual satiation. Once the curve goes flat, there's little hope of another surge. A house, on the other hand, can provide a steady rise in satisfaction. Not that I have to choose between the two. I can have my cake—white butter cream (thick muscle), red sugar rosebuds (small, hard nipples), pale green leaves (smooth skin shaded by beard) and eat it, too—right down to the last powdery crumb.

That night Marla goes to dinner at the Breymanns'. If she sees her life as a forked road, then this living room with the pale blue carpet, matching draperies, and blue-and-white floral couch, this walnut coffee table with the curved legs and stack of magazines—*Reader's Digest, Discover, Newsweek, TV Guide*, this mantelpiece with framed photographs of Breymanns formally posed in various stages of their lives, is the road she has not taken. For Marla, the evening becomes a series of events, each building on another like monotone transparencies placed one on top of the other, until she's formed a full-color picture, not only of Bobbie's life but of her own had she stayed in Cassandra, married a local boy, taken a regular job, become part of the community in which she'd grown up.

Bobbie, welcoming her at the door. Bobbie—a woman of slightlys: slightly heavier than she should be, slightly dowdier than she need be, slightly older than she need look. Marla imagines Bobbie in the hands of her California team: Sylvio, the hairdresser, Bonita, the cosmetician, and Bertram, the exercise and diet maestro to the rich and the famous. She would be shaped, pummeled, firmed, trimmed, pruned, and painted. But then it's doubtful Bobbie would ever go to Marla's make-over team. She was always resistant to change, an anchor to Marla's wild swings of imagination, holding fast against the rapid and changeable gusts of Marla's enthusiasms, hatreds, loves, and dismissals.

Dan, standing at the head of the dining room table. The chandelier, made of small glass drops, mirrors his bent head, reflecting dozens of blond crowns, hairs thinning and turning a dull gray. Marla remembers him from chemistry class. Dan Breymann: glasses with black frames, bony wrists, thin neck, ugly plaid shirts his mother bought at the boy's section of Walker's. Danny Boy—that's what the teacher called him. One hundred percent on the final exam, and the only student to win the teacher's prize, a dinner at Herlihy's Steak House. Dan, grown to manhood, is surprisingly tall and burly and almost handsome. Bobbie has put a frilly apron on him: "He's a messy carver." If Marla narrows her eyes, he blurs and becomes part of the meal— roast beef, scalloped potatoes, green beans—basic, nice, practical, not flashy.

* * *

Joel, entering the living room and earnestly shaking her hand. She catches a complex expression on Bobbie's face, such a tangle of pride, love, and anxiety that Marla realizes Joel is the pivot on which Bobbie's heart swings. He's a blend of Breymann and Gardiner—Dan's blondness, blue eyes, and broad, open brow, Bobbie's sweetness of smile—and a mix of boy and man. He has a boy's thin neck and bony wrists, but his shoulders are broad, there's the hint of a blond mustache over his upper lip, and he has an honest man's direct gaze. Marla can't help herself. She kisses him on the cheek and is delighted by the embarrassed dip of his head. His skin is smooth and smells of soap and cologne.

"I understand you're buying the Hiller house," he says carefully, and she sees he's been coached. *Say hello and ask her how she is. But I don't know her, Mom, so it would sound stupid. Then find a subject of conversation you have in common. Like what? Well, she's buying the Hiller house. You know the Hiller house.*

"That's right," Marla says.

"When I was a kid, I thought it was haunted."

"By who?" Marla asks. "Anybody interesting?"

He thinks for a minute, shrugs, and gives her his sweet smile. "Nah. Just your basic generic ghosts."

On a tour of the house with Bobbie, who keeps saying, "I know it's not very exciting compared to Malibu." The master bedroom decorated in pale blue and green has its own bathroom. Joel's room is pure boy: captain's bed with a blue-and-brown bedspread, sports equipment and posters, a collection of model airplanes. The second bathroom, blue again, is off the hallway. The television room has an old, comfortable couch and rocking chair. The view off the dining room encompasses a lawn and the patio, gas barbecue, and deck chairs. Down in the basement is a rec room with a wet bar, similar to the one that the Hudsons had at 68 Willow. It has its own small sink, counter, and refrigerator, and behind it are shelves of glasses and bottles reflected in a background mirror.

"Do you remember how we used to play barmaids in my rec room?" Marla asks.

Bobbie looks startled. "Did we?"

"We'd mix awful concoctions from sodas and make believe they'd get us drunk?" Marla remembers staggering around and singing at the top of her lungs while Bobbie collapsed in laughter.

"Isn't that funny," Bobbie says. "I don't remember any of it."

Candlelight flickering on sterling silver flatware and delicate bone china. The pewter holder is shaped into a loop that spirals upward so the slender, white candles appear to be climbing. Marla recognizes a wedding gift, stored in its felt bag and taken out only for momentous occasions like birthdays, anniversaries, and dinners when friends who have to be impressed come to visit. There's a wedding photograph of the Breymanns on the mantelpiece. Dan, sporting a mustache, is in a tuxedo and a thinner Bobbie wears a long white dress and a frothy veil. Their smiles are young and confident. Marla never had a formal wedding. She was a rebel in the late sixties, disdaining ceremony and ritual. She and Sean went to a justice of the peace, and they wore jeans, matching flowered shirts, beads, and headbands. How cool they thought they were, how anti-establishment. How clichéd. Six years later, she thought it absurd to wear white for her wedding with David. Her suit was a pale mauve and pink with a creamy white blouse, his suit was blue with a blue-and-red striped tie.

But didn't she secretly yearn for white, for ecru and tulle? For a delicate tracery of beads over her breasts and satin heels dyed to match the long, flowing silk? For most of her senior year, she lulled herself to sleep by fantasizing about her wedding: the organ notes swelling, her father's arm, her mother's tears, the misty world beyond her veil, Christian waiting for her, standing tall before the altar.

"More roast beef?" Dan asks, knife poised over the platter of meat.

"Yes, thanks. It's delicious." Marla nods and smiles, but when she looks into the staircase of flame, she sees that the candles are slowly dissolving, first into fire and then into thin wisps of curling smoke, elusive as her dreams.

Talk over dinner about how Cassandra has changed. Bobbie and Dan are determined to bring Marla up to date. They talk about properties changing hands, streets being widened, school expansion, the cost of a new road west of town, the increase in garbage pickup fees. It's like a film running before Marla's eyes, a disjointed, nonlinear film.

"The new medical building opened in nineteen eighty-four," Dan says.

"But Dr. Peters was here before that," Bobbie says. "He took care of Joel when he had the mumps. When was that? Nineteen seventy-nine."

"I was only six then," Joel says. "I got the mumps when I was nine."

"Chicken pox then." Bobbie turns to Marla. "Joel got every infectious disease going."

"Remember the year we couldn't go to Disney World because I got that sore throat?"

"Strep throat," Bobbie says. "You were ten."

"Two days before we were supposed to leave," Dan says to Marla. "We were all packed and ready to go."

"I still wanted to go," Joel says.

"He tried to tell us he was fine," Bobbie says, "except all he could do was croak."

The three of them smile at one another, and Marla thinks of all the moments and myths she and Didi cannot share. Did she ever tell Didi the story of her first tooth—how it didn't come and didn't come even though Didi was teething for months, drooling and chewing on everything in sight? How she kept rubbing her finger along Didi's bottom gum vainly waiting for those two small front teeth to emerge. How one day she was feeding Didi cereal and heard a clink on the spoon, but when she pulled down Didi's lower lip there was still nothing there. Contrary, that's what Didi's teething pattern had been. The tooth that had emerged was the right upper canine. What had she been saving that story for? Didi—when she had her own babies?

Marla takes a sip of wine and chokes.

"Are you all right?" Bobbie says.

"Fine," Marla says. "I'm fine."

Talk about the Deacons' daughter in low, concerned voices. There've been searches around Cassandra, and the police have issued an All Persons Bulletin across the country, but it seems as if Caroline's disappeared into thin air. Everyone is one hundred percent positive that Caroline wouldn't run away—not Caroline Deacon, a nice girl with a good head on her shoulders who wouldn't think of putting her parents through such a thing—and the town is already abuzz with rumors about rape, murder, a serial killer. Not that they're saying such things to the Deacons, mind you. They're bringing casseroles to the Deacons and a cornucopia of pies, muffins, cookies, breads, and platitudes. They're saying, "She's going to be fine, I just know it," and "The police'll find her, that's what they're trained to do," and "If there's anything I can do to help, you know you can just call on me," but across the width and breadth of Cassandra, a different sort of conversation is taking place at the dinner tables, words and undercurrents swirling together into a disturbing mix of gossip, emotion, excitement, and fear.

"A girl was raped and murdered in Elverton a year ago," Bobbie says. "They never found who did it."

"I heard there was a green pickup truck near the school," Joel says. "Nobody in town has a green pickup truck."

Dan shakes his head. "This is pure speculation and it's causing a lot of anxiety."

"I feel so bad for the Deacons," Bobbie says. "Molly says the worst is the not knowing."

And suddenly Marla is pulled directly into the words, the undercurrents. She knows all about not knowing: the times Didi came home late, the nights she didn't come home at all, the strange boys who called at two o'clock in the morning, the lies about school, the lies about where she'd been, the brush-offs—"Just get off my case, okay?"—and the silence.

Marla felt as if she were floating in a pool of anxiety, all the more frightening because the pool had no shape, no definition, no hook on which she could comfortably hang the weight of her fears. She understands the unknown Molly, trapped in her own private hell.

"And Frances told me Ben is taking it hard," Bobbie continues. "Ben is the son of our friend, Frances Phillips. He's been going out with Caroline for—how long has it been?"

"About a year," Joel says.

"She says he's throwing himself into schoolwork, it's his way of escape, but he's up until three and four in the morning. She's afraid he's going to be sick."

"The trauma team talked to us today," Joel says. "They want to know if everybody's freaking out."

"At the school," Bobbie explains to Marla. "They've brought in a psychologist and social worker. A lot of the girls are frightened."

"They asked if we're having nightmares," Joel says. "They're real interested in how we're sleeping."

"How are you sleeping?" Marla asks.

"Oh, pretty good."

"Joel could sleep through a rock concert," Dan says.

"Not if it was a good band," Joel says.

Reminiscences over chocolate cake, coffee, and their high school yearbook. Bobbie and Dan know what happened to most of their graduating class.

"Sammy Key. He was killed in Vietnam."

"Remember Mary Alice Dobson? She teaches school in Oneonta."

"Skip Romer married Sandy Brasseau. Two weeks after graduation."

"How pregnant was she?" Marla asks.

"About three months, I think."

"We guessed they were sleeping together, didn't we?"

"Bill Hahn works with me," Dan says. "He's married, two kids. Lives in Laurel Grove."

"Mr. Preston retired in—when was it, Dan? Seventy-two? Anyway, he died last year. Liver cancer."

They study their own photographs, their young smooth faces.

"That horrible hairdo," Bobbie says. "It looks artificial."

"It was artificial," Marla says. "Ninety percent hairspray."

"Those glasses make me look like I'm trying to be fifty years old," Dan says.

Marla hasn't seen her graduation photo for twenty-five years. A pretty girl with a dark flip and an arrogant gaze stares back at her. She looks as if nothing can stop her from getting what she wants (the picture was taken before Christian's death). Beneath the photo is written:

Likes: T. S. Eliot, Old Spice, boys the speed of light.
Memories: the Junior Prom, a blue Chevy, moonlight
  on a special rock.
Favorite phrase: "It's real cool."
Ambition: to be a star.

"Moonlight on a special rock?" Dan asks. "What was that?"

"My poetry place," Marla says.

"That big boulder they bulldozed behind the school," Bobbie says.

"I used to read my poetry to the moon." Marla remembers standing on the rock, eyes closed, head tilted back, while she sent words of love and destiny and pain to a star-studded sky. "Dramatic, wasn't I?"

"I thought it was romantic," Bobbie says. "You wrote reams of love poetry. I was really impressed."

Dan turns a page, and they see the blank where Christian's picture was supposed to go. The yearbook was already in the process of being printed when the accident happened, and there was no opportunity for the printer to close the ranks.

"I burned all that poetry after Christian died," Marla

says. Dramatically, of course, sitting in her room, lighting each piece of paper with her cigarette lighter and dropping it into the wastebasket. Crying hysterically throughout, but even through her tears noting, with the writer's eye, the pastel-colored Mother Goose scenes on the wastebasket: three smiling mice, a jolly cow jumping over the moon, Little Bo Peep's fat pink cheeks. She'd used those details in her first novel to great ironic effect in the scene where the narrator burned her diary.

"You know," Dan says, "I saw Faith the other day when I was going to work."

It takes Marla a minute to make the connection. "Christian's sister?"

"She lives in Laurel Grove," Bobbie says.

"She's married and has a son. He played in Little League with Joel," Dan says.

"You're thinking of Faith Ohms," Bobbie says. "Not Faith French."

"Faith Ohms?" Dan says. "She works for Aetna Life."

"Faith Ohms works at the bank," Bobbie says. "Faith French never married and works as an X-ray technician at Laurel Grove Hospital."

"Do you think she'd talk to me about Christian?" Marla asks.

"Why not?" Dan says.

"The Frenches hated me."

"That was a long time ago," Bobbie says and, standing up, begins to pick up the dishes. "They don't live here anymore."

Leaving after dinner, saying thank you. Marla compliments Bobbie on the food, her house, and her hospitality and says good-bye to Dan.

"Now, keep in touch," he says.

"Joel," Bobbie calls out. "Our guest is leaving."

Joel obediently emerges from his bedroom, where he was doing his homework. "I hope everything goes okay with the Hiller house."

"Why, thank you, Joel, I hope it goes okay, too."

"There weren't any ghosts, by the way. That was just kid stuff at Halloween."

"That's too bad. I think I'd like a few ghosts."

She's earned his startled, sweet smile. "It was nice meeting you," he says, extending his hand.

He has a firm, manly handshake. "It was nice meeting you, too," Marla says, and sees Bobbie and Dan, standing side by side, smiling proudly.

I have this theory that my life is a forked road with Christian's death as the intersection. If he hadn't died, we would have married and lived in Cassandra. I'd be a drama teacher (I said I'd be a star in the yearbook, but in my heart I was more realistic), and he'd be a . . . what? He wanted to be a trial lawyer, but his grades were shit. Whatever—we'd have children, a nice house, funny family stories—in short, the better, happier road not taken, closed off, no entry, keep out!

But life isn't a forked road. Life has prongs, hidden pathways, and dead ends. It's more likely we'd have married, hated one another, and divorced. Who was Christian anyway? I thought I knew him and owned him, because we touched each other's secret places, but at seventeen I didn't know that such intimacy is only skin deep, or that my hold on him was so flimsy.

Now I know no one belongs to anyone, not husbands, lovers, or children. The need to possess is a human weakness. We take what we think is there, only to discover later that it's not what it seems. I think that beneath his facade Christian was frightened, confused, and angry. I think that what he wanted from me was the reflection of himself as he wanted to be, not what he really was. And wasn't I the perfect mirror? In my eyes he was cool, sexy, passionate, and enigmatic—the James Dean of Cassandra, and he was mine.

Marla soaks in a hot bath, ignoring the motel's horrible color scheme: pale green linoleum, pink ceramic, darker pink walls. She lies in the water, her head resting against the curved edge of the tub, her eyes closed, letting the tenseness seep away. Her calf muscles ache as if she'd been climbing a mountain instead of reacquainting herself with her home-town. She knew coming back was going to be hard, but then the first steps are always the hardest, aren't they? Meeting Bobbie, playing down her own successes, making sure the friendship was still there. She knows she can't easily reenter Cassandra and revisit the past without Bobbie's help. Of course, she still likes Bobbie, her open smile, her goodness. She always envied Bobbie's goodness without ever trying to equal it—that depth of decency seemed like a trait that was right for Bobbie but not for her. In her fourth novel, *Crimson Dreams,* she created a character based on Bobbie, a married woman who had an affair with her best friend's husband but was too honest to lie when her own husband asked her about it. Marla remembers the rule of thumb she used every time the character had to make a decision. Is this what Bobbie would say? Isn't that what Bobbie would do? One critic had described this character as "an accurate and moving portrayal of small-town propriety at agonizing odds with big-city iniquity." Marla sighs as she gets out of the bath, remembering that *Crimson Dreams* was her last novel to get uniformly good reviews.

She's just got on her nightgown, when there's a knock at the door to her room.

"Yes?" she says through the wood.

"Tony Molino, your friendly real estate agent."

"Just a minute." She's expected Tony to make a move, but not quite so fast. But then she's forgotten about the "mad" Molinos, the town's motorcycle freaks and speed demons. Hadn't Guido been infamous for collecting more speeding tickets on Route 240 than anyone else in town?

She pulls on a bathrobe and opens the door. Tony raises an eyebrow at her and then the bottle of scotch he holds in his hand. "Some J & B? To celebrate?"

"The offer's been accepted?"

He walks in and shuts the door behind him. "Signed, sealed, and delivered. Thanks to time zones and fax machines." He puts the bottle on the table, opens the paper bag he's carried in his other hand, and takes out two shot glasses.

"You've thought of everything," Marla says.

"Even the ice." He takes out a plastic container that holds several ice cubes. With motions imitating great fanfare, he puts an ice cube in each glass, pours an inch of scotch in each, hands a glass to her, and then raises his high. "From the Hiller house to the Hudson place."

"To the Hudson place." Marla can't help smiling. It's like a third-rate movie from the forties. The set: the motel room, tacky and threadbare, with the bed as the focus of the scene. The protagonists: the single woman alone and unhappy, her breasts loose beneath her nightgown, her skin flushed from her bath; the man lonely and needful, his suit tie loosened, his hair attractively tousled. The dialogue: corny.

"You don't mind my coming this late, do you?" Tony asks as he takes off his jacket and makes himself comfortable in the only chair in the room.

Marla sits on the edge of the bed. "No, I don't mind."

"I remembered something else about you when I was back in the office."

"Oh?"

"A school assembly where you got up and read this poem."

"Was it any good?"

He shrugs. "I was watching your legs."

Marla sips her scotch and smiles the enigmatic smile of the movie heroine.

"You were wearing this plaid skirt with red, black, and yellow colors. It had—whatchyacallit?" He motions with his hand.

"Pleats."

"Yeah, pleats. All the way around. How's that for recall!"

"Excellent. I'm impressed."

But the dialogue is like so much dust, and Marla discovers she's impatient. She wants to brush it aside, flick all the words, innuendos, and preliminaries away. In the past, she would have enjoyed a prolonged and delicious flirtation, curious to see what he'd say, what she'd say, his maneuvers to get her into bed, her responses, noting and remembering the phrases, the tone of voice, the look in an eye. Hadn't she used Sean's verbal foreplay in two of her novels? David's anticipatory habit of rubbing his crotch in *Fly Away the Night?* Every detail is material, words and expressions are provisions to be stocked against a later need, even her own reactions gauged and measured and stored for future use. But tonight, she can't bear the thought of the territory Tony will want to cover. She doesn't care about his memories, his wife, his separation, his children, his job, his brothers. She doesn't want to spend the next hour scrambling over the verbal hills and valleys of his sadness, his joys, his loneliness, his horniness. And she's sick of lonely nights, empty beds, and her own fingers for satisfaction.

Marla puts down her scotch. "Are you going to fuck me?" she says.

His head, that dark, handsome head, moves back sharply as if his body, running full tilt, has hit a wall. "Now?" he asks.

"Now."

Chapter
6

Since I was a child, libraries have been places of solace, of comfort and satisfactions. When I was growing up, the town's library was situated beside the fire department in a four-room wooden building that had once been a schoolhouse. It hadn't been used as a school since the war, but the floors still showed the scuff marks of many heels and the scraping of desk chairs on the wood, and there was a smell of children's sweat—a slightly sour odor—embedded in the walls. I loved that library and spent hours in it. I read my way through the children's section by the time I was eleven years old, and had to get written permission from my parents to take out books in the adult section. There was no such thing as young adult reading in those days. I went straight from *Little House on the Prairie* to *The Bridge over the River Kwai*. I remember the thrill of reading my first adult book. I had the same sensation as a diver poised over a pool of blue water. Opening to the first page was like cutting into that water in a clean dive, a breathless, arced leap into the unknown.

Mrs. Morgan was the librarian then, a thin woman nearing fifty with dyed ash-brown hair and the wrinkled face of someone who smokes too much and sits in the sun more than she should. The librarian's position was a part-time job that she got because her husband, Newty, was the fire chief, and she could bring him his lunch at noon and sit in the library until he was ready to go home. "And Newty's not fussy about supper," she'd tell me. "He doesn't mind leftovers and if there's nothing made, he'll settle for PB and J." PB and J was Mrs. Morgan's shorthand for peanut butter and jelly, and I was shocked that she'd serve to Mr. Morgan the kind of sandwiches my brother and I ate. He was the biggest man in Cassandra, three inches over six feet, thick biceps, a protruding stomach, and a military crew cut. Besides, my mother would never serve sandwiches at supper. In our house, supper meant a roast, mashed potatoes, and vegetables, followed by pie or cake. My mother said that my father worked hard all day with numbers, and his brain cells needed sustenance so he could face another day tomorrow.

When Mrs. Morgan realized that I came like clockwork to the library every afternoon, she began to save up the returned books for me to shelve. I was immensely proud of this unpaid job and pushed the book cart around in a self-important fashion, not only shelving the returned books but searching for misplaced books and putting them back in their rightful places. I was also entranced by the Dewey Decimal System, in which every subject in the world— tatting, rock climbing, Henry VIII, keeping salamanders as pets—had its own place on the shelves. While I worked, Mrs. Morgan knit and talked. The result was that I heard a lot about Newty and got a glimpse of a marriage that differed dramatically from that of my parents. Unlike my father, with his closet of suits and his drawers of rolled-up socks and folded boxer shorts, Newty was a slob. "Balls of socks kicked underneath the bed, underwear at the bottom of the closet," Mrs. Morgan would say while her knitting needles clicked. "And the cigar ash. Mark my words, Barbara, don't marry a man who smokes cigars. You'll be vacuuming until kingdom come." And even worse, Newty played poker with his cronies, a weekly event that Mrs.

Morgan found a trial because of the food consumed, the beer drunk, and the mess created.

My father didn't believe in gambling. This belief had nothing to do with any religion but with a spiritual respect that he had for money. He liked to put his money into his bank and watch it grow, and his idea of a flyer was to invest in municipals and utilities. I often sat and watched him pay the bills while he talked to me about money. His hands were narrow, and every once in a while he'd sit back and pass a slender thumb and forefinger over his pencil mustache. "The important thing is to choose solid investments," he'd say. "Not dramatic, but safe. What you have to be careful of is speculation. You know what speculation means?" He'd lean forward and I could smell his brisk aftershave and see the comb marks in his dark hair. "Speculation is putting your money into risky investments. Sure, you may stand to make a lot if it goes, but what if it doesn't? What then?"

My father didn't have to elaborate. I had a frightening vision of my small bank account, that repository of baby-sitting money and birthday gifts, shrinking into nothing. One day, I'd take my bank book with its gray, grainy cover and the embossed gold crest of the First National to the teller and discover that, due to speculation, gambling, or some reckless disregard for money on my part, the balance had disappeared. All that hard-earned money evaporated, like so much steam, into the cool air.

So Newty's Friday-night poker games had the thrill of the forbidden for me, even if the details were secondhand. I listened to Mrs. Morgan's recitals of the sandwiches she'd had to make, the vacuuming she'd done afterward, and the way the cigar smoke irritated her throat so she had to suck on special lozenges the doctor had given her. Sometimes she'd tell me about big plays Newty'd make, and later I'd say phrases to myself like *straight flush, aces high,* and *five-card stud,* although I wasn't sure precisely what they meant. Sometimes Newty made a bundle, but a lot of the time he lost something terrible.

"The trouble is he doesn't believe in that penny-ante stuff," Mrs. Morgan would inform me. "He likes stakes to mean something." Her thin lips turned down at their wrinkled corners and she squinted at her knitting. Although she and Newty had no children, her specialty was baby sweaters in pale blue or pink popcorn stitch that she made for the annual Firemen's Craft and Rummage sale.

"Did Mr. Morgan lose a lot of money?" I would ask with a delicious little shiver down my spine.

"That Newtson would bet our house if I let him," she'd say. "Why, he'd put me on that table if white slavery wasn't illegal." I wasn't sure what white slavery meant either, but I'd imagine skinny Mrs. Morgan stretched out on the card table, eyes closed, arms straight at her sides, while cigar-smoking men eating ham-and-cheese sandwiches called out bets over her still body.

When I came back to Cassandra with my library degree in hand and took the job as head librarian fifteen years later, Mrs. Morgan met me on the street, congratulated me on the job, and then told anyone who'd listen until her death in 1977 that she'd taught me everything she knew. It took me several months into my job, several months when Mrs. Morgan failed to come to the library, to realize that the keeper of the books, the owner of the key to the treasures of my childhood, didn't like to read and had never had any interest in literature. I also realized what a boon I must have been to her. How bored she must have been sitting there hour after hour, checking books in and out, and having meaningless (for her) conversations with the book lovers who used the library. Enter little Barbara Gardiner, a willing ear, possessing not only the patience to listen to the humdrum details of Newty's imperfections but also the naïveté to be impressed by her burdens and sacrifices. And I was pliable and eager. How relieved she must have been when I jumped at the chance to reshelve books, relieving her of the burdensome necessity of learning the Dewey Decimal System.

The library I work in now was resurrected from the ashes of the old library when it burnt down in 1970. It's a small, brick building with big windows that let in a lot of light. The upstairs houses the adult fiction collection and nonfiction section, while the children's books are in the basement in a room that has been decorated with small tables and chairs and many bright pictures. Mona Criado, who handles the children's section, and I are the only full-time librarians. We have two other women who work part-time and a large staff of volunteers who help at the front desk, prepare new books for circulation, reshelve books, and keep order during the preschoolers' story times. As head librarian, I report to a board of trustees that meets twice a year. Two board members are elected town officials, and three are volunteers from the community who are interested in literature. This year, Edgar and Frances are serving along with Eileen MacDonald, who's in her eighties and has been on the board for as long as I can remember. This board votes on my proposals and reports and makes recommendations to the town council, which provides our funding. It's a system that's worked smoothly, although we always request larger budgets than we receive and recent cutbacks in state funding to municipalities don't augur well for next year's book purchases.

I'm working on book orders in my office, a small room situated in the back of the building, when Mona sticks her head in the doorway. "Good morning."

"Good morning," I say, smiling. "Come on in."

Mona is my right-hand woman, and I liked her the moment I interviewed her. She came to us straight out of library school and is now in her late twenties. She's proven to be everything I thought she'd be—bright, cheerful, easy to work with, and good with children. She has a pretty face and beautiful coloring: dark hair, dark eyes, and a creamy complexion. She's also fat in a warm, inviting way, and I've noticed that the preschoolers like to burrow into her soft lap and lean their heads against her large breasts.

Mona sits in the chair opposite my desk. "Did you know about the candlelight vigil for Caroline Deacon at my church tonight? Everyone's invited." Mona goes to St. Matthew's Episcopalian, as do the Deacons.

"Yes," I say, "we'll be there."

"What an awful business."

I sigh.

"You know something? I think the kids are taking out more horror novels than usual," she says. "Funny, isn't it. I'd have thought reading those books would make the fears worse."

"Maybe they help the kids work through the fears."

She gives a little shudder and her dark curls shake. "They'd make me worse. I'm already having trouble sleeping at night. I hear every sound in the apartment. I swear that's the worst thing about being single."

I smile internally at this, because Mona has one of the most active love lives of any single woman in Cassandra. The preschoolers aren't the only people in town attracted to her pretty smile and inviting bulk. She may be single, but she's rarely alone.

"Why not have Tony over for protection?"

"He's toast."

"Already?" I ask, although I'm not surprised. Tony Molino and Mona have been an item since February, but I hadn't thought it would last. Mona likes books, intellectual movies, and interesting conversation. Tony doesn't even own a library card.

"He's still attached to his wife and kids. You know what these Italian guys are like. Their wives are madonnas and, even when they're separated, their girlfriends are whores."

She says this cheerfully, and I'm a little shocked. "Surely not."

She gives a careless, little shrug. "I wonder who he's sleeping with now."

Mona is almost like the sister I never had—the younger sister who confided in me and took my advice because I was older and wiser. When she moved to Cassandra, I took her under my wing, helped her find an apartment, and introduced her to the most eligible men in town. She hit it off with Peter Zimbrowski, our insurance agent, and I had great hopes for a wedding, but the relationship didn't last and he got another job in New Jersey. This was a blow to my matchmaking ambitions, but I also realized that Mona had no real intention of settling down for a while. What had begun as a maternal sort of possessiveness—looking back, I now see that I was trying at first to make Mona into the daughter I never had—slipped into a more relaxed, sisterly attitude. Now I have no dreams of nuptials but instead listen with a fond tolerance to the ups and downs of Mona's many romances and allow myself to be pleasurably titillated by the sexual activities of the town's single men, separated, divorced men, and married men who can't keep their fingers from Mona's succulent flesh. It's a side of Cassandra I wouldn't have known existed.

"Now for the items on the agenda," she says briskly, and waves a clutch of papers at me.

"Hit me gently," I say. "It's still morning."

We discuss the children's spring readings, the school library tours, and the volunteer program, which has been disrupted by the illness of its coordinator. Then Mona says, "Marla Hudson. Did you ask her?"

"Not yet. She's been busy house hunting." When I told Mona that Marla was moving back to Cassandra, she immediately hit on the idea of having Marla give a series of talks at the library.

"If we don't get her," Mona says, "Timothy will. He's got more money."

Timothy O'Hara heads the library in Laurel Grove, and we're in friendly competition. "I know," I say. "I'll ask her just as soon as she's a bit more settled."

"Did you see her on the Channel Five news?" I shake my head. "She was asked if she'd come back to Cassandra because she'd run out of things to say about California and needed new material. Imagine if she'd said yes—no one in town would talk to her. Anyway, she sidestepped it neatly. She said she'd been away for a long time and needed to touch her roots."

"Marla's always been clever," I say.

"I heard she's bought the Hiller house. Edgar says she's going to renovate it from top to bottom."

"How does Edgar know?" I try to think my way through the connections of people that would result in Edgar's knowing Marla's business almost as soon as it's transacted.

"You know Edgar," Mona says. "If I wanted to know something juicy about my own life, I'd ask him first. Then it wouldn't be such a big surprise."

I laugh and she glances down at her papers. "Have you gone through your mail yet?"

"No."

"There's a letter from Arlene."

"Not again," I say. Arlene is a gadfly, stinging us with requests to censor books that she considers dangerous to Cassandra. So far the board has squelched her requests and she's abided by their decisions. "Is it *The Catcher in the Rye?*"

Mona nods. "She's got a new twist, though. She says that Caroline's disappearance can be directly linked to increasing violence in our society, which can be directly linked to decreasing respect for authority, which, in turn, can be directly linked to books like *The Catcher in the Rye.*"

I sigh. "Okay, I'll handle it as usual." "As usual" means I write her a polite letter informing her that her request will be considered at the board meeting in June. "Anything else?"

"Frances Phillips phoned. She'd tried to reach you at home but you were already gone. She needs to talk to you urgently, but she can't be reached because she has a class. She says she'll phone a little after eleven, and would you please be here to take the call."

I raise my eyebrows. "I wonder what that's about."

"She sounded really upset about something."

We finish our meeting a little after eleven, but Frances doesn't phone me. Although I want to check some books in the reference section, I stay in my office and worry, because it isn't like Frances either to call in a panic or not to call when she says she will. I'm reading some correspondence when the door bursts open and bangs against the wall. I stand up in alarm because Frances is breathless, her face too pale, and she looks as if she's been crying.

"I couldn't stay at the college," she says. "I just couldn't. I don't even know how I managed to get through that class. I can't remember a word I said." I sit her down on the chair and press a cup of tea into her trembling hands. "I'm a mass of nerves. What a ridiculous thing to say. Have you ever thought about it? We're all masses of nerves right to our fingertips. It's a meaningless statement."

"Frances, what's happened?" I say.

"It's Ben. They want him to take a lie detector test."

I was standing next to her chair, but now I sit on the edge of my desk. "The police?"

"They came by this morning before he went to school. Reg says it's pro forma and nothing to be worried about. He says they're talking to all of Caroline's friends. But I'm not kidding myself. They're not asking all her friends to take lie detector tests." The perfect symmetry of her face cracks, then distorts, and she starts to cry. "They think he murdered her."

I take the cup of tea from her shaking hands and hold her icy fingers in mine. "They don't," I say. "I'm sure they don't really believe that. They're just being careful. And besides, who knows if she's dead? Nobody knows that."

"Then we're burying our heads in the sand, Barbara, because it's been three days and where do you suppose she is?"

Of course, Frances is only saying what we're all thinking but can't bear to say out loud because the words would be so painful to our ears. "I'm sure it's just standard procedure," I say. "Reg has known Ben since he was in diapers. Didn't he coach Ben's Little League team?"

"I've said all of this to myself a thousand times." She pulls her hands from mine and wipes her eyes. "It doesn't help."

"How's Ben taking it?"

"A lot better than I am. He's so calm. He said, 'It's okay, Mom. It's just their job.'"

I think of Ben, a tall, handsome boy who's inherited Frances's fine bone structure and coloring and his father Paul's cool reserve. Although he and Joel aren't friendly anymore, they were best friends during grade school, and we often had him at our house. Even when he was playing cowboys and Indians or cops and robbers, he had an air of coolness about him. Joel would race around, scream and yell, and, when shot by a gun or pierced by an arrow, fall into a flushed and overexcited heap. But Ben played as if a part of him was the audience and the other part was the actor. He had dying down to an art. At first he would stand very still, his head cocked to one side. Then he would put a hand to his chest and breathe heavily. Finally, he fell to the ground but not with Joel's abandon. Rather, his was a careful collapse with his arms and legs arranged in a starlike pattern and his back in an arch of simulated agony.

"Look at it this way," I say. "He'll pass the lie detector test and that'll be it."

"No, it won't," Frances says. "Everyone knows those tests aren't accurate. He'll still be under suspicion. You know why?"

I shake my head.

"I followed Reg out of the house, Barbara, and I argued with him. I told him that Ben and Caroline hadn't been going together that long, that they were more friends than anything else, and you know what he said? He said I was wrong, and I said I wasn't, that Ben had told me he wasn't that serious about Caroline and she wasn't serious about him. They liked each other, sure, but it was more a convenience thing, you know, for dates and the prom. And then you know what Reg said?"

I shake my head again.

"That they were sleeping together. That it was common knowledge—all of Ben's and Caroline's friends knew. And that Caroline was on the pill, but you know how girls are. They could have been forgetful so the police can't rule out the pregnancy factor. So I went back to Ben, and you know the first thing out of my mouth? Even I can't believe it. I screamed at him, 'What about condoms? You're supposed to use condoms.' And he said, 'Sometimes we did, Mom, but sometimes they just got in the way.' I'm just shaking, Barbara. Just shaking."

The tears trickle slowly down her face, and I take her hands again and massage her thin fingers with their pale, bluish nails. I stroke them as if the heat of my skin, the warmth of my pity, can be absorbed into her flesh. "Oh, Frances," I say. "I'm sorry. I'm so sorry."

And it's true. Sympathy has a physical shape. I feel it rising in my heart and overflowing like water. But this flood, this waterfall, doesn't conceal another shape, the nugget of relief that lies solid in my chest. I can't help it. I'm glad it's her and not me, her son and not mine. I'm glad Joel isn't fully developed, glad he's not that interested in girls, glad that I don't have to think of him as a sexual being, yet. For, if I try to imagine Joel erect and ready, handling some girl's breasts, entering her, coming to orgasm, I can't keep any images in my mind. The pictures keep sliding away, as if I were sitting rigid in a train, eyes staring straight ahead and, out of the corner of my eye, catching forbidden glimpses of a passing landscape, a frightening, unwanted landscape.

There but for the grace of . . .

Dan and I arrive at St. Matthew's a little late. Sophie Rundle, who went to school with my mother and lived next door to us when I was growing up, is manning the desk at the door. She's a tiny woman with a pronounced bosom and stomach and white hair permed into tight curls.

"So glad you could come," she whispers. "Such a tragedy, just awful, so terrible for the Deacons. My heart"—she presses a liver-spotted hand, decorated with hot pink nail polish, to that ample chest—"just hurts for them. But I'm just thrilled by the turnout. It's wonderful, everyone coming and praying for that dear, sweet child. God just has to listen, don't you think?"

We murmur sympathetic agreement, and I think how silly Sophie has always been: fluttery, foolish, inane. She drove my mother, who did not believe in speaking ill of anyone, to comment that when God gave out brains, he must have had something very special in mind for Sophie.

She gives each of us a candle, lights them, and points us to empty seats. The church is crowded with people whose candles flicker like fragile beacons in the dim evening light. Our pew is in the rear of the church, but I see the backs of the heads that I know: Daphne and Matt, Frances, Virginia and Raymond, and the Deacons—Brian's sandy fringe, Molly's dark curls, and the blond ponytails of Caroline's younger sisters. They are sitting very straight and still, except for Brian, whose head is bowed and whose sagging shoulders speak to me of a burden too heavy and painful to bear.

"Friends," the minister is saying, "we've gathered here tonight to pray for our daughter and our friend, Caroline, and to ask our God, who cares for all things large and small on this earth, to bring her back safely to us." He pauses as if gathering forces for this request. "Caroline Deacon is a child who lives close to our hearts. She is a good daughter to Brian and Molly, a loving sister to Missy and Tracy, caring of her friends, respectful of her teachers and a handmaiden in our church. She has helped with our Sunday school activities and sings in our choir. When we were raising money for repairs to our roof, Caroline spent many hours helping us organize our bake sale and our rummage sale."

St. Matthew's has better acoustics than our church; I can hear the minister quite clearly even though we're in the back row. His prayer makes me think about my relationship to God, which is an uneasy one. My parents were churchgoers, and as a child I believed wholeheartedly in His existence. While I rarely got what I prayed for—requests such as new ice skates or that Willie Smith, who sat next to me in school, would stop pinching—I did notice that God was benevolent about my misdeeds. Lightning didn't crack open the heavens when I lied about taking my brother's favorite coloring book, or when I said nasty things about Susie Saperstein to my best friend, Phyllis McLeod. As I grew older, I had the belief that God had good things in mind for me, because nothing really terrible ever happened in our family. The days of my childhood rolled along without catastrophe, major accidents, deaths of close relatives, or scandals like divorce. During my adolescence, this belief underwent attack. My parents' decency began to grate on me. If only they knew, I thought, about all the indecent and turbulent emotions I was feeling, but they didn't seem to notice. They thought I was the same good little girl I'd always been, only taller.

"Are you ready, Barbara?" my mother called up the stairs one Sunday morning.

"No."

"We're waiting for you."

"I'm not going."

"Aren't you feeling well?"

"I feel fine."

"Then what's the matter?"

"Nothing. I'm just not going."

There was a long silence and then light steps on the stairs and a knock on my bedroom door. "Barbara, can I come in?"

At my grunt, my mother opened the door. She was wearing her spring Sunday best, a blue dress with white polka dots, a white handbag and gloves, and a hat with a blue ribbon. She did her hair in pin curls before church, and I could see the little crimps in the curls where the bobby pins had held the hair in place. I was still in my pajamas, lounging on my unmade bed, my hair loose and unbrushed.

She sat down on the edge of the bed. "Why aren't you coming to church this morning?"

"I don't believe in that junk anymore."

"Since when?" she asked.

Her calm threw me, because I'd wanted a very different reaction, shock at the very least, outrage preferably. "Since a long time," I blurted. "Since I've noticed that God doesn't care about this world."

"How doesn't He care?"

I pointed to the book I was reading, *Exodus*. It had made a great impression on me. "He didn't care about the way people killed each other, or the Jews, or the concentration camps, or else why did He let them happen?"

Now that I'm the age my mother was then, I see that I'd have handled the situation much the same way she did. At the time, I wanted answers to questions overt and secret. How can God let there be murders, rapes, and wars? How can He let me hate Fiona Meara because she's prettier than I am? How can He let me act so stupid when Dennis Ackerman said hello to me on the way to English class? Why does He let me get so sad sometimes that I cry myself to sleep? And does He know I use my fingers to stroke that unmentionable place between my legs?

Perhaps my mother guessed at the hidden questions, perhaps she didn't. What she did recognize was that I was too old to be satisfied with easy answers to complex moral dilemmas. "That's a hard question that many people have trouble with. I hope God will help you find the answer someday."

"I don't believe in God," I said with some impatience.

My mother refused to rise to the bait. "I believe in a God who has reasons for what He does. Those reasons might not be obvious to us, but they're there all the same." She stood up. "If you're going to stay home, would you make some biscuits for dinner? You know how much your father loves biscuits."

I was married in my parents' church, but I didn't join until Joel was three years old. Dan wasn't religious at all and only agreed that we should join a church to provide Joel with a structure that would reinforce our own moral beliefs. Needless to say, that didn't make steady churchgoers out of us. We're recreational worshipers, attending church at those important junctures in time such as Easter and Christmas when the spiritual and the secular worlds intersect in ways that can't be ignored. My relationship to God, if there is a God at all, remains ambiguous. I don't think of Him ninety-nine percent of the time. There is, however, that one percent, like tonight, when I find myself saying His name, bowing my head, and hoping that the God of my childhood does exist and that He will wrap Caroline in the same warm and generous benevolence.

"Dear God," the minister says, "hear our prayers for Caroline, because they come from our very hearts and souls. We pray that Caroline is well, and that she knows that our thoughts are with her, that her family is praying for her, that her friends are praying for her and that her town is praying for her."

There is the sound of sobbing to the left and front of us; heads turn and then eyes look away politely. A group of teenagers sits there, Caroline's friends. Ben is among them, and Sarah, Virginia's daughter. Joel should be with them, but he refused to come. Dan and I agreed not to push him. Although Joel seems to be handling the tragedy well, the candlelight vigil is maybe more than he can take.

"So let us stand now, friends, and pray for the health and well-being of Caroline."

There is the rustle of many bodies standing up, and the candles sway, and as the flames move, they leave shadows behind, dark images that are the shape of flames, blacker than the dusk. Suddenly I remember the midnight walk held after Christian French died. We gathered, his friends and classmates, at Misty Lake and walked with our candles blazing to the curve in the road where Christian's car had crashed into a tree. No adult had organized the walk, and we had no minister to lead us. The word simply went around school—no one knew who started it—to show up at the lake at midnight with a candle, and we did, about a hundred of us.

Marla and I went in Brian's car. He drove while I sat in the backseat with Marla, my arm around her shaking shoulders. She hadn't cried once during the three weeks that Christian was in a coma but had hardly stopped since his funeral. She hadn't been able to come to school some days or, if she came, she would burst into tears in the middle of the class and have to go to the nurse's office. The doctor had prescribed a sedative for her, but Marla refused to take it. "It's my grief," she told me fiercely, "and I don't want them to take it away from me."

I had taken on that grief and anguish as if it were my own. I would go with Marla to the nurse's office, walk her home, help her with schoolwork, stay overnight and try to get her to school the next morning. I spent so much time at the Hudson house and the circles under my eyes got so dark that both my mother and Marla's became concerned.

"I know how you feel," my mother said, "and I think you're being a wonderful friend, but you've got your own life, too. You need to study for the Regents. They're important. You've got college next year."

"I am studying," I said.

"Why don't you stay home tonight and get a good night's sleep and—"

"No! I can't."

"Honey, this isn't your responsibility. Christian's death isn't your fault."

"You don't understand!"

Mrs. Hudson was more blunt. She took me aside one evening while Marla was in the shower. "Bobbie, Martha can get over this without you. She's very dramatic, you know. I'm not saying she's putting this all on, but there's a strong element of drama here."

I shook my head vehemently. "She needs me."

"This isn't going to bring Christian back."

"I know."

"And you need to sleep in your own bed. I'm afraid you're going to get sick."

"I'm fine, Mrs. Hudson. I'm really fine."

Nothing short of chains, I was sure, could have kept me from Marla's side. I was both Marla's comforter and confessor, and such was the power of death that both mothers were afraid to lay down a rule that would force me to stay at home. Instead, Marla would crawl into her bed, and I would turn off the lights. I'd climb into the other bed, which we'd pushed against hers, and then it would begin: the tears, the wails, the sobbing, the guilt, the recriminations, and the self-flagellation. We revisited her version of the Honor Society barbecue at Misty Lake over and over again until I knew it by heart, until I almost came to believe it had happened to me as well as her. I saw myself lying on that blanket in the woods under the cover of darkness, and hearing the crackle of the fire and the laughter in the distance. I knew the breeze had a slight chill to it so that when Christian undid the buttons of Marla's blouse, she shivered and he pulled the blanket up around them. I felt his kisses on my mouth and neck, and the slight rasp of his shaved chin against my flesh. I knew the sensation of his hands slipping to my back and my own arch that allowed him to unhook my bra without struggle. When Marla cried and spoke of the touch of his tongue on her nipples, my own nipples went hard and I closed my eyes in ecstasy.

"And then," Marla would say, her voice breaking, "he wanted to do below-the-waist. You know."

I knew. All the boys wanted *that*. Brian Deacon wanted that. The hand slipping into the waistband of pants or a skirt and the tightening of your legs as if locked-together knees could protect that soft, hidden sanctum. Or maybe the boy's wrist would have to be grabbed to stop his hand from moving lower. Or maybe you let the fingers inch lower and lower until you panicked, and the fear overwhelmed the overwhelming need to be touched and you finally jerked away and said, "Stop."

"Just let me feel it."

"No."

"Just a little."

"No, please."

"I won't hurt you."

"Please don't. Please."

And most boys obeyed, because they were frightened, too, or because the more confident of them believed there would always be another chance. But Christian was different. He hadn't given up. A month before the Honor Society barbecue, he'd finally touched Marla there, although she'd begged and pleaded, and then she'd touched him, and the touches had gone from tentative to frenzied. His hand had been everywhere, outside, inside, and she hadn't been able to stop him, because it felt good, oh so good Bobbie I never knew it could feel so good. In the darkness of her bedroom, I pressed my face into the pillow to hide my tears, which were understandable, and the unbearable bubble of hysterical laughter which began somewhere in my abdomen and rose to my mouth where it threatened to explode into a thousand horrifying fragments.

"He wanted to go all the way," Marla said between sobs,

"and I told him no, I can't, I don't want to get pregnant, I just can't, and he said I didn't understand, that it hurt, that he physically hurt, that I was torturing him."

I imagined the furious whispers under the cover of the blanket, then the angry words spoken above the rustling over the trees, and finally Christian springing up and standing over Marla while she hurriedly zipped up her jeans and buttoned her blouse. I saw Christian toss his dark hair back in that impatient way he had, his fingers running from the temple over his ear to the nape of his neck. And I heard that final exchange.

"Where are you going?"

"Forget it."

"Don't go. Please!"

"I can't stand this shit."

"I'm so scared. You don't understand!"

"If I don't get the hell out of here . . ."

"What?"

"Figure it out for yourself."

"Chris, please. Don't leave me."

She put her arms around him and pressed her mouth to his, sliding her tongue against his closed lips, willing them to open. For a second, he stood very still and then roughly shoved her away so that she fell to her knees on the blanket. "Cockteaser," he said, and turned on his heel while Marla collapsed into sobs.

In St. Matthew's, the organ sounds a few notes, but I'm thinking how ignorant we were then of all things sexual, of the physical compromises that could have been made in those prepill days, and the tragedies and grief avoided. While voices rise around me in song, my head lowers and Brian's car reaches Misty Lake where the milling crowd of our classmates is lit by the headlights of cars. As I open the car door, I hear voices and nervous laughter, but the crowd grows silent as Marla steps out. From that time on, no one speaks. In some uncanny way, we have all agreed that the memory of Christian must be honored in silence. Someone steps forward and lights our candles, and then without a word uttered, other matches are struck, other candles lit and the headlights extinguished. Our faces become pale ovals with dark holes for eyes, and we are surrounded by night sounds: the rasping of crickets, the croaking of frogs, the hooting of an owl.

The crowd parts and then follows as Brian and I escort Marla through the parked cars to the road. She's no longer crying but is calm, holding her candle so steadily its flame doesn't even flicker. When we reach the road, Marla turns to watch the lights assemble behind us, and when she decides we're ready, she begins walking. As far as I can tell, Marla never looks behind her once during that fifteen-minute walk. But I do. Brian tries to hold my hand, but I won't let him. He doesn't yet know that I don't want to go out with him again, that I don't want to sit in the backseat of his car and park near the quarry, and I never want to kiss him again or feel the clumsy tips of his fingers on my skin. As the tears begin to fill my eyes, I turn and look behind me. Through the prism of those tears, the river of tiny flames waver and then coalesce into one brilliant, incandescent sun.

I feel Dan's shoulder push against mine as the minister asks us to sit once again. I put my mouth near his ear. "Did you go to the candlelight walk for Christian?" I whisper. His quick nod tells me he's remembered, too, and I wonder how far back in the crowd he was—probably last, I think, behind Christian's friends, the football team, the cheerleaders, and all the girls who dreamed of Christian and hated Marla. He probably came with his friend, Bill Steen, another gawky, pimply boy who has since become a lawyer in Atlanta. I put my hand next to his and his palm turns so that our fingers entwine. The heat of his skin is a warmth and a comfort.

"The ways of God," the minister is saying, "can be mysterious. We don't always know the whys or the reasons why things happen the way they do. But what we have to remember is that God's purpose is being served."

A movement at the right of the room catches my eye, and I turn to see Marla enter and slip into a seat. She doesn't see me, and I watch as she presses one hand against her mouth, and the flame of her candle trembles. I wonder if she can still cry for Christian, but I know that later, when we meet outside the church, I won't ask her. I'm not seventeen anymore, and I no longer have a need for vicarious mourning. Besides, I've learned grief is a private affair, no matter how public its face.

Chapter
7

THE SUN'S RAYS ANGLE THROUGH THE WEST-FACING WINDOWS and slant across the double bed, which is rumpled and smells of love. The cottage belongs to Tony's family and is used for fishing. It's small and has a stove and refrigerator, Formica table and chairs, an old couch, the bed, a cot and a pile of nets, rods, and tackle boxes. A cross holding Jesus' sagging body hangs over the bed, while the Virgin Mary watches over the sink. There is grime on the windowpanes, the marks of dirty boots on the floor and a layer of dust on every surface. Only the bed is clean. Tony brought up pillows, sheets, and blankets, and assured Marla that the mattress was new. Not that she really cares. She's tired of the motel room, and Tony doesn't have a place of his own. Since his separation, he lives with his parents.

"They think I'm taking a buddy fishing," he explained during the drive to the cottage.

"Does that mean you have to bring back some fish?"

"Shit, I didn't think of that. You like fishing?"

"I detest fishing."

Marla stretches and watches Tony sleeping. A spear of light touches him, making a halo out of the dark hair on his bare shoulder. She's discovered that she craves the physicality of him: the beard shadowing his chin, the triangle of chest hair, the weighted genitals, the muscular buttocks. Celibacy created a hunger in her that seems insatiable. Tony can't satisfy her no matter how many orgasms she has, and he is no sooner out of her than she finds herself caressing him again, taking him in her mouth, tasting herself on his skin. He, of course, is delighted, mistaking her avarice for appreciation. How useful the male ego can be. It found them this cottage for the weekend, the view of the pretty lake, the hours Marla will need for surfeit.

Marla reaches for her journal, which lies on the floor beside the bed, and Tony opens his eyes a crack. "Shit," he says, "not that." And promptly closes his eyes and turns his back to her.

Marla finds Tony's dislike of the journal amusing. At first he was curious about it, particularly because they'd just made love and he was lying on his side, fondling her breast, when Marla picked up the journal and opened it.

"What's that?" he asked.

"Where I write down ideas for my next novel."

"You going to write about us?"

"Maybe."

"And what we do?"

"Maybe."

"They'll print stuff like that?"

"Why not?"

"Kinky stuff?"

"It's not kinky."

He licked the lobe of her ear and then whispered, "It feels kinky to me."

"Did you and your wife only do it in the missionary position?"

"My wife was a virgin when I married her," he said. "You gotta understand that."

"We were all virgins once. We're born that way."

"She used to get upset."

"About oral or anal sex?"

"Listen, we never did any of that stuff. She was brought up very strict. Hey, what're you writing down?"

When it happened again, he tried to stop her, snatching the journal away and holding it too high for her to reach.

Marla refused to play. "Give it to me," she said.

"Come and get it," he said, and then when Marla got out of bed, "Hey, what's the matter?"

"You want to fuck me anymore?"

He put the book down on her pillow. "I was only kidding," he said, and looked sulky.

She got back into bed. "Don't ever touch that book again."

"Jeez," he said. "Pardon me for living." Now, when she writes, he ignores her, feigning sleep.

Marla holds the journal open on her lap, the pen in her hand, and thinks about the candlelight vigil for Caroline. She went out of curiosity but then discovered how powerful her memories were of the vigil they'd held for Christian twenty-five years ago. She hadn't thought of that night for many years, but the sight of dozens of solemn flames flickering in the dark brought back the emotions—the grief and guilt, the sadness and despair—as if she'd felt them only yesterday. She tried to slip away afterward, but Brian Deacon caught sight of her as she came out the church doors.

"Martha!" he said, and surprised her by giving her a hug and holding on tight for several minutes. "Barbara said you were back in town."

Brian was almost unrecognizable: stout, bald, double-chinned. The only feature she recognized were his eyes, which were an unusual shade, almost turquoise, outlined by dark lashes. Back in 1961, she and Bobbie had agreed those eyes made Brian Deacon one of the sexiest boys in their class.

"Brian, I'm so sorry about—"

"Yeah, this is a pretty bad thing. I don't think they make them rougher than this." Then he shrugged and gave his head a little shake. Marla recognized the efforts of a man trying to swim out of deep water where he's suffocating and find some air he can breathe without his chest constricting. He said, "Remember those double dates? You and Chris, me and Barbara?"

She smiled and said, "I remember doing ninety-five down Route Two-forty one night."

"I'd forgotten that. Chris was driving, wasn't he?"

"You dared him."

"Those were the days, weren't they?" He shook his head. "Yeah, those were the days."

But he could hold off the present for only so long before it came rushing back, drowning him once again. Marla saw Brian's face sag, the skin of his jowls sinking beneath the weight of his sorrow. He turned to the woman beside him. "Molly, meet Martha Hudson. We went to high school together."

Molly was short, also plump, with brown eyes and brown hair. She looked as if she hadn't slept for days. There were dark circles under her eyes and the skin at the corners of her mouth was shiny and strained as if it had been stretched beyond its limits. She smiled wearily at Marla. "Thanks for coming. We think every prayer counts."

"I prayed enough for two," Marla said, although she hadn't prayed for Caroline at all. When she'd found herself in prayer, she'd been shocked to discover she was asking forgiveness for herself.

"Do you have children?"

"A daughter."

"Then you know."

"Yes," Marla said, and suddenly she had the sensation that the ground had moved. She must have swayed, because Brian caught her arm. "You okay?" he said.

"Yes, fine."

"Come around and see us sometime, will you?"

"Of course," she said, but as she walked away, she knew she couldn't afford to get too close to the Deacons and their anguish and grief. She knew all about those emotions. They were capable of creating a whirlpool, a swirling, circling rush of feelings so powerful she'd be caught and sucked in.

Look how close she'd come, standing next to Molly and having the earth try to tilt her into that vortex.

There were other people clustered on the church grounds as if they were afraid that by leaving the vigil their departure would make Caroline's safe return more precarious. Bobbie caught sight of her and beckoned her over to a group of women and men. Marla was introduced to Frances, who taught literature; Virginia the illustrator, and her husband, Raymond, a traffic engineer with the city of Laurel Grove; Daphne from high school, who now works at city hall, and her husband, Matt, an editor with the *Laurel Grove Leader*. The men separated from the women and talked about cars—Raymond had just bought a Mazda. The women asked Marla about her move, the house, her writing.

"Are you going to write a book about us?" Virginia asked.

"I don't think so," Marla answered.

"We're boring," Bobbie said. "Let's face it."

"Who says we're boring?" Daphne said. "We have a little of everything around here. Sex, affairs, divorce, adultery."

"Speak for yourself," Bobbie said.

Everyone laughed and the conversation took a somber turn. They talked about Caroline and what a lovely girl she was and what a tragedy this was for the Deacons. Virginia said she was afraid the tragedy wasn't going to stop at the Deacons but involve the whole town, and Marla caught Bobbie looking at Frances, who shook her head. Then they talked about how scared people had become, how girls only went out in pairs and how parents were having their kids check in even if they were just going to the mall. Their voices lowered as they discussed the Deacons, the way Molly was holding up even though she was hardly eating and sleeping, just look at her, smiling and thanking everyone.

"I couldn't do that," Bobbie said. "Not if it were Joel."

"Me either," Frances said.

"Maybe we don't know how much strength we have inside until we're tested," Virginia said.

"Spare me such tests, thank you very much," Daphne said.

Virginia persisted. "We can't predict how we'd be or what we'd do or say. There'd be a new person inside our skin."

"I think it would be ourselves," Frances said, "only intensified."

The conversation moved on to other topics, a canceled school trip, the book Virginia was working on, a sale at a furniture store in Laurel Grove. Marla listened, nodded and smiled, acknowledging their niceness and friendliness, but she thought that their pleasant smiles, even Bobbie's, were like closed doors, hiding something else.

Daphne: I remember her from high school. A big girl with too much bounce and not enough grace. Her loudness is still there, but she's transformed it into a bold humor. She wants to shock people but hopes to make them laugh at the same time so that they'll still like her. She doesn't like me, though, probably never did. Hostility came from her as we smiled and shook hands. I felt it in the grip of her hand and the rigidity of her wrist. She's married to Matt, who is large, rumpled, graying, and balding, the kind of man who appears to be more interested in ideas than appearances. But there's a secret and interesting vanity there. His hair, which curls, grows to his collar, and he preens it, running his fingers through it and separating the strands, not even aware of what his hands are doing.

Virginia: she's pale, tiny, and slight, she looks like a feather that could be picked up by any stray breeze. She illustrates children's books, she told me that right away to establish a bond between us—we're the creators. She's not happy. I sense shadows around her, pale, mauve shadows like the ones beneath her eyes and at the skin of her temples. She makes an awkward pair with her husband, Raymond, who is big, good-looking, and filled with a suppressed energy. They're the sort of couple one can't imagine screwing with any suppleness, because their bodies don't seem to fit together.

Frances: she's unmarried and beautiful in an oddly uninteresting way. It's possible she doesn't know she's beautiful or she doesn't care, and that's why I eventually lost pleasure in watching the expressions cross her face. Or maybe it was the tension in her, which I felt humming as if she were made of electrical circuits. Maybe that distracted me from her eyes and the perfect structure of her bones. Or maybe it's simply that, after a while, beauty in itself becomes boring when it lacks self-knowledge or self-interest.

As she writes, Tony shifts again, opens his eyes and sighs as if in defeat. "What're you writing about now?"

"Frances. I don't know her last name."

"Frances Phillips? She teaches at the college?"

"That's right."

Tony slides his hand onto her stomach. "What're you saying?"

"That she's beautiful."

"Frances? I wouldn't call her beautiful."

"What would you call her?"

"Okay-looking. Not sexy." His hand slides down her belly to the line of her pubic hair. "Tell me what you're going to say about me. That I'm good in bed?"

"That you're a superb animal."

His hand stops moving. "What does that mean?"

"It's a top-notch performance rating."

"Yeah." He slides his warm, heavy leg over hers. "I guess we're not in this for a real relationship."

"I don't think so."

"Most women want all the emotional shit, too."

"Not me."

"You don't even want to hear about my marriage breakup, do you?"

"I've had two myself. It's enough."

"See, you get most women in bed and you know what they want? To get into your psychology. They want all the sad stories like why your marriage didn't make it, and who did what to who, and whether your heart's broken. That stuff."

"Mmmm."

Tony props himself up on an elbow, peers at what she's

writing, and reads aloud, " 'Bed is the place where men want women to talk about their psychology. It makes them feel interesting.' Hey, wait a minute. I didn't say that shit."

"I said it."

Tony studies her profile and then says, "Okay, I get it. You don't want to talk about me. So what do you want to talk about?"

Marla lets the notebook drop, the pen clattering to the floor. With her forefinger, she traces a line from the hollow in Tony's throat, between his nipples, to his pubis, pushing the blankets down as she goes. He's half-erect, and she circles the glans and then strokes the sensitive cord beneath it. His penis swells to an upright position, thick and hot.

"Jesus," Tony says, lying back, eyes closing. "Don't stop."

As she leans over him, Marla glances across the room at the Virgin Mary. For a second, the two women stare at one another, and then she bends her head and takes Tony in her mouth.

Tony insists on taking Marla out on the lake on Sunday morning. As he rows the boat parallel to the shoreline, Marla sits back in the chair he's put between the seats and lets the sun imprint golden circles on her eyelids. For a while, there's nothing but the sound of the oars slapping against the water and the occasional splash as a fish jumps.

"What're you thinking about?" Tony asks.

Marla doesn't open her eyes but says, "Who killed Caroline Deacon."

"Some people think she's still alive."

"I doubt it."

"A lot of people think it was a kidnapping, some stranger coming through town and picking her up."

Marla lets one hand fall over the side of the boat so that the cool water trickles through her fingers. "Wishful thinking," she says.

"Yeah. A friend of mine—one of the cops in town— thinks one of the boys did it. Maybe her boyfriend, Frances Phillips's son."

Marla opens her eyes and stares into the clarity of the sky.

She remembers the look Bobbie and Frances exchanged. "Maybe a lot of boys liked her. From the posters, it looks to me like Caroline was one of the prettiest girls in town."

"Yeah, she was. She baby-sat for us."

Marla closes her eyes again. "If I wrote mystery novels, I'd make you one of the suspects."

"Me?"

"Why not? Father of two goes crazy for beautiful teenage baby-sitter. It's happened before."

The oars stop their motion. "Jesus," Tony says, "is that how writers think?"

And on the drive back on Sunday evening after stopping in Laurel Grove and buying fish at the Grand Union. "You know what I don't get?" Tony says. "Why you're here. If I could live in L.A., I'd of never come back."

"I want to find out why Christian died."

"He was like Guido. He drove too fast."

"We had a fight that evening, because I wouldn't sleep with him."

"Shit, most of the guys in this town should be dead then. Maybe he was drunk."

"The autopsy report said he hadn't had that much to drink."

Tony thought a bit. "Maybe it was dark that night."

"There was a moon."

"You know what most seventeen-year-old guys are? Complete assholes. I had two ambitions when I was seventeen, to make the football team and get laid. I made the football team."

"When did you get laid?"

"You won't believe this. I was a virgin when I got married."

"Really."

"Italian guys who dated nice Italian girls in those days didn't get any unless they were real lucky."

"Poor Tony."

"Yeah, it was rough. You girls never understood how really rough it was."

Tony: I am such a score for him that he refuses to notice my contempt. He still sees me as that girl standing up before the school assembly—distant and desirable. I doubt he even sees the gray in my hair, the wrinkles beside my eyes, that heavy flesh on my legs. Several years ago, I saw the play *M. Butterfly*, in which the main character so fantasized about his lover of 20 years, a Chinese opera singer, that he never realized she was male. I found the premise hard to swallow then, but no longer. Even when I deliberately attempt to tear the veil from Tony's eyes, he persists in pulling it closed once more.

Chapter
8

THE TOWN'S SEARCH FOR CAROLINE TAKES PLACE ON A WEEKEND when summer is in the air. The sun is blazing, the ground has a smell I associate with warm, damp earth and green shoots, and crickets are already singing in the underbrush. I look out over the hillside and think how hot I will be before the afternoon is over. I don't dare wear shorts or a short-sleeved shirt, and I'm covered from head to toe in hat, jacket, jeans, socks, and sneakers. The ground is thick with brambles and thorns, and there are ticks hidden in the tall grasses. When I was young, my friends and I used to roam through these woods, playing Indians and fighting the frontier wars of two centuries earlier. It was the only time in my life I could be androgynous, switching easily between white scout and Indian maiden, white girl and Indian warrior. I'd crawl on the ground, ducking from bullets or arrows, hide behind bushes, sniping at the enemy, and race through the trees, imagining the wind whipping through my loose hair or warrior braids. The only part I didn't like was being tied to a tree and being held as a hostage, although as we got older a certain romanticism crept into the game that I began to enjoy. Captives had been just captives before, but now they were always maidens in distress. About the time I gave up playing Indians forever, I'd begun to imagine myself tied to a tree, helpless and quivering, awaiting my Apache or Davy Crockett hero.

Whenever I think back to my childhood, I'm both astonished by our innocence and pained by its loss. I don't think Joel and his friends have ever known the freedom that I and my friends knew as children of the fifties. Our innocence was created by the deceptions practiced by our parents, teachers, and the town itself. I know now there were unhappinesses of all kinds in Cassandra—marital incompatibilities, alcoholism, abusive husbands and fathers, wife beating, sexual assault—but such problems were hidden from me, and I played in happy ignorance. I didn't even know the word *fuck* until I was in high school or that homosexuality existed until I was in college. Joel and his friends, on the other hand, have witnessed violences, verbal and physical, since they were old enough to understand music lyrics and what was happening on the television screen. How shocked I was at Joel's ninth birthday party when one little boy called another a fag, or to overhear two boys in the library referring to their grade eight math teacher as a motherfucker, or to listen to Joel describe the possibilities of Caroline's disappearance—abduction, beating, rape, slashing, murder—with the nonchalance of a hardened veteran of the streets.

"Mom?"

"Mmm?" I was in the basement folding sheets, and Joel joined me, leaning against the doorway of the laundry room.

"You think Caroline's still alive?"

This wasn't the first time Joel asked this question, and I understood that while his sleeping hours may be tranquil, his waking hours were not. "I don't know," I said. "Nobody knows."

"You know what I think?"

"What?"

"I think she got picked up by some serial killer coming through town, and there's not much chance she's still alive."

We had a parents' night at the school where the trauma

team discussed the effect of Caroline's disappearance on students and made suggestions on how parents should handle their children's questions. The experts agreed that the best response was not to deny the possibilities of what might have happened to Caroline but to focus on our children's emotions by asking them how they felt or making a statement about feelings such as "That must frighten you."

"That's a scary thought," I said carefully.

"Yeah," Joel said. "I saw a TV movie about a guy who was crazy and had these hallucinations. When they came on him, he had to kill someone. He was driven to do it; he thought Satan was telling him to do it. Anyway, he picked up this girl in a parking lot near a doughnut place. He took her to his house and sort of tortured her and raped her and finally strangled her with his belt. He killed five more girls before the police caught him."

The trauma team hadn't prepared me for this one. "How did that make you feel?" I asked.

"I thought the guy was really gross and disgusting. And the point was, Mom, that he didn't really do it for sex, but for power, because he had this, like, powerless life. He worked as a janitor."

"Do you think television is the same as real life?"

Joel thought about this for a minute. "I think it's about real life but uses the worst examples."

"Why?"

"So we'll keep watching, right?"

I said what I thought had to be said. "I don't know if Caroline is alive or dead, Joel. I only hope that if she's alive she's okay, and if she's dead, it happened very quickly."

"Yeah," he said slowly, and watched for a few minutes as I folded a pillowcase and put it in the laundry basket. "Mom?"

"What?" I asked, steeling myself for the next impossible-to-answer question.

"Have you washed my football shirt? Hey, just kidding."

* * *

Today's search covers the area northwest of town between Route 240 and the river, and the police are organizing us into sections. Although they've already searched all around Cassandra with dogs, it requires more than a five-man force to go through every square inch of territory, and the call went out for volunteers the morning after the vigil. The area east of town was searched on Saturday. I had to work, but Dan participated along with about fifty other people. They spent three hours beating through the brush, finding nothing but beer bottles, pop cans, bits of metal, pieces of clothing, old tires, crushed tissues, and used condoms. Dan came home tired, sunburnt, and discouraged. "I don't know what's worse," he said. "Finding something or finding nothing."

More than a hundred people have shown up today, and we make a line along the ridge that overlooks town. The men are going to cover the area where the terrain is steeper, the trees thicker, and the river runs stronger, while the women will be walking through an area of rolling hills and thickets. I can see Dan and Joel in the distance, but only because I recognize the red of Dan's cap.

Daphne is on my left and Sarah, Virginia's daughter, is on my right. Virginia couldn't come because she's home nursing a bad cold. No matter how often I see Sarah, I'm always overcome with a feeling of surprise. She takes after Raymond and was always tall for her age, but since puberty she has shot up to just over six feet. This in itself would be striking enough, but she's also died her brown hair black and greased it in spikes, wears five or six earrings in each ear and a diamond stud on the left side of her nose, and dresses in funereal black: black T-shirt, black jeans, black shoes. The blackness seems to have sucked the color from her face. Her skin, which is slightly freckled, has a sickly, greenish pallor. "Sarah's turned into a member of the Addams family," Virginia announced at our bridge game the day Sarah dyed her hair, and that perplexed crease appeared between her pale, wispy eyebrows.

"How's your mom?" I ask Sarah.

"Sneezing and stuff," she says. "And running a fever."

"She's been sick a lot this winter," I say.

"Yeah, she's always getting something."

Sarah says this with the faint surprise that the intensely healthy hold for those who are less fortunate. Like Raymond, she's solid and robust, her face wide, her features large and even. I see a Nordic type of beauty beneath the black spikes, mascara, and eyeliner, but I suspect it will be a long time before Sarah discovers it for herself.

"Well, we'll be lucky if we don't get sunstroke," Daphne says. "I bet it gets into the eighties today."

"All right, ladies!" Reg Burton stands down the hill from us and is calling through a bullhorn. "Please line up with your arms outstretched and your fingers touching your neighbors'. That's it. Now, everybody take a few steps to your left. That's good, and you can drop your arms." A line of girls and women, each spaced equally apart, now stretches through the brush. "We're looking for any object we can identify as belonging to Caroline. She was wearing a blue nylon slicker, a white blouse with white buttons, blue jeans, white socks, and blue sneakers with pink-and-white laces. She was carrying a red canvas book bag. Walk in a straight line toward the river, try to stay the same distance from your neighbor, and keep your eyes on the ground. If you find something, don't pick it up and don't move from the spot where you found it. Just holler, and we'll come to you. And if your neighbor finds something, don't move from your own path. We don't want a hundred people trampling evidence. Any questions? Okay, let's go."

We walk forward, and the sound of crickets is muffled by the sounds of so many steps, of so many feet crushing twigs and leaves beneath their soles, and so many arms and legs brushing aside shoots and branches. I feel the sun on the fabric between my shoulders and on the back of my neck. I think how burnt my neck will be—I burn easily—and wish I'd thought about bringing sun-blocking cream.

Daphne says, "Did you hear about the psychics?"

"No," I say, watching the ground.

"Three psychics have called the police with clues to where Caroline is."

"I didn't know we had psychics in Cassandra."

"We don't. One is from Laurel Grove, one's in Syracuse, and the other's in New Jersey. They all heard about it on the news."

"What do they say?"

"The one from Laurel Grove said she sees white metal and chrome, the one from Syracuse has the sense of electric wires nearby, and the New Jersey one is convinced that Caroline is in or near water."

Something blue catches my eye, and I bend down to investigate. Trapped among the dead leaves is a child's knitted left-hand blue mitten with half the thumb gone. I stand up. "Are the police taking them seriously?"

"Reg says they're following every lead no matter how crazy. We now know there are seventy-two white cars and trucks in Cassandra. Two of them belong to town councillors. Oh, isn't this nice."

I glance at Daphne, who's crouched over the ground. "What is it?"

"It looks like the cardboard part of a tampon. How does stuff like that get up here? Anyway, the police have also looked by the electric towers and the power station, and as for water, we have the river and how many lakes?"

"Too many."

"That's the problem."

When I was nine years old, my parents took our family to New York City. We did the usual tourist activities such as going to Macy's, attending a show at Rockefeller Center, and visiting the Statue of Liberty, but what I remember best was a trip we took to the ocean. My father had an air force buddy who had settled with his wife and children in the Rockaways. We went to their house and then walked to the beach. I remember smelling the salty scent of ocean several blocks before coming in sight of it, and then hearing the roaring of the surf as we drew closer. Being a child of small freshwater lakes and streams, I could hardly believe the sight of that vast body of water stretching as far as I could see in all directions, the miles of hot, white sand and the continuous crash of waves breaking on the beach.

Our two families set up a cozy nest of blankets, umbrellas, coolers, and a playpen for the baby. Although Rob and I were good swimmers and dancing with impatience to get into the water, we were only allowed to go when my father took us down to the water's edge, where he explained about breakers and undertows and let us feel the sucking motion of the water as it receded from the beach. It pulled so hard as it swirled around our ankles that the grains beneath our feet seemed to evaporate and we sank slowly into the wet sand.

I was cautious for a while, playing in that part of the surf closer to the beach where the gray-green water had already tumbled over itself and was now foaming forward in a white rush to make huge dark arcs on the beach. But as the day progressed, I got braver and ventured out farther, moving from knee-high water to waist-high water. I began to imitate Rob, who had learned to dive into the waves before they broke, his head popping out in the smooth water on the other side. I got progressively cockier and more reckless until I misjudged a wave. Instead of diving through it, I was sucked into the middle of it, caught in the rising water, the abrupt break as the wave reached its pinnacle and the swirling cascade of water downward. I was driven forward, tumbling over and over, and pieces of shell and sand scraped my skin. But when I tried to cry out, my mouth filled with salt water and my throat seized. I couldn't breathe, my lungs burned, and my heart pounded. I forgot about the stings on my skin and tried to scream for my mother. It was then that the water flung me closer to shore, and my father caught me.

"There," he said, patting me on the back as I coughed and choked. "There, there."

"Is she all right?" my mother called.

"She's fine," he said. "Just a little shook up."

I was too young to say he was wrong. I didn't have the words to describe what had happened to me—that I'd felt the touch of death. It had gripped me by the throat, squeezed the air out of me, and pressed the heel of its hand hard against my chest. When I finished choking and opened my mouth, all that came out was a loud wail, and then I was running to my mother to be wrapped in her healing arms.

Now when I think of Caroline and water, this experience comes back to me. It is still my only personal knowledge of death, and I shudder even though the heat of the sun is causing sweat to appear on my upper lip and to trickle between my breasts.

To take my mind off this, I talk to Sarah. "How's school going?" I say.

"Pretty good."

"What's your favorite course?"

"Spanish is kind of neat."

"You like languages?"

"Not really. I like the teacher, Mr. Graves. He's kind of neat."

"Joel likes him, too."

The conversation peters out, and I think how teenagers keep their enthusiasms close to their chest for fear someone may discover that they're not as cynical and world-weary as they'd like to appear. I remember holding Sarah in my arms the day after she was born, when Virginia and I exchanged babies for a few minutes to see how it felt, and she started to cry, her mouth a huge open square, her eyes squeezed tight, face bright red, her cry as piercing as a siren. I recall that she was louder than Joel, who had a little, fussy cry and was much more wiggly, when suddenly she blurts out, "You know what I think about all the time? Like at night when I can't sleep?"

"No," I say.

"I wonder if Caroline's hungry or if someone's buying her any food. I wonder if he knows she really likes McDonald's Chicken McNuggets."

I wish I could comfort Sarah the way I did then with a change of position and a rocking motion. "I hope so, too," I say lamely.

"And you know what I wonder most of all? I wonder if she has any clothes on"—she starts to cry—"or if she's naked somewhere and cold and wet. I can't stop thinking about that."

That night, when we're going to bed, Dan and I talk about the search. Nothing was found during the afternoon that could be connected to Caroline. When we gathered together at the end of the day, we were hot, tired, and discouraged. Reg thanked us on behalf of the police, and Brian thanked us on behalf of his family. Then he broke down and cried, and Reg had to lead him away. For the first time since Caroline's disappearance, I cried, too. I stood in the crowd of searchers and felt the tears slip down my cheeks, salty tears that irritated the skin at the corners of my mouth and stung the tip of my tongue.

"I was talking to Reg," Dan says as he pulls down the blankets and sheets. "He says that without a body, they have no evidence and their hands are tied. They've called the state police and have even gotten in touch with the FBI, who have a special unit that profiles serial killers."

I climb into bed beside him. "But do they think it's a serial killer? They're taking Ben in for a lie detector test."

"They suspect everybody."

"There was that girl killed in Elverton last year. They didn't find her murderer, did they?"

"I'm sure they're checking that out, too."

He switches off the light and we lie in the dark, side by side on our backs. I take his hand and our fingers entwine. "I'm beginning to look at everybody with suspicion," I say. "Yesterday I saw Doug Blackburn walking down Main Street and I remembered how creepy he was in high school. He never could look you in the eye, and he once asked me to meet him after a basketball game and never showed up."

"That doesn't make him a kidnapper or murderer."

"I know, but look what this is doing. It's making me feel uncomfortable in my own town. I'm not as scared as the high school girls, but I find myself looking over my shoulder whenever I'm walking. And I don't want to be alone in the library. We're adding volunteer shifts."

"I think it's good to be cautious."

"It's different for you," I say, suddenly angry. "You're a man. You don't feel threatened, not personally."

"I'm threatened that something will happen to you."

I give his hand a squeeze. "I'm sorry. I'm beginning to feel like a victim, and I don't like it."

Dan pulls me into his arms so that my head rests on his bare shoulder. "I had a dream last night that I was searching for Caroline, not outside of town, but right here in the house. We had a lot more rooms, and I had about a hundred doors to open. I was terrified as I went up to each door and then weak with relief when she wasn't behind it."

I stroke his top of his leg where the hair ends and the smooth skin of his thigh begins. "I think you're afraid of the condition she'll be in when she's finally found."

He's silent for a moment and then says, "Actually I knew, even in the dream, that what I was really frightened of wasn't finding Caroline, but finding me behind one of those doors."

"Oh, Dan," I say, and we instinctively turn to one another as if the thought of death, that loneliest of human experiences, compels us into a connection. I'm suddenly ravenous for him, for his tongue in my mouth, for his hands on my breasts and between my legs, for his penis to fill me until there is no empty, untouched space left. We're generally kind and gentle lovers, but tonight we take each other with an unusual speed and an unexpected violence, our fingers gripping each other's flesh, our bodies slapping against one another, our breaths fast and guttural. How I want that pain and those sounds, I can't get enough. I grasp Dan's buttocks, guiding his strokes so that they are faster, harder, deeper.

In. Out. In. Out.

Deep, deeper, deepest.

Feel, feel, feel.

That night I dream not of Caroline but of Sarah. I dream she gives birth to a baby, and it's greasy and slick as if it's been oiled. The doctors can't wipe the substance off no matter how many baths they give it or how hard they rub it with towels. "Take it to the library," our family doctor says to me. "Try to clean it there." But I can't hold the baby. It's skin is too slippery. It shifts in my hands, slowly and then more rapidly so I'm juggling it, frantically trying to stop it from hitting the ground. Despite my efforts, the baby finally slithers out of my grasp onto the floor. That's when I see it isn't a baby at all. It has the darkened, puckered genitals of a woman and pubic curls as red as Caroline's hair.

Chapter
9

THE TUESDAY FOLLOWING THE SEARCH FOR CAROLINE, MARLA picks me up and we drive to Syracuse to shop for the Hiller house. It's my day off, and I like the idea of doing something other than cleaning the house and running errands. Besides, shopping with Marla was always exciting. As a teenager, she was a reckless spender although her family didn't have as much money as ours. Her father was an insurance salesman, and I once overheard my father telling my mother that Paul Hudson had recently upped his mortgage principal to cover some debts. In our house, upping a mortgage rather than paying it off was tantamount to selling one's soul to the devil. I never said anything to Marla, but it was then that I began to look for and find signs of monetary stress in the Hudson house: their sofa was threadbare at the arms, Marla didn't get as many Christmas presents as I did, and when Mrs. Hudson's car broke down, she didn't get a new one for six months.

But the precarious state of the Hudsons' finances didn't stop Marla from spending all she had. While I put a percentage of baby-sitting money and allowances in my bank account, Marla never saved a cent. I pointed out the dangers of this one day when we were cruising through Walker's Five and Dime, and Marla was accumulating lipsticks, scarves, and perfume.

"I don't believe in saving money," she said. "I may die tomorrow and what good would it do me?"

I was shocked. "But what if you don't die? What if you live to be a hundred?"

"I'm going to make a lot of money."

"Doing what?"

"I don't know, maybe being in the movies."

"It's hard to get into the movies," I protested. "You have to be discovered like Lana Turner was."

Marla picked up another lipstick. "I just know I'm going to be rich," she said airily, "and I'll never have to worry."

Well, Marla has proved me and all the financial acumen of my parents wrong. I saved religiously all my childhood, and when I married Dan, we saved with the same care and spent with equal prudence. Our caution and sacrifices had their rewards: a comfortable house, a trip to Europe, functional cars, nice clothes, and a good portion of Joel's future college expenses socked away in solid investments. As Marla and I go from the drapery store to the paint store to the plumbing store to the kitchen designers, I learn that all the reckless spending of her past, her lack of foresight, and her seemingly impossible dreams haven't hurt her at all. I don't try to add up the cost of her plans by the time we go to lunch, but I know she'll spend thousands on only the best: rich fabrics, specialty paints, expensive fixtures, marvels of plumbing.

"A productive day," Marla says as we get into the car and leave the parking lot. "Thanks for helping."

"I didn't help much," I say. "You knew what you wanted."

"What I can't get here, I'll find in New York. I'm flying down tomorrow for a few days."

"When do the renovations start?"

"Mid-May after we close on the house. The architect is still working on the plans and then he has to get tenders from contractors."

"You can stay with us while the renovations are being done," I say. "Otherwise you'll be in that motel all summer."

"Thanks, Bobbie, it's nice of you to offer, but I'm going to put a bed and camp stove in the turret. It's not in bad shape."

We're silent while Marla passes a trailer truck, and then I ask about something that's been puzzling me. "What about Didi?"

"What about her?"

"Will she come for a visit when the house is done?"

"I don't think so. Maybe I'll go to L.A."

I don't understand Marla's relationship to her daughter. It's like a chain with several missing links. She doesn't want to talk about her and doesn't seem to have any pictures of her. And when Marla was over for dinner, I was surprised when she told us Didi was going to be living with friends in L.A. after she finished summer school. I tried to imagine how I'd feel moving several thousand miles away from Joel and leaving him in the care of others. My imagination couldn't make the leap. Joel's an unfinished piece of work, not fully grown, not yet mature. I wouldn't want friends, no matter how close, to have the responsibility and pleasure of watching him take the final steps into adulthood.

"It must be hard having her so far away."

"We talk on the phone. She's fine."

Marla's tone is dismissive so I quickly change the subject. "I tried to reach you on Sunday, but the motel people said you were gone for the weekend."

"I went to my lover's cottage." Marla glances at me and smiles. "You should see the look on your face."

"It's none of my business," I say.

"You're dying to ask. Come on, it's okay. Remember, we never had secrets, we're best friends."

"It's different now."

"It's the real estate agent. Tony Molino." She glances at me again and laughs. "I've really shocked you now."

Well, Mona had wondered who he was sleeping with now. I clear my throat. "I don't know him very well."

124

"Neither do I." Marla says and, throwing back her head, lets out one of her rich peals of laughter.

I can't help myself, now I'm laughing, too. "You're amazing," I say. "You've been here just a week."

"He's had a yen for me ever since high school, and the chemistry's good."

"Marla, he doesn't know what a book is."

"We don't read to each other."

"Okay, but you know what Cassandra is like. Everyone talks about everyone else."

"We're being discreet."

"Besides," I say, "there are some nice men in town who might be more suitable."

"Bobbie, I'm not looking for suitable. I never want to get married again. I don't think I'm constitutionally designed for it."

I rarely question the path my life has taken. It always seemed preordained to me that I wouldn't stray far from my roots. I went to college in Syracuse and came back to Cassandra after graduation to marry Dan and become the town's librarian because Mrs. Morgan was retiring. When I became pregnant with Joel, a house Dan and I had admired went up for sale and we bought it. I've always believed the timing of these pairs of events was indicative of their rightness, as if my life were a jigsaw puzzle and all the pieces fit neatly into place. Now I wonder what would have happened if I'd gone elsewhere to college, if I'd considered the entire United States when I was looking for a job, if I hadn't married a town boy but looked for someone more exotic whose past differed markedly from my own. Would I still be married and faithful? Or would I be like Marla, independent of men and taking lovers when it pleased me for no other reason than chemistry?

"Christian and I used to talk about getting married," Marla is saying. "I fantasized about having his baby. It would have dark hair and those incredible eyes. Remember how green they were?"

"Remember how we used to fight over who had more beautiful eyes, Brian or Christian?"

125

"Who won?"

"Brian, but it was close."

"Christian and I had our first date after that unbelievable game with Laurel Grove when he made that basket in the last seconds," Marla says. "We went to Howard Johnson's and had ice cream." A few rain drops spatter on the windshield. "Remember that cheer—'Two, four, six, eight, who do we appreciate? Christian, Christian, that's who.'"

"Remember those little skirts with the tassels and the gold braid?"

"I don't care how sexist cheerleading was," Marla says. "I loved being on the squad."

"Me, too."

"Do they still have cheerleaders?"

"There's a pep club with boys and girls and unisex outfits. Shorts and tops."

The spatter of drops on the windshield becomes streaks and Marla turns on the wipers. "You know something I feel awful about? That Christian died a virgin."

"Marla—"

"He wanted it so badly, and it would've been so easy. But I couldn't do it. I didn't care whether my father would kill me or not or what the neighbors would think if I got pregnant. I was terrified of screwing up my life, my future stardom. I wouldn't even trust a rubber. But then I think what an unsatisfactory experience it would've been anyway. All that ignorant fumbling and no orgasm, and either rocks or a gear shift digging into your back. Still . . ." Her voice trails off and the only sounds are the humming of the engine and the swish of the windshield wipers. "I lost my virginity in college. To a bad poet with acne. What about you?"

"A biology major."

"My first orgasm with a man was with Sean when we started going together. I thought I'd arrived at heaven, but after we were married, the sex got terrible. Something happened to my orgasms. They got, oh, I don't know, thinner somehow and then they disappeared altogether." She pauses and then laughs a little. "I just had a funny thought. Do you suppose Sean is sitting around with one of his men friends talking about his orgasms with me—'Marla was such a nutcracker, I could barely get it up.'"

I try and fail to imagine Dan discussing our sex life. "Dan wouldn't. He'd talk chips and circuitry."

"I like Dan. He's solid."

I wonder if she also means boring. "He's a good husband and father."

"Mmmm." She maneuvers the car around a sharp turn in the highway and then says, "Of all those women I met at the vigil, who are you closest to?"

"Daphne."

"She hates me, you know."

This shocks me almost as much as Marla's revelations about Tony. "She doesn't. I'm sure she doesn't."

"She hated me in high school. She told me once I was a stuck-up snob. I told her she was a loudmouth."

"I didn't like Daphne back then either," I say, "but we saw only one side of her. Daphne's the kind of person who'd give you the shirt off her back. I had a miscarriage when Joel was two, and she was really there for me."

"I could feel the hostility," Marla insists.

"Well, Virginia and Frances were very taken with you."

"Frances fascinates me—all that dead beauty."

"Dead beauty!"

"What I mean is, there's nothing behind it."

"Frances has a lovely personality."

"I'm sure she does, but most women who are beautiful know it and make the most of it. Hers isn't—how can I say it?—illuminated within."

"Her beauty's not dead," I protest. "I see it all the time."

"But you're not threatened by it, are you?"

"She's a good friend."

"That's my point. The only divorced woman in your circle, stunning besides, and none of you worry about your husbands."

I'm so astonished by this comment that it takes me a few seconds to respond. "We're not like that. I guess we're not as sophisticated as people in L.A."

"Bobbie, I'm sorry. I've offended you."

"I'm not offended," I say, but this isn't true. While I'm not blind to the fact that Cassandra probably has as many adulterers as any other community, I believe my friends to be loyal and responsible. I've never looked at their husbands with sexual intent, and I trust they don't look at mine. Our friendship is too important to us to destroy it with messy affairs and jealousies. Instead, we're held together by the bonds of decency, civility, and compassion. I think, with a nasty turn, that Marla's statement is a telling comment on her own life. She may have many humorous stories about this writer, that critic, editors, producers, actors, artists, and directors from New York to L.A., but it's clear this crowd is made up of a thousand acquaintances and few friends. For all her charm, her curiosity, and the seductive appeal of her laughter, I'm beginning to wonder if Marla's connections to other people aren't too thin, too flimsy for real friendship. In fact, I wonder if I'm the only close friend she's ever had.

It's Marla's turn to quickly change the subject. As she takes the exit ramp to Laurel Grove, she begins to talk about Caroline, the futile searching, the useless leads. "What're the police going to do now?"

"I don't know."

"I heard they had her boyfriend take a lie detector test, but he passed it okay. That was Frances's son, right?"

I nod and tell her about the last time I saw Caroline. "The day I got your letter saying you were coming back to Cassandra, Caroline was working in the post office. We talked about how she wanted to be a writer, too, a journalist, and she was so impatient to get into her future that I assured her she'd be out of high school before she knew it. And she said, 'It's never going to happen.' Of course, I didn't believe her, did I?"

"Caroline from Cassandra," Marla says, "a town named after a woman doomed to speak the truth and never be believed."

"I didn't think of that," I say. "It's eerie."

"It just occurred to me—has anyone said if Caroline Deacon was wearing hoop earrings the day she disappeared?"

"I don't think anyone's mentioned jewelry."

"Remember that earring we found at Misty Lake?"

I suddenly get it. "Oh, no," I say.

"It's possible, isn't it?"

"We sat there talking, skipping stones . . ." My voice trails off as I imagine Caroline floating just beneath the surface of the water, red hair forming snakes around her face, her naked body bifurcated by the arcs and dips of those unfeeling stones. My stomach reacts to this vision as if it's been punched hard. I feel a visceral pain and an inability to draw a breath.

"I think I put the earring in the pocket of the jacket I was wearing that day."

"You'd better bring it to the police."

My voice trembles, and I feel her glance at me. "Bobbie, are you feeling okay? Should I just take you straight home?"

The plan was that she would drop me off at Dan's office, and he and I would go out to dinner because Joel had a late football practice. "No," I say. "Leave me at Dan's."

"You sure?"

I feel a wave of nausea that I think only Dan's comforting presence will be able to alleviate. "I'll be fine," I say. "Really."

The rain stops and Marla decides to visit Misty Lake on her way to Cassandra. It's the first time she's been back since the day she arrived. That afternoon she was troubled by the difference between her memories of the lake and its reality. Her imagination, so precise on the details of the Hiller house, had embellished Misty Lake, heightening the trees, sharpening the rocks, making the water darker and more sinister. Places are innocent, she thought then, people are not. Now as she stands by her car, staring down the lake to where a small boat with two fishermen is trolling near the shore, she thinks that, yes, the lake is still innocent, even if it seems to have a propensity for tragedy—hers, Caroline Deacon's perhaps, and maybe that of others who have come here, friends who've quarreled, lovers breaking up, husbands cheating on wives.

There's a scurrying sound of a small animal like a squirrel behind her, and she turns to face the hill of trees and rock. Sunlight breaking through the clouds gleams on the needles of fir trees and tries to finger its way to the dark, shaded ground. Marla believes the key to Christian's death is here, on this hillside, somewhere among the branches and bark, the jutting rocks and the soft, leaf-cushioned ground. The police, trying to find the cause of the accident, studied the skid marks, tested the steepness of the curve, had Christian's blood analyzed for alcohol, and checked what they could of the brakes and steering of the car. They found nothing and declared the accident a case of too much speed and not enough caution. Marla knows otherwise. Something happened in the shadow of these pines and conifers that so impaired Christian's judgment he'd driven off the road and rammed his car into a tree.

This is not a conclusion she's arrived at easily, because her guilt over his death was overwhelming and persuasive. For years she was convinced of the facts as she knew them that night. She refused to sleep with Christian, and as a result he was blinded by dammed-up arousal, swollen testicles, and sexual rage. A simple equation, a truth that was self-evident. The late fifties/early sixties girl was responsible for every aspect of sex from enticement to seduction, virginity to pregnancy. It took only one extrapolation further to be convinced she was also responsible for death.

Marla walks to the edge of the shore and sits on the rock she shared with Bobbie a week ago. The water is so clear she can see the pebbles of black, ocher, and cream that lie on the bottom. She thinks of Christian, that fascinating mixture of cool and emotion. He had a way of looking at her with his eyes slightly narrowed, the green just a glitter in the dark lashes, that made her shiver with sexual excitement. He had a way of standing with his thumbs hooked into his belt and his head tilted that made her think of a hawk poised for flight. Then there was the Christian capable of blowing sky-high. Certain people enraged him: a teacher who had it in for him, the fucking forward on the Laurel Grove basketball team, who elbowed him in the groin, and his father, who thought he could capture Christian's restless spirit and bind it with rules, commands, lectures, and punishments that did nothing but make Christian want to escape, man, just get the hell out of this lousy town. Hadn't she loved him best when he was enraged, even though he frightened her? She loved the way his skin stretched tight over his cheekbones, the passion in his voice, the clenching of his fists, the quick rise and fall of his chest.

And that's how he'd been that night, enraged at her, stalking off into the dark and driving into his destiny. Or so she'd thought until several years later when the grieving finally came to an end and her guilt began to lessen. When she told the story to Sean, he shrugged it away.

"What's the big deal? The guy could've gone into the woods and jerked off."

"Maybe he didn't do that sort of thing."

"What? Are you kidding? Listen, babe, most guys begin jerking off between diaper changes."

Or her first therapist who gently led her to figuring out that, like many children and teenagers, she'd been so egocentric she couldn't imagine herself as someone other than the central player in all the dramas enacted around her. He pointed to her belief that her rebellious behavior was the cause of her parents' bad marriage even though she knew they were incompatible and had serious money problems.

"But I made Christian angry," she said.

"Why was he angry?"

"Because I wouldn't have sex with him."

"Is that a good reason to be angry?"

"You mean there might have been other reasons?"

"There might have been many reasons and not all of them had to do with you."

And finally, there was the memory that had been submerged in the guilt and self-recrimination. After Christian left, Marla lay facedown on the blanket and sobbed, her head buried in her arms. When she could cry no longer, she turned over and stared up at the sky, wondering how the stars could still be so bright and the blackness so smooth and velvet. If she were in a novel, the sky would be rent by her despair, lightning would slash through the darkness, thunder would roll overhead, and the wind and rain would drive the trees into torment. But she wasn't in a novel, and she was beginning to get cold. She got up, wiped her eyes, and walked down the hillside to the fire, where the others were singing and drinking beer. She sat down next to Brian and hugged her knees to her chest. Her face grew warm from the flames but her back was still cool. She shivered and butted him with her shoulder to get his attention.

"Hey," she said. "Can I have a beer?"

He reached into the cooler beside him. "You seen Bobbie?"

"Where she'd go?"

"Thataway." Brian pointed in the direction of a copse of trees behind several high rocks where the girls went to pee.

"Maybe she got lost." She'd read somewhere that laughter was close to tears, and it was true, because she felt a giggle start in her chest at the thought of Bobbie wandering through the woods in search of the girl's john. The giggle also made her brave enough to say in a nonchalant way, "Do you know where Christian is?"

Brian gave her a beery, puzzled look. "He just left."

Marla hadn't remembered these final words of Brian's. She'd lost them somewhere between the finding of Christian's unconscious body by the wreck of his car and his death three weeks later. They remained lost until she was working late one night on her last novel, and for no particular reason, they popped into her head. She began to wonder how long she'd lain on the blanket crying and then staring up into the sky. Ten minutes? Fifteen? And, if so much time had elapsed between Christian's walking away and her arrival by the fire, the sequence of events as she envisioned them could not have happened. Christian hadn't gone straight to his car, switched on the ignition, slammed the car into first and revved it out of the parking lot, spewing pebbles from under the wheels. He hadn't driven down the highway, cursing her under his breath and slamming his fist against the steering wheel over and over again. His eyes hadn't filled with tears of anger and frustration, blinding him to the coming curve in the road. And his scream hadn't caught in his throat like that of a trapped animal when he suddenly realized he was hurtling through black space toward that ever-widening tree—all because of her.

For the first time in years, this sequence, which had run like a horror film through her head, came to a halt as if the celluloid had snapped. In its place was a blank, a ten- or fifteen-minute gap of missing activity. It was an enigma, but then Christian was an enigma. Marla picks up a stone and turns it over in her hands, its water-smoothed edges a metaphor for her own memory, which has been so eroded by time that the original outline of Christian has been worn to almost nothing. She can barely remember his face, gestures, smiles, words. The only thing she recalls with any accuracy is the raw stew of her own emotions whenever she came into contact with him—the yearning infatuation, the ache of sexual longing, the fear of losing him, her pride when other girls saw them together, her jealousy when he looked at someone else—the first and only grand passion of her life.

Funny how she can remember so many other things from that time. She can still conjugate some Latin verbs, the fights with her mother are as clear as a bell, and she could easily reconstruct those sleepovers with Bobbie and their whispered intimacies and hysterical laughter. But Christian is lost in time, and Marla is reminded of the way Brian has also disappeared, buried in jowls, three chins, and a paunch. Would that have been Christian's fate, too—to lose his thick, springing hair, the taut line of his jaw and his slender, muscled waist? Is there a certain mercy in dying young and at the height of beauty?

Marla throws the stone into the lake. As it splashes, she imagines the stone sinking through water that grows darker and colder as it approaches the bottom. If the earring did belong to Caroline, does that mean she and Bobbie just missed the murderer the day she arrived? If her plane had been earlier, would they have come upon whoever it was dumping the body? She reaches into her purse, pulls out her notebook, and writes:

Who killed Caroline Deacon? The temptation would be to write this as a mystery novel with every boy and man in town under suspicion. I'd have the two women inadvertently witness the murder—perhaps the tail end of it such as a man pulling away in a boat. They don't really understand they've seen a killing, nor does the killer realize they were there until one of them casually drops a remark to the effect that she's seen his boat on the lake on the day of the murder. The murderer must then try to kill both women before they figure out what they've seen and go to the police. The plot would thicken like porridge, and the novel would fill with dead bodies, frantic police, and frightened townspeople.

The detective could be a young, savvy woman lawyer who's at the end of a turbulent affair with a local businessman separated from his wife. The killer would be a man esteemed in the community, an attentive husband and doting father, a pillar of the church and town government, a fund-raiser and a district Boy Scout supervisor. What is his motive for killing Caroline? The secret lusting, of course, the year of following her with his eyes, the planned abduction, the shameful, bungled rape, and the act of strangling, done more in sorrow than in anger.

Marla puts down her pen and thinks how comforting it would be to create a world where mayhem is so well organized, where a murderer leaves appropriate clues for the clever detective and perplexing problems always have tidy solutions. But real life isn't like that, is it? It's messy and confusing, a tangle of ambiguities, puzzles, and problems with no solutions: her parents' bad marriage, Christian's death, her two divorces, and Didi. *Didi.* Why couldn't she tell Bobbie the truth about Didi? Marla closes her eyes, that mental door is forced open, and she falls helplessly back onto the old battlegrounds.

"Leave me alone!"

"It was a dangerous thing to do."

"It wasn't."

"Didi, you didn't know those boys and you didn't know that part of town."

"They weren't going to do anything to me."

"How did you know that?"

"I just did."

"But you only met them an hour before."

"I can tell about people, that's why."

"They're dropouts, kids who hang around the streets. They're probably doing drugs."

"They're nice, Mom. Not that you'd ever believe that!"

"There are lots of other nice kids around who don't hang out in bad neighborhoods."

"You don't understand."

"Explain it to me."

"I could explain my whole life long and you'd never get it. It's how I feel, okay? And you've never really understood how I feel!"

The old painful sensation of not getting anywhere. Trying another tack. "Do you know what it was like sitting here until two in the morning waiting for you to come home?"

Flippantly. "I'm sorry."

"I almost called the police."

A bored, insulting shrug.

"Don't you care?"

"Do *you* know what it's like living here and having to answer every stupid question and having you watching me all the time? I hate it. I hate you!"

The fishermen pull their lines out of the water, rev the motor and speed off. Marla reaches for a stone. She grips it tightly in her hand, seeking comfort from its smoothness, its well-worn surfaces, and then presses it hard to her chest over the beating of her heart.

I love you, Didi. I hate you. I loved you.

Chapter
10

OUR BRIDGE NIGHT HAS ROTATED TO DAPHNE'S HOUSE, AND our mood is sober, which isn't surprising considering the week we've been through. Virginia is still getting over her cold, and her thin nose is pink at the nostrils. Daphne has spent several evenings sitting with the Deacons, trying to be optimistic and cheerful even though her own spirits were drooping. Frances believes Ben is still under suspicion, although she's calmer since he passed his lie detector test. And as for me—I'd been in a state ever since Marla suggested the earring we found at Misty Lake might have belonged to Caroline. I couldn't eat during my dinner out with Dan and I hardly slept that night, tossing and turning with frightful, broken dreams about bodies and water, hair and naked limbs, mud and cold. The next morning I had to pick up a prescription for Dan, who's developed eczema in his ears, and Edgar and I talked about Caroline.

"A terrible thing," I said.

"Terrible." He made a tutting sound as he typed out the label for Dan's prescription. "Makes you wonder what this world is coming to. A nice girl like that."

"They got the posters out fast enough," I said. Edgar had put a poster of Caroline in the window where his third

repudiated art print had once hung. HAVE YOU SEEN THIS
GIRL? the poster asks over Caroline's high school photo.
*Caroline Deacon, 17 years old, disappeared April 14, 1990. If
you have any information, please contact . . .* The poster is
large and in color and cost a fortune. There have been three
bake sales to help pay for the printing: one at the Deacons'
church, one held by the cheerleading squad of which Caroline is a member, and another by the Women's Auxiliary of
the Fire Department. Every time I see the poster in Edgar's
window, I think how much I preferred the nude that
preceded it, and I wonder how many other people in
Cassandra recognize that there are other forms of obscenity
besides nakedness.

"They've got those posters across the country," Edgar
said. "There's a national organization that does that—
distribute posters of missing children. And there've been a
lot of tips. Of course, most calls are a waste of time, but
they're following up every single lead."

"I guess they have to."

"No stone unturned as they say." He wrapped the label
around the vial of ointment, put it in a bag, and handed it to
me. "Voilà. This should fix up Dan's ears in no time. I've got
the same problem, you know."

"No, I didn't."

"Hereditary so they say. And maddening. There you are
in the middle of a dinner party and suddenly your ears go on
you. Itch, itch, itch. And I ask you—can you stick your
knife in your ear in polite company?"

I smiled at Edgar and thought how smart he is to keep his
professional and community life separate from his sexual
activities. Everyone in town knows Edgar is gay, but no one
knows who he's gay *with*. His grandfather was the town
pharmacist when I was a baby, and his father was the town
pharmacist when I was growing up. Edgar followed in these
familial footsteps, working with his father after he finished
college and taking over the drugstore when his father died in
1981. He lives with his mother in the house in which he was
raised and takes care of her—she has severe osteoporosis—
with great diligence. I sometimes see them on Sunday

mornings when he brings her to church and then to lunch at the Tea Room. He holds her carefully by the arm, his own back curved solicitously to match hers.

He is equally diligent about his pursuit of culture. In addition to his push for an art gallery and sitting on the board of the library, he plays with a recorder group and is on the committee for Cassandra's annual Arts and Crafts Fair. He also belongs to a poetry club in Laurel Grove and has season tickets to the Syracuse Orchestra. My suspicion is that those are the places where his sexual life happens, outside the confines of our small, too intimate town and in the safe anonymity of a city. His caution means there's nothing to feed the gossip mills—no affairs and no flagrant behavior—only an effeminacy that makes us smile now and then with affection. After all, Edgar is an Ashley, and Ashleys have been a fixture in Cassandra for over one hundred years.

Our conversation turned back to Caroline, and I told Edgar about the hoop earring Marla and I found at Misty Lake.

"Oh, no," he said, "that wouldn't be Caroline's."

"It wouldn't?"

"She had infections in her lobes from cheap pierced earrings. You know what these girls are like. Vanity before common sense. They think nothing of putting the worst trash on their bodies. Mind you, there's some people that have the reverse—an allergy to gold, believe it or not. They can wear trash from morning to night, but put gold next to their skin and they're in trouble."

"The earring might've been gold," I said.

Edgar pursed his lips under his thin mustache and shook his head. "She had to wear studs to keep the holes open and the doctor prescribed an antibiotic cream. It's been an uphill battle, mind you. Molly was in here just the day before Caroline disappeared, saying that the infections weren't clearing up that fast."

The knowledge that the earring wasn't Caroline's and her body wasn't likely to be in Misty Lake lifted the heavy burden of dread that I'd been carrying and even gave me a sense of euphoria that lasted all day. While I recognize that my euphoria is inappropriate, I can't help the way I feel. I play bridge with a lightheaded and slightly giddy sensation that comes from a combination of intense relief and lack of sleep. The result is that I don't count my cards well, and Virginia and I go down to immediate defeat.

"Bad cards," Virginia says, shaking her head.

Daphne starts to deal out another hand, but the conversation turns to the effect of Caroline's disappearance on our children, and we don't even pick up our cards.

"Julian's stomach is nauseated all the time," Daphne says. Julian was Daphne and Matt's afterthought, now fourteen years old and conceived during a holiday when Daphne discovered she'd forgotten to pack her pills and thought: what the hell. "The doctor said it's pure anxiety. He said he's seeing a lot of that—kids who throw up before school, kids who can't sleep, kids who want to sleep all the time."

"That's Joel," I say. "He sleeps right through the alarm. We can hardly get him up in time for school."

"How's Ben doing?" Virginia asks Frances. Although Frances hadn't wanted me to mention the lie detector test to anyone, news that Ben had to take one was all over town by the next day. I heard it from Frieda Doerman, who's a library volunteer, and Mary Morris at the dry cleaner's.

"Ben is Ben," Frances says. "He studies for hours. He looks pale, and I think he's lost weight, but he doesn't show a thing, just like Paul. It amazes me that although he hasn't lived with his father for most of his life, Ben's just like him."

"Does Paul know about the test?" I ask. Paul doesn't live in Cassandra anymore. He moved to Maryland, married again, and has two daughters.

"I don't know if Ben told him or not. The father-son relationship is a place I'm not allowed to get close to. It's verboten."

She says this with arched, ironic eyebrows, but I think it must be painful. Of all of us, Frances has been the fiercest mother, the most protective, the most likely to intervene when she thought Ben was not getting what he deserved from teachers, coaches, doctors, the world. I don't criticize her for this, she's the only one of us who has had to raise her child alone, but I see that Ben has, in turn, learned to protect himself by erecting barriers between them, cool defenses against the heat of her love. I think of Joel, whose adolescent rebellion takes the form of small, difficult moments—chores badly done, spats over use of the car, homework he's neglected—that are tolerable because when they're over he reverts to the Joel of his childhood, sweet, affectionate, and connected.

"I think Ben must find it hard," Virginia says, "to equate who he is with what the police think of him. Imagine going through the throes of the teenage identity crisis, when you have so much trouble defining yourself, and finding that people can actually believe you're capable of a crime like murder. It must be terrible for him."

"He won't talk," Frances says. "You know how it is, I'm only his mother." She makes a helpless gesture, throwing out her hand and tilting her head. The lamplight falls on her face differently, an angle of illumination that highlights the right side of her face, the pure lines of her temple, cheekbone, and jawline. I remember what Marla said about her beauty, how she didn't seem to care about it, and I note that she wears no makeup, that her hair, pulled back into a chignon, is in the same style it's been as long as I've known her, and that the colors and shapes she wears are subdued: pale cream in the pearls at her ears, pale gray in her blouse, a slim gold wristwatch, darker gray slacks, flat shoes. I recognize that Frances is not stunning or breathtaking or sexy. Her face is merely perfect in a modest way. While I resent Marla's suggestion that we're only friends with Frances because she doesn't threaten our marriages, I acknowledge that if she were truly dazzling in that cleavage-baring, eye-turning, husband-stealing way, we might never had become friends with her at all.

"I'm really worried about Sarah," Virginia says. "She's

obsessed with Caroline's disappearance. She talks about it all the time, and now she's spending as much time as she can over at the Deacons'.''

"Doing what?" Frances asks.

"Helping Molly with housework as far as I can tell. Of course, she wouldn't think of doing any housework at home, but that's not what really bothers me. I don't think it's healthy for her, but if I ask her to stop, all hell breaks loose. She just screams at me. She's so intense."

"She wasn't that close a friend to Caroline, was she?" I ask, thinking about the way I stuck to Marla after Christian died.

Virginia sighs. "They weren't friends at all. That's the weird part of it."

"Did you know three hundred kids a year disappear and aren't found?" Frances says. "I heard that on *Geraldo.*"

This number silences us for a minute, and I think about the three hundred unhappy families and the three hundred communities that suffer along with them. "These kinds of crimes sometimes bring the worst out in people," I say, and tell them about the letter I received from Arlene requesting that *The Catcher in the Rye* be banned from the library.

"That old chestnut," Daphne says with disgust.

"I got one, too," Frances says. "Just today."

"That's a new strategy," I say slowly, "sending each board member a copy. Usually she's satisfied to have me present it at the board meeting."

"And adding Caroline like that," Virginia says, shaking her head. "That's taking advantage."

"It's playing to the galleries," Daphne says. "It'll put extra pressure on the board."

"That woman," Frances says, "is really a nuisance, isn't she?"

"I hated her when we were kids," Daphne says. "She was such a goody-goody. Remember, Barbara? Remember those white gloves she wore to school that never ever got dirty? She made me want to puke."

I don't recall the white gloves, but I do remember Arlene

well. In grade school she had dark, glossy braids, a pug nose, a well-scrubbed freckly face, and an irritating air of moral superiority. Teachers liked her and she was always winning awards, not for academic achievement but for good penmanship, the most organized desk, and the neatest math homework book. Arlene wanted to be a missionary when she grew up, and she did a project in grade eight that showed how the unfortunate heathens in darkest Africa would benefit from Christianity. I remember being duly impressed but also wondering if the heathens would love Arlene as much as she said she already loved them. I, for one, found it very hard to like Arlene then and find it impossible to like her now.

She never did get to go to Africa. I believe that the closest Arlene got to that continent or an African was a lecture held by a Nigerian bishop on *Educating Our Children* in Syracuse in 1978, which she told me about during one visit to the library. Instead of being a missionary, she married her high school sweetheart, Barry McPherson, who is the town controller and local accountant. She has three children and a career of volunteerism in church groups, the PTA, the Women's Auxiliary to the Fire Department, the March of Dimes, and other worthy causes. Although time has transformed her dark braids into short, graying curls, faded her freckles, and diminished the impact of her pug nose by widening her face, it hasn't made a dint in her air of moral superiority, which remains unfortunately intact.

As we pick up our cards and fan out our hands, the conversation shifts to less disturbing topics: gardens, backyards, houses, and house repairs. Virginia sighs and says they need a new roof. Daphne mentions that Peter Mailer, the architect for Marla's renovations, was at the town hall getting permits for the Hiller house. "He didn't say in so many words," she says, "but it's going to cost her a mint."

"You get a book on the best-seller list," Virginia says, "and you don't have to worry about money."

Daphne leans forward. "I also hear she has a thing going with Tony Molino."

"The real estate agent?" Virginia asks. "That Tony Molino?"

"Phyllis Gruber saw them shopping together at the Grand Union in Laurel Grove."

"That's fast," Frances says.

"She must be lonely," Virginia says, "coming here after all these years all by herself. It must be hard."

I once envisioned the foursome that Virginia, Daphne, Frances, and I have created as a square and wondered if Marla would be able to cross the boundaries of that square and step inside. I now see that the geometry is more complex than that. Her confidences have created their own boundaries, lines drawn between me and the others, lines of information that can't be crossed without betraying those confidences. I also see that Marla was right about Daphne. The reach of adolescence is a long arm extending into our adult selves. That reach pulled me back into the circle of Marla's charm, into liking her all over again, just as it has repelled Daphne once again. They rubbed each other the wrong way in high school, and they're rubbing each other the same wrong way twenty-five years later. They're too alike, I think. They're both bold and like to shock, and the hard edges of their personalities strike sparks when they meet, like two swords crashing against one another. I wonder why the hard edges don't bother me, Virginia, or Frances. Perhaps our softness deflects their aim, perhaps the way we yield blunts their sharpness.

"What about Marla's daughter?" Daphne asks, turning to me. "Didn't you say she had a daughter?"

"She's in summer school in L.A.," I say. "I think Marla's going to visit her."

Virginia frowns, that tiny crease cutting the pale skin between her eyes. "That's odd," she says.

"What?"

"I met Marla in front of the deli yesterday, and we were chatting, and I asked her about her daughter. Didi, I think that's her name. Anyway, she didn't mention summer school. She said Didi was a counselor at a camp in the Rockies."

I stare down at my cards and remember the uneasiness I felt about the offhand way Marla talked about her daughter. "That is odd."

"Maybe not," Frances says. "Maybe she's doing both. One month summer school, one month camp."

"Maybe," I say.

Daphne, who's dealt, says, "Are we going to play or keep this chitchat going all night?"

"Who's winning?" Frances says.

"You are."

"Then we're playing."

"I have lousy cards," I say.

"Watch it," Daphne says. "No table talk."

That night I sleep well, deeply, and if I have dreams I don't remember them. The alarm is set for 5:00, because Dan has to drive to Syracuse to catch an early plane to Albuquerque, where he's attending a large computer conference. I awake with a feeling of well-being and energy. I get up with Dan, prepare breakfast, see him off, make the bed, neaten the living room, wake up Joel, and get two laundries done by 7:45. By the time I'm dressed and drinking my last cup of coffee before going to work, I'm glowing with that inner pleasure only another wife and mother would recognize. It's a satisfied feeling of being one step ahead, of having beaten the household odds and winning that endless battle—Mom versus dirt and clutter, 1–0.

Joel is in the shower when the doorbell rings a little before 8:00. Curious as to who would come by so early in the morning, I peer out the curtains that hang beside the front door and see Reg Burton standing on our front stoop—the official Reg Burton, a big, burly man with a graying crew cut dressed in his cop's outfit: pale blue shirt with the Cassandra police insignia on the sleeve, brown belt, darker blue pants, brown shoes. Behind him, parked up against the sidewalk, is the cop car, white with a blue stripe and the circular insignia.

I open the door. "Reg," I say. "Good morning." I look beyond him to the street and wonder why he's here. Has there been a disturbance? A neighbor burglarized? Someone hurt?

"Hello, Barbara," he says. "Can I come in for a minute?"

He walks past me into the foyer as I say, "Would you like some coffee?"

"No thanks, I just had some. Actually, I've been cutting down. I got chest pains last year and the doctor said to ease off the caffeine."

"What about decaffeinated?" I ask as he steps into the living room and sits down on the couch. "Would that be all right?"

"That's what the missus is after me to drink," he says, "but I can't. It just doesn't have the taste, if you know what I mean."

"No, it doesn't. Not really." I've never noticed what long eyelashes Reg has. They're dark and curl upward like a woman's does after she's applied mascara and a curler. They're at odds with his face, the narrow, dark eyes underlined by half-circles of flesh, a thick, broad nose, heavy jowls mottled pink.

"So I have my one cup in the morning and that's it."

"Reg," I say, sitting down opposite him, "what's this about?"

"Is Dan home?" Reg asks.

"He left on a business trip this morning."

"Joel around?"

"In the shower?"

"Well, I'd like to talk to the two of you."

I think of Ben and my heart lurches, literally. I feel it bump hard in my chest. "Reg," I say, rising in my chair.

He puts both beefy hands up, palms facing me. "Barbara, this is just standard procedure. It's nothing to get worried about."

"Mom?" Joel's voice precedes his arrival from the kitchen. His feet are bare, and he's wearing jeans and a white T-shirt with a green tree on it that says SAVE THE FORESTS. His hair is still damp and curls around his forehead. I know he's almost grown, that his body is thickening, that he spends time after his showers now to shave two small patches of facial hair, one above his upper lip and one on his chin, but to me he still has that bony vulnerability of a boy, a sweet angularity that clutches at my restless heart.

Joel stops at the sight of Reg, looks warily at both of us, and then says, "Oh, hi, Mr. Burton."

"Reg wants to talk to us," I say.

He sits down, his knees jutting upward, and cracks his knuckles. It's a habit I dislike and I give him a warning look. He drops his hands to his lap.

Reg clears his throat. "This business about Caroline is turning out to be very difficult for everybody, and we want to get to the bottom of things just as fast as we can. Now, as Joel knows, we've spent a lot of time talking to Caroline's friends and classmates. In some cases, we have no problem ruling out kids as suspects. In other cases—"

"Are you telling me Joel is a suspect?" My voice rises uncontrollably on the last word.

"Now, Barbara, I said this is standard procedure, nothing out of the ordinary. We're looking at all the boys whose activities that day can't be pinned down tight. That's all we're doing here." He gives me an intent look to make sure I've got the message. "We'd like Joel to take a polygraph test."

I think how I can't believe this is happening and yet hate it at the same time, and how I wish Dan were here and am angry that he's not only out of Cassandra but untethered to earth, to us, to me. I think how content he is in that stasis an airplane creates, that sensation of standing still while really going hundreds of miles, the engines' roar only a pleasant hum in the background as he sips at his coffee, eats a Danish, and listens to music on the earphones, ignorant of what is happening below.

"Does he have to?" I ask.

"No, we can't force him to, and whatever he says is not admissible in court. That's the law in New York State."

"Then why do it?"

"Now, Barbara, I told you there's nothing to worry about here. It's just a tool. Joel takes the test, we know he's innocent, and that's all there is to it."

"Suppose he's nervous and it's not accurate."

Reg's hands go up, those supposedly calming palms. "We've got specially trained operators that know the ins and outs of this procedure. They take everything into account. Again, as I say, this is just a tool to help us sort this mess out. And you know that until this thing is solved, this town is going to be on pins and needles. I'm sure I don't have to tell you what it's doing. We got fear, we got anxiety, we got trauma. We've got kids of twelve who're going to have nervous breakdowns if we don't get some answers."

I'm wondering, frantically, if we refuse to let Joel take the test, whether we should get a lawyer, when Joel says, "Okay."

I look at him. "You don't have to."

He shrugs. "It's okay."

"Barbara," Reg says, "it's for the best. Believe me."

"Is he the only one?"

"No, we've got a few others."

"And what's the reasons, Reg? Why Joel?"

"We're looking at alibis, motives, and ability to commit."

"Commit what?" I ask sharply.

"Now, Barbara, easy does it."

Easy does it—easy for him to say. How would he and the missus feel if the situation were reversed, and I were sitting in their living room, suggesting that one of their three sons had committed murder? I remember a school picnic where Reg's wife, Jean, and I shared the job of dishing out the baked beans and potato salad, and she told me, with such pride, about their older son, John, who'd made the dean's list his first year at university.

"Joel went to school that morning," I say.

"Yes, but there was a time spell there after you left the house and before he got to school." He sees I'm about to object. "I know that happens every morning. Joel's said so, but there's no one that can account for his actions. You see what I'm saying?"

"I'm sure that's true of a hundred kids."

"Then we looked and asked ourselves who had access to a car, because if it's someone in town, then that someone moved Caroline out of the immediate vicinity and would need a car."

"Joel doesn't take a car to school," I say.

"But you walked to work that morning. He had access to your car."

"You're fishing, Reg. Isn't that what this is?"

The appeasing palms go up again. "We're taking a serious look here at the boys who went out with Caroline or asked her out. Joel asked her out."

I look at Joel, whose head is bent as he intensely studies his hands. "You asked her out?"

Reg answers. "A year ago. She turned him down."

"That doesn't mean anything," I say hotly. "She was a pretty girl. I'm sure lots of boys asked her out."

Reg is standing up now and talking to Joel. "We'll be making an appointment for you at the county sheriff's office in Syracuse. It'll probably be tomorrow." He turns to me. "And don't you worry, Barbara. It's just a formality, that's all."

I smile, I see Reg out, and say good-bye as if his call has been only a neighborly chat. If I were Frances, I'd probably run out after him, pursue him with questions, and find out what I don't want to know. But I'm not Frances and Joel isn't Ben, is he? We talk, we communicate. I close the door and face Joel, who's still sitting in the chair, knees jutting out like sharp corners, his knuckles cracking.

"Stop that," I say.

He stops and begins to chew on a nail.

"Is there more to this?" I ask. "Is there anything else you haven't told me about?"

"Like what?"

"I don't know. I'm asking you."

"There's nothing."

"No other reason why they're taking you all the way to Syracuse?"

"No."

I study his upturned face with its clear blue eyes and broad brow. It's the face of my baby with its innocent fat cheeks and sunny smile. It's the face of my little boy who could not tell a lie without assuming a telltale shifty expression with guilt written all over it. It's Dan's face, honest and straightforward.

"You asked her out, she said no, and that was it."

"Yes."

And I believe him.

PART II

JOEL

Chapter
1

IT USED TO BE THAT WHEN JOEL WAS SWIMMING IN THE POOL during practice, he could imagine that he didn't live at 55 Steeplechase Street, Cassandra, New York, but in some other place where the air was turquoise, there was no sound but his own heartbeat, and his body could cut through the atmosphere like a knife. He used to imagine this during the twenty-lap warm-up: pull, kick, somersault, turn, pull, kick, somersault, turn. Sometimes he swam the whole warm-up and couldn't remember a stroke. Sometimes he swam and played out this fantasy where he was an alien who'd come to this weird world of turquoise air and was an instant celebrity because of his endurance and speed. He could beat the natives, who looked human but were not and could speak English (just like aliens in *Star Trek: The Next Generation*), in every stroke—freestyle, back crawl, breast stroke, butterfly—and every event.

Their sportscasters would fall all over him. "What's your secret?" they asked.

"Technique," he'd say modestly into the microphones, but it was more than that. It was muscle: pecs and quads, delts and abs firing under his skin, pulsing with power and strength. And you want to know the amazing thing? He didn't have to work at it, it just came naturally. Born to be king, man. King of the world of underwater weirdness.

Of course, he knew the fantasy was stupid, a kid thing, a holdover from when he was fourteen and began to worry about himself. That was the year he asked for weights for Christmas and kept a tattered copy of *Playboy* hidden at the bottom of his closet. He'd got it from Gene who'd gotten it from Pete who'd gotten it from Andy who said he'd found it in his father's dresser and there were a lot more where that came from.

But even at the best of times, the fantasy didn't go beyond the warm-up, because Joel swims with the C group, four other guys whose times match his so they don't climb all over one another when they're doing lengths. The A group is the fastest guys, like Ted Snedecker, who went to the state competition and brought back a silver in the 400-meter breast. But then Ted is amazing, everyone says so. His whip kick could jump-start a fucking motorcycle.

The C group is okay except for times like now when Joel finds himself swimming parallel with Dennis Morehouse, a B group swimmer, and Dennis slowly pulls ahead of him. It doesn't matter how much steam Joel puts into it, he can't make his pace any faster without his breathing going all to hell. Every time he turns his head, he sees another part of Dennis pass through his line of sight: head, shoulders, chest, hips, legs, and feet until all that's left is a trail of bubbles. That's when he's reminded there's no turquoise fantasy world, only a pool painted turquoise with black lines, no admiring sportscasters, only a yelling coach, and no adoring alien girls who like to swim naked beside him.

"Breymann! Breymann!"

Joel swims over to the side of the pool, pulls himself up, and balances his weight on his elbows. He tugs off his goggles and pushes them up onto his forehead, feeling the rim left by the rubberized edge around his eyes. The coach squats down beside him. Mr. Boehm, who also teaches math, is tall, lanky, and hairy everywhere except for his scalp, which is bare but for a dozen splotchy freckles. He has frizzy dark hair on his shoulders, thin shins, and bony knuckles and toes. His secret code name among the members of the swim team is Spiderman.

Mr. Boehm grew up in Cassandra and swam for the high school team back in the sixties. Framed photographs of that team hang in his office, twenty half-nude, grinning guys with full heads of hair, none of whom look anything like Spiderman does now. Whenever he sees those photographs, Joel wonders whether future students will study the 1990 photographs of the Cassandra Dolphins and not be able to find him, Joel, in the second row, third from the right. Mr. Boehm's team won the state all-around in his senior year, and Spiderman swam the third leg in the fastest relay team in state history. He doesn't let the modern-day Dolphins forget it. After every meet, he does his locker-room performance where he paces up and down, hands whirling like chopper blades.

"You had a problem out there in the pool today, Peppert? No? What about you, Mavinsky? No? This is amazing, a truly amazing happening. You want to know why? Because I have a team here without a problem. Not a single, solitary problem. We've got perfect A-one swimmers. An entire Olympic team. But there *is* a problem. You know what that is? Breymann, you have a hunch? No? Well, here's the mystery—nobody knows Cassandra has an Olympic team. It's the best-kept secret in central New York. That's right. We're a hidden force. We're under wraps. We've got guys here who could break state records, *world* records, but we're holding back." He pauses and studies their faces. "I say to myself, we've got to get to the bottom of this. We've got to solve this mystery or the Dolphins are going to be in the basement for the rest of the year. So I ask, what's missing here? What's the missing ingredient? Snedecker, you know what it is?"

They all know the answer to this. "A clear mind, sir?"

"Right!" Spiderman roars. "When we get in that pool, we've got to let everything go, school, family, the whole outside world. You've got to have your mind as clear as a bell, nothing in it but the water and the stroke. No homework, no wondering what you're going to do on Saturday night, none of those lovey-dovey thoughts about girls." This always evokes a snigger. "To win another all-around for Cassandra, we've got to have a clear mind. You know why? Morehouse?"

"To concentrate, sir."

"Right!"

A clear mind and concentration, Joel has noticed, translate into more practice, more drills, more timed swims, more sprints. But it hasn't done Joel any good. He can't keep his mind clear, he can't concentrate, he loses the thread of what he's doing, what he's thinking, and even the fantasies get muddled.

"What's the matter, Joel?"

"Nothing."

"You feeling okay?"

"Yeah."

"Anything on your mind?"

"No."

"You sure?"

Joel nods.

"I have this feeling, Joel, that you're daydreaming in there."

"I'm trying not to."

"You focusing on keeping that mind clear as a bell?"

"Yes, sir."

"And thinking only about the water and the stroke?"

"Yes, sir."

Mr. Boehm puts a hand on Joel's shoulder. "Your butterfly is really coming along, Breymann. It's almost there."

"Yes, sir."

"Okay," Mr. Boehm says, standing up. "Okay."

Joel puts his goggles back and pushes himself off the edge. The water closes over his shoulders and his head. He looks down at the bottom of the pool, the black lap line angling into water that gets bluer as it gets deeper, and he wishes he could skim along its surface forever, never having to rise upward, never needing to breathe, at home in the alien, turquoise depths.

* * *

"How was practice?" Dan asks.

"Okay."

"There's a meet next week, right?"

"Yeah."

"Who's the meet with?"

"Binghamton."

"A good team?"

"Yeah."

"You worried about them?"

Joel shrugs.

"I have time on Friday night," Barbara says, "to go with you to the mall and get some shirts."

Joel had been nagging his mother for weeks to take him shopping. "Maybe."

"You said you needed shirts."

"I may be busy."

"You going out?"

"I don't know."

"When will you know?"

"I don't know."

"Is it something you're doing with Andy or Pete?"

"Maybe."

Joel shrugs and catches his mother looking at his father in that meaningful way as she passes the bowl of rice to him. There've been lots of looks like that since he took the lie detector test. Eyes meeting, arched brows, small shakes of the head. They don't think he sees it, but he does. Sometimes at night when he goes to the bathroom and passes their bedroom, he hears murmuring behind the door, an agitated humming. He knows it's about him. He imagines their conversations. *He's acting strange . . . very strange . . . less open . . . not the old Joel . . . it's just a reaction . . . do you think so? . . . maybe a phase, too . . . they all go through phases . . .*

He doesn't know what it is himself. He couldn't describe it if he had to. It started as a bad feeling somewhere deep down in his gut the day the police came to school to interview Caroline's classmates. By the time Mr. Burton got to Joel, he knew about Joel asking Caroline out and her turning him down. He didn't know what had gone on before it, and Joel wasn't about to tell him. It wouldn't have been easy to pinpoint the day when Joel suddenly noticed Caroline in a different way than he had before. She'd been a fixture in his life forever, one of the busy little girls who jumped rope in the playground, one of the tall, lanky thirteen-year-olds who stood in clumps before their lockers, whispering and giggling, and one of those brainy types that teachers went nuts for and whose homework was always neat. He ignored her except for birthday parties arranged by their parents. He was invited to hers and she to his. He always knew her birthday present to him would be something from the hardware store. The most memorable was the small hammer and screwdriver she'd given him the year he was eight.

Then something changed, too slowly for him to fix on the moment it happened, and Caroline ceased to be an object of no particular significance and stepped forward into his consciousness. Aspects of her that he'd never noticed before became important, like the way her hair curled at her temples, the dimple in her cheek when she smiled, the thrust of her breasts beneath her blouse. He could handle each of these details separately, but not the combination of them together. The whole of Caroline was more than the sum of her parts, and he was dazzled and blinded by her. He couldn't look at her directly and spent the year he was fifteen watching her out of the corner of his eye at school and having real stupid fantasies about her, like the two of them stranded together on a desert island and him saving her from starvation by miraculously finding food and protecting her from savages with his strength and cleverness.

On his sixteenth birthday, Joel promised himself he'd ask Caroline out even if she was popular and a lot of other guys wanted to go out with her. It took him two months to pull his resolve together and make the move. He'd noticed that Caroline always went to the library during third period when they both had a spare. She sat alone at one end of a table and did her math homework. Joel sat down opposite her one day and asked her if she knew the answer to one of the algebra problems. Then he did an imitation of their math teacher, Mrs. Benevenuto—"See, Caroline, I bet you never thought you'd understand that, but you did, didn't you?"—in her breathless shrill way, and Caroline laughed. After that they did math together every third period. Joel expanded on his repertoire of impersonations—the principal's pomposity, the librarian's ferocity, Mr. Boehm's emphatic gestures—discovering a knack for imitation he hadn't known he possessed. When Caroline laughed at something he'd said, Joel felt wittier than he'd ever felt before. He wondered whether he might not become a stand-up comic, which was a far cry from being an engineer, a career his parents were pushing.

Joel thought he was really getting somewhere, making huge, giant steps towards Caroline (like in the game he used to play as a kid) that would end with her agreeing to go to a movie with him. He didn't think about the actual date but focused on the asking. He practiced the words: *Busy on Friday night?* or *There's a great flick at the Odeon* or *I won a quiz on CKWU and have two tickets to . . .* He practiced in front of his dresser mirror, deepening his voice, smiling nonchalantly at himself, looking deep into his own blue eyes. He was so single-minded and intent on success that his friends noticed his distraction and the way he watched Caroline. They teased him, poking him when Caroline went by and his head swiveled.

"Don't look now, but Joel's love life is passing."

"Ooh, she's cute."

"She's got the hots for you, man. You could do it tonight."

"Nah, she's on the rag."

"Got a boner on, Joel?"

"Shut up, you assholes."

He finally got up the courage to ask Caroline out at the end of a third period spare when they were gathering up their books and papers. He'd adroitly switched the conversation from math to movies, mentioning he'd seen *Lethal Weapon 2.* He figured that was a safe bet, considering the way girls flipped over Mel Gibson.

"Did you like it?" Caroline asked.

"Yeah, it was great."

Even when Caroline frowned, she was pretty. Her brow furrowed adorably, and she fluttered her dark lashes. "I don't much like violence in movies."

Shit. "Yeah, I know what you mean."

"Even when it's cartoonish, it's still violent."

"Yeah."

His plan had been simple. When Caroline said how much she loved Mel Gibson, he'd say he wouldn't mind seeing the movie again and ask her if she'd like to go. He was going to do this so casually, so coolly, she'd think he didn't care what she said. He should've quit when his plan was shattered but he was driven forward, as if a huge fist were pressing against his back. The days of building up his courage, of replaying a dozen scenarios in his head, of heroic fantasies had a momentum all their own.

Joel rushed ahead, knowing he was doomed, hating himself, but unable to stop. "Um . . . I . . . would you like to go to the movies on Friday? There's probably something not so violent . . . I mean, I don't know, but I can check . . . I'm sure there is."

"Oh!" Caroline looked startled, her blue eyes widening, and pressed her books against her chest. "Gee, I'm sorry, Joel, I'm . . . like, busy on Friday."

His face felt hot. "Oh . . . well."

The bell rang.

"I've got to go," she said. "See you."

Her embarrassment and desire to get away from him were painfully obvious. Joel felt them twist in his gut, but he couldn't let her know that. "See you," he said, shrugging as if he didn't care.

His humiliation hadn't ended there. Caroline must've told her friends. When he passed Megan Sheehan and Carol Poole on the way to American History, they turned to each other and giggled. He walked on as if he hadn't noticed, but he was thinking, Why not broadcast it? Fuck, why not make it the frigging lead article in the *Cassandra High Chronicle?* And it didn't stop with Caroline's friends. The story of his failure worked its way through the cliques and circles until his friends got wind of it.

"Didn't you know she's going out with Ben Phillips?"

"Bad luck, man."

"What a bitch."

"What a cunt."

Their crudity was designed to make him feel better, to make all of them feel better, and even though Joel knew it was ugly, it worked. He laughed and felt his humiliation lift. "She's a ho and a real slut," he said. "That's why I asked her out."

And that's what Mr. Burton knew, a year later, when Joel sat by the desk in the vice principal's office, which had been turned into an interrogation room for the police. In the corner of the room by the window was a cop, someone Joel didn't know, who was taking notes. Behind the desk was Mr. Burton, who was studying a big file of papers in front of him. While he waited, Joel shifted uncomfortably in his seat. The interviews had gone on most of the day, and most kids had said they were a snap, nothing to worry about, no problem-o, man. Even so, Joel didn't like the feeling he had in the room, as if he were already wrong, guilty, and on the defensive.

"Joel," Mr. Burton said, "how're you doing?"

"Okay, sir."

"Your teachers tell me you're doing fine in school, except for Spanish. You don't like Spanish?"

"No, sir."

"I didn't like French. Flunked it three years in a row." Mr. Burton looked at the other cop. "You do well in languages, Stu?"

"Fair."

Joel knew that they were trying to make him comfortable, trying to make him feel like this was nothing more than a pleasant chat.

Mr. Burton turned back to Joel. "Now, you know why we're here."

"Yes, sir."

"To get to the bottom of Caroline's disappearance."

"Yes, sir."

"And the way we're going to do that is if everyone cooperates and everyone tells us what they know. Sometimes even little details that don't seem to matter might be important. So I want you to think hard and don't be afraid to tell us anything you can think of."

"Yes, sir."

"Now, you've been in school with Caroline since . . . when?"

"Kindergarten."

Mr. Burton checked his file. "And you're in four of her classes."

"Yes, sir."

"Were you friends with her?"

"No, sir."

"You saw her in class and that was it?"

"Pretty much."

"You didn't socialize with her or her friends."

"Sometimes we might be at the same party. But not really."

"People tell me she's going with Ben Phillips. Now, you and Ben used to hang out together. Weren't you two in Cubs?"

"We were friends then, but we're not in the same crowd now."

"Why is that?"

"I'm into sports and Ben isn't."

"Is he kind of a loner?"

"You mean like he doesn't have any friends?"

"Yeah, like that."

Joel didn't think of Ben as a loner, but more as someone who was self-sufficient, cool and aloof, the kind of guy who wrote poetry for the school newspaper and still dated the most desirable girl in Cassandra. "I don't know about his friends, sir."

Mr. Burton switched gears. "Tell me about that morning, Joel. About going to school."

"I got up about seven-thirty and had a shower and stuff. I left for school at eight-thirty."

"You walk?"

"Yes, sir."

"You see anything along the way? Anything unusual?"

"No."

"You're sure of that?"

Joel tried to remember that morning, but it blurred with all the other school mornings in his life, the daily routine repeated thousands of times. "Yes, sir."

"No strangers? No unusual vehicles?"

"I didn't see anything."

"Okay. When did your dad leave?"

"Before I got up. He goes in to work real early."

"And your mom?"

"A little before me."

"Did she take her car?"

"Uh . . . I don't think so."

"She walked to work?"

"Sometimes she does when the weather's nice."

"And it sure was a nice morning." Mr. Burton sighed and shifted the subject again. "You think Caroline's a pretty girl, Joel?"

"Yes, sir."

Sexy?"

"Uh . . . I guess so."

"You guess so?"

"She's one of the prettiest girls in our class."

"Is there a difference between pretty and sexy?"

"Uh . . . I don't think so, sir."

"Do you know if Ben and Caroline were sleeping together?"

Joel looked at that thick pile of paper and wondered what everyone else had said. "I heard they might be," he said cautiously.

"You don't know this for a fact?"

"I guess I do, sir."

"You ever date Caroline?"

"No, sir."

"You ever want to?"

Joel felt his face get as hot as it had when Caroline turned him down. "Yes, sir."

"You think Ben has a good thing going?"

"I beg your pardon, sir."

"You jealous of Ben going out with Caroline, having sex with her?"

"No, sir."

"It doesn't make you angry."

"No, sir."

"But you wanted to go out with her."

"Last year."

"Did you ask her out?"

"Yes, sir."

"And what happened?"

"She said no."

"Were you upset?"

"A little."

Mr. Burton checked his papers again. "According to some people, you called her a ho."

His friends had acted like a police interrogation was nothing, but now Joel sees that everyone had been so scared they'd spilled their guts right into Mr. Burton's file.

"Would you define a ho for me?"

"It means hooker, sir."

"You ever seen a hooker?"

"Uh . . . only the movies."

"Is Caroline a hooker?"

"No, she isn't."

"Is she a slut?"

"No, sir."

"So why did you say those things about her?"

"I guess . . . I was angry then."

"Okay." Mr. Burton turned to the other cop. "That cover the territory, Stu?"

"I believe it does."

"That'll be all, Joel. Thanks very much."

* * *

When Joel was a little boy, his favorite TV reruns were *The Bionic Woman* and *The Six Million Dollar Man*. In those days he was painfully aware of being small for his age, one of the shortest boys in his class, and nothing his mother said ("Everybody grows differently" or "One day you'll be as big as your dad") really convinced him that things would ever change. It wasn't surprising that he loved those shows and the idea of miraculous transformation even though it had to be through a terrible experience like a fire or accident. He wanted to wake up in a hospital someday and discover that he wasn't just Joel Breymann, four feet five inches, who had to play infield because he couldn't throw the ball far enough, but a new Joel with superhuman powers who was stronger and faster than any boy alive. He'd be able to throw the ball clear into the bleachers, beat up anybody at Cassandra Elementary, especially Billy Boehm, who was really mean, and amaze his father by being able to lift up the car when it had a flat. He dreamed about fighting bad guys, crime guys, so they ended up in jail and having the president pin a medal on his chest for making America a safer place to live.

Of course, he grew and, as it turned out, his mother had been right. He was a late bloomer, and by the time he was fifteen, it was clear he was going to be tall and maybe taller than his father. But the notion that someday something unusual would happen that would make him bigger and stronger than everyone else never quite left Joel even after he knew that the bionic woman and the six million dollar man were just figments of some writers' imaginations. He thought it might happen in sports—that, if he just kept at it, one day the miracle would occur and he'd find himself swimming faster, throwing farther, jumping higher.

What he had not known was that there could be other types of transformations—ones that could make you smaller, lesser, and divide you in two. The bad feeling started during his interview with Mr. Burton and persisted, sitting in his gut like one of the weights he'd gotten at fourteen when he wanted more than anything to look like Sylvester Stallone. The bad feeling made him shrink into himself as if he were losing height. It screwed up his concentration during practice. It made him trip over his words in class so that he looked like a complete asshole.

But that wasn't as bad as the change that took place during the lie detector test. He was seated in a special room in the sheriff's office in Syracuse, attached by wires to a box of tape and tracing pens, and asked questions. What was his name? How old was he? Did he live at 55 Steeplechase Drive? Did he go to Cassandra High School? Did he know Caroline Deacon? How long had he known her? And had he had anything to do with her disappearance? As he said no, he felt the transformation happen. It was like in *Ghost,* when Patrick Swayze died and his ghost left his body. Joel felt a part of him slide out and stand to one side, watching. He saw himself, a thin, awkward, blond boy sitting straight in a chair. He heard himself answer, no, he hadn't seen Caroline that morning, and no, he had no idea what happened to her. And the sensation of watching himself didn't go away when the test was over. Mr. Burton thanked him, his parents were relieved, and his mother even cried a bit. And, all the while, the other self was there, watching him go through the appropriate moves: Joel being polite to Mr. Burton, talking to his father, patting his mother on the shoulder. That other self was even there when he talked to Andy and Pete.

"Did you feel anything?" Andy asked.

"Like what?"

"I don't know. Electric shocks?"

"I wasn't being fried, you know."

"Man, I woulda been shitting," Pete said.

Joel watched himself shrug like he took lie detector tests every day. "It didn't bother me."

There was the Joel on the surface, the one everyone could see, who acted like nothing important had happened. The other Joel was secret, hidden, and knew that everything had changed.

Everything.

Chapter

2

JOEL LEAVES HIS BIKE IN THE GARAGE AND ENTERS THE HOUSE through the back door into the kitchen. Hearing the voices of his mother and her friend Mrs. Hudson in the living room, he tries to slip down the hall to his bedroom, but his mother has heard him and calls out, "Joel?"

He steps into the curved archway that separates the dining room from the living room. "Hi, Mom. Hi, Mrs. Hudson."

"Where've you been?" Barbara asks.

"Just around."

"Around where?"

"Around."

Barbara sighs. "Your father wants you to mow the lawn this afternoon."

"Okay."

"And then go down to Deacon's, get another cord for the hedge clippers, and pick up some fertilizer for the garden. You can take my car."

"Okay."

"Joel," Marla says. "I've been meaning to tell you—there *are* ghosts in the Hiller house."

"Oh, yeah?" Joel shifts from one foot to the other. Mrs. Hudson isn't like his mother's other friends. For one thing, she's a lot richer. His mother is always regaling him and his father with stories of Marla's purchases and renovations. *Marble imported from Italy,* she says, shaking her head, *prints from Liberty's in London.* He thought his mother might be jealous, but then he once overheard her telling his father that Marla may be rich in wealth, but she was poor where it really counted. Then he figured his mother felt sorry for Mrs. Hudson, because she was divorced, didn't have a husband, and her daughter lived in L.A.

Another thing was that Mrs. Hudson didn't talk to him the way his mother's other friends did. Whenever the bridge group was at the house, and he came into the living room, the first thing they'd say to him was, "How's school?" Too bad he couldn't win any money by betting with himself on how the conversation would continue, because he'd have made a million by now.

"So, Joel, how's school?"

"Okay. Math's a little tough." Sometimes this wasn't true, sometimes he was breezing his way through math, but this comment always brought a sympathetic murmur.

"You still on the swimming/basketball/football team?"

"Yeah, working out real hard."

"You going to beat Laurel Grove?"

"We're going to try."

This always brought sounds of satisfaction, and then they went back to playing cards, and he was off the hook until the next time one of them visited the house or the bridge game rotated back, and the same conversation would be repeated all over again. What he couldn't figure out was why he was the only one who seemed to know what was going on.

Of course, he'd thought Mrs. Hudson was going to be more of the same, but she wasn't. She never asked him about school or his teams, and he had no idea what she might say to him from one time to the next.

Once it was "Great shirt, Joel, the green brings out the blue in your eyes."

"Thanks," he answered with a small shrug as if it was nothing to him, but then he went into the bathroom and studied his image in the mirror, pulling the collar up higher and widening his eyes. He hadn't noticed it before, but the color of his eyes did seem darker if you studied them long enough. He ended up wearing the shirt a lot more than he used to.

Another time when she was over for dinner and his parents were in the kitchen, she asked him if he'd ever dreamed that someone was trying to murder him. She'd had a dream like that the night before. He said yes, and she told him there was a theory that all the people in your dreams were really reflections of yourself.

"You mean—like I'm trying to waste myself?"

"Yes."

"That's really weird."

"What I wonder is if the killer is the angry part of yourself let loose in your dreams. You think that's what it might be?"

It was a good thing his parents came back then, because he really didn't know what to say. But he felt different about his dreams from then on. It was as if Mrs. Hudson had compelled him to open the top of his head and peer in. What he'd taken to be ordinary—dreams were just dreams, weren't they?—could in fact be extraordinary, mysterious, even sinister.

Finally, Mrs. Hudson was different from his mother's other friends, because she was . . . well, sexy. Joel knew she was the same age as his mother and had a daughter his age, but that didn't seem to change the way she was. Her voice was husky as if she'd just gotten out of bed and hadn't cleared her throat. It made her sound sleepy and inviting. Then there was something about the way she dressed or maybe it was the fabrics. His mother wore blouses and skirts that were like her—basic colors, sensible, not frilly. Mrs. Hudson wore dresses whose fabrics glowed or slithered and gleaming jewelry that made you want to look at her ears or her neck. But most of all, it was her eyes. Not their color or shape, but the way they looked at him. He knew that when his mother's friends looked at him, they didn't see who he really was but the Joel who'd eaten, slept, and played at their houses since he was in diapers. Mrs. Hudson never looked at him like that. When her eyes met his, her glance was direct and intimate, as if he weren't just a teenager. Joel felt those looks right down into his groin.

"Ghostly little breaths," Marla is saying, "and tiny screams, mostly in the turret."

All Joel can think to say is, "No kidding."

"And feet sounds. Pit-pats."

"You're not serious," Barbara says.

"First, I thought it was the wind. Then I thought, maybe a cat's got in with all those carpenters and electricians coming and going and leaving the doors open. But I didn't find a cat. Now, I'm convinced it's ghosts. Did anybody die in that house?"

"Not that I know of," Barbara says.

"Actually, there's more than one."

"Marla, this is silly. There's no such thing as ghosts, but if you're frightened, you can stay with us."

Marla shakes her head. "I talk to them. 'Hello,' I say. 'Enjoying your visit?'"

Joel can't help his snort of laughter.

"Joel," Marla says. "You don't believe me."

And she laughs too—a louder, deeper, richer laugh than Joel has ever heard from a woman—and her eyes are laughing when she looks at him, and he feels shock waves right down to his testicles.

"I better go do the lawn," he says quickly. "'Bye, Mrs. Hudson, nice seeing you." And he's out of there as fast as he can go.

Joel finishes the lawn and goes to Deacon's to buy the cord for the hedge clippers and fertilizer for the garden. He dawdles a bit before making the purchases. He likes hardware stores. He likes walking down the aisles in the electrical section and looking at the variety of wires, sockets, plugs, and cords. He likes the section that has the hammers, screwdrivers, and boxes of nails and screws. He can remember Deacon's before it was renovated in the late seventies, and nails were still sold by the pound. In those days, you could pick up a pile of tiny, sharp nails and let them run through your fingers like sand. The game was to do it without pricking your skin. Joel guesses he likes the idea of reducing a building, which is complex, down to basics that he can see and handle.

But his favorite part of the hardware store is the power tool section. He's done some carpentry in school and with his father. He likes it, although the stool he made in shop never stood quite straight. He has a vision of himself some long way into the future when he's married, has a family, and owns a house. He has no real vision of his wife, just a fuzzy image of a woman much like his mother, and there will be kids, more than one, because Joel has always wished he wasn't an only child and would've liked a brother. He's a littler clearer about the house, which will be a lot like 55 Steeplechase Lane and have a basement shop where he can do repairs, make toys for his kids, and maybe even build furniture. Dan has a basement workshop, only most of the tools belonged to *his* father, and they're old-fashioned—like the corded drill. You can get battery-operated drills now. Joel picks a drill off the shelf and feels the heft of it. He likes the way tools fit in his hand.

"Hello, Joel." Mr. Deacon stands near him, wearing the red jacket that all the hardware clerks wear. This is to make sure the customers can find them. The trouble is that Mr. Deacon is fat, and the red jacket just makes him look fatter.

"Oh, hi, Mr. Deacon."

"How's school?"

"Okay, well, math's hard." It's the same routine he uses on his mother's friends, but he suddenly has a dizzying sensation as the other Joel slips out and watches the first Joel talk politely, very politely, to the father of the girl he's suspected of killing.

"Don't give up on math," Mr. Deacon is saying. "It's real important for later on."

"Yes, sir."

"This country is going to need people who know their math."

"Yes, sir."

"How's the folks?"

"Pretty good. We just got a new car."

"What did you get?"

"A Ford Taurus."

"Nice." Mr. Deacon's heavy jowls shiver a little as he nods. "Your dad let you drive it?"

"Not yet."

"Now, what can I do for you? You need a drill?"

Joel has forgotten the drill he's holding, and he puts it back on the shelf. "Not really. I was just looking."

Mr. Deacon smiles and pats him on the shoulder, and the two Joels come together as suddenly as they split. "Okay, then," he says. "You take care, son."

As Mr. Deacon turns to walk away, Joel has the horrifying sensation of tears rising behind his eyes. He blinks and blurts out, "Mr. Deacon?"

Mr. Deacon turns back. "Yes, Joel."

Joel has no idea what he's going to say, but the words are suddenly there. "You take care too, sir."

For a moment, they look at one another and then Mr. Deacon says, "Thanks, Joel. We're trying."

Joel's room is his sanctuary, and it's filled with his treasures. He has posters and pennants on the wall: Wayne Gretzky about to catapult a puck into the goal, Joe Montana with his arm cocked to throw, a Syracuse University pennant from a game Dan took him to when he was twelve. His fielder's mitt sits next to his swim caps and goggles, which, in turn, lay next to a soccer ball, a biking helmet, two pucks, and his jock strap. His World War II model airplane collection, representing three years (ages eight to eleven) of obsessive painting and gluing, sits on a shelf over his bed, and on his desk is a ghetto blaster and a stack of tapes of heavy metal bands like Metallica and Guns N' Roses. He likes to lie on his bed with the music on loud, letting the sounds wash over him like waves. He and his friends went through a period a couple of years ago when they thought they might form a rock band called The Suicides. It didn't matter to them that only Andy played an instrument, the drums. They figured that if they got electric guitars and practiced some chords, they could put a few words to music and be wildly popular. During this period, they'd spend hours watching MTV videos and grew their hair as long as they could. That seemed to be as important an ingredient of rock band success as being able to sing.

The rock band didn't pan out. Pete's parents rented a guitar for him to try out, and the boys discovered that, while it wasn't hard to learn how to play a few chords, creating music wasn't as easy as it looked, even though Pete had perfected an assortment of moves to go with the music—jumping, knee crawling, and a moon walk—that they thought was great. It wasn't easy to write lyrics either, since they really didn't have anything to say, especially about sex, which was the topic that seemed to sell the most records. Also, they argued a lot about the order of the songs they'd play and what real band's song they'd do first and who would sing what lyrics. The idea of forming a rock band slowly evaporated. Although they occasionally did air-band stuff when they were hanging out at someone's house, they eventually turned to other, more durable interests. Joel got into sports, Andy and his drums joined the Cassandra High School marching band, and Pete decided he wanted to be a mechanic and got a part-time job at the Shell station. Joel and Andy cut their hair short, but Pete left his long, pulling it back in a ponytail, and began to wear a small, hooped earring.

This evening as he lies on his bed and listens to music, Joel remembers this rock band phase. He thinks how dumb they were, calling themselves The Suicides and trying to write songs about sex, which none of them knew anything about, although Andy claimed to have put his hands on Sarah Silver's naked breasts after they shut themselves in the coat closet at Angie Dodd's Halloween party. He said they were about as big as the silver-dollar pancakes at Donney's Pancake House on Route 240. The thought of breasts, even silver-dollar breasts, is enough to make Joel's penis stiffen every time. He believes he spends way too much time thinking about breasts: their weight and shape, how soft the skin would feel, the way they move inside a girl's blouse when she's walking. When he starts obsessing about breasts when he's alone in his room, he masturbates, fantasizing about pictures from *Playboy*. When he starts obsessing about breasts when he's in school, he tries to think about other things like winning the 200-meter breast stroke or making a double play from first base to second.

Joel hasn't asked another girl out since Caroline, even though there are a couple of girls he likes—Mary Alice Potter, the principal's daughter, who isn't pretty but gives him these cute smiles, and Jenny Silko, who sits behind him in American History and is always tapping him on the back and asking him where they are in the book. He has a feeling she really knows and just wants to talk to him. She's not pretty either, but he likes the way her dark hair bounces on her shoulders. Lately, he's been wondering about asking a girl to the prom. He hasn't gone to most of the dances, or if he has, it's been with Andy and Pete. They've usually hung around the school gym, watching the dancers, commenting on the girls, and drinking the punch. Or they might go out into the parking lot where Andy and Pete would usually have a couple of beers or smoke pot. Since Joel was in training, he didn't touch the stuff, but he still liked horsing around in the dark and ducking whenever the door opened in case a teacher might be coming out. But those days are over. Andy has started playing with the school dance band so he won't be around to keep Joel company, and Pete's recently got a girlfriend and may not come to the dance at all.

Pete's going out with Stephanie Binda, who graduated two years before and works as a hairdresser at the Set 'n' Curl on Route 240. Stephanie got pregnant in her sophomore year and dropped out of school. Her parents take care of the baby, a little girl, while she works. Pete met her at the Shell station when she'd come by to get gas. They'd talk while he pumped gas, and then she started getting out of the car and standing by him while he cleaned her windows. Finally she asked him out on a date. Joel imagines this scene like something out of the movies. There's Pete in his overalls with the Shell insignia on the pocket, wearing the hat with the visor and his long, brown ponytail hanging out the hole in the back. Then there's Stephanie, who wears short black leather skirts and spike heels that show off her skinny legs and whose fine, dark hair is teased into a flag in the front and falls in a cascade of ringlets in the back. She's built, too—no silver dollars there. He imagines Stephanie leaning against her car door, smoking a cigarette and coming on strong.

"She looked at my crotch," Pete said, "like she could see through my pants."

"No shit," Joel said.

"She's hot," Andy said. "Man, what a babe."

But since Stephanie took Pete to see *Die Hard 2,* he doesn't talk about her much, and Joel sees a lot less of him after school. But then Joel's started hanging out more with the guys from the C group swim team anyway so it doesn't matter. Still, he has weird dreams about Pete and Stephanie. The weirdest one was when he dreamed that Stephanie came to the Shell station and she was only wearing panties. Her breasts were huge like those of a *Playboy* centerfold and the nipples were the color of brick. Joel was really turned on, but Pete didn't seem to notice. He unhooked the nozzle from the gas pump and waited for the numbers in the gauges to turn back to zero. But instead of feeding the gas to Stephanie's car, he fed it to her. Her head tilted back, her breasts arched forward, and the gas flowed down her throat. The weirdest part was that Joel should've been disgusted, but he wasn't. He wanted the gas, too, and after a struggle managed to wrench the nozzle out of Pete's hands. Then he tilted his head back, stuck the nozzle in his throat, and began to drink deeply. As the gasoline hit the back of his throat, cool and clear as water, he woke up and discovered the sheets sticky with semen. He wondered what Mrs. Hudson would make of *that* dream.

Joel has been discreetly checking out Mary Alice Potter and Jenny Silko. This is what he knows so far: neither of them is going out with anyone, neither of them has a crush on anyone, although rumor has it that Mary Alice had the hots for Ben Phillips before he started going out with Caroline. Joel finds he's leaning a bit more toward Jenny anyway, because he thinks it would be kind of heavy to date the principal's daughter, but what he really wants to know is whether they like him or not. You can't tell with girls. They look at you, but their eyes are veiled by lashes. They wear short skirts and tight tops, but there's something prim about the way they move. And they smile at you in the hallway, but as soon as you're past them, they giggle and whisper and glance back at you over their shoulders. Sometimes Joel wishes that girls were like sports where the rules are set, there are referees and judges, and the only thing you're fighting against is yourself.

There's a knock on the door. "Joel. Joel!" It's Dan.

"What?"

"Could you come into the living room? Your mother and I want to talk to you."

"Shit," Joel says under his breath as he gets off the bed and turns off the ghetto blaster.

His parents are drinking coffee when he arrives in the living room. Barbara is sitting on the couch and Dan is in the easy chair. They look comfortable and relaxed, but Joel knows it's a pose. A summons to the living room is the precursor of a family meeting, presided over by his parents, where the main topic is Joel's wrongdoings. There's the list of complaints—breaking of rules, chores not done, responsibilities forgotten—combined with frowns, talk of hurt and disappointment, requests for explanations, and attempts at compromise and reconciliation. Joel hates these meetings.

"I saw Charlie Boehm a couple of days ago," Dan begins as Joel sits in the rocker. "He says you haven't been to a couple of practices."

"I've been busy with school stuff."

"That's not what Phil Potter says," Barbara interjects. "He says you might flunk English if you don't pull your socks up."

Good-bye, Mary Alice, Joel thinks. Sometimes he wonders if there's a conspiracy of parents and teachers in Cassandra. He thinks it would be different in a big city where your swim coach wouldn't meet your father at the grocery store, and your mother wouldn't have the nerve to phone up a principal she didn't know just because she was suspicious.

"I didn't hand in a paper," he says.

"Why not?" Dan asks.

"I forgot."

He's said this so flippantly that Barbara shakes her head in disbelief. "Joel," she says.

"I'm not perfect, okay?"

"We don't expect you to be perfect, but we'd like a better attitude."

Then it's Dan's turn. "Charlie wanted to know if you were planning to drop off the team."

"I don't know."

"Don't be a quitter now," Dan says.

Joel can predict his father right down to the words as they come out of his mouth. *Don't be a quitter* is Dan's favorite motto, along with *Do the best you can even if it's not perfect.* Joel used to believe all that motivational shit, but lately it doesn't make any sense. What's the point of trying to get from the C group on the swim team to the B group or writing an English paper? What difference will it make? Who cares?

"Are you finding English hard?" Barbara asks. "Is there anything we can do to help?"

"Mom, I'll hand the paper in late, that's all. I'll get partial marks."

"Phil said you didn't pass the last two tests."

Fuck. Joel studies the pattern his foot makes in the pile of the carpet.

"Joel," Barbara says gently, "are you upset about something?"

"No."

When he was little, Joel believed his mother had a direct physical connection to him. She had cool fingers that made cuts feel better and warm arms that encircled him when his feelings were hurt. For several years, her lap was the safest place he knew. Of course, as he got older, he didn't need that baby stuff anymore. He played farther and farther from home, he went to school, he traveled to towns around Cassandra with his teams. There even came a time, when he was as tall as she was, that their positions were reversed. The summer he was thirteen, he and Barbara went on the Ferris wheel at the state fair together while Dan stayed below and took pictures. The wheel got jammed, and they got stuck at the top. Joel thought it was great, but Barbara didn't. She hated it up there, it made her stomach sick, she even turned pale. Joel put his arm around her just like his father would, and she leaned her head on his shoulder. He'd never felt so big as he did then, or when they finally returned to earth, and she told Dan that she didn't know what she would've done without Joel, who must have nerves of steel and a stomach of iron.

Recently, however, Joel's view of Barbara has started to change. He's grown critical of the way she looks and dresses. She's too plump and her clothes are dull. He thinks she should color her graying hair the way they do in the TV ads, but when he suggested it she said she planned to grow old gracefully, thank you very much. He loves his parents, but they're drab and boring, uncool and ignorant about the things that really count. And neither of them has a clue about what goes on in his head. They'd be shocked if they did. Boy, would they be shocked.

"Joel," Barbara continues, "this business with Caroline and the lie detector tests has upset everyone."

"I passed, didn't I?"

"Doesn't it feel strange to think that people might believe you're involved?"

"I don't care," Joel says.

"Has anything happened at school?" Dan asks.

"Like what?"

"Kids talking, anyone singling you out."

"No," Joel says, although there have been a few incidents when people have stared at him longer than they should or a conversation has broken off when he passed by. The other Joel takes care of those situations. He watches as Joel walks on, looking as if he didn't give a flying fuck what anyone thinks of him.

Barbara sighs deeply and picks up her coffee. Dan thumbs the newspaper that's been sitting in his lap. These actions signal what Joel thinks of as the last three minutes of play in the final period of the family meeting.

"We'd like to be able to count on better performance in the future," Dan says.

"And it would be a shame to waste all those practices," Barbara says.

Face-off!

"Okay."

"We mean it, Joel." *Dan has the puck. He skates down the ice.*

"I said okay." *Joel blocks him.*

Dan passes the puck to Barbara. "What about your English paper?" *she asks.*

"I'll do it." *The puck bounces off Joel's skate blade.*

Barbara retrieves it. "When?" *She shoots.*

"Tomorrow." *Thanks to those quick reflexes, Joel blocks the puck again.*

Dan picks up the pass and deflects it. "What's wrong with tonight?"

Joel stops the puck and holds it on his blade. "I've got a math test tomorrow." *He skates down the ice.* "I have to study for that, don't I?" *He shoots. There's a silence. He scores. The light goes on, the bells go off, and the crowd screams. He skates around the net, arms up in triumph, stick waving in the air, and the other guys on his team are skating into him, hugging him, whacking his helmet with their gloved hands. Man, what a game!*

Chapter

3

THE FOLLOWING MONDAY MORNING AS JOEL WALKS DOWN the hallway toward his locker, people fall silent and stop to watch him as he passes by. He keeps on walking but has a panicky feeling that there's something on his face that he didn't see in the mirror or that he's missing a critical piece of clothing. As he lowers his books to his waist and surreptitiously pats his fly, he notices a group—Andy, Pete, Dennis, Jenny Silko, Sarah Silver—clustered around his locker. When they see him approaching, their voices disappear one by one. By the time he reaches his locker, the only sound he can hear is his own breathing. He's about to ask what's happening, when he sees the words scrawled in black spray paint on his locker door: KUNT KILLER.

They're all studying his face, waiting to see how he'll react. He feels like crying, tears prick at the back of his eyes, but he can't do that, especially not with Jenny watching. Instead he says, "Shit," and it's the signal for all them to talk.

"You're not the only one," Andy says.

"Ben has one, too," Pete says.

"They all have one," Jenny says.

"All who?" Joel asks.

"Everyone who took the lie detector test," Dennis says. "You, Ben, Murph, Bobby . . ."

"Tim, Steve . . ."

"Paul . . ."

Joel thought the lie detector test would end the bad feelings that began when Mr. Burton interviewed him, but it has solved nothing. It's as if Caroline is a dead spider at the center of a living web that has caught any boy who'd gotten too close to her. Ben was her current boyfriend. Steve Nolan had taken her to the Christmas dance when she was a freshman. He, Tim Kyle, and Murph Miller had asked her out and been turned down. Bobby Palmeri was in the process of finishing an American History project with her when she disappeared, and Paul Stone had the misfortune to be her lab partner in Biology. Joel thinks he now knows what it must be like to be a fly or bee caught in a web. There's no escape. The harder he struggles, the tighter he's bound.

"It's so mean . . ."

"Disgusting . . ."

"It must've happened last night . . ."

"Or early this morning . . ."

"Maybe someone was drinking . . ."

"Or stoned . . ."

Joel sees their mouths moving, but he can only dimly hear the words, as if they're coming at him through thick insulation. He wonders if it's the other Joel, not sliding out this time, but standing between him and the others, blocking out the sounds. And maybe he's seeing through the other Joel's eyes, because he's noticing things he never would have seen before—like the fact that they're all looking horrified, but only Sarah really is. The others are excited, even Jenny. Her mouth forms a small, dismayed circle, but her eyes are gleaming. The only true distress comes from Sarah, who's recently gotten so weird—black clothes, black spiked hair, studs in her ears and nose. Joel can feel the upset radiate from her, and he mentally apologizes for all the times he laughed about her with his friends, poking fun at her height and her shape. "Here comes the GG," they'd say, or,

"Scopes down. It's only NET." GG meant Giant Girl, NET stood for Non-Existent Tits.

"It isn't just the words," Sarah blurts out, breaking into the buzz of speculation. "It's the spelling . . . the Ks. It's like they do in advertising or in the name of some fast-food place. It makes it even worse . . . don't you see?"

They don't see. As she breaks into tears and rushes away toward the girls' bathroom, they watch her and their mouths gape open.

"Geez," Andy says, "I just thought the guy couldn't spell."

"Or has a learning disability," Jenny says.

That brings a big laugh, and Jenny blushes but looks pleased. That's when Joel knows he's never going to ask her out. The fact is, he doesn't even like her.

That morning, the principal announces over the loud-speaker that there'll be an assembly for second period that morning for all classes, and that he'd like those people whose lockers have been marked to be in his office at the end of homeroom.

"Lucky stiff," Pete says, poking Joel in the back. "You'll miss Spanish."

But Joel doesn't feel lucky sitting with six other silent boys outside the principal's office. He'd rather be in Spanish even though he didn't do the homework. They don't talk to each other, but stare down at their hands or fidget with their books. Only Ben seems to be calm. He's reading a book, and Joel catches sight of the title, *The Fountainhead.* He's never heard of it, but he's impressed by its thickness. Joel remembers spending hours with Ben when he was small. They played cowboys and Indians and cops and robbers. They went to the arcade and played computer games. In the winter, they set up nets on the street and played hockey. But the year they were thirteen, their relationship changed. Ben started reading a lot and taking art classes in Laurel Grove, and by the time they entered Cassandra High School, they were going their separate ways. Joel became one of the jocks.

Ben got the highest grades in the class in English and History but somehow managed not to be a brain.

"Okay, boys," Mr. Potter says. "Come on in."

They file in and take seats around a small conference table. Reg Burton is standing near the principal's desk. When they're all seated, Mr. Potter tells them that the janitorial staff is busy removing the paint as he speaks. He says that erasing the words from the lockers, however, isn't going to erase the words from people's memories. He says attitude is going to do that—attitude on the part of the school to show people that he and the teachers won't tolerate that kind of behavior, attitude on the part of the victims, who can let others know that they're not going to stoop to that level, and attitude on the part of the student body by being cooperative and helping them find who did it. As he talks about his own shock and distress, he runs his palm repeatedly over the gray, thinning corkscrews on his scalp, which flatten and then spring up like miniature jack-in-the-boxes.

"And I want to get to the bottom of this," Mr. Potter concludes. "I want to find who did it and have that person appropriately punished."

Then Mr. Burton talks to them about malicious behavior from the police point of view. He describes small minds that get a big thrill out of hurting other people. He says paint on a locker door doesn't appear to be physically harmful, but such vandalism could escalate to involve property damage or worse, and he doesn't want to see that happen, not in Cassandra. He says he's got a job to do keeping the peace in this town and he intends to do it.

"Now," he says, "this may be just mischief, but I can't rule out that the person who did it may be involved in Caroline's disappearance."

There's a small snort from someone, and Mr. Potter says, "You have something to say, Murphy?"

"Why don't we just say she's dead? She is, isn't she?"

"We don't have a body," Mr. Burton says. "We have no evidence of murder."

Joel thinks of Molly Deacon. Everyone in town knows that, even though it's been four weeks since Caroline disappeared, she's quit her job to sit by the telephone, because she's convinced that one day it will ring with a request for a ransom or, much better still, with Caroline at the other end asking her mother to come and get her and bring her home. Joel's overheard Barbara talking on the phone to Daphne and saying how pitiful it was, watching the vitality just drain out of Molly and, although she herself understood how important hope was and would never want to give up, not for one minute, if you looked at the situation as objectively as you could, you could see how much better it would be if a body were found so that Molly could put this behind her and get on with her life.

After that, Joel thought a lot about the term *get on with your life*. It made life sound like a train running down a set of tracks—"Climb on board and get on with your *life!*"—and it reminded him of those pictures they drew in elementary school art classes to learn perspective. You began with two lines far apart and then drew them closer and closer together as you approached the horizon. Alongside these tracks, you drew trees or telephone poles, making them smaller and smaller as the tracks headed into the distance. The trick of it was that, even though the tracks looked like they were going to meet, they never did. He always liked drawing those pictures, because he could imagine the tracks going beyond the drawing, over the horizon and into infinity. He used to think his life would be like that, a train with a predictable schedule, preordained stops—high school, college, job, marriage, children—and no end in sight. But now he's beginning to think otherwise. The possibility of chaos, of life as a set of random, accidental events, has occurred to him for the first time. The train has disappeared and in its place is a thick fog, shrouding signposts, obscuring paths, and making each step forward unknown and treacherous.

"And this person, if he was involved in Caroline's disappearance," Mr. Burton is saying, "may thrive on sick kinds of excitement. He may want to keep everyone talking. He may like to have people upset. We can't rule out the possibility that he may hurt someone else again."

"Shit," Paul says under his breath.

Mr. Potter steps forward as if to admonish Paul, but Mr. Burton waves him back. "That's right," he says. "This stinks. Everything about it stinks, and that's why I would appreciate it if you boys could help us. This person is focusing on you, and I'd like you to keep your eyes and ears open, to notice any strange behavior here at school and to report it to us when you do."

"Why must it be someone at school?" Tim asks.

"It doesn't have to be," Mr. Burton says, "but no one forced any doors or broke any windows to get in here when the school was locked during the night. We think it was someone who hung around yesterday or came in very early and wouldn't be noticed, because he was a student. So that's why we—"

"Or a teacher," Ben says.

In the silence that follows, Joel sees this hasn't occurred to Mr. Potter. He flinches and glances helplessly at Mr. Burton.

"You're right, Ben," Mr. Burton says. "Or it could be the janitor or the school secretary or, hell"—he grins at Mr. Potter—"it could've been Phil." That gets the response he wants. The boys laugh and even Mr. Potter smiles weakly. He continues, "Eyes and ears, okay?"

They all murmur, "Okay," and Mr. Burton turns to Mr. Potter. "Back to you, Phil."

Mr. Potter runs his hand over his scalp. "Mr. Burton and I are going to talk to the rest of the school at the assembly this morning. I'll understand if you'd rather not attend, and give you permission to spend the rest of this period and the next in the library." They nod. "All right. You can go now."

They're silent as they file out of the principal's office, but begin to talk as they walk down the hallway to the library.

"They'll never catch who did it," Murph says. "They never caught whoever was stealing out of the lockers last year."

"They'll try to find out where the spray paint came from," Joel says. "If it was from Deacon's, someone may remember who bought it."

"Putt-putt did it," Tim says. Putt-putt is the school's nickname for Mr. Potter, because he's an avid golfer. "Dressed all in black, his face covered by a stocking . . ."

Murph picks it up. "He sneaks in as the clock strikes twelve . . ."

"Tiptoes down the hallway . . ."

"And hears a noise. He whirls around . . ."

"His deadly paint can held up high . . ."

Even Ben gets into it. "The nozzle pointed straight into the heart of darkness."

They can hardly stifle their laughter.

"But there's no one there," Bobby says.

"His pulse beats like a wild thing," Ben says.

They can't help their hilarity. As they enter the library, their laughter breaks out and shatters the peace. Mrs. Deans glares at them. She's the oldest member of the teaching staff and due to retire next year. She has a fearsome reputation for a sharp tongue and an acid personality—everyone knows she hates teenagers—and she guards the library quiet as if it were made of fine glass.

They quiet down under her stare. "Mr. Potter tells me you're here until third period," she informs them, "but if you think this is going to be party time, you're mistaken. There'll be no sitting together and no chitchat. Each one at a separate table. Right now."

Joel picks a table, sits down, and opens his Spanish book with the intention of doing the homework he should've done the night before, but he can't keep his mind on it. He keeps glancing over at Ben, who's at the next table, deeply immersed in his book. Joel wonders how Ben can handle everything with such cool. It has to have been much worse for him than anyone else. He was going with Caroline, he was sleeping with her, he may have even loved her. Joel wishes he could talk to Ben the way he did when they were ten and discussed everything without worrying whether the other guy would be offended or upset. Not that their subject matter was particularly offensive or upsetting, but they didn't pull punches if they were arguing over a football player or who got to be banker in Monopoly.

There are a thousand things Joel would like to know now, like how can Ben still think school counts, and how did he feel about the lie detector test, and does he feel weird a lot of the time the way Joel does? He thinks that maybe Ben would really talk instead of just shrugging or saying something dirty as if nothing really mattered and everything was a big joke. The thing is, it makes Joel uncomfortable to think of approaching Ben. At ten he was just another kid, but now he's somebody who keeps his thoughts and emotions to himself and maybe would prefer it that way.

Joel studies Ben's profile with its hawklike nose and strongly arched, dark eyebrow and wonders what it must be like to be so successful with the girls. Andy told him last summer that Sandy Solomon said he, Joel, was cute. Sandy was one of those girls, like Mary Alice and Jenny, who weren't exactly terrific but weren't woofers either. For a while, Joel watched Sandy every time he saw her at the beach, but then he saw what a big flirt she was, and that made him nervous. He couldn't be sure if she went out with him that she wouldn't be eyeing every other guy around.

The trouble is, Joel doesn't really know what girls mean when they call a guy cute. He's stared at himself in the mirror and sometimes he thinks it's his eyes, other times his mouth, or maybe it's his hair. Some girls really go for blond guys, or so he's heard. Actually, he finds girls very bewildering. The only female he can count on to be consistent is his mother, and what he expects is that eventually girls grow up and turn into women like Barbara, and that's when you can finally have a relationship with them. Everything that comes before is trial and error. X and Y go together for a couple of weeks, it's all perfect, but you bet they'll break up and they do. Then the girl walks around school with her eyes all pink, while the guy acts like nothing's happened.

This time when Joel glances at Ben, Ben is looking at him.

"You okay?" Ben asks, his voice just above a whisper.

"Me? Yeah, sure." Joel points to his book. "Except for Spanish."

"It's a bitch. I did it last year."

"Graves is tough."

"Memorize the vocabulary. That's what he'll get you on."

A shadow looms behind Joel. "I said no chitchat," Mrs. Deans says, "and I meant it."

Joel obediently bends his head over his book, but not before he's exchanged conspiratorial smiles with Ben. For a moment, it's just like the old days—he and Ben fighting side by side against the bank robbers, the enemy spies, the cow rustlers, and the raiding Apaches. But the camaraderie doesn't last. They're not kids anymore, the danger is real, and the enemy is hidden behind a scrawl of black paint. "Verbs in the Past Tense," Joel reads, and feels a weariness come over him that's so heavy it drags his eyelids down and presses his head into his folded arms. And, as the silence wraps him tightly in its shroud of soundlessness, he sleeps.

That afternoon, as he's walking away from the school, Mr. Boehm, the swim coach, pulls over in his car and winds down the door window. "Joel," he says. "Can I invite you for a doughnut?"

"Pardon, sir?"

"I sometimes go to The Donut Hole after school and pick up dessert for the family. Come on, hop in."

Joel knows what this is about and he'd rather not, but he gets into the car, because he's polite. On the way to The Donut Hole, Mr. Boehm talks about how he's always wanted to see the mountains so this summer he's renting a van and taking the family on a cross-country camping trip to the Rockies. Has Joel ever had a yen to see the Rockies? No? Well, he'd like to go to the ocean, too, but that'll have to be another summer. He has in mind the barrier islands of North Carolina. Has Joel ever been there? No? Well, that's where Kitty Hawk is and where America's first airplane flight took place. Right on the ocean dunes. Joel finds it weird to be talking about mountains and oceans in Mr.

Boehm's car, which smells like spilled milk and is filled with school papers, old candy wrappers, some Fisher Price people, and a dirty soccer ball.

They arrive at The Donut Hole and sit at a booth. Mr. Boehm orders coffee and a dozen chocolate-glazed doughnuts to go. Joel orders a doughnut with maple-walnut icing and a Coke. After the waitress takes their order, Mr. Boehm gets down to business.

"Pretty upsetting this morning," he says.

"Yeah," Joel says.

"I heard the police found the can of paint in the trash behind the school. It wasn't bought at Deacon's, probably at a store in Laurel Grove."

"Oh."

The waitress returns with their drinks and Joel's doughnut. He takes a big bite and savors the sweetness.

"You haven't been at practice for a week, Joel. I'm really disappointed."

"Sorry," Joel mumbles through his doughnut.

"You think you're going to stay with the team?"

"I haven't decided."

Mr. Boehm sips his coffee. "I'd like to tell you a story about something that happened to me when I was about your age."

Shit.

His feelings must be evident, because Mr. Boehm holds up a hand. "No, listen, this isn't a lecture or anything like that. It's what happened to me, and if you can get something out of it, great, and if you can't, well, I'll understand that, too. Okay?"

Joel shrugs. "Okay."

"The day after I turned sixteen, my father died. He was driving into town to get some feed, and the truck went off the road. It was raining, and everyone thought it was an accident. But I knew it wasn't. He had a mental illness, today I guess we'd call him manic-depressive, but in those days we just said he was moody. Over the years, the depressions got worse and worse and longer and longer, and he'd talk about killing himself. It scared me, and I know my mother was terrified, but we didn't know what to do. We didn't even talk about it. But when his truck went off the road, we knew it was no accident, although we didn't say anything to anybody. My mother had even tried to stop him from going into town that morning, because he'd had such a bad night.

"I think swimming was what saved me then. I was ashamed at what he did, and angry he did it, and grieving because he was dead. I was so mixed up and so unhappy, I could hardly see straight. My grades went down, and I thought about leaving school, but my mother begged me not to, and that's when I turned to the swimming. I got in that pool and found it was like another world. I could forget about my father and his suicide and the troubles at home. I could forget about how bad I felt." Mr. Boehm paused. "Am I getting through, Joel? Do you know what I'm saying?"

"Yeah, I know what you're saying." Joel also notes that strong emotion makes the flanges on Spiderman's bony nose tremble. He wonders if girls considered Mr. Boehm cute when he was in high school, and thinks of those team pictures from the sixties. All the guys in those pictures look like geeks with their hair greased back in funny looking waves, but then maybe girls had different standards back then.

"This business with Caroline . . ." Mr. Boehm shakes his head. "I think the police are picking on you boys because they can't figure what else to do, and they don't want to look like they're sitting on their butts and twiddling their thumbs."

"It could be someone in school."

"And it could be a neighbor, or someone she baby-sat for, or someone who saw her at the post office, or someone who watched her walk down the street. Everyone in Cassandra is a suspect."

"I guess so."

"Look, Joel, our last meet is with Laurel Grove. You know what a tough team they are. We can't afford to lose you."

Joel thinks disparagingly of his racing times. "Oh, right," he says.

"Listen, I was the slowest guy on our team. My times were worse than anyone else's, but I threw myself into it, and worked hard, and it paid off. Look, you don't have to give me an answer now. I just want you to think about what I've said."

Joel finishes his doughnut and drains his Coke.

"Promise you'll think about it?"

"Yeah, okay."

That night Joel dreams that he's swimming with the team, only the water is too thick. Mr. Boehm begins to check the chlorine levels, but as he does so, Joel notices that the water isn't clear anymore. It's turning a dark red, and he realizes they're swimming in Caroline's blood. Nobody notices this but him. He tries to ignore it, too, but he gags with every stroke as he puts his mouth in the water and tries to exhale. The gagging turns to choking, and he begins to sink to the bottom of the pool while the blood fills his mouth, a nauseating syrup. He knows he mustn't swallow it; if he does he'll die, too. Desperate for a breath, he tries to swim back to the surface, but now he can hardly move. The water is too heavy, it's pressing him down, farther and farther down. Suddenly he sees that the pool has no bottom anymore. He starts to scream, to thrash, but the blood pours into his mouth. *No! Stop!* He doesn't want to die! *No! Help!*

"Joel. Joel, are you okay?"

He swims out of the dream, opens his eyes, and blinks at the light coming in his door from the hallway. His mother's body in its nightgown makes a bulky shadow in the opening.

"I was dreaming," he says thickly.

Barbara comes in, sits down beside him, and puts her hand on his forehead. Her fingers feel cool on his skin, and he can smell the rose scent of the sachets that she puts in the drawer where she keeps her nightgowns.

"You're wet," she says. "Heavens, you're sopping."

She leans toward the table beside his bed to turn on the lamp, but he stops her. "Don't," he says. He doesn't think he can bear the light. He just wants to curl up in the dark next to his mother's comforting presence.

"That must have been some dream," she says.

"I dreamed I was drowning in Caroline's blood."

She expels a breath as if he's hit her. "Oh, Joel, that's awful." For a few minutes they're silent as she strokes his hair away from his temple. "The writing on your locker has really upset you."

He made light of the vandalism that night at dinner, imitating Mr. Potter's earnestness and joking about turning from a suspect to a spy for the police. But now, lying in the dark with Barbara's cool fingers on his flushed skin, it's different. "I'm not a killer," he says.

"Of course not."

"But then someone says I am and what can I do? Nothing. I don't even know who did it."

"I know."

"It's not fair, Mom."

"No, it isn't."

"And why does it have to happen to me? Just because I asked her out once. It wasn't such a big deal. It really wasn't. So why does everything in my life have to be about that one stupid thing? Why?" Her fingers move steadily across his brow, and now he shakes them off. "Shit, it makes me so fucking mad!"

He's not supposed to use language like that in the house, but Barbara doesn't remark on it. "Oh, Joel," she says gently, "I'm so sorry."

He starts to cry and buries his face in the pillow. The sobbing shakes him, and Barbara strokes his back. "It'll be all right," she says. "Eventually it'll be over and everything will be all right."

"No, it won't," he sobs. "Nothing will ever be the same."

"Barbara? Joel?" It's Dan's voice. "What's going on?"

At the sound of his father's voice, Joel stops crying and his body goes rigid beneath Barbara's calming hand. It's one thing to cry in front of his mother—his tears have always been safe with her—but his father is different. Dan has never said so, but Joel's quite sure his father wouldn't think it right for his seventeen-year-old son to be curled up next to his mother and sobbing like a baby.

"It's okay," Barbara says. "Joel and I were just talking. We're almost finished."

"Anything I can help with?"

"No, I don't think so."

His father's footsteps fade away, and Barbara says, "Joel, do you want to see someone?"

"What do you mean?"

"A counselor or psychologist. Someone who could help you deal with your feelings."

"I don't want to see anybody."

"But, honey, this is really upsetting you, and I want to help, but I'm not sure I can."

"No."

"There's no shame in seeing someone."

"No!"

"All right," she says, "but I want you to talk to me about what you're feeling. It's not good to hold that stuff in, it eats away at you. Do you know what I mean?"

"Yes."

"Promise?"

"Okay."

But after Barbara leaves, Joel turns over on his back, stares into the darkness, and goes down a mental checklist of all the things he can't discuss with her.

Girls: her advice is to smile and be nice and girls will like him, but as far as Joel can figure out, this has nothing to do with being popular. Scowly guys with great bodies like Ted Snedecker have girls calling them all the time. Aloof guys like Ben end up dating the prettiest girl in the school. Joel could smile until his face cracked, and it wouldn't get him anywhere.

Sex: he sure as hell isn't going to tell her about the erections and frequent masturbating, his obsession with breasts, or dreams he has like the one with Stephanie Binda that leave his bed damp with sperm. Guys don't tell their mothers stuff like that. Guys don't tell anyone about stuff like that. They just make their mothers happy by getting real interested in doing their own laundry.

The swim team: if he told Barbara that he doesn't want to

swim anymore, she'd be just like Mr. Boehm, laying on the pressure and expectations. She'd tell him some story about how *she* faced obstacles and persevered as if her life could be applied to his. She wouldn't understand that he no longer cared about cutting ten seconds off his 200-meter butterfly or gave a shit if Cassandra beat Laurel Grove.

And then there's the other Joel with his cool, appraising eyes: if Barbara knew about him, she'd make him go to one of those shrinks who mess with your head and try to get you to talk about private things like erections and obsessions.

As he turns back over and pulls the covers over his shoulders, Joel has a memory that goes back to a time when he was very small. He remembers being terrified that he'd lose Barbara whenever they were in places like the mall where there were crowds of strangers, and that he'd suddenly be all by himself, alone and helpless. This fear was so strong that he'd cling onto her fingers with one hand and grasp her skirt or pocketbook with the other. Sometimes when he attached himself to her like this, he couldn't walk beside her without stumbling. "Joel," she'd say to him, "it's okay. I'm right here. I'm not going anywhere."

As he falls asleep, Joel has another image of himself. He stands with one hand clasping onto his mother, while the other reaches into a space, his hand spread wide, his fingers reaching to nowhere.

Chapter
4

ONE OF THE THINGS JOEL LIKES BEST ABOUT WORKING FOR Mrs. Hudson—she says to call her Marla, but that makes him feel strange so in his mind he still calls her Mrs. Hudson—is that he sometimes gets to drive the Taurus to her house on Saturday and Sunday afternoons. His parents have two cars. His mother's is a 1982 Toyota Tercel, standard shift, on its last legs, and it's the car he usually gets to drive. The Tercel doesn't have power steering and brakes like the Taurus or the comfortable upholstered seats, the clean-smelling interior and stereo system. It's the newness of the Taurus that has given him the chance to drive it. His parents turn into garden freaks when the weather gets warm and spend their weekends fertilizing the lawn, putting in the vegetable garden and planting flowers. Dan doesn't want to get the Taurus dirty by using it to transport plants, bags of soil, and gardening equipment from the hardware store and nursery to the house. "Drive carefully," Dan says whenever he gives the Taurus's keys to Joel. "No fancy stuff."

As Joel drives away from the house, he switches the radio to a rock station and turns the volume up high. He can feel the beat of the drums in his chest and replicates it on the steering wheel with his fist. *Da-da-dum. Da-da-dum.* He feels great when the car's power surges at the slightest pressure of his foot, the windows are open, and wind ruffles through his hair like the fingers of an imaginary girl. When he drives the Taurus, the ties and responsibilities that bind him to Cassandra seem to weaken. It's as if he's flying free and skimming the surface of the earth.

And he likes his new job clearing the grounds of the Hiller house, gardening for Mrs. Hudson and doing other odd jobs. Joel knows Barbara cooked this job up for him after he dropped off the swim team, because she thinks it's unhealthy for him to spend so many hours in his room. But he doesn't care. He's getting paid a dollar more than minimum wage and he can use the money, and then there's Mrs. Hudson—*Marla.* After he works for a couple of hours, she brings him a Coke or glass of lemonade, and they talk before he heads home. The best part is that they don't discuss Caroline or what's happening in school but talk about things other people might find weird, like the shapes of clouds and what it would be like if humans could smell the way dogs can. He liked the way Mrs. Hudson laughed when he suggested that maybe there'd be sniffways in parks where people could leave scents for other people to follow. He likes the way she discussed her landscaping with him, asking him where he thought the pool should go and taking his answer seriously. He also likes the way she watches him work. Sometimes she stands in the doorway, and he can feel her eyes on his bare back as he digs out roots and tosses away stones. She never says anything, but he feels his muscles move more powerfully, the sweat shimmer on his skin, and his hair gleam silver in the sun.

As he drives up the winding road toward the house, Joel turns off the music. Mrs. Hudson doesn't like heavy metal. She says people have different ways music works in their brains, and her pathways can't accommodate what Joel's can. He thinks her point of view is a whole lot more open-minded than that of his mother. Barbara can't stand the music he plays. She says it has no melody, and she only likes music she can sing to, which is a pretty narrow way of looking at things and doesn't apply to those Beethoven symphonies either. But when he pointed that out, his mother said classical music was different.

Joel parks the car in the driveway. There's another car next to Mrs. Hudson's Honda, a blue New Yorker that Joel hasn't seen before. The front door opens, and Mrs. Hudson stands there. She's wearing white sandals with slender thongs and a dress Joel likes, because it's made of delicate, pale blue fabric that seems to float when she walks.

"Hi, Joel," Marla says as he gets out of the car.

"Hi," he says.

A man appears beside her in the doorway, a man with thick, dark hair and a stocky build. He's wearing jeans, a crisp white T-shirt, and a gold watch. "Joel," Marla says, "do you know Tony Molino?"

The man gives Joel a smile. "We've seen each other around. Right, Joel?"

"Yeah," Joel says. He hardly knows the guy, but there's something about him he doesn't like. Maybe it's the way Tony's sneakered feet are planted, spread wide as he stands in the doorway, sort of as if he owns the place.

"Tony was the real estate agent who sold me the house."

"It's looking good," Tony says. "Whaddya think, Joel?"

"Yeah."

Tony turns to Marla. "Are you going to get another estimate on the fireplace?"

"Peter says Therontos does good work."

"That Greek is a crook."

"Wouldn't the architect know that?"

"I'm telling you, Marla, he's going to rip you off."

"And which of your many relatives could do the job better?"

Tony winks at Joel as if to say *what a woman* and spreads his hands wide in a helpless gesture. "Now, Marla," he says.

Joel leaves and walks around the house to the shed where the garden tools are kept. The house is looking good on the inside, but the grounds are a mess. The contractors' trucks tore up what little grass was left in the front, and the rest of the lawn, front and back, is weeds and overgrown bush. Mrs. Hudson wants to put in a terraced back deck of weathered cedar with benches, archways, and latticed ceilings. Joel can't quite imagine how it will look, but it sounds pretty. Then beyond that will be the pool, kidney-shaped, surrounded by a tiled deck. There's also a part of the property that is treed as thick as a forest and angles down to the river. This part of the river runs quickly, a rush of water over rocks and around curves that's deafening up close and can even be heard as far as the back door of the house when there's no wind rustling the trees.

Mrs. Hudson wants to create a pathway through the trees to the water, and near the river bank, a clearing under the trees with a flagstoned floor. She says she'll put chaise lounges there for when it's hot and listen to the music created by the water. But that's all in the future. Right now, Joel's job is to work on the garden at the west side of the house that can't be rototilled until he pulls out all the rocks. He strips off his shirt, clips a Walkman to the belt that holds up his shorts and puts the earphones on. He likes listening to music as he digs. He can get a rhythm going—shovel in, up, turn, in, up, turn. Whenever he finds a rock, he squats down, picks it up with his gloved hands, and throws it into the wheelbarrow. The sun heats up his skin and hair, and every once in a while, he stops, pulls out a handkerchief, and wipes his face.

When the wheelbarrow is almost full, Mrs. Hudson appears at the back door and waves at him. Joel takes off his earphones. "Time to quit," she says. "You're getting burned."

He walks the wheelbarrow through the trees and down to the river, where he dumps the rocks. Then he puts the wheelbarrow and shovel back in the shed. By the time he's finished, Mrs. Hudson has brought out the lemonade and set up two chaise lounges in the shade of some trees. She's sitting in one of them, shading her eyes with her hand and looking toward the garden.

"Where did you suppose all those rocks originally came from?" she asks as he sits down.

"I don't know," he says, and picks up a glass that's already beaded with drops. He closes his eyes and drinks deeply, enjoying the cold, tart flavor of lemon sliding down his throat.

"I wonder," Marla says, "if the house appreciates this."

Once Joel would have said that houses don't have feelings, but he's learned that Mrs. Hudson isn't interested in the obvious. "It's kind of like surgery," he says.

"It is, isn't it? Ripping and tearing, removing the old and broken parts, rewiring and replumbing. Sometimes I hear the house sighing. Not painful sighs, but an easing of its spirit. You know what kind of sigh I mean?"

"Like at the end of the day."

"That's right," she says, and takes a sip of her lemonade.

When Joel looks at Mrs. Hudson a certain way, he can see that she's as old as his mother. When she bends her head back to drink, there are the same lines on her neck that Barbara has. She's also going gray like Barbara and has wrinkles at her eyes and a softness in the flesh below her chin. But he doesn't often look at her that way. In fact, he doesn't look at her directly if he can help it. Like Caroline, she's too dazzling. So he sneaks looks at her like when she's drinking or closing her eyes and putting her face up to the sun. That's when he sees that her body is different than Barbara's. It's leaner, not as soft, and her breasts are bigger, pointier. Joel feels his penis stir and gulps down some more lemonade.

"Do kids still go to Misty Lake?" she asks.

"Sometimes." Barbara has told Joel about Christian's death, and he's curious but afraid to ask Marla directly about it. He picks his words carefully. "My mom says one of the guys from her class was killed near there."

"He was my boyfriend."

"Were you, like . . . serious?"

"I thought we were going to get married."

"Yeah, that's serious." They both laugh a little, and he says, "You must've been really torn up when he died."

"I thought about suicide, like stabbing myself or jumping off a mountainside, but then I had a dramatic streak."

"And there aren't any mountains around Cassandra anyway."

"And I don't like pain. I had to reconcile myself to living."

"Was my mother serious about Mr. Deacon?"

"Your mother wanted a boyfriend, and Brian just happened to be there. He didn't seem all that upset when it ended either."

"Why'd they break up?"

"I never really knew why." Marla takes another sip of lemonade and looks back at the house. "You know, I spend a lot of time wondering what happened in this house when the Hillers lived here. I don't really believe in ghosts, but I think you can feel things. I had a very strange experience once. I was traveling to Oregon on business and stayed with a friend. We went to a party, and she introduced me to an acquaintance of hers. As we talked, I got a terrible feeling from this woman, just hideous vibes. Later, after we left, I said to my friend, 'What kind of cancer does Marlene have?' and she said, 'How do you know that?' I don't know *how* I knew, I just did. Isn't that awful—to sense something like cancer in a stranger?"

"Do you ever feel good things?"

Marla turns completely toward him. "That's very perceptive of you, Joel."

He feels his chest swell with pride. "It is?"

"Because I don't feel good things. Just disease and death."

"Maybe good things don't send messages."

"You mean bad things want to send messages?"

Like many of their conversations, this one has taken an abrupt turn into the unknown, and Joel has to struggle to find his way. "Maybe bad things want to be recognized."

"I see," Marla says slowly. "Like the cancer being evil and wanting me to know it."

"Yeah."

"Do you believe in God?"

Although God isn't someone Joel has thought much about, and he doesn't consider himself religious, a couple of months ago he would have said yes. Now he says, "No."

"Me either." A crow alights on a branch near them and begins cawing. Marla glances up at it and adds, "If I put this in a book—two people denying the existence of God followed by a crow screaming at them—readers would think the crow had something to do with the denial."

"You mean a messenger from God?"

"Or from the devil if you're literal. Or maybe that the crow simply represents the lack of spirituality in my characters' lives."

Joel believes that this is the most adult conversation he's ever had in his life. "Is your next book going to be about Cassandra?" he asks.

"It's going to be about Christian and why he died."

"Wasn't it an accident?"

"Yes, but the question is why. He was a good driver."

"Was he drunk?"

"No, I think he was angry and upset about someone."

"Mom says you had a fight that night."

"We did, Joel, but something happened after it, after he left me. He talked to someone else."

"Who?"

"I don't know, but I'm going to find out." Marla glances at him. "Maybe you could help."

"Me? How?"

"Ask your mother what happened that night."

"Why don't you ask her?"

"I have, but she doesn't want to talk about it to me. Maybe she'll talk to you." She reaches across the table that holds the lemonade glasses and grasps his forearm. "Will you?"

Joel has felt a shock—like an electrical shock—at the touch of her cool fingers on his warm skin. Now the residue of that shock, a tingle of excitement, slips under the skin, enters his bloodstream, and pulses through his arteries. He shudders slightly and says, "Yeah. Okay."

The next Saturday night, Pete, Stephanie, Joel, and a girl named Katrina Doyle go to see *Total Recall* at the Cassandra Cineplex. Katrina works in the same beauty parlor, the Set 'n' Curl, as Stephanie. Her job is to sweep up hair, clean mirrors and tables, and give manicures. She isn't from Cassandra but lives with her parents in Banting, a small town on the other side of Laurel Grove. According to Pete, who talked Joel into double-dating, Katrina did have a boyfriend but they broke up about a month ago, and she was real depressed. Stephanie thought she should start getting out more and asked Pete if he had any friends that Katrina might like. Joel finally said yes to Pete's urging, because if Katrina were anything like Stephanie, she'd be a hot number, and Joel has a belief that he wouldn't be so obsessive about breasts if he had access to a hot number.

But Katrina isn't like Stephanie. She's not tall and thin and built but short and plump with thick ankles and a small double chin. She has big blue eyes that Joel likes, soft features, and a halo of blond frizzy hair, but she also giggles a lot and that makes him uncomfortable. Even worse, Joel has the feeling she doesn't like him. He's noticed that she doesn't look at him if she can help it. When they said hello, her eyes slid to a spot over his shoulder, and before the movie she talked mostly to Stephanie. During the trailers, he went to the bathroom and looked into the mirror to see if something had happened to his face, but it was the same face he saw every morning in his own mirror at home. The violent parts of the movie, when Arnold Schwarzenegger was fighting the villains, didn't improve intimacy either. During those parts, Stephanie gave little screams and buried her face in Pete's shoulder. Katrina just covered her eyes with both hands, although Joel thought a couple of times that she leaned against him, but the pressure was so light he could've imagined it.

By the time the movie lets out, it's close to eleven o'clock. It's a warm night, and a sliver of moon illuminates their faces as they walk toward Pete's car, which is parked down a side street. They talk about going for a pizza, but no one's really hungry. Then Pete says, "Let's go swimming."

"The water'll be too cold," Stephanie says. She gives Pete a playful punch in the shoulder nearest to her. "Besides, I just washed my hair."

"I don't have a suit," Katrina says with a nervous giggle. She's still not looking at Joel, although they're now holding

202

hands. He twitches his fingers experimentally, but her hand doesn't respond. It lies like a small, limp animal in his palm.

"You don't need a suit," Pete says, looking over his shoulder at Joel and giving him a sly smile. "Right?"

"Yeah," Joel says, trying to sound enthusiastic and macho. The boys in Cassandra often go skinny-dipping in the summer. On hot nights you can usually find some of them at Misty Lake, drinking beer, laughing, joking, and doing crazy dives off the big rock into the water. Joel's fantasized about skinny-dipping with girls, but now the thought of it doesn't turn him on the way it usually does. He can almost feel the cold water on his genitals, shriveling him into virtual nonexistence. He thinks girls have it lucky when it comes to being naked. They don't have to worry about swelling and shrinkage and having their state of mind visible to anyone who wants to know.

When Pete heads out of Cassandra onto Route 240, Stephanie lights up some pot and hands the toke around. They all take drags, and then talk about the movie, whose action takes place in the future. The hero goes to a company called Recall, where he's plugged into a machine that can probe his mind and send him on a fantasy vacation.

"You know where I'd go if it were me?" Stephanie says. "To one of those Club Med places. I'd tan all day and dance all night."

"You have a tendency to burn real bad," Katrina warns.

"You wouldn't on a fantasy vacation," Stephanie says. "That's the point."

There's a silence while they absorb all the fantastical possibilities of vacations where the traveler gets to choose all the options. "You know what I'd do?" Pete says. "I'd go as a NASCAR race car driver to Indianapolis. And I'd arrange it so I won. Man, that would be great."

"I'd go to Disney World," Katrina says. "My cousin Ralph—you remember him, Steph?"

"The one who sweats all the time?"

"He does not sweat *all* the time. Only when he's nerved up."

"You should see this guy," Stephanie says to Pete. "He asked me out once, and I thought he was melting. It was gross."

"Anyways," Katrina says, "he's been to Disney World three times."

It's Joel's turn. He's never thought much about traveling except when the swim team had a chance to go to Albany for the state meet, but his big ambition has always been to go to the Olympics wherever they were held. He wonders if he should say that, except that he's not doing sports anymore and would it really be a vacation if he were a competitor? Joel tries to think of another choice that would make him sound the most cool, but the pot's made him a little dizzy. Finally, he says, "I'd go to Vegas with a million bucks."

But Stephanie's already moved on. "That nail polish was pretty neat, wasn't it?" she says to Katrina. In the movie, a receptionist changes the color of her nails with a wand attached to a computer pad. "If we had that today, you'd be out of a job."

"Yeah, but who would do the shaping?" Katrina asks. "Who would do the cuticles?"

"They'd have machines for that, too."

"They probably wouldn't need hairdressers either," Katrina counters. "They'd probably use robots for that."

"A robot couldn't look at a face and know what cut would be best, Katrina."

As they argue, Joel looks out the window at the passing landscape. In the past he'd have gone to see a movie like *Total Recall,* liked the special effects and the science fiction stuff, and not thought much about the violence. Actually, he would have liked that, too. It's always satisfying when the bad guys get mowed down in a bath of blood and gore. But tonight he can't help wondering what Mrs. Hudson would say about the movie if she'd seen it. He thinks there are things he's missed or not understood, deeper meanings in the bloodshed, the mutants on Mars, the way the hero was brainwashed, and whether a vacation is truly pleasurable if you have a hundred percent control.

"Here we are," Pete says, taking the turn to Misty Lake too quickly so that Katrina's thrown against Joel, the softness of her breast brushing against the back of his hand. Joel thinks of the mutant woman in the movie who had three breasts and how pink her nipples were. He wonders what color nipples Katrina has and what they would feel like. He wonders if she has blond pubic hair. He's heard a rumor that nobody has truly blond pubic hair, it's always darker than the hair on your head. This is true for him. The hair on his head and legs is blond, but the hair at his groin is light brown. Pete drives up to the lake and cuts the headlights. The moon makes the water look as if it were made of ice and turns the tops of the trees silver. Beneath the trees, the ground is black and shadowed. Joel thinks it's going to be too dark to see much of anything.

Stephanie is out of the car first, followed by Katrina. They kick off their shoes, run down to the water, and poke in their toes. Their little screams punctuate the stillness of the lake.

Joel is about to follow them when Pete pulls him back. "She digs you, man," he says in an undertone.

"What?"

"Katrina, asshole. She told Steph you were kind of cute."

"Oh." Instead of cheering Joel up, this news depresses him. It isn't that he doesn't want Katrina to like him. It's just that if she's been sending messages, it's clear he's too stupid to read them. On the other hand, when he thinks of those sideways glances and limp hand, he's not convinced she likes him at all. And what is "kind of cute" anyway?

Stephanie is back. "You're going to freeze your balls off," she says.

"Not with this." Pete pulls a flask of rum out of the glove compartment, takes a swig, and hands it to Stephanie.

She takes a big swallow, coughs, and says, "If I get pneumonia . . ."

Pete is already opening the trunk of the car and bringing out a blanket. "And I'll get you warm afterward," he says.

Stephanie holds the bottle out to Katrina, who's come up behind her. "Want some?"

"No thanks."

"You going in?"

"No."

"Come on," Stephanie says. "Don't be such a chicken shit."

"I'm not going."

"Just because you don't have a suit."

"Steph," Katrina says in a low warning voice.

"Oh, yeah," Stephanie says. "You're on the rag."

Katrina's voice goes up a horrified, breathless notch. "Oh, thanks, Steph, thanks a lot."

Joel and Katrina stand by the car and watch as Stephanie and Pete take off their clothes, turning themselves into pale ghosts, and run into the black water. There's a lot of hollering, laughing, and splashing, and then Pete yells out, "It's great in here, you guys." But the swim doesn't last long. They're soon out, wrapping themselves in the blanket and disappearing into the shadows. Joel and Katrina hear a stumble, a muttered "Fuck!" and then nothing.

Joel clears his throat. "Want to sit in the car?" he asks.

"Okay."

They sit in the backseat, near each other but not quite touching. Joel can smell the scent of the shampoo that Katrina used in her hair, but the light from the moon is so weak that he can barely see her. Her profile is a pale oblong with a dark hole for her eye. For a few seconds they sit in silence, and Joel has the sensation of the other Joel slipping out and perching on the steering wheel watching them. From that perspective, what he sees are two strangers stuck together in a car, both wishing they were somewhere else.

He shifts slightly and puts one arm on the seat behind her. "You ever been on a blind date before?" he asks.

"This is my first."

"Me, too." There's another silence and Joel continues, "The movie was okay."

"Yeah."

"I don't think Arnold Schwarzenegger is a very good actor."

"He was okay."

Joel thinks of the ways Mrs. Hudson might examine the Schwarzenegger character and says, "He never said anything interesting."

"What?"

"He was always reacting to things. He never had an interesting idea on his own."

"He was brainwashed," Katrina says. "That's why."

But Joel has had an insight. "Maybe the people who made the film knew he couldn't act well enough to handle a more interesting part so they put all the clever stuff in the special effects."

Katrina thinks about this. "I thought he was okay," she says.

Having hit a dead end, Joel tries another tack. "Pete said you were going with somebody up until a month ago."

"Yeah."

"Do you want to talk about it?"

Katrina shrugs, leaving Joel in a quandary. Does she or doesn't she? Since he can't think of any other subject of conversation, he says, "Why'd you break up?"

"He wanted to go out with somebody else," Katrina says, and starts to cry.

The blind date from hell. Joel's first instinct is to open the car door and run. But the other Joel is cooler, steadier. It's the other Joel that makes him put his arm around Katrina and pull her toward him. "It's okay," he murmurs, and brushes her soft hair with his hand. "It's okay."

Katrina sobs for a while, big, racking sobs that shake her body. When these subside, she takes deep, shuddering breaths. Then she rests against him, her face buried against his now wet shirt. Joel gives her a small, tentative kiss at the crook of her neck. When she doesn't pull away, scream, or slap his face, he applies a series of kisses near her ear, having read somewhere that the skin just below the earlobe is very sensitive. This has an appropriate and gratifying effect. Katrina tilts her face so that their lips meet, and Joel finds himself deep in a busy French kiss with her tongue probing his mouth and wiggling against his teeth. It's not his first French kiss—there've been kisses at various birthday parties and school dances since grade seven, but nothing ever came of them.

It's surprisingly easy after that—up to a point. Katrina doesn't say anything when he pulls up her blouse and even helps him unhook her bra. Her breasts are like small apples with tiny hard stems. Each one fits into the curve of his hand. She lets him fondle her breasts, but when he tries to put his hand between her legs, she presses her thighs together. "No," she says, and he remembers she has her period. He can't imagine what that's like, bleeding from between your legs, but he has a horror of finding out so he stays away and focuses his attention on her breasts. He cups them, lifts them, and buries his face between them. He thinks he's reached heaven when she arches her back slightly, and he understands that she wants him to take her nipples in his mouth.

By this time she's lying on the backseat and he's crouched down beside her, kneeling on the floor. When he lifts his head from sucking on her breast, he sees her face illuminated by a ray of moonlight as it angles through the car window. Her eyes are closed, her mouth slightly open, her breathing light and fluttered. It's the other Joel who recognizes what's happening, the more adult part of himself that sees more, understands more, and knows more than he has ever wanted to know. It's the other Joel who realizes that Katrina's not thinking about him at all. Behind her closed lids, she's replaced his mouth and fingers with those of her old boyfriend. In her imagination, he's someone else altogether. A sadness comes over him, a dimming of his spirit, but it doesn't stop him. The surging of blood in his groin, the tightening of his testicles, the biological imperative drive him on. He bends his head again, takes a small, hard nipple between his teeth, and thinks: *Fuck it.*

The next morning, Sunday, he wakes up way too early— 8:30—and can't fall back to sleep. Even with his curtains closed, the sun is too bright in his room. He gets up, pulls on a pair of jeans, and steps outside. It's one of those clear mornings that promises a hot day to come. The sky is an uninterrupted blue from horizon to horizon, and he can already feel heat in the patio stones. Hearing a banging sound near the garage, Joel walks around to the driveway, where Dan is squatting beside the lawnmower, tools spread around him.

Dan glances at him. "You're up early."

"I couldn't sleep."

Dan picks up a screwdriver and starts to remove the cover from the motor.

"What're you doing?" Joel asks.

"Changing the points. They're burned out."

"That mower's pretty old, isn't it?"

"Older than you," Dan says. "It doesn't owe me a thing."

"Want some help?"

"Pass me the wrench, will you?"

Joel passes him the wrench and watches while Dan takes off some bolts. "How was your date?" Dan asks.

"Okay."

"How was the movie?"

"It had good special effects."

"Let's see if we can get this flywheel off," Dan says. Using three screwdrivers and gently applied force, he and Joel lift the flywheel up the drive shaft. Then, while Joel holds it, Dan taps the drive shaft with a piece of wood so that the flywheel pops off.

"There," Dan says. "That should do it."

This is how Joel relates best to his father, when they're working together and not making too much conversation. It didn't used to be like that. When Joel was little, he could climb on Dan's lap and get a hug. If he fell down and hurt himself, Dan was just as good as Barbara at making his cuts feel better. But as Joel got older, a rift grew between them, widening until it no longer could be breached by outstretched arms. The rift isn't Dan's fault; Joel feels the need of it himself. He has a feeling that if his father gets too close or knows too much about him the space will shrink, constricting his chest until he won't be able to breathe anymore.

"What was the name of the girl you were with?" Dan asks as he begins to remove the old points with a screwdriver.

"Katrina Doyle."

"Doyle . . . Doyle. Do we know any Doyles?"

"She comes from Banting."

"Oh."

Joel watches his father work. Dan is methodical and careful. Each tool has its place around him, and he lines up each part in a row so he won't lose any pieces, screws, or bolts. Between steps, he wipes his fingers on a clean cloth and studies his handiwork before moving on to the next job. Joel wonders if Dan ever had to worry about girls like Katrina, the kind you didn't like but you knew you could have if you wanted. Was it wrong to take advantage of her unhappiness? But then wasn't she using him, too, making believe he was someone else? What I'd like to know, Joel thinks, is when do two wrongs make a right? But he can't ask Dan those questions, so he says, "I think I'll go over to Mrs. Hudson's this morning before it gets too hot."

"How's the house coming?"

"They're putting a bathroom in the turret now." He pauses. "Dad?"

"Mmm?"

"Was Mrs. Hudson, well, was she like different in high school?"

"She had something, a kind of charisma. She attracted people."

"You, too?"

"In a far-off sort of way."

"What was her boyfriend like?"

"Christian? What we called BMOC in those days—big man on campus, football star, basketball captain, lots of pretty girls around him."

"Were you at Misty Lake the night he got killed?"

"Yes." Dan picks up a paper bag and dumps out a new set of points.

"Do you know why he had the accident?"

"There've been a lot of theories, Joel."

"Mrs. Hudson says he was angry about someone. Not her, someone else."

Dan rocks back on his heels. "That's interesting," he says, "now that I think about it. You see, I heard a girl crying and then saw him come out of a clump of trees and head for his car. I figured he'd been with Marla, they'd had a fight, and he was drunk. I always felt bad that I didn't stop him. Not that he'd have listened to me anyway."

"So who was crying then?"

"I don't know." Dan adjusts the new points on the motor. "Pass me the wrench again, will you?"

Joel's driving the Tercel, but that doesn't diminish his pleasure as he heads toward the Hiller house. He's thinking how delighted Mrs. Hudson's going to be when he shows up so bright and early—she never sleeps in, she hates wasting one minute of the day—and how interested she'll be in the information he's gotten from Dan. This pleasure takes something of a beating when he sees the blue New Yorker parked in front of the house, and he wonders sourly how long a real estate agent is supposed to hang around after making a sale.

He parks next to Mrs. Hudson's Honda and knocks on the front door since the doorbell hasn't been installed yet. When no one answers, he opens the door and is assaulted by the smell of wood shavings and freshly applied paint. Bright morning light pours through the uncurtained front windows and illuminates thousands of dust motes hanging in the air.

"Mrs. Hudson?" he calls out. "Marla?"

There's no answer, and he steps inside, skirting around a ladder and several cans of paint. He walks through the downstairs and sees two styrofoam mugs half filled with coffee sitting on a kitchen counter. Most of the kitchen isn't functional yet. The cooktop, the oven and dishwasher haven't been hooked up, but Mrs. Hudson isn't like Barbara, who had headaches the whole time the Breymanns renovated their kitchen. She either eats out or makes meals in a microwave and uses paper plates. He stands at the bottom of the stairs to the turret and calls up, "Hello? Hello!"

His voice reverberates in the silence, and he turns back toward the front door. From this perspective, he sees for the first time how dramatically Marla has changed the Hiller house. The staircase has been moved, the wall between the living room and music room taken down, the fireplace rebuilt, and an antique wooden mantel installed in place of the old, discolored brick. The house was already spacious, but Marla's made it seem even more so by painting the walls off-white, replacing the tall, narrow windows with larger ones that let in more light, and sanding the darkened floors down to a lighter finish. Golden oak, that's what Marla calls the stain.

Joel steps outside and walks around the house to the back, but no one's there either. He hears crickets singing, birds calling overhead, the hum of the river. Maybe that's where she is, enjoying the music made by the water. He follows the path that he's used when bringing stones down to the river in the wheelbarrow. It twists and turns, avoiding small rises and thick clumps of bush, and he has to watch his sneakered steps because of fallen branches and jutting stones. The air is cooler under the trees, and he can catch glimpses of the river glittering in the sunlight through the foliage as he heads downhill. Just before he reaches the break in the trees at the river's bank, he hears a sound over the gurgle and rush of water. The sound—the high pitch of a woman's half-laugh, half-scream—stops him in midstride.

For a moment Joel stands still, and then the sound comes again. He walks forward cautiously until he reaches a large oak. Slowly, he looks around its trunk toward the river and feels his heart give a violent thump, his scrotum grow tense. A naked Marla and Tony are in the river, the water swirling around their thighs. Tony splashes water at Marla, and she makes the sound Joel's been hearing. Then she leans over and splashes back. Her hair is wet and gleaming, her shoulders white, her buttocks full and heavy, a reverse heart. She twists and he sees her breasts, large, pale, their tips dark and pointed. When she tries to run from Tony, stumbling and laughing, they bounce from side to side.

Joel is caught between two opposing and urgent desires. The first is to stay, watch, savor, learn, and possess her just by knowing everything there is to know—what she looks like naked, how she acts when she makes love, what her hands will do, what her body will do, the expression on her face when she comes. The other desire, equally violent, equally urgent, is to run as hard and fast as he can, because there's a part of him that doesn't want to know, that hates Tony, that can't bear to see her entered by another man, that hates himself for wanting to watch. And it's this part—the shamed, guilty Joel—that finally makes him turn and run up the hilly path, stumbling over roots and stones, falling once and scraping the palms of his hands, his breath raw and painful in his lungs. He has to hold his arms in front of his face to ward off the branches whipping past him, because he can barely see. There are images blocking his sight—white water rushing over stones, Tony's thick, ruddy erection, droplets glistening in the dark triangle between her legs, his hand outstretched, her foot rising, a bent knee, a smiling mouth. But no matter how hard Joel's feet pound the earth, no matter how hard he throws himself forward with the wind in his eyes, the image doesn't disappear. It seems to harden on his retina as if seared on the flesh, locked forever in his mind's eye.

PART III

SUMMER

Chapter
1

I ENTER JUNE WITH BRUISES ON MY SPIRIT, HOPING THAT THE beginning of summer—the heat of the sun and the warm breezes—would heal me, but it doesn't, even though we have extraordinary weather, one beautiful day following another. I sense that the blue sky with its unraveled skein of clouds is like the false fronts of old western towns that made buildings seem grander than they were. If I could see behind this facade, I think I'd find something less pleasant and ominous, as if thunderclouds were building to the west and the air was unstable and electric. But my fear is only an undertone, an uneasy humming beneath the steady pace of work, home, and friends. Dan and I dig out an old cedar hedge from the back of our property and plant oaks in its place, an optimistic act that is equaled by our purchase of a new mattress for our queen-size bed. I think of these acts as statements of faith. We go on. We continue. We endure. We celebrate our twenty-second wedding anniversary on June 5 by eating at Au Gavotte, an expensive French restaurant in Laurel Grove. Dan wanted to do something fancier, like take a trip to England, but I'm hesitant to leave Joel.

My bruises are from Joel, from what has happened to him

and the way he's changed. He's grown enormously in the last few months, and the final remnants of boy are being quickly absorbed into the man. His shoulders have thickened, the softness at his jawline is gone, and his face is all hard angles and planes. He looks less like Dan than he used to. His features are sharper, and his eyes less candid. One day when I was leaving the library, I had the shocking experience of not recognizing him. Two boys in jeans and T-shirts were walking down the street toward me. I recognized Andy right away, but not the blond boy next to him until they drew closer. It was his walk, I realized. He'd developed that swagger of the hips, that young male saunter, an oiled motion composed of thickening bone, heavier muscle, and testosterone.

I accept this growth into physical manhood with some equanimity, because it's happening at its natural and preordained pace. What I can't accept with any calm is the way Caroline's disappearance has wrenched Joel out of his childhood and thrown him into an adult world without adequate preparation. I think how it must feel for him to have Reg, who was his Little League coach, turn into his interrogator. I imagine how difficult it must be when he sees people he's known, trusted, and felt safe with—teachers, friends, neighbors—look at him with suspicion. He's had to learn to watch his back, to curtail what he might say. I've noticed that he's lost that direct gaze he once had, and that open, guileless curiosity that could turn so easily into delight. Even his dreams have lost their innocence. I want to cry when I remember his nightmare of drowning in Caroline's blood.

So I'm not surprised that the new Joel is difficult and moody. He spends hours in his room or off somewhere with his friends. The rest of the house, including Dan and me, is merely a runway that he lands on and takes off from as quickly as possible. When he's with us for those brief periods, I discover that what I miss most are his sweetness and sense of humor. He's acquired an expression of sullen resentment that turns his face into an unpleasant mask of hooded eyes and downturned mouth. I notice he rarely smiles anymore.

This new Joel has also dropped all his sports, thrown away his trading cards, put his equipment in the garage, and even pulled down his sports posters. I was shocked when I saw the bare walls but said lightly, "I'm going to miss The Great One."

"That was kid stuff," Joel said.

"What are you going to put in his place?"

He shrugged. Sometimes it's difficult to hold conversations with the new Joel. When he's in one of his moods, his vocabulary is reduced to shrugs and words like *no, maybe, yeah,* and *'bye.*

"I thought you liked hockey and swimming and baseball," I persisted.

"I wasn't any good." Joel gave me an angry get-off-my-case look and said defiantly, "Okay?"

This new Joel is dating a girl I don't know and he doesn't bring home. She comes from a town on the other side of Banting and works at a hairdresser's. I have uncomfortable suspicions: that she dropped out of high school, that she's a bad influence, that he's only going out with her for sex.

"What's Katrina like?" I ask one rare evening when he's having dinner with us.

"She's okay."

"Just okay?" I say with some surprise.

"Yeah."

"Is she funny, nice, clever, whimsical, thoughtful—?" I run out of adjectives and glance at Dan, who shakes his head at me. I recognize a warning to leave Joel alone, but I ignore it. "What kind of personality does she have?"

Joel doesn't answer but takes another mouthful of mashed potatoes. That's one thing, his appetite hasn't changed.

"Would I like her?" I ask brightly.

Joel looked up from his dinner. "Mom, *you* don't have to like her."

This has the desired effect. It shuts me up immediately, and I don't ask him about Katrina anymore. Dan tells me

I've got to learn to let go, that Joel was bound to grow up someday and his sex life isn't any of my business.

"I think he doesn't bring this Katrina around because he's ashamed of her."

"That may be," Dan says, "but you can't do anything about it."

"And what about pregnancy?" I ask. "What about AIDS?"

"He knows all about birth control and safe sex."

"Should we buy him a supply of condoms?"

"You're going to have to trust him," Dan says. "You can't sit next to him when he's on a date and tell him what to do."

"Would you talk to him?"

Dan sighs. "If my father had tried to talk to me about sex at seventeen, I'd have run in the other direction."

"Please."

"Barbara, you've got to give him space."

Space—a parent's final frontier. That place where you step back, close your eyes, and pray. I talk to my friends about Joel. Frances sighs in commiseration, and Virginia tells me how Sarah hates even to tell her where she's going when she's out. Daphne says, "He's settled down in school, hasn't he?"

"Well, I think so. I haven't heard from Phil lately."

"So what are you worrying about?"

"Who is she? Is she a bad influence? I don't know anything, that's the problem."

"My philosophy is, you bring up your kids as best you can, you set a good example, you instill values, and then you let them go."

"I guess it's hard for me to accept that he's probably having a sexual relationship."

"He's seething with hormones. Don't you remember what it was like?"

"I do," I say, "that's the problem."

I don't discuss my anxieties with Marla. We talk about her renovations, my job, people in Cassandra, the past, her books, but not Joel. Why exactly I don't know, except that I'm uncomfortable at the thought. I wonder if I don't want to share confidences about children, because I think Marla is hiding something about her daughter. Perhaps I feel Joel's sex life is none of her business. What I know for certain is that my friendship with Marla is evolving, awkwardly. It isn't what it was when we were teenagers and Marla was my other half, the only person who fully understood me. Now Dan is my other half, and no one can ever fully understand me, not even myself. At seventeen I thought I had to find out who I was. I refused to accept my parents' definition—a nice girl—and explored my boundaries by pushing hard to see if they'd push back. My boundaries proved to be flexible but only to a point. I tried smoking for a while but didn't really like cigarettes. I thought about becoming a lawyer or astrophysicist but ended up being a librarian, one of my mother's suggestions. I dated different kinds of boys but married a man much like my father, steady, loyal and reliable. I've turned out to be a good wife, mother, and friend, but I've learned that, even within that framework, I am capable of surprising myself, making unexpected and occasionally alarming choices. At forty-three, I accept this mystery of self. Sometimes I even enjoy it.

My friends are mirrors, reflecting back facets of myself. Daphne allows me to be earthy, Frances intellectual, Virginia analytical. This sounds as if I've made my choice of friends in some methodical, cold-hearted way, but that isn't the case at all. I didn't seek out my friends. Our initial meetings were accidental, our liking based on unexpected recognition. A close friendship between two women is like a triangle. One line represents a mutual delight in each other's uniqueness. The second line represents the pleasure of common sympathies and understandings. And the third, the base, is the ability to provide comfort. If I have a problem, I can talk to Daphne, Frances, or Virginia and feel better, calmer, consoled.

I'm still attracted to Marla, to her vivacity and unusual perspectives, and I take pleasure in the past we share, but she no longer comforts me. She has a self-absorption that undercuts any sympathy she expresses, and when I look back in time, I wonder if she was always so self-centered, so intent on her own needs, so bent on her own agenda. I think she was, but the difference is that when I was seventeen, I found those needs and agenda exciting. She was hungry for excess and forbidden experiences, and I got a vicarious thrill from her drinking, her spending, the term paper she didn't write, what insolent thing she said to the principal, the smoking on school grounds, how far she'd let Christian go. Listening to her was almost as good as doing it myself. Today I'm not interested in rebellion, but I sense that Marla still lives on an edge. I don't know what that edge is, but I'm wary of being drawn close to it.

So we call each other a couple of times a week, and I see her occasionally. She travels to New York frequently—she goes for the theater and concerts—and is very busy with her house. Rumors of her extravagance are keeping Cassandra agog. I hear from Mona that she has dozens of unbelievably expensive oriental carpets, from Daphne that she's importing tile from Italy for the pool, and from Edgar that she's putting gold fixtures in the bathroom in the turret. I'm made so curious by this gossip that I visit on my day off and get the grand tour.

"So," Marla says, "what do you think?"

"It's going to be beautiful," I say. There are three oriental carpets in rolls in the living room and brass fixtures in the bathroom. The pool, as far as I can figure out, is being installed by a company in Syracuse with American tile manufactured in Illinois. This doesn't mean Marla hasn't spent a fortune. She's replaced the heating, plumbing, and electrical systems, pulled down walls in some places and put up others elsewhere, plastered, painted, sanded, and polished. Her kitchen in cream and blue has the latest appliances, she's installed a sauna and Jacuzzi in one bathroom, and the planned landscaping will change the grounds near the house completely.

"Joel worked over there," Marla says. We're standing at the back of the house and she points to an area of dirt near the trees.

"I hope he's been helpful."

"He's been great. He removed every stone and carted them away. I'm putting him to work on the path to the river now. The trees need cutting back, and there's a lot of overgrown brush. Anyway, I thought I was going to put in a garden in that area where the stones were, but now I think I'm going to do a cupola. That spot has an especially pretty view of the hills toward town."

"A cupola," I say as we sit in the chaise lounges and sip at lemonade. "You'll be the talk of the town."

"I already am," Marla says. "Tony says a lot of people think I'm crazy."

I look up to the turret, where Marla has replaced the old, small windows with floor-to-ceiling panes of glass. From the outside they appear to be mirrors, reflecting back the blue sky and the foliage of the trees. From the inside they create an illusion of nonexistence, as if there were nothing between the bedroom and the outdoors. During my tour, I exclaimed over the view, but I was secretly thinking what hard work it was going to be to keep those windows clean.

"Cassandra's conservative," I say. "We're not used to celebrities."

"Do you think I'm a celebrity?"

"You were on *Oprah.*"

"So are wife beaters, child molesters, and murderers."

"You know what I mean," I say.

"It's fleeting," Marla says. "My last two books didn't do well, and I haven't been asked to do a talk show in a year."

I make polite murmuring sounds as if I don't agree, but the quality of her writing has changed. As a loyal reader, I bought my own personal copies (an extravagance for a librarian) and recommended her titles to readers at the library. But even I noticed that her latest novels didn't have the smooth flow and depth of her earlier works. The narratives wandered as if she'd lost interest in her stories, and the endings were unsatisfactory as if she herself didn't believe in them.

"I lost my touch," Marla says, "so I knew it was time for a change."

I want to ask whether Didi had anything to do with Marla losing her touch, but I don't dare. Instead I say, "I'm just afraid you'll get bored here. Nothing much happens in Cassandra."

Marla gives me a surprised look. "How can you say that? A girl disappears, half the town is under suspicion, and somebody is malevolent enough to spray obscenities on lockers."

"Ordinarily, nothing happens."

"I must hear about a different side of Cassandra than you do."

"I'm not naive. I know there's stuff going on."

"But you've created this safe enclave," Marla says. "Everything can be in turmoil, but you're protected by your husband and your friends. Sort of a charmed circle."

But the drawl she puts on the word "charmed" sets my teeth on edge. "You make that sound dull," I say.

"Don't get me wrong. I envy you." Her honesty pleases me, but then she says, "But not always. I need change."

"I don't," I say with a vehemence that surprises me.

"Bobbie," she says, "it makes you grow."

I shake my head, thinking I've grown enough, thank you very much. But even as I think this, I realize I'm being overtaken by change whether I like it or not. I can dig in my heels, I can lower my head so I don't see what's coming, I can resist with all my might, but that part of the world I once controlled—Joel, my role as mother—has started to spin away from me, and I don't know where it's headed.

Marla must sense my discomfort, because she changes the subject. In the past, we could say anything to one another, speak on any topic, explore any idea no matter how repugnant. Now we tiptoe carefully around sensitivities, inadvertently pushing each other to a point of uneasiness and quickly shifting to another, safer, conversational tack.

"I met Frances's son, Ben," she says.

"Oh?"

"He came to interview me for the school newspaper, but what he really wanted to know was how he could become a writer."

"He writes poetry, I think."

"He's writing a novel now."

"Good heavens."

"About the death of a girl and its effect on a sensitive young hero."

"That sounds like a healthy form of catharsis."

"That's what I told him," Marla says, "although not exactly in those words. I told him I was going to write a book about the death of a boy and its effect on a sensitive young girl. I said I should have written the book right after it happened instead of letting it fester inside. We talked about sadness and grief, and he was very insightful. I don't remember any boys like that when I was seventeen. Do you?"

"There was Wayne Crozier. He wrote poetry for the school newspaper."

"Sonnets," Marla says, "and they were bad."

"Wayne lives in Delaware," I say. "I think he repairs refrigerators and air conditioners."

"Do you remember Christian almost flunking English?"

"He liked your poetry."

Marla gives her rich laugh. "Of course he did. It was about him."

"Imagine if you'd married him," I say.

"Imagine," she echoes.

When Marla and I talk about the past, I have the sensation that I'm falling backward into a soft, luxurious chair. No matter how I sit, I'm never cramped or pinched. Rather, the chair adapts its shape to fit me, fluidly changing as the conversation shifts and meanders. The sensation becomes even more pleasurable when we speculate on what might have been. That brings me back to Marla's bedroom at 68 Willow, and those wonderful dark nights of gossip and giggling when we talked about anything and everything.

"I don't think the marriage would've lasted," I say.

"Probably not," Marla says.

"I can't see Christian diapering babies."

"He seemed like James Dean, didn't he? Wild, rebellious,

225

and untamable. We projected all kinds of fantasies onto him."

"I suppose we did," I say.

"When we were with Christian, we felt like we transcended Cassandra and our parents and our school and all our miserable, insignificant problems. On the other hand, he was also impatient, aggressive, and short-tempered. Lousy husband material." She turns to look at me. "Bobbie, where were you when he left that night?"

"Me?" I try to remember. "Drinking by the fire?"

"No, Brian said you'd gone to pee in the woods."

"I don't remember." The chair no longer fits me properly. Rather, it envelops me, pulling me down into its depths. I begin to feel tired and sleepy, my eyelids grow heavy and weighted. I think of all the errands I ran in the morning and wonder why I call it "my day off."

"He didn't leave right after our fight," Marla says. "That's the point. He hung around."

I close my eyes, lean my head against the back of the chaise lounge, and turn my face upward to the sun. My eyelids grow warm as they reduce the sun to smooth gold disks. "Mmm, that feels good," I say.

"I've found out that he was with someone before he left. A girl."

"Who?"

"I don't know. You didn't see him with anyone?"

"I would have told you."

Marla sighs. "Why is the truth so elusive?"

"I don't know," I say, and squeeze my eyes tight, causing the gold disks to fracture along black, jagged lines.

I finish my day off with a visit to Molly Deacon. Right after Caroline disappeared, I made an attempt to stop by for a chat at least a couple of times a week, but in the past month, the number of my visits has tapered off. It isn't that I don't want to see Molly, it's just that I seem to have been so busy at work preparing for the June board meeting and too busy at home with spring cleaning and gardening. On the way back from Marla's, I pick up a pan of lemon squares that I baked the night before and arrive at the Deacons'.

"What a treat," Molly says when she opens the front door. "You make the best lemon squares in Cassandra."

"Thank you," I say. "The trick is fresh lemons."

"Come on in."

A rich, chocolate aroma fills the house. "It smells good in here," I say.

"That's Sarah. She's making cookies."

"Sarah?"

"Sarah Silver, Virginia's girl. She comes after school and helps me."

I remember Virginia's concerns about Sarah's visits to the Deacons'. "Every day?" I ask.

Molly nods. "I wouldn't know what to do without her. Here, let me find you a seat."

The Deacons' living room has piles of paper on every surface. "Letters I've received. Letters I've sent." Molly reels off the litany as she removes several piles from the couch. "Extra posters. The scrapbook." The Deacons live in a house similar to ours, a bungalow with an L-shaped living room and dining room, and three bedrooms and a bath down a hallway. But their taste is different. While we lean toward comfortable modern, they like the colonial style: braided carpets, furniture made of maple, and upholstery in rust, green, orange, and gold plaid. Molly has an étagère that holds her collection of Royal Worcester figurines, and a picture of a mountainside in fall foliage hangs over the mantelpiece.

"What scrapbook?" I ask as I sit on the couch and put the pan of squares on the coffee table.

"For Caroline when she comes back."

"Oh."

Molly sits next to me and opens the scrapbook between us so I can see and she can explain. It begins with Caroline's high school photo—big blue eyes, a tumble of red curls, that dazzling smile—and continues with clippings of newspaper articles, letters to the editor, condolence cards, the church announcement of the candlelight vigil, handbills for different bake sales, the bill from the company that printed the posters, and a math test—marked 100%—handed back after Caroline's disappearance. Every item has been carefully placed and glued down, and every page enclosed in a plastic cover. Neatly written tags indicate dates.

"The newswires carried the story all the way to Albany," Molly says.

"I didn't know that."

"We'd have liked more exposure out of state, and we did get some in Pennsylvania, but so far that's it. We've also been trying to get on a talk show—*Oprah, Geraldo,* one of those—but we haven't had any luck. They've already done missing-kid shows this spring."

Molly's fingers trace a headline, CASSANDRA CHEERLEADER DISAPPEARS, and I remember how she once kept her nails so beautifully manicured. As one of the best real estate agents in Cassandra, Molly dressed for success. She had elegant suits and pretty jewelry, dyed the gray in her dark hair, and never appeared without makeup and lipstick. That Molly is gone, leaving behind a pale facsimile with white roots, bangs that won't stay out of her eyes, ragged fingernails, and a painful thinness that isn't hidden by her baggy, blue sweatsuit. But the worst is her facade. Molly smiles brightly and chatters with great sprightliness, but the wrinkles cut deep at her nose and mouth, and her eyes are so sad I can barely look into them. I think it would take only the slightest blow to break her into little pieces.

"Caroline will love the scrapbook," I say.

Molly looks gratified. "Well, that's what I think, but Brian says it's morbid. He says nobody would want to know about this stuff. And I tell him he's wrong. Take obituaries, for example."

"Obituaries?"

"Isn't it a real shame that you never get to read your own obituary and all the nice things people have to say about you? I'd rather know when I was alive, wouldn't you?"

"I never thought about it."

"Of course, I'm talking about people with terminal illnesses, not someone who dies suddenly. Oh, good, here comes Sarah."

Sarah enters carrying a tray with a coffeepot, cups, and a plate of chocolate chip cookies. "Hi," she says.

"Hi, Sarah. Those cookies look wonderful."

"Thank you."

I may be wrong, but I think Sarah's wearing more jewelry than she was the last time I saw her. I wouldn't have thought it possible to punch more holes in her ears, but little colored gemstones wink at me from the tops of her ears where they curve. She's also added a ruby stud to the diamond in her left nostril. But her clothing and hair styles haven't changed. Even though it's summer, she's wearing a black T-shirt with long sleeves, black jeans, and black shoes. And her hair stands up in black clumps.

"Sarah's like my right hand," Molly says.

Sarah gives me a proud smile as she kneels beside the coffee table. "Cream and sugar?"

"Yes, please."

"My own girls are always off somewhere with their friends," Molly says. I make sympathetic sounds, but I'm not surprised. I only have to look at Molly and her piles of papers to see that Tracy and Missy haven't just lost a sister. I wonder if Molly's obsession with Caroline also affects Brian in the same way when she adds, "And Brian is putting in all kinds of hours at the store. Of course, spring is a big season for him what with all the gardening, painting, and repairing people want to do. I'd have been overwhelmed if it weren't for Sarah. She's types all my letters and is real good on the computer. I haven't figured the program out yet. What is it?"

"WordPerfect," Sarah says. "We use it at school."

"And she goes shopping for me, because I don't want to leave the phone. You know we're getting about ten calls a day from the posters. They're all over the country now. Not that we've had a meaningful call, but you can't let one go, can you?"

I shake my head and nibble at a cookie.

"And Sarah's been helping me make dinner, too."

"Macaroni and cheese," Sarah says. "That's my specialty."

"Well, any time you want to come to my house," I say, and we laugh.

"And yesterday, we put Caroline's winter clothes away and took out her summer things. That was a job, wasn't it?"

Sarah begins, "Three loads of laundry—"

"I like to have everything clean."

"And six skirts and ten blouses to iron. I counted."

"I also hemmed her prom dress," Molly says. "The dance is this weekend."

I know that Caroline has been chosen to be in the court of the senior prom queen, which is not only an unusual honor for a junior girl but also means she's a shoo-in for queen the following year. "You're all set," I say, but my smile feels shaky.

"Is Joel going?"

"No."

"Well, it's not his senior year. That's the prom that counts. I'll never forget mine. I had such a beautiful dress, a pale pink organdy with a satin sash. And the boy I went with gave me a corsage of rosebuds and baby's breath."

"Did you go to your senior prom?" Sarah asks me.

"She went with Brian," Molly says.

Sarah's eyes grow big. "Really?"

"We were just friends," I say, and remember how unhappy I'd been. I'd told Brian I didn't want to be boyfriend and girlfriend anymore, and had been a little bit annoyed when he wasn't more devastated by the news. Still, we decided that, since neither of us had another date to the prom, we'd go together. But prom night turned out to be a horrible sham, despite getting my hair done in Laurel Grove, Brian's corsage, and the dress my mother had made for me. I hated being there, dancing with him, smiling at other people, and having to act like it was a celebration and it didn't matter that Marla wasn't there and Christian was dead.

"And Sarah's helping with the letter writing. I'm contacting Albany and Washington, trying to keep the momentum going."

"But Reg is—"

Molly shakes her head. "Reg is a small-town police officer with no experience in something like this."

"Hasn't he brought in the state police and the FBI?"

Molly leans forward. "They're giving up."

This isn't what I've heard. Just two days ago, Daphne told me that Reg and the two men with him were spending so much time on Caroline that there hadn't been a speeding ticket in two months. "But, Molly," I say, "I hear Reg is working night and day."

"He's spinning his wheels over the boys in town, when the fact is she was taken by someone driving through."

"Is there any evidence that—?"

"I just know it, Barbara. Right here." Molly presses a thin hand to her chest. "And she's probably far from Cassandra by now. A psychic in Syracuse told me she sees palm trees."

"Florida?" I ask.

"Or southern California," Sarah says. "Right?"

Molly nods. "More coffee, Barbara?"

"No, thank you. I've got to get home soon."

"Of course, the real point is," Molly says, "that people are forgetting already."

"They're not," I say. "I know they're not."

"You can't imagine the things people say to me." In imitation, her voice is shrill and nasal. " 'You've got to put this behind you. You've got to get on with your life.' As if I could just pick up the pieces and act like nothing's happened."

I'm stung because I've said these things, although not to Molly. "I think people are frightened," I say slowly, "and maybe they can't face it."

"Well, that doesn't help me, does it?" Molly's face is suffused with anger, her jaw set, the corners of her mouth inverted. "It doesn't help when people turn away like that and treat me like I'm crazy, because I don't think she's dead. Well, nobody can say she's dead, Barbara. Nobody!"

I'm shaken by this, but Sarah is transformed. She hasn't taken her eyes off Molly, and every emotion of Molly's—frustration, outrage, fury—is duplicated across her face.

"People mean well," I say lamely, and look down at a page of the opened scrapbook that holds three articles about Caroline from different newspapers.

"They may mean well," Molly says bitterly, "but they're deliberately putting her aside as if she didn't count, as if seventeen years of living didn't mean anything, as if she passed through this town, and it's like nobody noticed."

Each article is illustrated with the same high school photo of Caroline so that there are three sets of eyes, three tumbles of hair, three brilliant, dazzling smiles. Tears fill my eyes, and those smiles, those little scallops of black dots on white newsprint, begin to blur, slide, and merge as if all the losses—Caroline, Christian, my parents, my miscarried babies, Joel's growing up—have come together into one.

Chapter
2

ON THE MORNING AFTER HER BEDROOM FURNITURE HAS COME out of storage and been put into the turret room, Marla wakes up and knows for certain she was right to buy the Hiller house. She realizes that some people think she's crazy—Bobbie, for one, and Bobbie's friends. She's seen Virginia, Frances, and Daphne at various times, and although they always ask politely after the renovations, Marla believes she can hear their thoughts, which are disapproving and unflattering. They think she's recklessly wasting her money and trying to impress the town. They think she'll resurrect the Hiller mansion only to discover she doesn't belong in Cassandra in the first place. Marla's sensitive to these thoughts in different ways. Virginia's feel like dark, delicate threads, winding their way through her words. Frances emits a chill, even on a warm day and despite her smiles. And Daphne's thoughts are unbearably loud and shrill, no matter how low her voice. The last time Marla met Daphne—they exchanged pleasantries in front of the bank —she wanted to put her hands over her ears.

Marla hasn't admitted to anyone, not even Bobbie, that there have been times during the renovations when she's hesitated, not because of money or what Cassandra might think, but because the house might not turn out to be what she craves after all. After having grown up in 68 Willow with its cramped rooms and stifling atmosphere, Marla needs a house in which she can breathe. In the Malibu house, she had a sense that the walls were barely there, that she was enclosed and yet free since almost nothing stood between her and the ocean. When she thought about moving to Cassandra, she remembered the Hiller house with its big rooms, high ceilings, and vistas in every direction. Then, when she saw it again, she imagined it with fewer interior walls, more open spaces, and much bigger windows. The architect tried to dissuade her.

"This isn't California," he said. "It's colder here. You put in windows that big and you're going to have a heat problem."

"What about those new thermal windows?"

"In the size you're talking about? It'll cost you a fortune."

"Do it," she said.

Now, as she lies in bed, the pleasure of being right washes over her. The turret faces southeast, and the morning sun fights its way through the trees to bring the outside into the inside. The rays create a kaleidoscope of light and shade that plays on the cream-colored walls, the pale gray carpet, and the scarlet spread of her king-size bed that has her monogram in gray in the center. When the wind blows, as it does this morning, the patterns of leaves and branches don't hold still but form, shiver, break, and re-create themselves over and over again.

The trees have been trimmed back so that the branches don't reach the walls anymore and make hissing sounds on the brick and glass, but she can hear the creaking of bark and the rapid whispering of the leaves through the open casement windows. Of all the rooms in the house, Marla loves this one the most for its airiness and serenity. She's even extended it, tearing down the inner wall so that the bedroom flows into a sitting room that's also her office. Again, she's replaced wall with glass so she can sit at her desk and look through the tops of the trees and catch glimpses of the river below. The view of foliage, river, and sky is constantly in flux, leaves shifting and silvery water tumbling against a backdrop of blue and shifting white clouds.

The wind blows a branch back and forth, and a band of sunshine sweeps across the bed. "Christ," Tony says with a groan, turning over and putting his hand over his eyes. "You need some shades in here or something."

"I like it this way."

"What time is it?"

"Time to get up."

Tony leans up on one elbow and peers at the clock on the night table beside Marla. "It's not even seven yet."

"Rise and shine."

Tony groans again but doesn't argue. Marla knows he doesn't dare. Their relationship has thinned to a filament and even Tony, thick and obtuse, recognizes that it's close to breaking. Not, she thinks, that it ever had much substance other than physical pleasure. They had no common intellectual ground or any strong emotional links. She thought it would last longer than three months but, in Tony's case, familiarity bred contempt and intimacy aversion. It didn't take her long to realize that Tony's wife had kicked him out because he was seeing other women, and that Gale Real Estate kept him on not because he was a good agent but because the Italian community in Cassandra and Laurel Grove was loyal.

Marla doesn't really care about his wife or business, but now she suspects he's trying to screw her over. She knows how he thinks. The real estate business hasn't been so hot this spring, his wife—the bitch—is complaining that the support money isn't enough, and shit, the lady's swimming in it, isn't she? So he's been pushing relatives on Marla for her renovations: Mario the carpenter, Guido who does plaster, Sylvio, the best tile man in central New York, and Joe, the driveway expert. At first, she thought it was family loyalty, and she agreed to hire Sylvio before catching on to the fact that Tony was raking a percentage off the top of the contract. She figured that out when she refused Guido's services and Tony pushed a little too hard.

Marla wishes she could preserve sexual experiences the

way you do fruit and vegetables, and imagines a pantry lined with jars, labeled with names, dates and ratings. *Sean, April 1972, oral sex, good. David, June 1980, missionary position, fair.* Then, when she felt needy, she could dip into a past experience instead of having either to go without or hope she'll cross paths with an appropriate man. The problem is "appropriate." When you're wealthy and famous, how do you find a man who isn't in love with your money or prefers to bask in your success rather than create his own? During her last trip to New York, Marla met a man at a dinner hosted by her agent—Colin McIntyre, an investment banker, in his fifties, divorced and well-to-do. He's interested, he's even written her a short note after she returned to Cassandra, asking her to call him the next time she's in the city and they'll lunch. His stationery is impeccable, pale gray with black embossed letters.

But Marla's not sure. Although Colin talked intelligently about movies, books, and art, he's slender, and his hands are small. She glances over at Tony, who's lying on his back, his forearm over his eyes. She likes her men bigger, heavier, more muscular. She puts her hand on Tony's chest where the dark, curly hair is the thickest. Then she slides her hand down his abdomen to his erection.

"What're you complaining about?" she asks. "You're up."

"I gotta pee."

"So pee."

He lowers his forearm. "I have a biorhythm, you know. I'm a night person, not a morning person. It isn't as good for me in the morning."

"Close your eyes," she says. "Make believe it's still night."

"Jesus," he says, but he obediently gets out of bed and walks to the bathroom. As Marla watches him go, the muscles in his buttocks tightening and loosening, she thinks this will be the last time. *Tony, June 1990, every which way, great.*

Joel: white, gold, blue with a flush of pink beneath his cheeks. When I first came to Cassandra, he was still living in the innocent realm of the boy. Even though he was tall and his voice had deepened, he had a child's smoothness of skin and a childlike purity at his jawline and the nape of his neck. What attracted me to him most was his lack of shadow. His eyes were so clear that when the sun slanted across them, I was reminded of the blueness of water in the tropics and shallow lagoons where you could see every detail of the bottom. It was as if nothing more complex had ever crossed his mind than what cereal to have for breakfast or which friend he'd play with that day.

Had Christian ever been like that? I don't remember him in grade school or junior high, he was just another boy. But I can't imagine him without the shadow, that darkness of spirit that lay so heavily on him. He fought it hard, he craved release, I can see that from a distance of so many years. He drank, drove fast, played sports violently, and when it came to me, he wanted everything, fast.

I used to think that this violent, barely held in aggression was a natural part of manhood. I've seen it expressed in different ways: Sean's ambition, David's coldness, my father's anger. But I see that some men don't have it—Dan Breymann, for example. And I think Joel wouldn't have developed it, except that Caroline's disappearance has changed him profoundly. The shadow has crept into his glance; it's less open, shaded, darker. He doesn't look at me directly anymore, and I feel his sexuality in a way I didn't before. He tells me he's going out with a girl, but I sense he doesn't like her. The preshadow Joel wouldn't have dated her in the first place, but I think the new Joel—like Christian—seeks escape.

Ben Phillips has asked Marla if she would read the first chapter of his novel, and she's said yes although she usually refuses to read the work of beginning writers. During the year and a half between the selling of her first novel and its publication, Marla made extra money teaching a writing course for adults at a local high school and critiquing their manuscripts. But after the book went on the best-seller list, she didn't need the money.

She finds as she reads Ben's work that she's forgotten just how bad new writers can be. The dialogue is stilted, the transitions between scenes awkward, and the descriptions often banal. Ben has set the novel in New York City and made his hero a young poet living in poverty in SoHo. The girl he loves is a dancer with the New York City Ballet, tall and ethereal. In the opening, the young poet has a fight with his mother (there doesn't appear to be a father), leaves his home in Iowa, travels to the city, finds a garret, and meets the heroine on a windswept corner near an art gallery. Very little of it rings true, especially the setting—has Ben ever been to New York City?—and the girl, who is impossibly beautiful and falls for the hero with breathtaking speed. At the end of the chapter, the hero and heroine go to bed together in the hero's half-furnished garrett where the floors are dirty and the bed has no sheets. The sex scene is written as a fade-out, movie style, with the hero and heroine falling to the stained mattress in an obliterating embrace.

Still, there are a few sections that show promise. The fight between the hero and his mother has moments that sound authentic, and the yearning of the poet for fame and love, although overwritten, is heartfelt. Marla also finds the occasional turn of phrase that is just right, a metaphor that catches an emotion perfectly, or a notion of such intimacy and grace—"As Carola walks away, Jason felt himself caught in the abrupt turn of her ankle"—that Marla gets that sense of being uplifted that good writing always gives her.

Reading this first chapter brings Marla back to those days when she began writing and hadn't any idea what she was doing. She'd been alone then except for Didi, who was three years old. Sean was supposed to pay child support, but he was an unemployed actor and an occasional waiter, so the money he sent was infrequent. Marla got a job paying medical claims for Aetna Life Insurance and began a novel at night after Didi was asleep. She worked on an old Smith-Corona typewriter set up on the kitchen table with a broken *h* key, which meant she either had to avoid words with *h* or fill in the missing letters by hand. She wrote in fury and haste. Haste because she was in a hurry to see if she would be a successful novelist, and fury because she'd been cheated and betrayed, not only by Sean, who'd left her and immediately moved in with another woman, but by all those phony promises of the fifties that she'd swallowed lock, stock, and barrel despite the evidence of her parents' marriage. Promise #1: that marriage was forever. Promise #2: that her husband would be her lover, friend, and father all rolled into one. Promise #3: that good girls have happy endings. Her rage at being duped was so powerful that she typed in a white heat and finished her first draft in six months.

Luckily, she had an actress friend whose agent knew a literary agent in New York—Brian Lamm—who liked her novel but asked her for another draft before he'd send it to a publisher. The rest was publishing history: an extraordinarily big advance for a first novel, excellent reviews, and a quick leap and hop up the best-seller list to the number-one slot. Despite this success, Marla doesn't consider herself an exceptional writer. She believes she has good technical skills, but what made her career was being in the right place at the right time with the right story about a woman's coming of age in California. Like the surfers she watched at the windows of her Malibu house, she saw herself as cresting on that first wave of women writers who came into prominence in the late sixties and early seventies.

Success has made part of her very happy and not touched another part of her at all. She's lousy at picking men. But then she didn't have a good role model, did she? Her parents' marriage was a disaster, and she never learned the trick of marital harmony, only survival. Her mother taught her that you could only stand up to a man for so long and, after that, you did the dance of avoidance. You tiptoed, sidestepped, and ducked. You apologized, pleaded, and placated. Marla vowed she'd never humble herself the way her mother did, lying so flat on the ground as to be indistinguishable from the floor and carpet. Two failed marriages and numerous unhappy affairs later, she knows there has to be some middle ground between being stepped on and constantly battling for her integrity, but the trouble is she's never found it.

So she gave up trying to find happiness with men. Either it's too difficult or there's some trick to it she's never been able to learn. She'd thought Didi might be part of the answer to finding happiness, and she remembers Didi's birth, that incredible, painful moment when the baby slid out of her and established its independence with a lusty cry and a flailing of arms and legs. "Good work, Marla," the obstetrician said. "A beautiful girl." And she had a vision of small arms tight around her neck and soft curls against her cheek.

Marla puts down Ben's manuscript and lets the door in her mind open so that Didi doesn't have to slip in but can enter boldly as she entered life. She never was that cuddly, affectionate child of Marla's imagination but a banging, laughing, hollering, noisy presence. As a toddler, she tolerated hugs and kisses with impatience, wiggling to get out of Marla's embrace almost as soon as she entered it. As an older child she rarely sat quietly but was always on the move, a child who preferred the company of other children to Marla's. *Come,* Marla thinks, *come and let's remember the good times, the birthdays and Christmases, when we saw* Cats *in New York and you loved the music so much, the fun we had horseback riding in the Rockies, the trip to Paris when we discovered the bead store and spent several hours making necklaces.* Perhaps it's the calming effect of sunlight shimmering on the walls or the innocent swooping of swallows outside the window. Perhaps it's the passing of time that has blunted the sharp edges of her memory. Whatever the cause, this time Didi slips in silently and, instead of the fights and angry exchanges, Marla discovers she can remember the quietest time of all.

Like Christian, she died without a mark on her face. If I hadn't pulled the sheet down to see what they'd done to her, I might have been able to believe that life can slip away without trauma or pain. She looked more peaceful than she had been for a long time. And lovely. I'd been so angry and despairing for so long, I no longer knew she was pretty.

The police were very kind. One young policeman held my arm, because he was afraid I'd collapse or faint. He didn't know how the writer in me kept my back straight and my mind clear. I absorbed everything: the metal table, the chemical smell, the wash basins, the linoleum, which was dark brown with small cream-colored dots, the ovalish yellow stain on the sheet by her neck. It was the kind of stain that remains despite a hundred washings.

You don't have to look, they said, but I did. I saw the knife wounds in her chest. They weren't long but deep, and the skin was purplish at the cut edges. She'd been beaten, stabbed a dozen times, and left to bleed to death. A drug war, the police said. One wound was in her left breast at the edge of her nipple. I remember thinking: *she'll never be able to feed her babies now.* I trembled visibly, and the young policeman tried to comfort me. He knew about Didi, they had a file on her. "There wasn't anything you could've done, ma'am," he said. "There's no stopping some kids."

Marla's hand falters, the last word falls off the line, and she lowers her head so that her forehead rests on what's she written. And, for the first time in the year since Didi's death, she's finally able to cry.

"I like what you're saying here," Marla says, tapping the manuscript. "And I like your hero. He has a lot of character."

Ben leans forward slightly. They're having coffee at her kitchen table. "Do you think I can get it published?"

Marla doesn't laugh. Instead she says, "But I think you should consider a change of setting."

He sits back and frowns. "Why?"

Marla likes Ben's frown. He has Frances's build and her beauty—he's tall and slender with thick, dark hair and even

241

features—and the frown gives his brow a moody, Byronic splendor. He has other qualities she also finds pleasing. He's polite to the extreme. She smiled inwardly when they came into the kitchen, and he held out her own chair for her in her own kitchen. He's intelligent. He never answers questions right away but pauses slightly as if he's weighing his options and judging the heft of his words. And he startles easily. Marla likes to shock Ben so she can watch the quick turn of his head and the widening of his dark eyes. At those moments, he reminds her of a fine, high-strung animal, alert and wary.

"I think your story would have more power," she says, "if you put it in a high school setting. You know a lot more about high school than New York City."

"You mean, like here?"

"You can make up a town like Cassandra but give it another name."

He's silent for a moment. "Everyone will think it's about Caroline."

"Write what you know about. That's the best advice I can give you."

"But people will try to find themselves in the book."

Marla nods. "You want to know something funny? Most people don't actually recognize themselves if you do put them in. The truth is no one ever sees himself the way others do."

Ben frowns again, deeper this time, and his fine, arched eyebrows draw together. Marla thinks that girls must go crazy over him. "But if I set the story in a school and I write about what I know," he says slowly, "then, like, Mr. Potter, he's our principal, he'll guess he's the model for the principal of the school."

"Juggle everyone. Make the principal the girl's father. Make the girl's father a teacher. Make a teacher the police sergeant."

Ben stares at her for a second and then smiles. "Okay," he says, "I could do that."

"Has your mother read your book?" she asks.

Ben gives her that startled look. "No."

"She's the mother in it, isn't she?"

"Partly," he acknowledges.

"I liked the fight," Marla says. "It sounded just right."

He gives a uncomfortable shrug. "We fight sometimes."

Marla raises an eyebrow. "Really?" she drawls, and he smiles again. She leans forward. "Do you think a lot about Caroline?" she asks.

Now she's really shocked him. He quivers slightly and the pupils of his eyes enlarge. "Yes," he says.

"Do you think she's dead?"

"Yes."

"Who do you think killed her?"

"I don't know."

"But it's probably someone in town?"

"Yes."

"Does that make you angry?"

He makes fists out of his long, slender fingers. "Yes."

"Good," Marla says. "Keep writing. Get it out of your system."

Ben: a cool surface, a noncommittal smile, and slightly arrogant way of holding his head. He reminds me of Christian although he's not quite as beautiful as Christian was. Still, there's a sexual fineness about him that Christian also had. I'm not sure I can describe it, except that it's both pure and animal at the same time—an exotic, erotic mixture that Christian exploited and I doubt Ben knows he possesses. But Ben has a quality of stillness Christian didn't have. Christian was never peaceful. He didn't sit, he slouched with one foot twitching. He didn't walk, he paced with his shoulders hunched and his hands jammed into his pockets.

Ben's emotions are interior, concealed, and contained. Although he seems to be relaxed in that stillness of his, I sense turbulence in his bones and muscles, in his fingers and the ligaments of his hands. Sometime in his childhood, when his mother tried to possess him once too often, he must have discovered that the best way to protect his vulnerability was by raising shields. I can almost see those shields rushing into place when I've shocked him or caught him unawares. For a brief second, he's wide open and then it's over, his true self hidden once again. I think he's capable of being in love but will find intimacy difficult, because he holds his heart in such solitary confinement. It must feel safer that way.

Chapter
3

ON THE MORNING THAT I'M PUTTING THE FINAL TOUCHES ONTO
the budget proposal for the library board meeting later that
night, Mona comes into my office, closes the door, and sits
down. I see from her agitation and pinker-than-usual cheeks
that she's bursting with news.

"Someone's died and left the library a million dollars?" I
ask.

She shakes her head, and her dark curls tremble. "It's
Edgar," she says.

"Is he sick?" I ask with some concern. He's a member of
the library board, and I'm counting on his support to fight
Arlene's request to take *The Catcher in the Rye* off the
library shelves.

"Last night someone spray-painted 'Fucking Faggot' three
times on the drugstore window and once on the door of his
house."

I sit back in shock. "Oh, no," I say.

"The only good thing is his mother is practically blind.
According to Sophie Rundle, she never even noticed."

I think of silly little Sophie and her love of gossip. "I hope
she doesn't tell her."

"Not even Sophie would be that stupid. Mrs. Ashley already has one foot in the grave and the other on a banana peel."

I can't help smiling. "That's awful," I say.

"But true. Anyway, you can just imagine Edgar."

"He must be beside himself. He's always been so discreet."

"He's notorious in Laurel Grove."

"He isn't," I protest.

"In certain circles. He likes young men, the younger the better."

I shake my head. "Mona, how do you find out things like that?"

"From a friend who has a gay friend in Laurel Grove who does the bar scene."

I've never wanted to contemplate Edgar's sex life before and I don't want to now. I change the subject. "Do they think it's the same person who wrote on the lockers at the school?"

"My source says—"

"Who's that?"

"Mary Morris at the cleaner's."

"Of course," I say with a touch of sarcasm.

"Reg's wife brought in her muskrat coat for storage this morning, that's how come Mary knows. Anyway, the police think it's the same person."

I remember how Virginia once worried that the tragedy of Caroline's disappearance wouldn't stop just at the Deacons but would eventually involve the whole town. I didn't share her concern, because I had no idea what such involvement could be. Now I see that it's like a volcano, evil erupting from some hidden, secret place, spreading like lava on the surrounding countryside and trapping everyone and everything that stands in its path.

"Edgar's a good member of the community," I say. "He doesn't deserve this." Mona agrees with a sober nod, but I see she has more to tell. Her cheeks are still a hot pink. "What else?" I ask.

"Guess who called me last night?"

"I haven't a clue."

"Tony Molino."

"Really," I say.

"He asked me out."

"Well, well."

"Did your friend get tired of him?"

"She doesn't talk about it with me."

"He *is* an illiterate boor." She pauses. "But good in bed."

I put my hands over my ears. "No more gossip," I say. "I can't stand it."

Mona stands up. "Don't you want to know if I said yes?"

I lower my hands. "Okay. Did you say yes?"

"Absolutely not. I'm not a doormat." Her indignation is so vehement and physical that even her fat shivers. "I asked him who the hell he thought he was and told him he could go fuck himself for all I cared."

The library board meets in a conference room in our town hall, a two-story cement building at the corner of Main and Webster. Usually there are only six people at such meetings, myself and the five appointed members of the board: Edgar, Frances, our mayor, Stuart Crawley, who also owns a GM dealership, town councillor Marty Sylvestro, who's partners with his brother in a trucking company, and one of Cassandra's oldest residents, Mrs. Eileen MacDonald. She's close to eighty years old and has sat on the library board since its inception. As far as I can tell, she's been knitting the same pair of argyle socks in red, yellow, and black since I became head librarian in 1977.

The library board meetings are usually informal and friendly. We chat, we discuss library business, we look over my budget proposals, we have a slight tug-of-war over how much dint the library can make on the town's balance sheet, and we adjourn until the next meeting. But when I drive my car into the parking lot, I realize with a sinking feeling that tonight is going to be different. There are far too many other cars in the lot, and I see several friends of Arlene's entering the building. When I go in, I discover the meeting's been moved to a larger room to allow for our unexpected audience of about thirty-five concerned taxpayers. Where, I wonder, was Edgar's grapevine when this movement was taking root? Some people are carrying placards with awkwardly printed messages such as THE RIGHT BOOKS FOR GOOD KIDS and CATCHER IN THE WRONG. Deborah Constable, who owns and manages the *Cassandra Gazette* with her husband, Stan, is busy interviewing people, notebook in hand. She waves her pen at me and says, "Can I have a word with you later?"

I nod, but I'm not happy. It's the first time since I've been librarian that voters, other than the community members on the board, and the press have shown the slightest interest in our board meetings. I'm not the only one who doesn't like this sudden community participation. Our elected representatives are visibly nervous, particularly Marty Sylvestro, who's seriously overweight and sweating profusely as he helps set up extra chairs even though the building is air-conditioned. And Stuart is welcoming people with a nauseating obsequiousness. "Arlene," I hear him saying, "how good to see you. And, by the way, did I mention what a marvelous job you did on the heart drive? I did? Well, let me just add that—"

There are also other undercurrents in the room. As I join Edgar and Frances at the coffee machine, Edgar is saying, "I almost didn't come."

"I'm glad you did," Frances said.

Edgar turns to me. "I'm going to be a handicap," he says. He's pale, and his mustache is twitching.

"No, you're not. We need you."

He gives a bitter little laugh. "You think anyone's going to listen to what I have to say about corrupting youth after what happened this morning?"

"Edgar," I say, "you're a respected member of this community, and your opinion is important."

"And your vote's important," Frances adds. "Do you think Marty and Stuart are going to support literature? Books aren't going to re-elect them."

"I know," Edgar says gloomily. "That's why I'm here."

The meeting, chaired by Stuart, begins quietly. Frances

reads the minutes of the last meeting, and the first item on the agenda is my report on the estimates for repairs for the toilet in the men's bathroom and roof leakage in the back of the building. Stuart discusses these issues in excruciating detail, right down to the cost of replacing the ball-cock supply valve in the toilet tank. I can't decide whether this unusually prolonged discussion is designed to bore the audience, thereby convincing them never to attend a meeting again, or to show the Cassandra electorate what a fine mayor Stuart is, the kind of elected official who leaves no stone unturned when it comes to spending the taxpayers' money.

Then we move onto the book acquisition budget, children's and adults', and the costs of periodical and newspaper subscriptions. Marty now shows an unusual interest in whether or not we should continue to receive the Sunday *New York Times Book Review*. We bat that subject around for at least five minutes . . .

Marty: The point is whether enough people read it or not.

Me: I can't give you exact numbers.

Marty: Could we improve on that system?

Me: Which system?

Marty: Keeping track of what comes in and what goes out.

Me: The *Book Review* doesn't go out. It's newspaper and too fragile. People have to come in and read it.

Marty: I wouldn't think people have a lot of time to do that.

Me: A lot of people do.

Marty: But you don't know how many.

Edgar: I think we can take Barbara's word with respect to the quantity of readers.

Frances: And it is the most influential book review in the country.

. . . and finally voting to keep the subscription, while Frances, Edgar, and I struggle to maintain straight faces and avoid looking at one another for fearing of showing what we think.

Eileen keeps on knitting, only stopping when Stuart calls for votes. She's a grandmotherly type with little curls of white hair and a plump, smiling face. Her husband was a farmer, and she lived outside Cassandra until his death in 1965. She told me once that she couldn't have survived being a farmer's wife if it weren't for books. They were her salvation, taking her away from the fields and the barns and into other, more exciting worlds.

"So when Harvey Anderson, he was the mayor back in thirty-four, thought Cassandra should get its own library, I wrote letters and drummed up support. Of course, George didn't like it. It took time away from him, the children and"—this with a twinkle in the blue eyes magnified in her trifocals—"the cows."

Unlike the rest of us, Eileen seems quite unfazed by Arlene and her cadre of supporters. Her hearing isn't what it used to be, she wears an aid in her left ear, and perhaps she can't hear how restless the audience is getting as the meeting goes on. People rustle, they shift in their seats, and they whisper to one another. I watch her calmly purl her way down one row, adding and dropping colors, and wonder how she's going to vote on Arlene's request. Edgar and Frances will vote against, Stuart and Marty will vote for. Eileen holds the future of censorship in Cassandra in her small, knobbly hands.

"Well, that completes the budget," Stuart says. "What have we got under other business?"

I clear my throat. "As you know from the letters sent to you, Arlene McPherson is requesting once again that we remove *The Catcher in the Rye* from the library shelves."

"I'll allow discussion on this issue, starting with Barbara here, and then opening it to the floor. Barbara?"

The room has gone completely silent except for the clacking of Eileen's knitting needles. I look at the audience first to bolster my nerves, because I know almost everyone in the room, and I think I'll find that comforting. It's an audience mostly of women with a sprinkling of husbands. Bev Stapleton. Neil and Suzette Basset. Sandy Carelli. Rosemary Meszaros. I'm not close friends with any of them, but they're acquaintances, women I see in the bank and post office, women I chat with on grocery lines and when I'm working at the reference or checkout desks at the library. But tonight I don't see a friendly face, and I look nervously at my collection of index cards. I'm not used to making speeches, even little ones, and while I did practice this one on Dan, what I've written now strikes me as pompous. But it's far too late to change it, and I have no skills at improvisation.

"Arlene says in her letter," I begin, "that books like *The Catcher in the Rye* promote disrespect for adults and for authority, and lead to a tragedy like Caroline Deacon's disappearance. I respect and share Arlene's deep concern for the children of Cassandra, but I can't support her position on the censorship of literature. I don't think we can point our fingers at one book and ask it to bear responsibility for the problems that teenagers have today. Our children are influenced by thousands of messages that come from movies, television, radio, music, magazines, and other forms of media.

"Also, *The Catcher in the Rye* isn't a book of questionable taste. It's a classic, a story of a teenager going through the pains of growing up. It's a book with important messages about hypocrisy and dishonesty in the adult world. I don't believe we have a right to censor a book just because we don't like its message. Oscar Wilde once said, 'There is no such thing as a moral or immoral book. Books are well written, or badly written. That is all.' Therefore, I recommend that the board turn down this request for censorship of one of the classics of American literature."

There's now a murmuring of voices and a couple of scattered boos. "Quiet," Stuart says. "Arlene?"

Arlene stands up but doesn't look at her notes. Instead, she gives me a triumphant glance. "I'm surprised, Barbara, that you'd quote Oscar Wilde. He was imprisoned for being a notorious homosexual."

I hear Edgar take a sharp intake of breath, I see Dorothy scribbling frantically in her notebook, and I feel terrible. I thought the Oscar Wilde quote was a nice touch. It hadn't occurred to me that Arlene would twist my good intentions to her own uses.

"Just a minute," I say angrily. "You don't judge a book by the life-style of its author."

"Why not?" someone yells from the audience.

Stuart uses the flat of his hand as a gavel. "One at a time, please. Arlene, continue."

Arlene reads from her notes. "Since Caroline disappeared, I've watched our town turn from a community of trust to one of doubts and suspicion. I've talked to the police, and we're going to have to face the facts. Chances are that Caroline was murdered by someone right here in Cassandra, and that someone is one of our teenagers."

"I object!" Frances has flushed scarlet, and before Stuart can slap his palm on the table, she adds, "Not one boy in this town has been accused of anything. Not a single one!"

There are hollers from the audience.

"Arlene's right!"

"You think you know better than the police?"

"Get real!"

Stuart says, "Silence!"

Arlene waits calmly as the room quiets down. "All of us here know how impressionable children are. They don't have the maturity of mind to understand fully what they see, hear, and read. So they believe everything. This means that we who are their parents and teachers have to make sure that they read the right books, see the right television shows, and watch the right movies. *The Catcher in the Rye* is an example of the kind of book that makes children misbehave. It's disrespectful and mocks adults. And what do books like this do? They teach our children not to listen. They teach them to be rebellious. They teach them to ignore what their parents say, what their teachers say, and what their church says."

As she takes a breath, I'm forced to concede that Arlene's put together a far better speech than I did. She's also impressive. She's a big woman and heavier than she used to be. That extra weight imparts something to her words so they feel like blue-chip stocks, backed by caution, deliberation, and solidity.

"So how do we stop this?" she goes on. "Where do we

start? Barbara's right. Children are influenced by many things in our society, and we can't control the whole world. We can't change the rock stars who sing obscene lyrics. We can't change Hollywood producers who want to make violent or obscene movies. And we can't change the people who make television shows that glorify sex and murder. But we do have a voice in Cassandra, and we should use it. Let's get rid of the bad influences in this town that can hurt and contaminate our children. And let's begin by getting rid of books like *The Catcher in the Rye*." She sits down to tumultuous applause and cries of "Right on!" and "That's telling them."

I'm surprised to see Edgar stand up. "The question is," he says, his voice pitched a little too high, "where does it end? I mean, if you start with one book, well, what's next? And who decides what's harmful and what isn't? Who picks the judges?"

He sits down, and I hear one of the men in the audience mutter, "Not you, that's for damned sure."

Horrified, I glance at Stuart and see that he's also heard this comment and senses the ugliness brewing in the audience. Quickly, he stands up and makes a show of checking his watch. "It's getting late," he says, "and it's a workday tomorrow. I don't know about you folks, but I need my beauty sleep. And you know Meg. She'll give me heck if I miss my curfew."

This brings a small laugh, because we all know Stuart's wife, and although she looks like she wouldn't say boo to a goose, rumor has it that Stuart is the most henpecked husband in Cassandra. I understand suddenly that Stuart is a lot more clever than I've thought. He's deflected ill will by poking fun at himself and made sure there wouldn't be a lot of time for acrimonious argument about Arlene's letter by asking interminable questions about toilet and roof repairs.

"So," he says, "it's time we put this issue to a vote of the board. All those opposed to Arlene's request that we remove *The Catcher in the Rye* from the library shelves, raise their right hands."

Edgar's and Frances's hands shoot up, but that's all, and a

few people in the audience cheer. Arlene looks smug, and Frances and Edgar mirror my own disappointment.

"All right," Stuart says. "All those in favor of Arlene's request that we remove *The Catcher in the Rye* from the library shelves, raise their right hands."

He and Marty raise their hands, but that's all, and everyone looks at Eileen, who's busily counting stitches. I think about the kind of books Eileen takes out of the library, primarily romance novels. I tried once to encourage her to read a novel I'd really enjoyed, *The Stone Angel,* by a Canadian author, Margaret Laurence. I thought the book would interest her, because it was written from the point of view of an old woman looking back on the happiness and tragedies of her life. "Oh, I'm getting too old to want to read about reality," she told me. "I just want happy endings."

"Eileen?" Stuart says, and then louder, "Eileen? Do you have your hearing aid on?"

Eileen puts down her knitting and fumbles with the hearing aid in her ear. "Battery's going down," she says. "I'm sorry, Stuart, you'll just have to speak up."

"We were voting on Arlene's letter asking us to take *The Catcher in the Rye* off the library shelves," he says in a loud voice.

"Oh, yes," she says.

"Did you hear the discussion?"

"Oh, yes. It was most interesting."

"We need to know your vote, Eileen. For or against?"

"Against," she says, raising her right hand and bestowing a grandmotherly smile on the audience. "I can't imagine what everyone's so afraid of. A book can't hurt anyone. Why, I've never heard of anything so silly in my life."

When I get home that night, close to eleven o'clock, Dan takes one look at my face and asks, "Coffee, tea, or a scotch?"

"Coffee, although getting drunk has some appeal," I say as I sink wearily down onto a chair in the kitchen. I hardly moved during that entire meeting, but my legs ache as if I'd run a marathon.

"It was that bad?"

"We had an audience. Arlene had drummed up about thirty-five people. Some of them were carrying protest signs." As Dan boils water in the kettle and sets up the cups, I tell him about the speeches, the angry undertones, the vote.

"So you won," he says.

"But for how long? The tenure of this board is only until next January. Watch what happens then. Instead of having to beat volunteers out of the bushes, I'll bet we have a dozen people—Arlene and her friends—requesting appointments."

Dan puts two coffees on the table, one for me and one for him. "Cross that bridge when you come to it," he says.

I wish I could live by Dan's philosophy of taking each day as it comes, but I know that the composition of our future board is going to trouble me for months. I'm going to fret about drumming up grass-roots support for my position. I'm going to worry about finding people to send letters to the town council so that more liberal candidates get serious consideration. Most of all, I'm going to have bad dreams about serving under a board made up of Arlene and her clones.

"The worst part of it was," I say, "that I looked around that room and understood, for the first time, how neighbors can turn on one another. You know, like Germany, when ordinary people turned on friends and acquaintances just because they were Jewish. Dan, when I got up to give my speech, not one person smiled at me. Not one. I could've been a stranger they'd never seen before."

"I've always thought of Cassandra as having two faces," Dan says. "The good face is the one the town puts on when something happens that pulls everyone together, like the way we did the search for Caroline and the financial support people gave to the Deacons. The bad face happens when we discover we have strong differences, like when we voted on the budget to build the school. Remember how people were? Russ Delaney called Joe Carelli a lousy wop, because he objected to putting the gym in a separate wing."

Claire Harrison

I think about these two faces Dan's described. I've loved
the intimacy and neighborliness of Cassandra and tried to
ignore the meanness, the pettiness, and the jealousies. "I
guess I can't reconcile those two faces."

"It's just human nature."

I shake my head. "I always thought Cassandra was
so . . . so safe."

Dan sips at his coffee. "Nowhere's really safe."

"Well, I hate that," I say with vehemence. "I could've
gone anywhere, but I stayed here because it felt safe."

Dan nods. "I couldn't have separated you from Cassandra
if I'd used explosives."

I look at him with surprise. "Did you want to?"

"I tried."

"When?"

"Remember the job offer from that company in California?"

"What job offer?"

"Just before we bought the house."

I remember the job offer now, although only vaguely.
"There was something wrong with it."

"It was too far away."

"No, there had to be something else."

"I tried to talk to you about it, but all you said was that it
was three thousand miles away and you didn't know anyone
in California. I couldn't budge you."

"Did you really want to go?"

"I thought it would be interesting."

"I'm sure you never told me that."

"Barbara, you panicked at the idea of moving. Don't you
remember?"

I shake my head. "Maybe you really didn't want to go
either. Maybe you exaggerated my reaction to support your
real feelings."

Dan frowns and studies his coffee. "Maybe you're right."

As we close up the house for the night, I think that
memory seems to be a faulty way of remembering the past.
Marla and I share different memories of times we spent

256

together, of games we did or did not play, and of nights that may or may not have been lit by the moon. Perhaps it was naive of me to think that Dan and I would be any different. But what other mechanism do we have to truly record the past? Suppose someone were to have followed us around with a video recorder, filming every moment of our married life from the most mundane events to the most passionate. Suppose we sat and watched this film of our lives, would we still agree on what was being played before our eyes? It's true we couldn't argue about what was said or what we wore or what gestures we made, but what about intuition, perception, and interpretation? *They* make no impression on celluloid.

Maybe the truth isn't important, I think as I lock the back door. But what a heretical thought for someone brought up the way I was. "Always tell the truth," my mother told me. "The truth will protect you." The result was that I suffered from a painful honesty for much of my childhood and wrestled with terrible moral dilemmas, because my mother also said, "You have to tell Aunt Jessie how good her chocolate cake is even if you don't like it. It's not polite to criticize," and "I know Uncle Bob is fat, but that doesn't mean you up and tell him." It was years before I was comfortable with the white lie, that untruth that lies in some ambiguous territory between right and wrong.

As I pass Joel's closed door, I hear rock music blaring. It's close to midnight, and he has his math final tomorrow morning at nine o'clock. He can't be studying, I think, not with that racket, and he should get a good night's sleep. I knock on his door, once lightly and then harder. When there's no answer, I open it and find Joel asleep, fully dressed, on his bed with his pencils, books, and papers around him. I switch off his radio and smile as I look at him. He sleeps the way he did as a small child, on his side with his knees drawn up and one hand tucked under his cheek. He looks younger in sleep, innocent and serene. His hair, which he's growing longer, makes silvery gold curls on his forehead and neck, and his skin is smooth and slightly flushed. A flood of love for him washes over me, obliterating all the anxieties and irritations of the past weeks. I take his books and homework off the bed, cover him with a light blanket, and turn off his light. His sleep is so deep that he doesn't even move when I lightly kiss his cheek. What does the truth matter, I think, when this is what really counts—that everyone I love is with me, under this roof, safe and sound.

Dan is undressing when I enter our bedroom, his back to me as he takes off his shirt. I sneak up behind him, put my arms around his chest, and press my cheek to his bare back. "Mmm," I say. "Nice heartbeat."

"Interested?" he asks.

"Could be," I say.

He turns in my embrace, cups his hands under my buttocks, and presses his forehead against mine. "I thought you'd be too stressed out, too tired."

"I'm not going to let Arlene McPherson ruin my sex life, too."

We kiss then, a fully satisfying encounter of mouths and tongues, and I think we should kiss like this more often. There are too many perfunctory kisses in marriage, those quick pecks on the cheek and hasty brushings of lips that pass for affection when two people with busy careers and often nonmatching schedules are rushing around, coming and going, trying to keep the house operating smoothly, the meals made, the laundry . . .

The telephone on the table beside the bed rings.

"Don't answer it," Dan murmurs.

It rings again and again, and we slowly break apart.

"Who'd call this late?" I ask as I walk over and pick up the receiver. "Hello?"

"Barbara? It's me . . . it's—" the voice cracks.

"Virginia? *Virginia?* What's the matter?"

She can only get the words out between the sobs. "It's . . . Sarah. She's disappeared."

Chapter
4

MARLA HATES HOSPITALS. THIS INTENSE DISLIKE DEVELOPED after Christian's accident when she spent hours sitting by his bedside, trying to talk him out of his coma, and was nourished by other unpleasant experiences: Didi's birth when the maternity ward was so crowded she almost had Didi in a hallway, and her father's terminal days when his cancer was painful and he had to beg for drugs. She hates hospital smells and textures, which are too antiseptic and too white, indifferent doctors and officious nurses who won't acknowledge emotional pain because they can't treat it, and the heavy atmosphere of misery and suffering that presses against her chest and constricts her breathing.

She didn't want to have lunch with Faith French, Christian's sister, at the hospital where she works as an X-ray technician, but Faith didn't give her any other choice.

"Faith French, please."

The voice at the other end of the phone was deep. "Speaking."

"Faith, this is Martha Hudson. I used to go out with your—"

"I know who you are."

"I've moved back to Cassandra."

259

Silence.

"I'd like to take you out to lunch."

Silence again, but Marla notices that Faith hasn't hung up. "I could pick you up at the hospital and we could go to a restaurant in Laurel Grove."

"I eat in the hospital cafeteria," Faith said. "I only have an hour."

"Could I meet you there tomorrow?"

A pause and then, "I guess so."

"At noon?"

"I go off duty at twelve-fifteen."

"How will I recognize you? You were twelve last time I saw you."

"I'm short, fat, and have a purple name tag," Faith said, and hung up the phone.

"What a fascinating description," Marla said into the dead receiver. "It'll be a pleasure, I'm sure."

Marla walks through the corridors of Laurel Grove General, passing people in wheelchairs and patients in beds being pushed by orderlies, and smelling that awful hospital smell that evokes so many memories. But she thinks that maybe meeting Christian's sister in a hospital is fitting after all. It was the last place she'd seen Faith, on the Saturday afternoon when it was clear Christian was dying and his mother asked Marla to leave the room. Marla, furious and crying so hard she could hardly see for the tears, screamed at Mrs. French, who turned her back and told the nurse in a high, shrill voice that she wanted Marla *out of there, right now, this minute.* As she was being pushed out of the room, Marla caught a glimpse of a terrified Faith standing in one corner, pressing hard against the wall as if she hoped she could merge into the plaster and disappear.

When Marla arrives in the cafeteria, she sees a short, fat woman with a purple name tag, tortoise-shell glasses, and cropped, graying hair, standing by the water fountain. She bears no resemblance to the Faith that Marla remembers: a skinny twelve-year-old with a head of unmanageable dark hair that she wore in a messy ponytail. But when she says, "Hello," and Faith turns, Marla sees that she takes after her mother, whose face was too round, whose nose was too long, and whose chin too short. Her only physical connection to Christian is her eyes. They are the identical shade of green, yellowish and crystalline.

Faith doesn't smile but tilts her head to one side and studies Marla as if she were an X ray. "You haven't changed much."

"I'm older."

"I hated you."

Marla thinks that Faith's use of the past tense is slightly encouraging. "I know," she says.

"Well, let's eat," Faith says. "I don't have a lot of time."

They don't talk again until they're through the cafeteria line and sitting at a table. As Faith takes a bite of her sandwich, Marla says, "I remember you wanted to be a dress designer."

Faith shrugs her heavy shoulders. "Well, we all had dreams, didn't we?"

"Are you married?"

"No."

"Never met the right man?"

"No."

"I've been married twice."

Faith puts down her sandwich. "I'm gay, okay?"

It's Marla's turn to shrug. "Okay."

"And I'm not interested in your life, your marriages, your kids, your triumphs, or your disasters."

This sentence is spoken so quickly and with such relish that Marla realizes Faith's been savoring and practicing words like these for years. "So why'd you agree to lunch?" she asks.

"I was curious, I guess."

"Look, I just want to know more about Christian."

"Why?"

"I'm a writer. I want to write about that time of my life."

Faith resumes eating.

"I didn't kill him," Marla says. "It wasn't my fault."

"If he hadn't of been going out with you, it wouldn't have happened."

"Nobody knows that."

"And if he hadn't of been going out with you, he might've spent more time at home."

Ah, Marla thinks. "What would have happened if he'd spent more time at home?"

"You have any idea what it was like to have a brother who was so good-looking that everyone went gaga over him? He was like a god or something. My mother worshiped the ground he walked on. It was Christian this and Christian that, and do you think Christian would like meat loaf for supper and don't be so loud, your brother's got a test. It was Christian who got the expensive bike and the record player and the really good birthday parties."

"I never—"

But Faith is in some different place now and doesn't seem to hear or even see Marla. "She cracked up after he died, you know. She went absolutely loony. She saw dirt everywhere and was washing floors and vacuuming all the time, even in the middle of the night. I think it was the noise of the vacuum cleaner that finally made my father put her away. It didn't matter to her that I was there, because I was just second best. I couldn't make up for what she'd lost, could I? Not with all her hopes and dreams gone down the tubes."

"Is she still alive?"

Faith comes out of the place she's been and focuses on Marla. "No, she died about five years ago."

"And your father?"

"He divorced her and married someone else. Lives in Ohio somewhere."

"You don't see him?"

"He could rot for all I care."

Christian rarely brought Marla to his house, and she'd only met his father a few times. She remembers a large, sullen man, who must have been beautiful once like Christian but whose looks were blurred by age and the extra weight he carried.

"What would have happened if Christian had spent more time at home?" Marla asks again.

"You mean you don't know?"

"Christian didn't talk to me about family."

"I don't suppose he would have. We didn't talk about it much to each other either."

"About what?"

"That my father used to beat the shit out of my mother." *Jackpot.* "And he didn't when Christian was there?"

"He didn't dare, not once Christian got older. He waited until he was gone. Of course, my mother never said anything, because she was afraid Christian would kill him if he found out."

"I'm sorry," Marla says. "I never knew."

"Yeah, well." Faith picks up her sandwich. "It was the deep, dark family secret. Nobody knew. He never hit her face, just places she could cover up."

I've had a glimpse into the heart of Christian's shadow, and it astonishes me that I never knew, that I never even guessed. How hard we worked in those days to present the picture-perfect family. How hard I worked to ensure Christian was the boy I wanted him to be—wild, rebellious, but ultimately tamable—the perfect romantic hero. There was no room in that fantasy for a boy with a real problem, he must have sensed that. So the problems were manufactured and acceptable: parents that nagged, too-early curfews, not enough allowance, fights over the family car.

When I looked into his eyes, I thought I saw into his soul, but what I really saw was my own image. I was prettier in that reflection than in any other mirror. I looked and looked, endless cycles of drowning in those yellow-green depths, thinking I could sink to the bottom of him, and then rise to take the plunge again. But all I was really doing was preening, studying the tilt of my own eyes, the way my eyebrows feathered, the curve of my nose. Me, Martha Hudson, Mrs. Christian Robert French.

Eyes aren't the windows of the soul, or even the mind. I was too young then to know that we hide things behind our eyes. They're like the shades we pull down or curtains we draw, opaque, colored facades. It's the musculature around the eyes that gives us away. There is a moment when someone is not telling the truth that the skin at the corner of the eyes tightens as if the muscles beneath it are shrinking back from the telling of the lie. I've seen this on different eyes: Sean when he lied about being unfaithful, Didi when she told me she wasn't doing drugs, Bobbie when she talks about that night at Misty Lake.

That night, Marla falls asleep early but wakes around two o'clock. The moon is full, and its beams create the same patterns on the walls and carpet as the sun did during the day, except that the effect is pale, muted, shadows playing on shadows. She doesn't know why she's woken up so suddenly, only that she's still tired but not quite ready to fall back asleep. She lies quietly and listens to the creaking of beams settling and the slight whisper of the trees. Marla thinks she can hear, if she tries hard enough, the sounds of the river, although it's no longer rushing as hard and as fast as it had been during the spring.

She wishes suddenly that she had a lover, not in Cassandra but a long-distance lover. Once, about a year after she'd divorced David, she met a man on a plane trip to Tulsa, Oklahoma, where she'd been invited to speak at a weekend writer's conference. He was a cattle rancher coming back from visiting his married daughter in Los Angeles, who had just had her first baby. He showed Marla pictures of the baby, and when they were landing, he asked her if she'd like to go out to dinner with him while she was in town. Richard Carruthers, that was his name: "But folks call me Rick." He wore brown slacks, a tan sports jacket, and a string tie with a silver eagle clasp. His wife had died three years back, he told her, and he had two grown children, the girl in L.A. and a boy who worked with him on the ranch. No, not a ranch, a *spread*. Like margarine, she said, and he laughed. He had straight brown hair that was gray at the temples, a square, open face and wrinkles at the corners of his blue eyes that were whiter than his skin.

Marla was the keynote dinner speaker for the conference, so she did her bit, skipped out during the meal, and met Rick outside the hotel. They went to a steak house, and she asked questions about ranching, or was it *spreading,* and he laughed and the wine flowed and, since she was always on a high after getting a speech over with, they ended up back in her hotel room. It was clear he hadn't gotten laid in a while, but then neither had she so they were a perfect match. At least, that's what Rick said when he left the next morning and asked her humbly if she minded if he phoned her now and then. "I know you're a big-time writer and all," he said. He hadn't had any idea who she was when they were on the plane, but by the time they met for dinner, he'd read the local newspaper, which had a big feature on her, including a photograph that took up seven column inches.

For a year after that, Rick phoned her very late at night about twice a month. At first they talked about what he was doing, what she was doing, and the distance between them geographically and otherwise. Rick always mentioned that he'd never met a writer before, not a one, and wanted to know if she was going to put him into one of her books. He told her stories about ranching that always made him out to be a hero like the time he saved a lost cow in the dead of winter. He always prefaced these stories by saying that he wanted her to get it right when she wrote about him: "You know, you gotta have the bigger picture." Marla always said she knew what he meant. Then they'd talk dirty, their voices lowering to almost whispers.

"Are you wearing a nightgown?" he'd ask.

"No."

"Are you under the blankets?"

"Just a sheet."

"Touch yourself there."

"Where?"

"You know."

"Tell me."

"Between your legs."

"You'll have to be more specific."

"The place between your legs. Where it's wet."

"Maybe it isn't."

"I know it is, baby. I can tell."

"You can?"

"Are you touching it?"

"It's wet, and you know what else?"

"What?"

"It's open, wide open."

He groaned then, and she knew he was masturbating. They hung up after he'd come, and although he always thought she had an orgasm too, she actually waited until after the phone call to finish it off. After about six months, the calls began to taper off. Rick never said anything, not even a final good-bye, but Marla guessed he'd found another woman who was a little closer to home and part of, you know, the bigger picture.

Now Marla wishes someone like Rick was in her life. It was pleasurable to lie in the dark and have the world reduced to a deep voice and the feel of her skin naked and cool beneath the sheet. It was intimate, erotic, and at the same time uncomplicated. Wasn't that the best part? That Rick wasn't there to bother her during the day, interfere in her life, get in the way? That she didn't have to deal with his quirks, his personality glitches, his unshaven skin, his bad tempers, his sulks, and his smells? And finally, there was that feeling of ultimate control. She could hang up anytime she pleased, just push the button down and he would evaporate into the air. *I want you, I want you not. I hear you, I hear you not.*

Marla yawns, stretches, and falls into a dozing state that is a prelude to real sleep, when it's hard to tell the difference between what is real and what is dreaming. She has a conversation with Tony in which he tells her he's so broke that the bank has put his empty account on the street where everyone can see it and cars can drive over it. She sees it, too, a limp leather bag in the shape of a penis with a drawstring where the root of the phallus would be. She rises out of that dream, feels a breeze on her shoulder, pulls the sheet higher, and sinks back into the pillow. Then she hears a light tread on the stairs that wind up the inside of the turret to her bedroom. The footsteps go up and down as if someone were climbing and then descending, and they have different rhythms: pat, pat, pat and then pat, pat . . . pat, pat. A child sings, but so faintly she can't distinguish the tune. Marla fights to get up, but she can't even open her eyes. She's heard the tiny, breathy voice and footsteps before. Sometimes there's more than one child, including one that's so small, it can only cry, a faint wailing that merges with the creaking of the branches outside and rustling of the leaves.

The children aren't strangers, she knows who they are: the babies Elvira Hiller wanted so badly but couldn't have. In the dead of the night, they come to the turret, where the nursery was going to be. They run up and down the stairs, clap their hands, play hide-and-seek in the railings, and sing to themselves. *Ring around a rosy . . .*

Caught behind her closed eyes, Marla imagines them, not as flesh and blood but made of other things—dreams and hopes, tears and anguish, prayers and heartbreak. They're only shadows, like real children who grow up and away, leaving nothing behind but the ghostly remains of memory. Outside, the wind picks up, and the trees toss their uppermost branches as if they were horses swinging their heads from side to side. A cloud passes before the moon, and the bedroom darkens. Marla slips deeper into sleep, and her breathing slows. Behind her eyelids, scenes come and go, but she'll remember very little when she wakes up except for snatches of color, a feeling of motion, shadowy figures.

. . . *pocketful of posies, ashes, ashes, we all fall down.*

Chapter
5

BY FRIDAY AFTERNOON, WHEN DAPHNE, FRANCES, AND I ARE sitting with Virginia in her living room, Sarah has been missing for more than twenty-four hours. She left the house at nine o'clock the morning before, telling Virginia she was going to be with her friend Katie all day, that they were going to go shopping and she wanted to sleep over. Virginia was so relieved Sarah was doing something as normal as hanging around the mall with a friend that when Sarah asked for money for summer clothes and sneakers, Virginia gave her a hundred dollars. Virginia had been worried because Sarah was spending so much time with Molly Deacon and talking constantly about Caroline.

"She's too young to be so morbid," Virginia says. "It's not healthy, is it?"

And we all agree that this is so. Virginia's pale and tense, clasping and unclasping her hands, and we're doing everything we can to be supportive, providing food, conversation, and sympathy. I've even cried at one point, remembering Sarah and Joel as newborn babies lying side by side in the hospital, and it was Virginia comforting me, holding me tightly and gently patting my back.

Virginia spent the day that Sarah disappeared working in

contented ignorance on illustrations for a children's book about herbs and spices. The plants were organized in alphabetical order, and she was up to dill and fennel. When Melissa came home after school, they went to Laurel Grove to buy her some shorts and T-shirts for camp.

"I thought of calling Katie and Sarah and seeing if they'd like to go with us," Virginia says, "but then I thought it wouldn't be fair to Melissa, would it? She needs time alone with me. It's not easy being the youngest when your older sister is so intense and dramatic that she hogs the spotlight most of the time." She twists her fingers so hard they crack and adds, "I thought I was doing the right thing."

We say that of course she was, that every child needs individual, quality attention, that there was no way she could have known what was happening.

The result was that Virginia and Raymond didn't know that Sarah had not gone to Katie's until ten o'clock that night when Katie phoned and wanted to talk to Sarah about a pair of shorts she'd seen that afternoon at The Gap. That phone call set off a flurry of further calls to other friends of Sarah's and finally to the police. Reg was at the Silvers' house by eleven-thirty, and this time there were no generalizations about teenage runaways and talk of waiting another twenty-four hours. When Dan and I arrived at the Silvers' at midnight, Reg was looking grim and weary. He and Virginia had already searched Sarah's room, but nothing had been taken from it. Reg said he intended to cover every base: getting an APB bulletin out as soon as possible, having one of his men go to bus stations and airports in Laurel Grove, Symington, and Syracuse with a picture of Sarah, and contacting the FBI again. He left shortly after we arrived, and Dan and I sat with Virginia and Raymond until about two o'clock in the morning.

They were both exhausted, particularly Raymond, who seemed to have aged twenty years in a day. This sudden aging didn't adversely affect his appearance. Raymond is the only husband in our group who's becoming handsomer as he gets older. Dan's face is jowled and full of creases. Matt Feller has heavy, dark pouches under his eyes and a bald spot that's widened to include his whole crown. But Raymond, who was already tall and attractive, is wrinkling in just the right way at the eyes and developing dignified, elegant lines in his cheeks and distinguished silver wings at his temples. Although he's a traffic engineer with the city of Laurel Grove, I've often thought he'd have made a good lawyer, not because he was especially articulate, precise, or logical but because he so perfectly looks the part.

Dan and I sat in their living room, while Raymond and Virginia tried to talk themselves into believing that nothing was wrong.

"She's so impulsive," Virginia said. "She could have taken off somewhere at the drop of a hat."

"Remember last month when she went to the Bennetts' and never called us?" Raymond asked. "Remember that?"

Virginia grabbed on to this as if it were a lifeline. "She just forgot," she said, turning to us. "Can you imagine?"

"She's the kind of kid," Raymond said, "who gets so caught up, she'd forget her head if it wasn't attached."

He got up, paced, and sat down. Then he repeated these actions all over again. Of all my friends' marriages, I find Virginia's to be the most mysterious. Virginia is quiet and thoughtful; Raymond can't sit still even in less stressful circumstances and has a mercurial temperament. I understand that opposites attract, but I'm not sure how they live together. Then there are Raymond's affairs. I know of two Virginia has told me about, but I suppose there could be more. These affairs are always short-lived and poorly concealed, he's always humble and contrite afterward, and Virginia always forgives him. I don't understand this arrangement, but then it's impossible to guess what goes on behind closed doors, even when one of your closest friends is involved.

While Raymond paced, Virginia incessantly rearranged the objets d'art on her coffee table: a ceramic cat, a tigereye paperweight, a carved wooden box with mother-of-pearl inlays, and a small modern sculpture in black and silver wires whose shape suggested a running woman. The Silvers have the most dramatic living room I've seen in Cassandra, and I attribute this to Virginia's artistic temperament. The carpet is white, and the two sofas are a brilliant green-and-blue plaid with thin lines of orange. Virginia's had the wall with the fireplace painted the same shade of orange, and added other touches of color such as a vase of peacock feathers and a huge Chinese fan in yellow. In the midst of all this distress, I found the brightness of these colors both painful and offensive.

"I'm sure Sarah's all right," Dan said.

"Do you think so?" Virginia asked.

"Oh, yes," I murmured.

"Absolutely," Dan said with conviction. He patted her hand, but I thought how, on the way over to the Silvers, he'd said things like "Jesus Christ, not another one," and "We're going to have to find this fucking murderer if it kills us."

At two o'clock we went home, took sleeping pills, and fell asleep, holding each other tight. The next morning at breakfast, we told Joel about Sarah. He stopped eating and looked so frightened that Dan said, "What's the matter?"

"I'm going to have to figure out everything I did yesterday, right?"

My throat constricted. "Joel," I said, "no one's accused you of anything."

"But they will, won't they?" he said bitterly.

"Do you know anything about this?" I asked.

"No!"

"Then you don't have anything to worry about," Dan said.

He tried to put his arm around Joel, but Joel pulled away as he usually does now when Dan tries to be affectionate. Instead, Joel hunched closer over his bowl of cereal as if he could make himself smaller, rounder, more compact, while Dan sighed and gave me a resigned look over Joel's head.

After breakfast I called Mona to tell her I wouldn't be at work that day.

"I heard about it," she said. "Frieda phoned me. You know what she's doing? Sending her girls to her mother's in Pennsylvania. She says Cassandra's too dangerous."

"I think that's a little extreme," I said, "don't you?"

"I don't know," Mona said. "I was so frightened I called Tony up and asked him to move in."

"You didn't!"

"It's only for a while. I don't want to be alone in my apartment."

"What about telling him he could go fuck himself?" I asked. "What about being a doormat?"

"It's better than being chopped liver."

When I got to Virginia's, I found Daphne and Frances already there, along with several other neighbors who had dropped by with sympathy and the inevitable tuna casseroles so dear to the hearts of Cassandrans when crisis hits their lives. When they were gone, we sit with Virginia and let her talk while Melissa, who's fourteen years old, wanders back and forth between the living room, where she huddles as close to Virginia on the couch as she can, and the den, where she watches cartoons on television as if her life depends on it. Melissa doesn't take after Raymond the way Sarah does but looks like Virginia with the same fine, pale hair, fair skin, and delicate features. Raymond comes and sits with us for a while. He doesn't say anything but listens to Virginia, who keeps rehashing the day before: what she thought versus what she should have thought, what she did versus what she should have done, what she said versus what she should have said. Then she cries and starts all over again. The three of us let it gush out, nodding and agreeing and sympathizing, but I sense the tension building up in Raymond. When he gets up and says he's going to clean the garage, Virginia doesn't notice, but I follow him into the kitchen.

He turns to me and says, "How can you stand it?"

"It's what she needs right now."

"Not me," he says, and the corners of his mouth twitch. "If I don't do something, I'll blow sky high."

"It's okay," I say. "We'll look after Virginia."

When I go back to the living room, carrying a pitcher of lemonade and a tray of drinks, Daphne is leading Virginia back into a memory of the past that we all share.

"Whenever I think about Sarah," Daphne says, "I remember the camping trip from hell."

Virginia's eyelashes are sodden with tears, but her mouth curves upward slightly. "That was awful, wasn't it?"

This trembly, one-sixteenth smile gives us encouragement, and we jump in enthusiastically.

"Where did we go again?" Frances says.

"Some campground outside of Watertown," I say, "I don't remember the name."

"Camp Nausea," Daphne says.

Melissa, who's wandered over and huddled next to Virginia, looks at her. "Was I there, Mom?"

"Everybody was there," Virginia says.

"It was nineteen seventy-eight," I say.

"There wasn't a kid over five," Frances says.

"No," Daphne says. "Celia was seven."

"You were two," Virginia says to Melissa.

"It was the hot dogs," I say. "I've always thought it was the hot dogs."

"Remember how great we thought that night was going to be?" Daphne asks.

"The kids all finally asleep in their sleeping bags," I say.

"The stars," Frances says, "the campfire, the singing."

"The vodka collins," I say.

"Who brought those?" Frances asks.

"We did," Virginia says.

"And then"—Daphne makes a dramatic pause and then says in a falsetto—"'Mommy, I don't feel well.'"

"It was Joel," I say. "Dan managed to get him outside before he threw up."

"Then Ben got sick," Frances says.

"It was like bowling pins," Daphne says to Melissa. "Then Celia, Julian, and you. Kids crying. Kids stumbling out of tents in their pajamas. Kids vomiting all over the campsite."

Melissa gives a little giggle.

"Everybody but Sarah," I say.

"She slept through it all," Virginia says.

"Until—" Daphne says, and starts to laugh.

Her laugh is infectious and catches us, even Virginia. Suddenly we're all smiling, while Melissa looks quizzically from face to face.

"Until," Frances says, "much later."

"Much, much later," I say.

"Everybody was finally asleep," Virginia says.

Frances paints the picture. "It was absolutely quiet outside the tents. Even the crickets had gone to sleep."

"And then from the Silvers' tent, we heard *'Mommy!'*" I say.

"But it was too late," Daphne says.

"Why?" Melissa asks.

"Sarah had thrown up in the tent," Frances says.

"All over everybody's sleeping bags," Virginia says.

"And you," Daphne reminds her.

"You should've heard the noises coming from your tent," I say to Melissa. "Your father scared away the wildlife for miles."

We're laughing now, although this event was far from funny when it happened. I remember how miserable and exhausted we all were, how Virginia's hair was full of vomit (she'd been next to Sarah), and how a disgruntled Raymond insisted on waking Melissa, taking down the tent, and driving home in the middle of the night. The rest of us milled around in the dark, whispering because of campers sleeping in the sites near us and trying to help Raymond pack and Virginia wash her hair when the only illumination was by flashlight. And, all the while, Sarah cried into a pillow, saying over and over that she didn't mean to do it.

A story like this one develops over the years. It acquires mythical proportions: the hour gets later, the adults drunker (we left this detail out with Melissa listening), and the vomiting more copious. At one party, several years later, Matt insisted it had also been drizzling, but everyone else agreed the night had been clear. The event becomes the apocryphal camping story in which all the hazards of parenthood—exhaustion, frustration, irritations, hangovers, foiled expectations, and the insidious smell of vomit

274

—are rolled up into one perfect, high-hilarity package. The joke's on us, but we love it.

And so it is this afternoon. Virginia, Daphne, Frances, and I laugh so hard we can no longer speak. We whoop, we gasp for air, we get tears in our eyes, we clutch our abdomens and bend over as if we're in severe pain. And we are. My insides feel as they're being strained to the breaking point. I don't think I can stand one more minute, but every time I get a glimpse of one of their faces, I'm sent into another gale of laughter.

It isn't until I wipe my eyes that I notice Virginia isn't laughing anymore. Her smile has become a rictus of agony, and she's making terrible animal sounds, a wailing and keening made up of great, gulping sobs with huge suckings of air in between.

"Mommy!" Melissa cries, and Virginia clutches her tightly.

We don't look at one another. Frances stares into space. Daphne chews on a fingernail. I study the sculpture on Virginia's coffee table. What's the point of looking at one another? We'd see the same fear, the same despair, and the same awful sense of helplessness mirrored on each other's faces. Instead we sit like prisoners, caught in the terrible bombardment of Virginia's cries.

Later that afternoon, I leave to run some errands before dinner. My place is taken by other Cassandrans, including Molly Deacon, who doesn't say hello when she enters but just folds Virginia into her arms. I wish I don't have a sensation of release as I walk down the Silvers' driveway to my car, but I do. I have a profound sense of the outside world: the greenness of the grass, the blueness of the sky, the brilliance of the sun. Every color is richer, the edge of every object sharper than it had been that morning. It's as if I've emerged from a cave after many years spent in cold darkness, and I think that this must be how Molly and Virginia feel, trapped in the cave with no way to get out.

I drive to the Baymont Mall, where I go to the bank machine and get some cash, buy ground beef for dinner, and stop at the dry cleaner's to pick up my raincoat. I try not to think about Sarah as I do these mundane things. Instead I let my mind fill with domestic trivia: bills unpaid and house repairs yet to be done. The comfort I get from this is ironic, and I wonder how much of my life feels safe only because it's set on a structure of obligations that I'm competent to handle. It's never occurred to me before that this structure is incredibly flimsy, built on the belief that my world runs and always will run according to some coherent, logical plan. There is nothing coherent or logical about Caroline's and Sarah's disappearances. They're like earthquakes, volcanic eruptions, terrorist acts—events that can't be controlled by anyone no matter how competent.

As I come out of the dry cleaner's, I see Joel walking toward me. He has his arm around a girl's shoulders, and she's leaning into him as they walk so that they stumble a bit and he's being pushed to one side. This is making him laugh in a way I haven't heard him laugh for months. The girl is short and stocky with frizzy blond hair and a spray of pimples on her chin. Her clothes are too tight, a white tank top that barely contains her plump breasts and a short black skirt that emphasizes the thickness of her legs.

When Joel sees me, he slows down and his arm drops from the girl's shoulders. The expressions on his face change rapidly, from shock to alarm to embarrassment. He whispers something to the girl, and her eyes dart toward me and then away. I feel Joel's dismay in a visceral way, but the edges of my mouth begin to turn upward as if someone were pulling on them. By the time we meet in front of Barton's Shoes for the Whole Family, my inadvertent smile feels like it's splitting my face.

"Well, hello," I say brightly.

Joel launches into introductions. "Mom, this is Katrina. Katrina, this is my mom."

"Hi," Katrina says, and her voice is breathless, a little girl's voice. She still doesn't look at me directly but sideways, as if my smile were the sun, too brilliant and blinding.

"Are you shopping?" I ask, trying to remember if Joel had told me he was going to be at the mall.

"We came for ice cream."

I turn to Katrina and aim for an appropriate conversational opener. Joel hates it when I give his friends what he calls "the third degree," so I have to be careful to sound polite rather than nosy. "Joel tells me you work at a hairdresser's."

"The Set 'n' Curl. Up on Route Two-forty." She finally gives me a direct glance, and I see that her eyes are pretty, big and blue and fringed with dark lashes.

"Have you worked there long?"

Those eyes slide away again. "A few months."

"A friend of mine gets her hair cut there. Her name's Daphne—"

"I don't do hair."

"Oh," I say.

"I do nails." We both study her short nails, which are coated with a silvery white nail polish.

"How nice," I say.

Joel has been shifting from foot to foot. "Mom," he says, "we have to go. We're meeting Pete and Steph."

"Okay," I say. "See you later."

"I won't be home for supper. I left you a note."

I feel the weight of the ground beef in my hand. I've bought too much. "When will you be back?"

"I don't know. We're going to a movie, I think."

"Well, don't be too late."

He shrugs with impatience, and I take a deep breath and smile again. "Well, it was nice meeting you, Katrina. Maybe you'll come over some night for dinner."

Katrina doesn't answer but glances quickly at Joel, who says, "Yeah. Maybe. Well, 'bye, Mom."

" 'Bye, hon," I say, but they're in such a rush to get away from me they're gone already.

As I head home in the car, I try to think nice things about Katrina. After all, if Joel likes her, if she makes him laugh, than she must have some pleasing qualities even if they're not obvious and I can't see them. She's shy, I say to myself, she's the quiet type.

Meeting Katrina brings me back to the time when I was

dating Dan and worrying if his mother was happy with me. I don't think about Mrs. Breymann often now—she died of a heart attack when we were only married a year—but I do remember two distinct things about her: her fragility and how excessively polite she was to me. She'd never been a strong woman, she suffered from some kind of colitis, and she was small and thin with soft, white hair. Although she was ten years older than my mother, she looked as if she came from an older generation and that Dan could be her grandson instead of her son.

Mrs. Breymann had grown up in Germany, married there, and then come to America before the war. Her Germanic formality was like a wall between us. When I had her over for dinner, she praised everything I made, even when a roast was too well done or my cake hadn't risen properly. When she opened the gifts I'd chosen for her the first Christmas after we were married, she was delighted by everything. "You have such lovely taste," she said. "Just like your mother." I never felt comfortable with this praise or her small, fragile smiles. It seemed to me that they masked what she was really thinking. After that Christmas dinner, I suggested to Dan that his mother didn't like me. He said that I'd got it all wrong, that she liked me a lot, but added as an afterthought that nothing in life really seemed to matter to her since his father died.

Now I wonder if I misread her politeness as insincerity. Maybe Mrs. Breymann truly thought I was a perfect match for her only son. After all, she'd known me since I was nine years old. My family wasn't particularly social with the Breymanns, but my father was their banker, and my mother and Mrs. Breymann were joint class mothers the year Dan and I were in grade five. I must have been in the periphery of her vision for years, biking on her street, acting in school plays, marching in the town parades with my clarinet. Maybe she'd always worried about the girl Dan would marry, maybe I was a relief to her, a known quantity, safe and respectable.

I know the world's changed, and it would be foolish to hope that Joel will date only girls I know and trust. And just because I don't know Katrina or her family doesn't mean there's anything wrong with her. She's shy, I say to myself again, but in my heart I think differently. I don't like the way she dresses, the color of her nail polish, the fact that she can't look me directly in the eye. I think she's sly, vulgar, and unattractive, and I'm horrified that Joel's going out with her. I'm also shocked by my reaction. I was brought up to be nice, to think the best of people, to know you shouldn't judge a book by its cover. The result is that I dislike myself intensely for disliking Katrina so much.

At dinner when I tell Dan about Katrina and my reaction to her, he says, "That's probably part of her appeal for Joel."

"That I don't like her?"

"You don't want to be safe at seventeen, Barbara. You want to live on the wild side, not go out with someone your mother would like."

"But she's so tacky."

"He's experimenting. He'll get tired of her eventually."

It doesn't make me happy, but I know Dan is probably right. I experimented, too, before I fell in love with him. My experiment was a fellow student in my biology class at college, a tall, thin Jewish boy who came from New York City and thrilled my upstate conservative sensibilities with his swagger, profanity, and long, curly black hair. Eugene didn't wash too often, but he could quote Beat poets and talk knowledgeably (or so I thought) about civil rights and politics. Three years later, long hair and cynicism about the establishment would be pervasive, but in 1965, at my small college, he stood out like a sore thumb or an exciting iconoclast, depending on your inclination.

The best part for me was that I knew my parents would hate him. "Like should marry like," my mother had said, and Eugene was about as unlike Cassandra as anyone I'd ever met. I had fantasies about bringing him home and watching my parents' reaction. They'd be kind and polite, bending over backward to make him feel comfortable. My mother would worry about his food preferences even though Eugene thought religion was shit and keeping kosher was pandering to autocratic assholes who were out of touch with reality. My father would try to assess his potential by asking what he planned to do with his life, a shocker right there because Eugene was only majoring in biology because his father wanted him to be a doctor. What he really wanted was to go to India and study meditation with a guru. I imagined my father's silence, broken by those small clearings of his throat that occurred when he was upset or agitated.

But if the best part of going out with Eugene was the thrill of the exotic, the worst part was bed: his sheets were dirty and he wasn't faithful. When I found out he was sleeping with another girl, a cheerleader of all things, I got furious and broke off the relationship with tears and cruel, hard accusations. But underneath I was relieved it was over, and when I saw Dan the following Christmas, I had the sensation of finally coming home.

My sleep that night is shallow, filled with fleeting dreams that I don't remember except that Eugene is in them, and I haven't dreamed about him in years. I wake up periodically, and when I check the digital display on the clock by the bed, I find that only an hour has gone by. I know this fitful sleep is partly the result of an upsetting day, but I'm also premenstrual and, for the past few months, I haven't slept well before my periods started. I've never had difficult periods before, I usually only feel a little tense on the first day, so I find this new pattern distressing. I'm not only tired but also anxious. The anxiety doesn't seem to arise from any specific reason but is a general feeling of foreboding that deepens as I get less and less sleep and become more and more exhausted until, by the time my period arrives, I'm so strung out I can barely function.

I attribute this pattern to stress, but Frances tells me it could also be a sign of lowering estrogen and a harbinger of menopause. "Every month I have these nights where I fall asleep at ten, wake up at eleven, and can't go back to sleep," she said.

"How awful," I said.

"You know what I do? Get a lot of work done. I correct

essays. I plan lectures." She paused and gave me a rueful smile. "And then I collapse during the day. I don't sleep, mind you. I just collapse."

Beside me Dan turns onto his back and starts lightly snoring. I give his shoulder a shove, and he obediently turns back on his side and breathes quietly. Lying in the dark, I hear things I wouldn't during the day. The house creaks, the refrigerator cycles on and off, a car goes down the next street. I hear Joel come in at one-thirty in the morning. He goes into the kitchen and opens the refrigerator door. When I don't hear it shut, I know he's standing in the dark kitchen staring into its lit interior and finally taking out the milk carton and drinking from it. How do I know this? Because I've caught him before. It's his late-night habit, which I haven't been able to break him of no matter how many times we discuss the cost of electricity and the unsanitary condition of the milk carton. The refrigerator door finally shuts, and he goes to his room.

I doze again—confusing dreams of Eugene and Dan meeting and going to a football game without me—and am awakened by the sound of a car door slamming and a motor revving. I glance at the clock—3:25. We live on a quiet street, and I can't imagine any of our neighbors being so impolite. I'm curious enough to get out of bed and look out the window, but all I see are red taillights disappearing around the corner. I'm not the only person roused by this. Across the street, I see a light go on in the Gages' bedroom and a curtain flicker. Now it's my turn to go into the kitchen, where I make myself tea and toast. When I finally get back into bed, it's almost four o'clock and I feel truly tired. I think it's a good thing it's Sunday and I don't have to get up early. I curl up in anticipation of deep, relaxing sleep, but I seem to have closed my eyes for only a moment when the telephone by the bed rings.

I pick up the receiver. "Hello?" I say, my voice thick. There's sunlight pouring into the bedroom, so I know I've slept even though I don't feel as if I had. Beside me Dan grunts, shifts, and rustles the bedcovers.

A hoarse voice says, "It's Virginia."

I go from sleepy to alarmed. "What's happened?" I ask, sitting up so abruptly I feel faint.

"We found her. She's okay."

"Oh, thank God," I say, and turn to Dan, whose eyes are now open. "They've found Sarah and she's all right."

Virginia continues, "She'd taken a bus to the Port Authority in New York City. A policeman spotted her sleeping in a corner and brought her in to the station. They didn't have any problem figuring out who she was from the APB. She's pretty distinctive."

"What was she doing there?"

"You're not going to believe this, Barbara. She was only making a statement."

"A *what?*"

"A statement. She felt everyone was forgetting Caroline. She figured her disappearance would bring Caroline's disappearance right back into people's minds."

I take a deep breath. "Well, she was right about that."

"I'm so angry. You know what she put us through? And to think she'd hang out in that Port Authority building. You know what could've happened to her?"

I hear Virginia's voice rising out of control so I change the subject. "How's she getting home?"

"They've put her on a bus back to Syracuse. We'll pick her up there this afternoon. Honestly, Barbara, what would you do? Hug her? Kill her?"

"Both," I say.

"Raymond wants to ground her for the rest of her life."

"I'll bet he does."

Virginia starts to cry. "I'm just glad it's over. I'm so glad it's over."

I make soothing sounds, suggest to Virginia she get some rest, and finally hang up. Dan is lying on his back staring up at the ceiling. I say, "Sarah was making a political statement about Caroline's disappearance. She wants to make sure no one forgets."

"Jesus," he says.

"At least Joel's political statements are less extreme."

"You mean you might even like Katrina?"

I cuddle up next to him. "I wouldn't go that far."

He puts his arm around me. "It's just a phase. He'll be fine."

"Promise?"

"Promise."

"Mmm," I say, and rub my hand over his bare belly.

"Mmm," he replies, and cups my breast.

I stretch luxuriously. "Mornings are my favorite time," I say.

"I know," Dan says, "and today you're going to get lucky."

We have breakfast on our patio, sipping coffee and glancing through the Saturday paper, which we haven't had a chance to read. Flower beds surround the patio, and the early blooms are out: red tulips, yellow daffodils, white hyacinth, and royal blue scilla. The lilac bushes are in bud, and I think how lovely it is when they're flowering and the backyard smells like my mother's sachets for about two weeks.

Joel comes out, yawning widely. He's only wearing a pair of shorts, and I can see that, like the flowers, he's in season, a glorious, golden brown bloom. His shoulders have thickened, muscle ripples on his abdomen, and blond hairs glint on his chest. My love for him is so fierce I'm suddenly afraid that the gods (whoever they are) might notice his beauty and destroy it. I say sharply, "Put a shirt on. It's too cold."

"Cold? Mom, it's almost seventy degrees."

"A shirt," I say.

"Dad? Do you think it's cold? Do you?"

Dan refuses to look up from the paper. "Your mother's always right," he says.

"Jeez," Joel mutters as he goes back into the house.

I smile and sip my coffee. Joel returns with a T-shirt on, picks up the comics, and starts reading. I sit back and let the sun warm my face. I think idly about what I'll do for the rest of the day and what we'll have for dinner. I'm contemplating making potato salad when our neighbor, George Gage, pokes his head around the side of the house.

"Sorry to bother you," he says. George is the oldest neighbor on our block. He's in his seventies, a thin man with a bald, liver-spotted scalp and a trim white mustache.

"Sit down," Dan says. "Have a cup."

"Thanks, but I came over to ask you folks if you'd seen your garage door."

"No," I say.

He shakes his head. "It's a real shame. That's what it is."

By this time, Dan and I are up and walking around the corner of the house to the front with Joel trailing behind us. George follows. "You know something? I think I heard them in the middle of the night. They woke me right up and I looked out the window, but they were gone. Well, I wondered, what was that all about?"

Our garage door is white and has two large indented squares on its upper panel. Both have been defaced with black painted scrawls. One reads CUNT, the other MURDERER. For a few seconds, we stand there and just stare at the words. Then, although I'm standing in the sun, I feel a chill run through me and I begin to shiver.

George hasn't stopped talking. "Then this morning, I looked out the window again, and I thought, good heavens, what's this world coming to anyway? That's what I'd like to know. Where it's going to end?"

"Goddamn," Dan mutters.

"Well," Joel says, "at least he's learned how to spell. That's something, isn't it?"

Chapter
6

BY MID-JULY, JOEL FIGURES HE'S HAVING THE WORST SUMMER of his life. This depresses him, because he's always looked forward to the summers, to getting out of school and having fun. Over the years his definition of fun hasn't changed much. It means no more responsibilities, even though he's had summer jobs for the past couple of years. The summer jobs—this year he's working at Video Heaven—don't really have an impact on his fun, because everyone else is working, too, and when he's not at the store, he doesn't have to think about it. Summer fun means hopping on his bike—now the car if his parents let him have it—and just taking off with the sun on his face and the wind in his hair. It means meeting his friends and hanging out wherever they want to hang out: at the mall, in someone's backyard, at Misty Lake. And it means lots of horsing around with girls at the lake, where you can tease them by splashing, dunking, or throwing them into the water. You don't do this alone. You're always with the guys, a free-floating group whose members change hourly. You do everything with these guys: chew the fat, dive off the rock, have spontaneous races, and torment the girls. Of course, the girls have their own group. They sunbathe together, comb each other's hair, and put sunblock on one another. Whenever the group of guys gets one girl and throws her in the water, all the girls scream and laugh. For most of his summers, Joel has associated the sound of girls screaming with all the other pleasures of the season: the heat of the sun on his skin, the sharp angle of a dive into cool water, the mindless hours stretching ahead until September.

The difference between this summer and the others, what makes this one the worst in history, is as Pete describes it, the "woman shit," which has ruined the horsing-around-with-girls fun, probably permanently. Now when Joel goes to the lake and sees the freshman and sophomore boys roughhousing and racing after girls, he recognizes that he's outgrown that kind of fun. Sometimes that makes him sad, and he wishes he could turn back the clock. But the carefree, unthinking Joel of a year ago is gone forever. It seems to him that he's merging now with that other Joel who appeared after Caroline disappeared, the one who sees reality so coldly, who has an uncomfortable sense of irony, who can make such acid comments on his own behavior. Now, when he sees himself with Katrina with that cool, unrelenting eye, he doubts he'll really enjoy another summer again or any other part of his life with the same abandon of childhood.

Both he and Pete are having trouble with the "woman shit." They don't talk a lot about it, but they spend a lot of time with each other. Pete's family belongs to a tennis club in Laurel Grove, and when Joel and Pete aren't working or going out with Steph and Katrina, they try to destroy one another on the tennis court. Although they're both rotten players, Joel is moderately better than Pete and usually beats him, but not until they're flushed beet red, dripping with sweat, and so exhausted they can barely lift their racquets. Then they take cold showers in the locker room and sit in the clubhouse restaurant eating fries, drinking Cokes, and having brief bursts of conversation.

"You shoulda gotten that serve," Joel says.

"Which one?"

"The last one."

"The angle sucked."

"It's your backhand," Joel says. "It's shitty."

"Fuck my backhand," Pete says.

"Fuck tennis," Joel says.

"Yeah."

They swig their drinks.

"Fuck women," Pete says.

"Yeah."

Pete and Steph aren't getting along too well. Steph says Pete is inconsiderate and immature. Pete says he doesn't know what the hell she wants from him. Joel's situation is different. He knows what he wants from Katrina, but she won't give it to him. He wants to lose his virginity, but she won't sleep with him no matter how hard he tries. They do everything else he can imagine, but she draws the line at intercourse, and nothing he says or does can change her mind. They have long, drawn-out discussions that go around and around in frustrating circles.

They're usually in the backseat of the car, parked by the lake. They've already been kissing, and her blouse and shorts are off. He strokes her breasts. It's already hot in the car, but Katrina won't let him open the windows because of the mosquitoes. She's got sensitive skin that shows every bite, and she hates being blotchy, it's too gross. He runs his hand down to the waistband of her panties and tries to tug them off. She pushes his hand away.

"Come on," he begs.

"No."

"You won't get pregnant. I've got condoms."

"Steph got pregnant on a condom."

"I'll use two."

"No."

"Jesus."

"Don't swear," she says in her prim, little girl's voice. "You know I don't like it."

"Why don't you go on the pill like everyone else?"

"I told you. They give me the worst headaches, and I get real depressed."

He kisses her again, very passionately, pushing his tongue as far back into her mouth as he can get it, and fantasizes that she's Marla. Katrina arches against him, her hand brushing his open fly. As the summer's progressed, she's graduated from rubbing her hand against him to releasing his penis from his pants and jerking him off. He's allowed to touch her inside her underpants, but that's all. Even though the movement of his fingers on her hot, wet flesh makes her squirm and pant, she won't let him take her underpants off. Recently he's managed to get a finger right up inside her, and whenever he imagines his prick there, he gets as hard as a rock and breaks out in a sweat.

"Come on, Katrina."

"No." She's wrapped her hand around his penis and is moving it up and down.

"Just take your panties off."

"No."

"Why not?" Joel can hear himself whining, but he's too aroused to care.

"It would be the start."

"It wouldn't."

"I said no."

"Please."

Her fingers stroke the sensitive cord below the glans. "No."

By now he can hardly breathe, but he renews his attack. "Come on."

"No."

"But you slept with Nick."

"I told you. He forced me."

Joel has heard about these so-called rapes—there were two of them—several times. At first he was horrified and sympathetic, comforting Katrina when she cried. But now he's confused, because he thinks if Katrina did to Nick what she does to him, maybe she drove Nick to it. Like sometimes she touches him for a while and stops, or sometimes doesn't want to touch him at all, and sometimes he feels so crazy with all his physical feelings when he's with her, it's all he can do to keep himself from pushing her harder. In his deepest, darkest moments, Joel also admits to himself that sometimes, rarely but sometimes, when she's at her most infuriating, he feels like hitting her.

He wishes he knew Nick. He'd like to sit down with him over a beer and talk man to man.

"She drives me nuts," he'd say to Nick.

"I've been there," Nick would say.

"I never know how far she'll let me go."

"I'm with you, man."

"Like, she encourages me, but then always draws the line."

"She's a real ho."

"I ask myself why I still go out with her."

"Why do you, man?"

"I guess because there's no one else."

"And you want some ass."

"Yeah."

They'd sigh and order another round of beer. Joel would say, "And you want to know something? Even though she says you raped her, she really wants you back."

"Women are weird, man. That's the truth."

The truth is that Joel doesn't like Katrina, but he wants her, and it's put him in a lousy, demoralizing bind. And that's not the only thing that's ruining his summer, although it's a big part of it. There's the defacing of the garage door. He wasn't the only target. The perpetrator, as Reg Burton calls him, wrote on the front doors or garage doors of all the boys who'd also had KUNT KILLER painted on their lockers. Joel hates having the finger pointed at him again and having to deal with the police. He hates having his family pulled into it. And it doesn't help when people tell him how sorry they are. It just makes him feel like a freak, as if those people are staring at him all the time.

Sarah Silver didn't help things either. Caroline's disappearance didn't get a lot of media attention outside their own area, but Sarah's disappearance and reappearance are a different story. All the major networks picked it up, including CNN. So she got what she wanted. Everyone's talking about Caroline again and rehashing what happened and who the suspects had been. A Syracuse television crew showed up at the Breymanns' house one Saturday afternoon, but they'd been forewarned because Ben and Frances were being bombarded by the media. Although the reporter asked for Joel, Dan acted as the family spokesman. He said that he and his wife and son were very distressed over what had happened to Caroline, they were working with the police to help them find her, and that was all he had to say. Joel watched from his bedroom window, and part of him was sorry he wasn't going to be on television. It was pretty exciting seeing people you knew and places you'd grown up in on the national news. But another part of him was intensely relieved. The thought of having his face fill up the screen so that his zits are as big as fucking strawberries makes his insides squirm.

Anyway, the Syracuse television station never showed the interview with Dan. "I guess I was sufficiently boring," he said with satisfaction. But lots of other people showed up on their set: a tearful Molly with Brian standing beside her, tiny Sophie Rundle saying what a well-behaved girl Caroline had been in her church, Arlene McPherson discussing the importance of morals in bringing up children, Reg Burton talking about the importance of ensuring that Cassandra was a safe environment for its citizens. Joel was surprised to see how well Sarah did during her interviews. She talked passionately about the importance of remembering Caroline and never stumbled once or sounded stupid.

Barbara noticed that Sarah was prettier on television than she was in person. "The camera fills her out," she said. "She doesn't look so angular."

"She wasn't wearing that nose ring," Dan said. "A vast improvement."

"You know something?" Barbara said. "I think Sarah is going to be lovely in an interesting sort of way."

Joel had never noticed that Sarah was pretty; actually, he'd thought of her as kind of weird looking. But when he imagined her without the spiked hair and the distracting jewelry, he saw that she had a pretty smile and dark eyes that were slanted and beautiful.

Ben was caught by the cameras one evening as he was coming out of the Happy Sombrero in Laurel Grove, where he worked as a busboy. He was amazingly cool considering the reporter just stuck a mike in his face and asked insulting questions.

"Could you describe your relationship with Caroline Deacon?" the reporter asked.

"We were going steady."

"According to the police, you were the prime suspect for a while."

"I had nothing to do with her disappearance."

"How did it make you feel to be put in that position and have to take a lie detector test?"

"The police were doing what they had to do."

"How do you feel about Caroline now?"

"I miss her."

"What would you say to her if you thought she was listening right now?"

Ben's dark eyes looked directly into the camera, and there was a slight quiver in his voice. "I love you, Caroline. Please come home if you can."

It brought tears to everyone's eyes, including the anchorwoman who was reporting the story, and Barbara was crying so hard she had to leave the living room and lie down in her bedroom. When she recovered, she called Frances and then cried some more.

After all the publicity, the Deacons and Silvers have been invited to be on the *Oprah Winfrey Show* in September. Ben had been invited, too, but he refused. Virginia came over and told his parents all about it while Joel was there. Actually, Sally Jessy Raphael also wanted them, so there were a thrilling couple of days when Molly and Virginia were being wooed by producers and being sent flowers and promised stretch limousines, but they decided Oprah would be the best, because they felt she was more sympathetic. They're going to be flown to Chicago and put up in a hotel and, in payment for having their personal lives bared on television, Oprah has agreed to show Caroline's picture several times on the show. Molly's convinced, Virginia told them, that this national exposure is going to get Caroline back for sure. In the meantime, Molly's scheduled a perm for two weeks before showtime so it has time to relax, and everyone but Sarah is shopping for the right outfits to wear on television. Sarah refuses to compromise her principles with regard to her appearance just because she's going on national TV.

Joel believes the only thing in his life that hasn't been ruined is his relationship with Marla. He isn't really working for her anymore, but he does go out to her place every week or so to chat and see how the house is coming. Marla's always glad to see him, and the best part is that Tony's not there anymore. At first, when Joel noticed his absence, he was afraid it was only temporary.

"Is that Mr. Molino finished with the house?" he asked.

Marla looked at him with curiosity. "Finished with the house?"

Joel could feel himself flushing. "I thought that . . . like maybe . . . he was helping you with the contractors."

"Oh." She shrugged. "I don't need him anymore."

So Joel feels a lot more relaxed about dropping by. He's even told Marla about Katrina, not every private detail, of course, but the general picture. She said it's important to try out different kinds of relationships when you're a teenager so you can figure out what's best for you. She talked about Christian and the fact that if he hadn't died they might have actually gotten married, and what a bad thing that could've been, because they hadn't really had a chance to go out with other people.

Joel has tried to help Marla with her questions about Christian's death. He told her what Dan had said: that Christian had been with a girl before he got into his car. Marla thought that was extremely helpful. Encouraged by this, Joel approaches Barbara one evening while she's making supper and he's setting the table. But before he gets to Marla's business, he has some questions of his own.

"Mom?"

"Mmm?" She's slicing cucumber for a salad.

"You and Marla were best friends in high school, weren't you?"

"Yes."

"But you're not now?"

Barbara's silent for a moment and then says, "I think a girl needs to have one girlfriend who really understands her. Maybe it's nature's method of letting her practice, in a safe way, the kind of intimacy she'll have later with the man she falls in love with."

"So now you're married you don't need her?"

"I still like her, Joel. We still have a good time together."

"But she's not your best friend anymore."

"Dad's my best friend now."

Joel likes hearing about his parents this way. It gives him a feeling of solid earth below his feet. "Yeah," he says.

"And besides, I have a lot of women friends. I don't want just one."

Joel puts out the knives and aligns one neatly beside each plate. "Marla told me all about her boyfriend and everything."

"Yes, that was very sad."

"You were there that night, right?"

"Uh-huh."

"Marla said he was really angry when he took off in the car."

"She and Christian had a fight."

"Dad says he met someone after that, a girl."

"Dad says that?"

"I asked him."

Barbara puts down the tomato she was about to chop. "Has Marla hired you as a detective now?"

She says this with a little laugh and Joel laughs, too. "She wants to write about what happened, but she can't quite figure it out."

Barbara begins to chop the tomato. "Well, good luck to her."

"You don't think she'll find the answer?"

"I think it happened too long ago."

"You didn't see or hear anything?"

"It was dark and there was a lot of noise. Someone had a guitar and was playing. Some people were singing." She sighs. "I didn't even see Christian leave."

"Oh," Joel says with disappointment. He's had this little

fantasy about finding out the truth for Marla. He's imagined the pleased look on her face and the way she'd congratulate him.

"You know something, hon? It isn't always a good idea to poke around in the past. The answers are never clear. Remember how you always insisted you cut your knee and got those stitches during that Christmas we spent with Grandma and Grandpa in Florida, but it really happened a year later when Grandma was visiting us? That's what memory does. It mixes things up. You can't trust it."

"Yeah," Joel says slowly. "Yeah, I guess that's true."

Joel wishes he had better news for Marla about Christian as he arrives at her house. He hasn't seen her since before Sarah disappeared and the graffiti appeared on the garage door, and he's looking forward to talking to her. He thinks she may understand how weird all of it makes him feel. He can't quite pinpoint all the emotions. Sometimes he's excited, sometimes he's depressed. And it's all mixed up with Katrina and the whole lousy summer. So, when he turns up her driveway, he's filled with an anticipation that suddenly dissipates when he sees another car parked in front of the house. It's not Tony's blue New Yorker but a white Pontiac Grand Am. He thinks maybe a contractor's come even though it's Sunday, but when he pulls a little closer and sees the sticker on the bumper—READING MAKES YOU LITERATE—he recognizes Frances Phillips's car.

He starts to turn the car around when Marla appears from around the corner of the house. She waves to him so he stops the car and turns off the ignition.

"Joel," she says, putting her head into the window on the passenger's side, "come and admire the pool."

"No thanks," he says, "I don't want to bother you and Frances."

"Frances?" she asks, and then laughs. "Frances isn't here. It's Ben."

The idea that Ben has taken to visiting Marla gives Joel the same bad feeling he had when Tony was around. But he obediently parks the car, gets out, and follows Marla around to the back of the house. Ben is stretched out on a cushioned chaise lounge on the upper level of the newly built cedar deck. Joel gives a nod to Ben as he and Marla sit down, and Ben nods back, the sun glinting off his sunglasses.

"Isn't the pool beautiful?" Marla says.

"Yeah," Joel says, but he thinks she's the one who's beautiful. She's wearing a white tank top and dark blue shorts that show off her slim, tanned legs. Her hair is different, Joel's not sure how, but it's softer and curlier around her face. A small diamond pendant glitters in the hollow of her throat.

"They're going to fill it tomorrow and check the filters. Then we'll be able to swim whenever we want." Marla picks up a pitcher on a table beside her chair and says, "Lemonade?"

"Sure."

"Ben and I were talking about poetry," she says, pouring him a glass.

Joel notices the *Norton Anthology of Modern Poetry* on the table and thinks: *Shit.*

Marla smiles. "But we can finish our conversation some other time. Right, Ben?"

"I'll bring that collection next time."

"Ben has a book of poems by writers from the central New York area," Marla explains.

"That's cool," Joel says. He sips at his lemonade.

"So tell me all about Sarah Silver." Marla stretches out, putting her face up to the sun, whose rays are broken by the latticework. "I can't believe what I've been seeing on the TV."

"She's kind of weird," Joel starts.

Ben interrupts him. "What she did to Cassandra," he says, "is like what Gandhi did to India. A nonviolent protest. She wanted to make Caroline's disappearance an issue again."

Joel sees Ben come down the ice, stick-handling the puck.

"Nonviolent in the physical sense, but not an emotional one," Marla points out. "I imagine her parents were devastated."

295

Joel leaps over the boards and bounds onto the ice. "But it worked," he says. "The Deacons are going to be on *Oprah.*"

"Was it fair to her family, though? Was it right?"

Joel tries to think this through, but he's confused. He knows how frightened and upset the Silvers and his parents were. "You mean, does the end justify the means?"

"Exactly," Marla says.

"I'm glad she did it," Ben says, his voice rough with emotion. "I wish I'd had the guts."

Marla lightly touches Ben's wrist and changes the subject. "Tell me how Sarah's weird, Joel."

Joel deftly scoops up the puck and races away with it. "It's the way she dresses. Everything in black and all the jewelry." He pauses and then finds a way to explain Sarah that he knows will interest Marla. "You can hardly see her for the nose studs and the earrings."

Marla raises her eyebrows. "How many nose studs?"

He's skating right toward the net. "Three."

"Two," Ben says.

Check!

"I'd like to meet Sarah," Marla says.

"She writes poetry, too," Ben says.

"Does she? What kind?"

The puck leaps from his stick to Ben's . . .

"Pyramidal."

"Pyramidal?"

. . . and hangs there as if it were glued.

"That's the shape she uses, and the words all run together." Ben pauses. "Actually, they're kind of hard to read."

"And what are they about?"

"Nature, the environment, commercialism. Stuff like that."

"You write about stuff like that."

"Yeah, but hers is more abstract imagery. Mine is more personal."

Joel's skating after Ben as fast as he can go, but he can't seem to close the distance. He clears his throat. "Are you going to have a party when the house is done?"

Marla turns toward Joel. "What a good idea."

Back in the action, he body-checks Ben in a corner. "An open house," he adds.

"I could have one now," she muses, "but most of the living room furniture won't arrive until October or November."

"A Thanksgiving open house," Ben says. "There's one every year."

"What do you mean—there's one every year?"

"Our families get together at Thanksgiving—us, the Breymanns, the Silvers—"

Joel smacks him on the helmet with his gloved hand. "The Fellers, sometimes the Deacons."

Ben slams him against the boards. "They move it from house to house."

Joel brings up one knee. "You could host it this year."

"Who does the cooking?"

Ben throws off his gloves. "Everyone," he says.

Joel throws off his gloves. "It's potluck."

Marla appears mystified by their sudden enthusiasm. "You'd really like me to do it, wouldn't you?"

Ben punches him in the face. "It would be cool."

Marla smiles. "I don't want to miss a chance to be cool."

The audience is on its feet, screaming, while the refs skate furiously toward them. Joel wants to knock off those fucking sunglasses; Ben wants to smash him in the nose. But the only way they can keep from crashing to the ice is to grab on to each other for balance. By the time the refs arrive, they're locked in a killer embrace, pushing and pulling, shoving and grabbing, swaying from side to side, and holding on for dear life.

Chapter
7

Caspar's hasn't changed in the six months since Marla lunched there last. The linen is still a pale pink and monogrammed with pink thread, the walls are still painted taupe and rose, and the service is still excellent. Marla notices only two exceptions. The prices have gone up yet again, and their waiter-writer is now the maître d'. He gives Marla and Harold big smiles when they come in and ushers them grandly to their table, pulling out Marla's chair and rearranging the origami of the napkin perched on Harold's wine goblet.

"Your waiter will be right with you," he says in a confidential undertone after they're seated, "but don't let him overwhelm you with the lamb. It's nice, very nice, a lovely hint of rosemary, but in my opinion, the salmon is today's star in the firmament. A very unusual presentation with orange, beets, and strawberries."

"Thank you, Peter," Harold says. "We'll keep it in mind."

"Bon appétit."

After he leaves, Marla says, "I don't think I can resist a star in the firmament."

"He doesn't know it yet," Harold says, "but we're having problems with his collection of short stories. The first ones were so brilliant that we signed the rest sight unseen. The last three aren't up to scratch."

"He'll have to rewrite."

"You know how most new authors are. He's touchy about revisions."

"He'll learn," Marla says.

"True. Very true."

They order lunch—the salmon so as not to hurt a new author's feelings any more than necessary—and discuss business. *Silver Crescents,* which Marla wrote in 1979, had been optioned by three film companies over the years, but no film was ever made. There were always problems with financing and getting a good screenplay. Marla even tried to write the script herself but found she didn't like screenwriting. She wasn't used to thinking visually rather than verbally, and she had difficulty translating her characters' thoughts into the action scenes that the film required. Finally, however, a fourth company optioned the book, hired a skilled screenwriter, and put the financing together.

Harold has invited Marla to lunch to celebrate the day that the film is going into production, but she knows there's more to the lunch than that. Brian has told her that Harold is planning a paperback reprint of *Silver Crescents* to be released simultaneously with the film. He hasnt' told her that Harold is filled with sweet visions of *Silver Crescents* once more being on the best-seller list, but Marla can see this is so. He's more jovial than usual, flashing that broad, toothy smile at her and ordering an extremely expensive bottle of wine. Six months ago, he treated her to a meal at Caspar's with a grudging kind of paternal affection. Today his generosity is spilling over.

"More wine?" he says.

"Thank you."

Harold fills her glass and then raises his. "To a blockbuster."

"One hopes and prays," Marla says. Their wineglasses meet with a vitreous tinkle.

Harold sips and sighs with satisfaction. "With Demi," he says, "it's money in the bank."

Marla would like to point out that even the greatest stars do not a blockbuster movie make, but why burst Harold's bubble? He's enjoying it so much. Instead, she says, "I'd like to add an introduction to the book and give the reader some idea how it fits into my life and work—the kind of thing you can't write while you're doing the book because you don't have that kind of perspective."

"A wonderful idea."

"And as for the new cover—"

"Yes?"

Harold's cautious tone makes Marla smile inwardly. She has no control over the artwork on the movie "tie-in" cover, but she realizes that Howard's been worried she might make a fuss about it anyway. "I like it," she says.

"Wonderful." Harold beams at her.

"It's better than the original."

"Really?"

The first cover had silver crescents on a background of bright blue. "That design was cold and uninviting."

"You didn't think it was sophisticated?" He has a slightly hurt look as if he'd designed the original cover himself.

Marla shakes her head.

"It sold a lot of books."

Marla could point out that it was her story and her writing that made *Silver Crescents* a best-seller, but it isn't her policy to fight with Harold over the small things, not when much more significant issues loom ahead—like Brian's negotiations for the advance of her next book.

"You're right," she says. "It did help."

Harold beams at her again as the waiter brings their salmon. The food, Marla sees, has been chosen for color. Almost everything on their plate is in shades of orange, pink, and red to match the fish. There are slices of oranges and the hulls of strawberries, sautéed red peppers, disks of beets, and julienne carrots. Even the rice is tinted a pinky orange. The contrasting shade is green, represented by sprigs of parsley and coriander.

"Lovely," Marla says to the hovering waiter.

"I've been hearing about Cassandra in the news," Harold

says as they begin eating. "Some girl there decided to teach the town a lesson, didn't she?"

"She was very successful. Another girl has disappeared, and she was afraid everyone was forgetting."

"And were they?"

"It's human nature, don't you think? To try to avoid thinking about painful things?"

"And is this other girl dead?"

"No one knows, but I suspect she is."

"How long has it been since she disappeared?"

"Almost five months." Marla takes a bite of her salmon. It's as delicious as promised. "It's put enormous pressure on the town, because the police suspect everyone, especially the boys she hung around with. I know two of them. It's very interesting."

Harold raises his eyebrows. "Ah—grist to the mill?"

Marla smiles. "I am thinking of a novel that intertwines the past and the present."

"The old and new tragedies."

There are times when Marla sees why Harold has climbed so far up the managerial ladder. He has an excellent memory. "Yes."

"You once said you were responsible for that old tragedy."

"I'm not."

"Do you know who is?"

"I think I know."

"And whose point of view would you tell these tragedies from?"

"From two points of view: the boy who died twenty-five years ago and a boy under suspicion now. Both are seventeen years old."

Harold's eyebrows went a notch higher. "You haven't tried writing from a boy's point of view before."

"I'm spending a lot of time with these two boys, talking and listening." Marla smiles. "I wish I'd been able to see through boys when I was seventeen the way I can now."

"The boy under suspicion in the novel—is he going to be the girl's boyfriend?"

Marla nods.

"And will he have killed her?"

"No. I don't think it matters who killed her, not for the purposes of the novel. I want to write about how people react under pressure."

"What's the connection between the dead boy and the boy under suspicion?" Harold asks.

"I haven't decided yet. They could be related. Maybe the first boy was the second boy's uncle. Or maybe his girlfriend was the second boy's mother."

"And it'll be set in a small town."

"Yes."

Harold nods his head slowly. "I like it. It has drama. How long do you think it'll take to write?"

"A year, maybe two."

"Then I take back what I said the last time we ate here. It seems to me your move has been a good one."

"I needed the change."

Harold lifts his wineglass again. "To your new novel," he says.

Marla raises hers. "To Cassandra."

Ben and Joel: They're fighting over me, which I find amusing. Joel isn't as good at it as Ben, who's more sophisticated and subtle. Joel's like a puppy, a golden retriever puppy, eager and easily satisfied. He's in love with me and a little frightened of me at the same time. I like to keep him on edge so he's constantly striving to maintain his balance. It's making his imagination grow and giving him the ability to think beyond the mundane and the clichéd. Sometimes he even surprises me.

Ben is deeper, moodier, darker. He finds his attraction to me torturous and conflicting. I'm an older woman, maybe I don't reciprocate the emotions, and what about his loyalty to Caroline? She pulls on him in one direction, and sometimes he doesn't show up for several days. But then I pull on him in the other direction. When he arrives, he talks with such a torrent of words I know he couldn't bear to dam up the thoughts and yearnings any longer.

And his body is so tense. No matter how cool he tries to appear, I can sense the rigidity, and when I touch him, his muscles shiver.

Marla meets Colin McIntyre at the bar in her hotel. He's the fiftyish investment banker she met at a dinner hosted by her agent several months earlier. He's written asking her to lunch with him the next time she's in the city. Marla isn't convinced she wants to commit to a lunch so she's called and suggested happy-hour drinks. They sit at a small table with a tiny lamp that barely illuminates their faces. Colin is as Marla remembers him: a slender face, small, narrow hands, silver at his temples, a gray business suit with a burgundy tie. He orders a scotch, Marla a martini. They talk about the weather, agreeing the city will be unbearable in another month, about the traffic congestion, which is always horrendous, and about the film being made from *Silver Crescents,* which Colin has read and admired.

"I couldn't put it down," he says, "and I couldn't get those characters out of my mind. They were so . . . intense. But all your books are like that."

"Thank you," Marla says. He's also admiring her and hoping to get laid. The message is subtle, conveyed in the flattery, the lean of his body toward her, the glances quickly masked. Marla wonders what he would be like in bed but can't decide if she's curious enough to find out.

"I know a lot of other authors, the kind that write economic and history texts. You're the first author of fiction I've ever known." He pauses. "I wish I could write, but then you've probably heard that before."

She acknowledges this with a smile. She divides readers into two categories, the wishers and the if-onlys. Wishers, like Colin, are humble. They'd like to write—they have stories to tell—but know they don't have the skills. The if-onlys are more arrogant. They're convinced that the only difference between Marla and themselves is time. They have great novels waiting to be written, they tell her, if only they could find the time to write them.

"I guess the part I find most mysterious is where characters come from."

"Anywhere. Everywhere."

"But you created them."

"They're composites of many people, many experiences." Marla's explained this so many times she can't keep the impatience out of her voice.

"You don't like analyzing your books, do you?"

"There's not much I can say. Readers bring their own emotional baggage to a book and then find what they want in it."

"But you're telling the story, bringing the characters to life, giving them emotions."

"I can only manipulate readers so far. They go the extra distance by themselves."

Colin shakes his head. "You talk about books the way I talk about banks."

"And how do you talk about banks?"

"Dispassionately."

He smiles slightly, and Marla thinks he has an attractive mouth. His upper lip is thin but beautifully curved.

"Writing is very private," she says.

"Then it must annoy you when people look for autobiographical details in your books."

"Intensely."

"So I shouldn't assume anything about you from what I've read."

"I wouldn't."

Colin studies her over the rim of his glass. "You're not what I expected."

"And what had you expected?" Marla asks this even though she knows the answer. In Colin's mind, she will be the embodiment of a female character in her novels whom he finds sexy and intriguing.

"More like the heroine in *Silver Crescents.*"

Valerie, who was rich and slept around because she was too lazy to say no—how disappointing. "She's more reckless than I would ever be, and not as intelligent."

"It sounds like you don't like her."

"I love all my characters," Marla says, "but I know their limitations."

He leans forward. "But surely, there's a part of you in her."

Marla suddenly discovers she's intensely bored. "Thanks for the drink," she says, reaching for her purse and standing up. "I'm afraid I have a dinner engagement."

If Colin is disappointed, he's too good-mannered to show it. He stands and smiles. "I hope we can get together the next time you're in town."

"I'll give you call," Marla says.

A good man is hard to find.
A hard man is good to find.
A found man is usually too good to be true.

They're all so boringly obvious, that's the trouble. I'd like some mystery, but there's precious little of that around. I'm tired of playing games where the rules are preordained and the outcome one of two possibilities, bed or not. I want to be surprised, but that doesn't seem to be possible anymore. I'd actually prefer either of my seventeen-year-olds to a divorced investment banker who's lonely and horny and thinks I might throw some business his way. At the very least, Joel and Ben possess a painful honesty.

This is my last entry in this journal for a while. I can feel the new book inside of me. It's been there since spring, growing the way bread rises, starting hard and compact, all the facts of it jammed together into a small space. Now it's expanded, it's lighter, and I can separate out the threads of the story. The novel will be a double helix, the two plots circling one another, while the main characters reflect one another like mirrors across the space of twenty-five years.

But nothing about the book is fixed or certain. This is what I know: who the protagonists are, the opening sentence, a few scenes, snatches of dialogue, and almost nothing about the world they inhabit, except that it's a small town not unlike Cassandra. This is what I don't know: how the novel will end, what secondary characters and subplots will appear, and what the writing will reveal about myself.

The coils of the double helix are uncharted territory, but I'm not worried. I begin my best books this way—with ignorance and anticipation. Writing is like courtship, that intimate journey into the other, the unknown. But it's more seductive and more mysterious than any courtship I've ever had, and ultimately more satisfying. What man can compete with *that?*

Chapter
8

THE DAY BEFORE DAN AND I ARE TO LEAVE ON OUR HOLIDAY, I tie up loose ends at the library. Mona will be acting head librarian while I'm gone, and we spend the morning discussing administrative details. We have a new volunteer, the schedule has to be shifted around to accommodate vacations, and the roof repairs are to be done while I'm gone. These repairs will require work inside and outside the building, and we've been told that workmen will be spending about a week taking out the damaged ceiling and replacing it. Since this section of the ceiling covers part of the nonfiction section—293.13 Nordic Mythology to 589.2097 Mushrooms and Molds—we've also just been informed that we'll have to remove the books and some of the shelving. We discuss how this will be accomplished without disturbing the readers in the rest of the nonfiction section.

"Do you think it could be done on a Sunday?" I ask.

"No problem," Mona says, "and I'll get some strong guys to do the books."

"I know Frieda's husband would help."

"I'll line up Tony and his thousand-and-one relatives."

When Mona invited Tony to stay with her after Sarah disappeared, I figured it would be a temporary arrangement. But time has proven me wrong. It's now mid-August, and Tony has moved in with Mona lock, stock, and barrel despite the objections of his parents, who don't like Mona because she isn't Catholic. Mona's conversation is sprinkled with "Tony this" and "Tony that" and "Sorry, but I can't come in on Saturday, because Tony's daughters are coming over for the weekend."

When I reminded her how she once felt about Tony, she said, "That was then."

"What's the difference now?"

"He's grateful."

"Grateful?"

"As in humble. I can thank Marla Hudson for that. She dumped him, and he took it hard, poor baby. And, besides, I've got him reading."

"Really," I said.

"Magazines," she said. "I started him on *Rod and Reel* and I'm aiming for *Newsweek.*"

My mother used to say there's no accounting for some people's taste, but Mona seems happy, and I suppose that's what really matters.

We finish our meeting, Mona goes to man the checkout desk, and I begin on all the odds and ends left on my desk. I'm contemplating a letter I have to write to one of our book suppliers, whose last shipment was missing three titles, when the phone rings.

"Barbara," Daphne says, "do you have time for lunch?"

I don't really, and I brought a sandwich to work, but there's an urgency in her voice. "We could meet at Brigg's," I say. Brigg's is a coffee shop near the town hall where Daphne works.

"Too public," she says.

"What's the matter?" I say with alarm.

"We're busy here," she says, and I understand she can't talk on the phone either. "Meet me at the park at noon?"

"Fine," I say. "We can split my sandwich. It's chicken salad."

"I'm not hungry," Daphne says. "I haven't eaten for days."

The park is a five-acre piece of property behind the town hall that was beautified in 1983 when the Ladies' Auxiliary of the Fire Department decided Cassandra needed a face-lift. We were besieged with posters and bake sales. The ladies solicited used goods and held a huge rummage sale in which we exchanged our junk for our neighbors' junk. I donated an old card table and chairs and bought a meat slicing machine that never worked properly. The most popular event was a "slave auction," in which members of the community offered services to the highest bidders. Dr. Peters, for example, donated a checkup, Myra Bailey, who owned the deli, offered a catered lunch, and Dennis Mitchell, a partner in a law firm in Laurel Grove, contributed a half hour of legal time. Each donor had to stand up on a stage while an emcee auctioned off their services. The bidding was especially lively when eligible bachelors donated themselves as dates, and really got raucous when Denise McLaughlin offered an hour-long belly dance lesson and Stuart Crawley, who's now our mayor, bid $350 for it. As far as I know, Stuart still can't belly dance, but we now have a true park behind our town hall rather than a dusty back lot.

I see Daphne at a table under the shade of an oak tree. The park isn't quiet at noon. A group of teenage girls lie on the grass eating ice cream, sunning themselves, and giving off occasional shrieks of laughter. Dozens of children run around the play area where there are swings, slides, and a jungle gym. Young mothers wheel babies through the paths that curve around picnic areas and a plaque commemorating those Cassandrans killed in World War I, the Korean War, World War II, and Vietnam.

At first, as I approach her, I think Daphne is looking unusually well. Her hair's gotten longer and waves attractively around her face, and she's wearing a pretty dress I haven't seen before, a green silky fabric with a darker green belt and pale orange piping on the seams. But when I sit down beside her, I see she looks tired. Her ruddy complexion is unusually pale, and she has dark circles beneath her eyes and lines of strain around her mouth.

"You don't have to say something nice," she says under my scrutiny. "I look like shit."

"Actually, you look as if you haven't slept."

"I don't sleep and I don't eat. Guess what? It's not conducive to survival."

I've spent the hour since her phone call trying to imagine what was wrong. Daphne isn't the type of woman who talks easily about her problems or asks for help. She's the toughest of us, poking fun at herself and avoiding self-pity. Some people think Daphne's attitude is bravado rather than bravery, because her laugh is too loud and her gestures flamboyant. I think otherwise. She's stalwart, loyal, and there when you need her. I'll never forget the way she helped me when my mother was dying from ovarian cancer. Although her children were still small and she was already working at the town hall, she made meals, baby-sat Joel, and visited my mother in the hospital to spell me. When I said I didn't know how to thank her, Daphne shrugged and replied, "You'd do it for me." But I was never sure I could have put out the same amount of effort into an equally unhappy cause with so much strength and cheerfulness.

When I think how strong Daphne is, I can come up with only one scenario that justifies her phone call to me—that her marriage is in trouble. This idea doesn't come to me out of the blue. Daphne and Matt are a tumultuous couple. If Daphne tells me the truth, she and Matt fight as often as they have sex, which is frequently. Unlike Dan and I, who are excellent roommates, the Fellers seem to argue over everything from the way Daphne pays the bills to Matt's methods of disciplining Julian. Matt says Daphne's poorly organized and a lousy cook, Daphne says Matt's a slob and a spendthrift—and I could go on ad nauseam. Frances says that some marriages thrive on conflict. Virginia thinks that without the excitement of fighting, the Fellers' love life would probably die of boredom. I think that Daphne's marriage must teeter on the brink most of the time, so it's not surprising that this is the first thing that sprang into my mind when she called.

"Are you and Matt okay?" I say as I sit down next to her.

Daphne gives me a startled look. "You thought we were splitting?"

"It crossed my mind," I admit.

"Matt and I are as usual. The Rock of Gibraltar has nothing over us." She gives a little laugh. "The problem is I'm pregnant."

"Pregnant!" I repeat in shock.

"Remember how I put my foot down about birth control and how it was all going to be Matt's responsibility now? Well, this is the result."

"How pregnant are you?"

"Ten days maybe."

"Have you missed your period? Have you been to the doctor?"

Daphne shakes her head. "Not yet. I just know, Barbara, just the way I knew when I got pregnant with Celia and Julian. I can tell within a few days. I stop sleeping, I get nauseated, and I feel different. I can't describe how, only that I feel different."

"What are you going to do?" I ask.

"I'd like to blow up the condom company for starters."

"It broke?"

"We think it was defective." She sighs. "Imagine being knocked up at forty-three when you already have a nineteen-year-old daughter. I should be worried about being a grandmother, not a mother. Anyway, I have to get a blood test just on the off chance that I'm actually wrong about this. Then I'll get an abortion."

I put my hand on Daphne's arm and felt her warm, solid flesh. "Are you okay?" I ask gently.

"Just pissed off mainly and thinking about getting my tubes tied. You had that done, didn't you?"

"No, Dan had a vasectomy."

"Right, I forgot. How did you manage that anyway?"

"Dan said he didn't mind."

Daphne gives a small snort. "You'd think Matt's balls were made of gold."

I saw Matt's balls once, long ago, by mistake. It happened when I dropped by the Fellers' on a Sunday morning to return a device that cored apples, which had belonged to Daphne's grandmother. When I arrived and handed over the apple corer, Daphne told me she wanted to give me a magazine that had an interesting article on toilet training. At the time I was obsessed with toilet training, because Joel, who was two and a half, was resisting with all his might. While I waited in the hallway for Daphne to find the magazine, Matt stepped naked out of the bathroom. He didn't see me at all but idly rubbed his wet hair, pulled on his testicles, and then headed for the bedroom. I remember two things about this incident: my shame at seeing what I wasn't supposed to see and my surprise at how similar Matt's genitals were to Dan's, except Matt's pubic hair was darker. Daphne returned from the kitchen with the magazine, and I never said anything. But in an odd sort of way, I've felt closer to Daphne ever since.

"I'm not going to try the hospital," Daphne is saying. "I hear they're hardly doing abortions anymore because of pro-life nurses. So I guess it'll be the clinic in Laurel Grove."

"They've been picketed, haven't they?"

"On and off."

"You know what makes me angry?" I say. "All those men marching for pro-life. I wish they could get pregnant."

"Or their wives and daughters."

"Wouldn't it be interesting if they had to bring up all the children they want to save?" I warm to this. "Wouldn't it be fitting if they had to support all those single mothers they want to create? I'd like to see them put their money where their mouths are."

"They better not try to stop me." Daphne clenches her fists and looks fierce.

I've seen ferocity in my other friends. Virginia wanted to kill Raymond when she found out about his first infidelity, and her ferocity was delicate and brittle. Frances has been fiercely protective of Ben, and her ferocity has an elegant,

ladylike quality. Daphne is different. She's large and loud.
When she gets angry, she can be truly intimidating.

"Don't worry," I say. "They won't dare get in your way."

Dan, Joel, and I have taken the same family vacation for
the past ten years. We stay at a Canadian resort that's about
a two-hour drive from the border, a big hotel that dates back
to the 1920s called The Rideau Manor. It sits in a beautiful
location near a narrows that connects Upper Rideau Lake to
Newboro Lake. The land is hilly and covered with pine and
elm, the lakes are clear, and their shores are home to ducks,
osprey, and heron. Because the narrows are a part of a
historic canal that runs from the St. Lawrence Seaway
through Ottawa and on to Montreal, there is a lot of
pleasure-boat traffic going in both directions, and Dan and I
often sit on The Manor's dock during the cool Canadian
evenings, watching the cabin cruisers motor past and speculating on whether boating's a life-style we would like. By the
end of our two weeks, Dan always decides that he's going to
buy a boat when he retires, a decision that he forgets as soon
as we're on our way back to Cassandra.

Everything about the interior of The Rideau Manor is
old-fashioned in a delightful sort of way, and guests have to
book a year in advance to be certain they'll get the holiday
times they want. The rooms have radiators, four-poster
beds, and hand-crafted quilts. The meals are as close to
homemade as you can get when you eat in a dining room
that serves a hundred at each sitting. And the grounds are
spacious, including clipped lawns that slope down to
Newboro Lake, carefully tended English gardens and flower
borders, and huge elms that shade clusters of lawn chairs
painted bright red.

We keep returning to The Rideau Manor because of the
family atmosphere (they don't serve any liquor and there are
always children for Joel to play with) and because Dan can
rent a boat with a motor and have miles of lake for bass
fishing, which he loves. Both Joel and I fish with Dan, but
what I like most is the peace I have to lie in the sun and read.
Contrary to public opinion, librarians never have the time

to read all the books they want. And if I want to be sociable I can be. The Rideau Manor's coziness encourages conversation, and I've met all kinds of interesting people: Canadians, other Americans, and Europeans. In fact, we still exchange Christmas cards with a Danish family that we met nine years ago whose son was the same age as Joel.

But this year is different. Within a couple of days, I realize with some sadness that this will be our last stay. It seems that our holidays have been like a three-legged stool, only balancing evenly because each leg was there and working well. The trouble this year is that Joel didn't want to come, and Dan and I can't seem to achieve an equilibrium without him. When he first said he wanted to stay home, we wouldn't even entertain the thought. This caused many unpleasant conversations.

Joel: I don't want to go.

Me: We can't leave you here all by yourself.

Joel: I'm almost eighteen.

Dan: It's not your age.

Joel: Then what is it? Don't you trust me?

Me: Of course we trust you.

Joel: Then what's the problem?

Dan: It's only two weeks, Joel.

Me: And you've always enjoyed it.

Joel: I just want to stay home.

Dan: We'll go fishing. I'll get you one of those reels we saw in Frey's at Christmas.

Joel: I'm too old for family vacations. I want to be with my friends!

When Dan and I were alone, we voiced our worries to each other. We wondered how we could leave him, what he would do on his own, whether he could handle an emergency, and would he know enough to eat properly. We worried that he'd get into trouble, not any specific trouble, but a generic, amorphous trouble that allowed us to worry in a way more frightening than if we'd had something solid we could picture in our overheating imaginations.

After the many unpleasant conversations, we realized Joel

wasn't going to come with us no matter how much we begged or pleaded. So we made arrangements: neighbors who would keep an eye on Joel and watch the house, friends who would drop by to see how he was doing or have him over for dinner. We left a long list of emergency numbers, meals in the freezer, and many verbal instructions.

"Water the plants in the house on Tuesdays and Fridays."

"Cut the lawn at least once."

"Call Matt Feller if anything goes wrong with the house."

"Don't forget to put out the garbage."

"And don't eat just junk food, okay?"

I'm sure Joel breathed a sigh of relief when we drove away, but I doubt he knew how close we came to turning around and coming back. For about five miles, neither of us said a thing and then we both spoke simultaneously.

Dan said, "I wonder if he'll remember to water and mow the lawn."

I said, "I have this horrible vision of Katrina in our bed."

We looked at each other and Dan said, "We've got to stop this or it's going to drive us nuts."

"You're right," I said. "Actually, you know something? This is the first vacation we've had alone in years."

Dan gave me a sideways glance that he thinks is sexy. "It could be a second honeymoon."

"It could," I said.

"It could get really wild and crazy." He jiggled his eyebrows at me suggestively, and the car swerved.

"It sure will be," I said, "if you don't keep your eyes on the road."

But there's no second honeymoon that can equal the first, when we had no cares and no children and our only responsibility was to give each other as much pleasure as possible. Although we make love frequently, and we're much more proficient at it than we were twenty years ago, we find ourselves too alone, even with each other, without Joel. I've never realized how much of our time he absorbs just by being there, and how much companionship he offers. Joel fills my days with his comings and goings, his needs, his noise, his chatter (even though he hardly talks to me anymore), and his clutter. A part of my brain has been reserved just for Joel.

Dan and I don't talk about this during our first few days at The Manor. We argue instead.

"I've got to get up early tomorrow," Dan says. We've just made love very satisfactorily under the puffy quilt, which is made of pale pink and blue squares and dotted with small blue bows. "I was talking to Orvil and he says that this year the fish are really biting at dawn."

Orvil, who's over seventy if he's a day, owns The Rideau Manor and greets all his guests by their first names. He also can remember with astonishing detail their fishing habits, what bait they like or lures they prefer. Plus he knows every nook and cranny of the lake. I've spent many trips trying to decipher Orvil's hand-drawn maps and directing Dan to that perfect fishing spot where they were "biting like the bejeezus last week."

"How early is early?" I ask.

"Five."

I stretch. "Well, just don't wake me up."

"I thought you'd come with me."

"No thanks," I say. "I'll just settle in with a good book."

"You like it when they're biting."

"Not that much."

"Come on, Barbara. Just this once."

"I went with you yesterday."

"It wouldn't kill you, you know."

The irritation rising in me suddenly spills over hard and fast, and I find I don't care that Dan doesn't like to go alone or that he misses Joel, who was always an enthusiastic fishing partner. "I don't *want* to go fishing," I say. "I don't like it that much."

Dan sits up. "I thought this was supposed to be a second honeymoon."

"We didn't go fishing on the first one."

"You know what I'm saying. We're supposed to be doing things together."

"Well, let's do something else," I say.

"Like what?"

"I don't know—walks, a drive into town. There's a lot of antique stores around."

"My favorite things," he says.

Dan's sarcasm is rare enough that it should stop me from escalating the argument, but I'm too annoyed to care. "Why do I always have to do what *you* want?" I say. "This is my vacation, too."

For a long second we look at each other, and then Dan says in a quiet voice, "Maybe we should leave."

I turn away and curl onto my side. "Maybe we should," I say.

I hear Dan get out of bed, get dressed, and leave the room. We don't eat breakfast together that morning. When I go downstairs, our waitress is clearing the table. She's a pretty teenager who obviously sees nothing wrong when a husband and wife don't eat together.

"Good morning, Mrs. Breymann," she says. "Beautiful morning, isn't it?"

"Beautiful," I say.

I usually eat far too much breakfast at The Rideau Manor, but today I can manage only juice and a little coffee. My stomach feels queasy, but I can't stand the thought of going back to our empty bedroom. Dan and I may bicker occasionally, but we rarely fight in any serious way, and I don't know what to do with myself. I dawdle over my coffee and finally leave the hotel and wander down to the dock where several boats are anchored. I nod good morning to a boater who is swabbing down his front deck when I see Dan standing at the far end of the dock and staring out over the lake, his hands jammed in his pockets.

I walk up to him and notice that, in the sun, his hair is no longer that bright gold it was when he was young. There's too much gray in it now, and its sheen has dulled. "Dan?" I say.

"What?"

"It's Joel not being here, isn't it?"

He turns around, and I see that something has also dulled inside of him. "This vacation isn't working."

"We miss him."

"It's more than that. Maybe we need him."

"What do you mean?"

"I wonder what's going to happen to you and me."

"We have to get used to the fact that he's growing up."

"It's more than that, Barbara. We've been parents for so long that maybe there's nothing much between us without him."

I wrap my arms around myself even though it's not cold. "Maybe this happens to everyone when their kids grow up."

"Maybe."

"And maybe the trouble is that The Manor is really for families and not couples who need a second honeymoon."

Dan sighs. "Do you want to leave?"

"We paid in advance."

"I don't suppose Joel would be too happy to see us either."

"No," I say, "we'd be ruining his holiday away from us."

We smile at each other, small smiles of recognition, and walk back down the dock. The boater has finished washing down his deck and is now taking out several jars and rags.

"Keep up the good work," Dan says as we pass by.

"It's nonstop polishing," the man says, "from spring to fall."

Dan takes my hand, and we thread our fingers together as we always do. I think that marriage is like a boat except it has no seasons, it's nonstop work year round.

"Joel's left a big space," I say.

Dan nods. "Like getting a tooth pulled."

"Remember when he was born," I say, "and we brought him home and couldn't believe what he did to our lives."

It had been a cold March and there was still snow on the ground. I was afraid Joel would catch a cold during the walk from the hospital to the car and the car to the house, and I'd dressed him in a sweater, a hat, a miniature snowsuit, and three blankets. His face was covered and he was so wrapped up, he bore a strong resemblance to a huge, pale blue Chinese egg roll. He began to cry when we got into the house, and I immediately assumed he was starving, although when I look back I think that maybe he was only suffocating.

"I couldn't believe that something only eight pounds would require all that equipment," Dan says, "or be so noisy."

"And need to be fed every two hours—remember that?"

"Vividly."

"All those diapers," I say.

"They blew the washing machine."

"That Bendix was on its last legs anyway." We're silent for a minute, remembering, and then I continue, "It's funny how parents can't wait in some ways for their children to grow up and leave so they can get their lives back, but then when it happens, they don't know what to do with themselves."

"I don't think it's a matter of getting our lives back. That *was* our life, being parents. Now we have to create something new."

"He hasn't left home yet," I point out.

"No, but we're superfluous, don't you think?"

"He'd sure like us to think so."

"You're right," Dan says. "We're not finished being parents yet."

"We can still set standards."

"And offer guidance."

"Even if he doesn't take it," I say. "Which is more often than not."

Dan squeezes my hand. "We're going to get through this," he says. "You'll see."

I squeeze his hand back and think how optimistic Dan tends to be. The moment on the dock was the lowest I've seen him since my second miscarriage, but he's already bounced back with a resilience and buoyant spirit that I don't have. I think we've come to a time in our marriage that will be as difficult as that first year when we had to adjust to living together. Our marriage has metamorphosed from newlyweds to parents of a teenager and will change yet again. In the seventeen years since we were a couple last, connections have broken and pathways we made toward one another have disappeared. New links have formed, but they're built around Joel and around being parents. We've gotten rusty at being responsible just for each other.

"Let's try that little bay tomorrow morning," I say, "the one where you got the five-pounder."

Dan looks at me with astonishment. "That was six years ago," he says.

"He probably had a big family, and his children have grown up."

Dan picks up on the game. "Maybe he has grandchildren, too."

"Big grandchildren," I say. "*Humongous* grandchildren."

"And we can go into town and do some antiquing this afternoon."

"That would be lovely," I say. "I'd like that a lot."

PART IV

MISTY LAKE

Chapter

1

Even though the beginning of school marks the end of summer and its freedoms, Joel has usually been excited to go back. There are new clothes, new binders and pens, and new kids mixed in with the same old bunch. But this year is different. Even though he's a senior now, top of the heap, he dreads the classes, the teachers, the work, and all the people he's been going to school with since he was five years old. There'll be no surprises. He'll have the same teachers he's had during the past three years—Graves for Spanish 4, Sunmiller for Journalism, Browning for Physics, Parisio for Economics, and Delmore for College Algebra. And the school year will unfold as expected. Ben will be elected class president, chosen prom king, and serve as editor-in-chief of the school newspaper. Sandy Solomon will head the yearbook committee, Murph Miller will be voted class clown, and Ted Snedecker will win the athlete of the year award.

The only mystery will be the identity of the prom queen. Everyone knows Caroline had it in the bag, and no one can agree whether Lisa Ann Lemonte is prettier than Sheila Bailey or not. Joel doesn't really care. Lisa Ann has never even noticed that he existed, and although Sheila was his lab partner in Biology in their sophmore year, she doesn't say hello to him anymore. Joel thinks he agrees with Sarah Silver and her group of friends who want the whole queen-and-her-court stuff stopped. She wrote an article for the school newspaper, saying that prom kings and queens are a hangover from the fifties, most schools don't even have them anymore, and they're an example of how society portrays women only as sexual objects and undermines confidence in their intellectual abilities. A lot of the guys made rude jokes when the article came out, but Joel can see what she means. When you're not one of the handsomest guys in school, you wish girls were more interested in what you were thinking than what you looked like. Overall, Joel doubts he'll even go to the senior prom, although it might be a kick to go stag with Pete and get stoned or drunk.

He and Katrina have broken up by default. Pete and Steph's relationship finally hit the dust, and since he and Katrina usually double-dated with them, this means they don't go out anymore either. They never actually said anything to one another. What happened was that one Saturday night they had their usual tussle in the backseat of Pete's car, and the next Saturday night Joel had nothing to do and nowhere to go. It was kind of a relief actually, although he doesn't say so to Pete. When Pete starts talking about how they've got to find some more girls and get some ass because he's so used to getting laid, Joel nods his head as if he were used to getting laid, too. But he knows why it never happened. Katrina knew he didn't like her, and it stopped her from going that extra step he wanted so much. Deep inside, Joel believes he deserves all the frustration and anger he felt every time he was with her.

Of course, his mother can't hide her relief. "Aren't you seeing Katrina anymore?" she asked one Saturday night.

"No."

"What happened?"

"Nothing."

"Did you have a fight?"

"No."

"It just ended?"

"Yeah."

Barbara paused for a moment and then said, "I'm sorry, Joel. That's too bad."

Sure, Mom, and tell me another.

Then there's the college thing, which is already getting him down even though it's barely started. This is the Year of the College Applications, and once upon a time he knew he wanted to do something with sports and recreation, but he closed that door when he gave up the teams. Now he's got to make decisions he finds almost paralyzing, like what he wants to be when he grows up. Plus his grades last year were kind of shitty, and Mrs. Petrino, the guidance counselor, keeps saying he can redeem himself by hitting the books and getting good marks at Christmas. She also wants him to retake the SATs to bump up the scores he got last spring, which were only average. She thinks some colleges might overlook the dip in his grades if he really pulls up his socks and shows he has what it takes. His parents keep the pressure up by talking to him about the future just about every fucking day. His father's decided the best bet might be a general arts degree.

"You can start off with a variety of subjects," Dan says, "and then if you take a course that sparks your interest, you can think about specializing."

"Okay," Joel says. "I could do that."

"Unless you have some good idea now what you might like to do?"

Dan asks this question every time they talk as if Joel isn't the same person from day to day but someone who will change overnight from ignorant to brilliant and suddenly know exactly what he wants to be for the rest of his life. Most of the time Joel shrugs, but sometimes he gets a glimmer of something, like a flicker of light at the end of a long, dark tunnel.

This time he says, "I like kids," and it suddenly strikes him as true. He does like kids. Doesn't he enjoy fooling around now and then with Davy next door, who's only eight? Throwing a baseball back and forth? Getting him in a headlock and mussing his hair?

"Teaching?" Dan muses, and then gets enthusiastic. "That might suit you."

"Yeah." He thinks about being a teacher and marking papers and being able to send kids to the principal. It might be cool to be standing at the front of the classroom instead of slumping in a seat at the back. "Yeah, I might like it."

"Then we should think about teacher's college."

"Okay."

Joel knows his parents are anxious about him. He overheard Barbara worriedly describing him to one of her friends as "drifting." He has an image of himself as a boat that's come loose from its anchor and is floating off to nowhere. He'd like to make his parents feel better, he really would, but he can't seem to hook himself onto anything. Some days nothing seems to matter at all, so why bother trying to make decisions about anything? Other days everything assumes an importance so huge he can't bear to think about what's coming, what it means, and what he's going to do about it.

He envies guys like Ben who seem to have their shit all together. Ben gets top grades, he does the best extracurricular stuff, holds down a part-time job, and his SAT scores were so high the first time around, he doesn't have to take the tests again. Everyone knows he'll get a scholarship to Harvard or Yale or one of those Ivy League places. Ben wants to be a writer, but he's planning to go into law, because he's realistic enough to realize that fiction writing can be a precarious existence. Joel knows all this, because he heard Frances telling Barbara and because he keeps meeting Ben at Marla's. Ben's doing short stories now, and Marla gives him feedback. Joel started a poem—"The leaves tell us about the end of summer"—but he couldn't think of the second line or a word that rhymed with *summer*, so he gave up. It wouldn't have been any good anyway.

Actually, the truth is he's hated Ben in a visceral kind of way ever since that day at Marla's. Joel's never really hated anyone before, he can see that now. Sometimes he was pretty jealous of the guys on his teams who were the stars, and sometimes he disliked some girl who didn't seem to like him either, but nothing he's felt before approaches how he feels about Ben. It's jealousy, resentment, distrust, and loathing all rolled into one horrible feeling that coils in his gut like a dark serpent. Ben is in his Physics class, and whenever he asks a question or answers the teacher, Joel has to mentally remove himself from what's going on. He has to think about something else, or he thinks he might go for Ben's throat. On the days he's been to Marla's, and Ben's been there, too, his hatred makes him physically sick. He's so nauseated he can't eat supper or if he does, he throws it up. Barbara's become so concerned about him she made an appointment with the doctor.

"I'm not going," Joel said when she told him. "I'm not sick."

"You're throwing up and you're not sick?"

"You know I don't like chicken in that tomato sauce."

"And what about the hamburgers we had on Thursday and the ham last week? You didn't like those meals either?"

"Leave me alone, Mom," he said. "Just get off my case."

But then Dan sat Joel down and told him you don't mess with your health, and he was going to have to go to Dr. Peters and get his problem looked at. So Dr. Peters did the usual doctor stuff, asked Joel if he had a regular girlfriend, and sent him to take a test where he swallowed gross stuff and another doctor took X rays of his stomach. Dr. Peters told Barbara that Joel was basically fine but probably suffering from stress. He prescribed tablets to settle Joel's stomach, but they're not much use. Joel doesn't think any doctor or any medicine can help him with the way he feels about Ben.

At the end of the second week of school, Mr. Browning takes the science class on a field trip to a slope of loose, fragmented rock that lies beneath a cliff about an hour from Cassandra. It's part of a two-week Earth Science unit that Mr. Browning added to the Physics course. It won't be on the Regents exam, but Mr. Browning majored in geology in college and thinks students should learn something about the landscape around them. Joel has seen the cliff many times before but never realized the layers of rock you could see in it were sediments laid down by an ocean that covered all of central New York and that the cliff was cut by the river that now flows near Cassandra. He finds this mildly interesting, proof that he and his problems are nothing more than a little speck of nothingness in the vastness of time. He wishes this realization made him feel better about his life, but it doesn't. In fact, it just makes him feel more depressed than ever.

The point of the field trip is to see the way the layers of sedimentary rocks in the cliff have tilted and curved over time, and to find specimens of specific rocks that they can later identify in the lab. Mr. Browning has shown them samples of limestone, shale, dolomite, and chert and says that, for collecting purposes, they can do a preliminary identification by color and whether a stone breaks smooth, curved, or jagged. But when the bus stops, Joel thinks it's going to be hopeless. As he looks up the hillside, he thinks all the rocks look the same, a dirty, grayish brown. Mr. Browning gives them thirty minutes to collect their samples, and everyone gets out of the bus and spreads out across and up the slope. Even though they've been told to wear sensible clothing—T-shirts, jeans, and sneakers—a couple of girls are wearing short skirts and dress shoes. The cliff is steep enough that they do a lot of sliding and squealing. Joel notices that Sarah and her friends, Katie and Carol, are dressed okay, but then they're wearing the weird stuff they have on every day: long-sleeved tops, oversized pants that sag and droop, heavy black Docs, and lots of jewelry.

Joel and Pete work their way to an edge of the cliff as far from Mr. Browning as they can get and talk about a problem Pete is having with the carburetor on his car. Every once in a while they pick up fragments and put them in their backpacks. It's pretty boring, but Joel thinks it's better than being stuck in English class, where they're reading that incomprehensible shit in *The Merchant of Venice*.

Suddenly a voice says, "Hey, watch what you're doing!"

Joel and Pete look around and see that Ben, being about

five feet below them, has been hit by stones slipping out from under their shoes and sliding down the slope.

"Fuck you, Phillips," Pete says good-naturedly.

They move out of the way, but not before Joel dislodges more stones that cascade down and hit Ben on his shin. "Cut it out, will you?" Ben yells.

Joel feels the other Joel, his observer self, slip out. With those ironic, knowing eyes, he sees the setup clearly—the two of them confronting one another like those stags with the huge antlers you see on nature films who are in rut and about to battle over does during the mating season. Joel sees he has a choice. He can be civilized or he can be an animal. He can say he's sorry or bend his head and charge. But then he feels a surge of hatred, a vicious bubble of bile and acid, rise up his gut and into his mouth, obliterating the other Joel.

"Fuck you, Phillips," he says, and doesn't even try to imitate Pete's lightness of voice.

Ben straightens up and they stare at each other. That's when Joel realizes Ben hates him as much as he hates Ben. His rush of triumph is so wild and exhilarating that he has to do something to express it. He gives Ben the finger and says, "Fuck your ass, man."

For a second Ben seems on the verge of saying something, but then he turns away and starts down the cliff. Joel follows him, sending stones skittering ahead. "Fuck your tight ass, Phillips. Fuck it good," he yells, and doesn't care that heads are beginning to turn in his direction.

Ben whirls around, and now they're only about two feet apart. Joel can't see Ben's eyes, he's wearing those goddamn sunglasses, but he can see the grimace on Ben's face, his clenched jaw and lips stretched tight over his teeth. Joel knows it's a mirror of his own grimace, his own glaring rage.

"Keep away from me," Ben says in a low voice.

"Keep away from me," Joel echoes mockingly.

"You're asking for it," Ben says.

"So what," Joel says. "You think I give a shit?"

When they were children and playing together, there was

always a moment when Joel and Ben would pause before trying to wrestle each other to the ground. During this moment they stared at each other in imitation of the wrestlers they saw on TV. Then, when they couldn't stand it any longer, they'd leap on each other, arms and legs entangling, and tumble into a heap of flailing, wiggling bodies. For a brief second now, Joel captures the flavor of that pause, which was filled with excitement and anticipation, and always ended with a surge of pure happiness as he threw himself on Ben. Then Pete says, "Hey, fuck it, Joel," in a careful, frightened voice, and the tension that's holding Joel still explodes.

He lashes out, his fist connecting with Ben's cheekbone in a satisfying crack. Ben's head snaps back, and his sunglasses fly off. Ben straightens up, looks into Joel's eyes, and says, "You asshole." His punch catches Joel in the side of the head, and then they're on each other, trying to smash each other's faces, crashing onto the rock and sliding down the slope as they struggle.

As they roll down the slope, parts of Joel are protected by his jeans, his backpack, and Ben's body. But the sharp, jagged rocks cut, scrape, and abrade his arms, hands, his left ear, and the side of his face. Joel doesn't feel the rocks or the impact of Ben's fists. He doesn't hear the screams of the girls or Mr. Browning yelling at them to stop. It's as if the world has collapsed to a narrow cylinder of space that encloses only their bodies and the rocky, bumpy surface of the ground. Nothing exists outside that cylinder, not the sounds of hollering voices, not the hands trying to pull them apart, not the knowledge of the punishments to come. Joel's too gripped by fury and exultation, too absorbed by the smell of their mingled sweat and the feel of muscle straining against muscle, bone crunching against bone. He will be an adult, a married man with two children, before he realizes that, in the midst of that crucible of hatred and rage was a love for Ben—his childhood playmate, his twin in love, the boy he wants to be—that was pure and white hot, burning him into absolution.

* * *

Over the summer, Marla and Edgar Ashley have developed something less than a friendship, but something more than just being mere acquaintances. He came up to her one day when she was walking the aisles of the drugstore looking for sunblock and introduced himself.

"Marla Hudson," he said.

She glanced at him in surprise. "That's right."

"You probably don't remember me."

Marla studied the pale blue eyes and wispy brown mustache above the thin chest in its white pharmacist's jacket. "I'm afraid I don't."

"Edgar Ashley. I was two years ahead of you in school."

Marla now remembered a bony adolescent with many pimples on his chin. "Ah—the Ashley boy," she said, "all grown up."

He smiled with delight. "I wrote poems for the school newspaper. Perhaps you remember one—*Pretty Bicycles?* My teacher had me send it to a Rochester newspaper and it got published."

"Vaguely," Marla said, although she didn't remember this event at all.

"And I've kept track of your career, too," Edgar said, dropping his voice into a low, confidential whisper, as if discussing books were an undercover operation in Cassandra. "I subscribe to the *New York Times Book Review*. Of course, some people around here read it in the library, but I want my own copy. I need to digest it, if you know what I mean."

"Oh, I do."

"Of course, I've bought all your books, every single one. I'm a book buyer in hardcover."

He paused to see if she caught how important his buying habits were to her success. "That's wonderful," she said.

"Oh, I'm a dying breed, they tell me. Everyone else waits for the paperback. But a paperback doesn't give you the same kind of read, does it? You don't get that feel of the book in your hands. That heft of it. But then there are so many people who don't understand the arts today. It's television, of course, I blame it all on television. Catering to

331

the lowest common denominator so the rest get pulled down, too." He made a tch-tching sound and shook his head. "Well, I soldier on here, trying to introduce art to the hoi polloi, but it can be a heavy burden sometimes." A dolorous sigh. "A heavy, heavy burden."

After this conversation, in which she said little but was vastly amused, Marla discovers that Edgar now believes they are kindred spirits. He engages Marla in conversation whenever he sees her on the street or in the drugstore. He's rereading her early books and discusses her plots and characters: "The depth of personality," he says, "that's the trick, isn't it?" He asks her advice on other authors, and he's thrilled that she's agreed to give four lectures on fiction writing at the library. He even makes broad hints that she should join him on the committee for Cassandra's annual Arts and Crafts Fair.

Edgar would be a nuisance, except his admiration for her is endearing and he's a such a caricature of a small-town intellectual. At first Marla wonders how he survives in Cassandra, but then she sees that his pharmacy is just a cover for his real stock in trade, which is knowing more than anyone else and thereby making himself invaluable.

"Did you hear about the fight yesterday?" he says one afternoon when Marla drops into the drugstore for shampoo.

She's been out of town, visiting the set of *Silver Crescents,* which is being shot in South Carolina. "What fight?"

"Between Ben Phillips and Joel Breymann on a school trip." Edgar registers the quick turn of her head with pleasure. "They used be friends when they were kids. They used to come in here and buy candy all the time. M&M's mostly."

Marla knows that if she shows too much interest, she'll arouse Edgar's curiosity and become an object as well as a receiver of rumor, gossip, and innuendo. She reaches for a bottle of shampoo and studies the instructions on the back. "Was anyone hurt?" she asks.

"Bloody noses, and I heard Ben had quite the black eye.

Dr. Peters told me he'd never seen so many cuts and bruises in the arm and head area on both, but then they were on that nasty slope of broken rock on the other side of Laurel Grove. You know which one I mean? And if you ask me, they were lucky they didn't break anything. The gods must've been watching *that* day. Anyway, Joel needed ten stitches in his arm from here to here." Edgar slides his forefinger down the top of his forearm. "Not a pretty sight, I gather, and Barbara had to get him painkillers. Aspirin wasn't doing the trick. And she told me his spirits were low. A week's suspension from school, you see. Well, I'm not surprised. I heard it was vicious, just vicious, and there were obscenities. It took Keith Browning about five minutes to get them apart."

He watches Marla avidly as she puts back the bottle of shampoo and picks up another. "Boys will be boys, I suppose," she says.

Her indifference doesn't faze him. "And Frances is just distraught over Ben what with college applications. I heard she's been in to see Phil Potter, but of course it's going on his record. Phil can't bend the rules because Ben's an honor student and will probably be valedictorian, can he? He's talked to both the boys and tried to get to the bottom of it, but they're not talking. Not a word. Of course, there are theories."

"Such as?"

"That a fight that bad would have to be over a girl."

"Who?"

Edgar's smile is sly and gleeful at the same time. "Well, now, that's the rub, isn't it? No one knows."

But Marla knows, and it's a first. In her long career of husbands, lovers, and one-night stands, she's never been physically fought over before. But then she's never attracted seventeen-year-olds before either. In the few occasions, like dinner parties, where two men have vied for her attention, the conflict took the form of intellectual sparring matches— aggression and muscle flexing converted into boasting and exaggeration. As she drives home, she feels an odd mix of emotions: sorrow, concern, curiosity, and amusement.

When she gets back to the house, she decides to call Bobbie and ask how Joel is doing. Just as she lifts up the phone, the doorbell rings.

"Marla Hudson?" A burly, uniformed man with a graying crew cut fills the doorway.

"Yes."

"Reg Burton with the Cassandra police." He flashes a badge at her. "I wonder if I can come in and have a chat."

For a second a sharp pain of dread stabs Marla below the sternum as she's transported back in time to the other ringing doorbells and the other policemen who've stood so hesitantly on her doorstep. They all look alike in their uniforms and insignia, those generic bearers of bad news: the policeman who came to the door when Didi still lived at home, wanting to talk to Didi about drug dealing at school; the policeman who came to the door after Didi had moved out, because her name had come out during an investigation of a theft at a 7-Eleven; and finally the two policemen who came to the door, their helmets turning nervously in their hands, to tell her Didi was dead.

"Are you okay, ma'am?"

The dread recedes, leaving the customary ache behind, a pain that she can tolerate, a pain that lets her breathe. "Sorry," Marla says. "What's it about, Officer?"

"Joel Breymann and Ben Phillips, and please call me Reg."

"Come on in."

Reg follows her into the kitchen, eyeing the house as they pass by the still unfurnished living and dining rooms. "I heard you were making big changes," he says, as he sits on one of the stools by the counter, "but this is really something."

"Thank you," Marla says.

"You must be planning to stay around for a while then."

"A while. Will it be coffee or tea?"

"You got instant decaf?"

"Yes."

"I had these chest pains, and the doctor ordered me off

regular coffee." He shakes his head. "I miss the stuff, but I'm making do."

Marla smiles, fills a cup with water, and puts it in the microwave.

"I take it you heard about the fight between Joel and Ben."

"Edgar Ashley told me."

Reg's laugh is a short, dry, and unamused bark. "That man's better than the *Gazette.*"

"I've noticed."

"Well, as Edgar no doubt informed you, it was a pretty bad fight. They were going for each other's throats. But when you ask either of them what happened, they clam up."

The bell on the microwave rings. "Do you usually investigate fights between boys?" she asks as she takes the cup out. "Milk, sugar?"

"Both," he says, "and no, not usually. If I had to worry about every squabble in town, I'd be in trouble. But we got a missing girl here and no answers."

Marla puts his coffee in front of him. "You think the fight had something to do with Caroline?"

"I think maybe one of those boys knows something or said something. I think there's feelings coming out that've been hidden for a long time."

Marla sits down. "I don't know how I can help you," she says.

"I heard Joel worked up here this summer, and Frances told Jean—that's my wife—that you've been helping Ben with his writing. Has one of them said something to you that if you think about it, might be a little suspicious?"

Marla shakes her head. "I never heard anything suspicious."

"Okay." Reg takes a sip of his coffee and starts on another tack. "My wife, Jean, she's read all your books."

"I hope she enjoyed them."

"Very much. She says you're real strong on character development."

"That's a nice compliment. Thank her for me, will you?"

He nods. "So I got thinking about your books and what's going on here in Cassandra."

"I don't write mysteries."

He puts up a hand. "I know that. No, my mind's working in a different direction. See, most of the folks around here have known these boys since they were little guys—hell, they were on my Little League team—but you come with an outside point of view, if you know what I mean. And what with your writing . . . well, you might have some insights we've missed."

"Are you asking me if I think Ben or Joel was capable of murdering Caroline?"

Reg gives her a sharp glance. "Nobody said anything about murder."

"I may not write mysteries, but I can put two and two together."

"Until we have a body, we got nothing here but a disappearance." Marla smiles, and he gives an angry shrug. "It's the company line, but at least it's keeping Molly and Brian's hopes alive."

"But how do you feel about it?"

This turns out to be an inspired question. From the torrent of words that follows, Marla understands that the people of Cassandra don't often ask Reg how he feels. They expect him to uphold the law, keep the town running smoothly, solve crimes from vandalism to murder, and keep his emotions to himself.

"You know what I think? That Caroline never even left town. That she was picked up here, killed here, and hidden somewhere close by, but we've combed every goddamn inch of ground from here to the county line, and we've brought up zip. Then I think, okay, what about the river? So we patrol the banks for ten miles in every direction. Nothing. Besides, I think if she'd been under some rock or log, she'd have come dislodged during the spring flooding. She'd have floated down to the reservoir and we'd have found her then. And when it comes to lakes . . ." He sighs angrily. "I don't have the money or manpower for that."

He pauses for a breath, and Marla has a vision of Reg at

home, out of uniform, repairing kids' bicycles, oiling the hinges on the screen door, and worrying about Caroline.

"But I'm gonna find the bastard that killed her, so help me God. This girl was one of ours, and you didn't know her, but she was the best—pretty, smart, talented, a really good kid—the kind that can make a town real proud. I tell you I'm gonna get the fucking bastard and screw him to the wall, if it's the last thing I do." He slaps his beefy hand down on the counter and then blinks at the sound of the slap as if he's forgotten where he is. He clears his throat. "Sorry about that. Pardon the language."

"I've heard worse."

He grins at her. "So I put it to you. You think either of those boys could've killed her?"

She shakes her head. "No, I don't."

Marla believes this as she says it, but it isn't until Reg is gone and she's sitting up in her office, staring at the blank screen on her computer, that it occurs to her she would never have thought that Ben and Joel would go for each other's throats either. She's thought of Joel as too sweet, of Ben as too refined. She types: "What does anyone know about the interior of the human heart, even when it's your own? The heart is an organ of chambers, blocked by valves that permit the flow of blood in only one direction. What happens when the blood is insistent? When it flows the opposite way? When the valves lose control?"

For a long time, Marla stares at these words as the computer hums and the cursor blinks under the final question mark. In her years of writing, she's learned that mentally reading what she's written doesn't always give her the true cadence of the sentences, so she speaks the words out loud and listens. If anyone were to ask her what she was listening for, she could only describe it as the way the words sit on the air or, conversely, the way the air wraps itself around the words. After her moment of listening, she changes the verb *flows* in the second question to *pumps*, highlights the paragraph as a block, and saves it to a file she labels NOVEL/IDEAS/HEART.J&B. When the screen is clear, she types *Prologue* and continues writing.

Chapter

2

Despite her best-laid plans, Daphne doesn't have her abortion until mid-October, when she's more than two months pregnant. The night after we spoke in the park, she developed severe pains in her upper abdomen and ended up having her gall bladder removed in emergency surgery at the Laurel Grove Hospital. I didn't find this out until after we came back from our vacation. When I visited her then, she still wasn't well but having complications from the surgery, nausea and diarrhea. I was shocked at how she looked. She'd lost more than ten pounds, and her face was gray and drawn.

She'd taken up residence on the living room couch and lay under an old blue electric blanket with a torn binding that trailed on the floor. The coffee table was overflowing with newspapers, magazines, bills, and letters, while a plate with a half-eaten roast beef sandwich lay on the floor beside a half-filled glass of apple juice. I could see cracker crumbs on the carpet and dust balls underneath the couch and two wing chairs. Daphne and Matt's taste for interior design runs to large furniture in muted colors that show dirt and wear. Daphne was never much of a housekeeper at the best of times, and no one else in the house picked up the slack at the worst of times. In fact, the evening I was there, Matt was off playing golf while Julian was in the basement rec room watching television. Celia's gone away, her first year in college, but her leaving doesn't seem to have made any noticeable difference in the mess. My mother would have expected God to strike down the Fellers in some suitable way for their lack of cleanliness and overall sloppiness, but I've always found Daphne's house to be more comfortable than anyone else's, even my own sometimes. In my house, no one eats in the living room or puts their feet on the coffee table.

"The pregnancy isn't helping," she said after I removed the cat from one of the chairs and sat down. "It may be causing some of my stomach problems. The doctor said the surgery might have brought on a miscarriage, but no such luck. The damn thing's lodged in there so tight, it's going to take a crowbar to get it out."

"The abortion's still on then?"

"Are you kidding? I'm too old to have this thing. It's killing me already."

"Have you made an appointment at the clinic?"

"The doctor wants me to get some stamina back first. I feel like shit, Barbara. Absolute shit."

"If it's any comfort," I said, "you look terrible, too."

As I'd hoped, this elicited a smile. "Cassandra's own Florence Nightingale," Daphne said.

I patted her hand. "At least I didn't bring a tuna casserole."

She laughed and then groaned and pressed her hand against her side. "Don't make me laugh," she said. "It hurts."

By the time she was feeling better at the beginning of October, the clinic was bombed by a pro-life group called the Baby Rescuers who claimed the damage for God and Jesus. Although they smashed several windows, broke down the front door, and ruined some equipment, the clinic was expected to be closed for only about a week. Daphne calmly rescheduled her appointment. "I don't know what cosmic forces are out there," she said, "but they're not going to stop me."

Sarah called me several days after the bombing. "This is Sarah Silver," she said, "calling on behalf of the Actions Rights Abortion Alliance."

"Well, hello, Sarah," I said. "How are you?"

"Fine, thank you," she said.

"And how's school?"

"It's okay."

"Have you decided on colleges yet?"

"I'm thinking I might go to an all-girls' school."

"Have you picked a major?"

"Political science and women's studies."

"That's interesting," I said. "And what will you do with it?"

"I don't know yet," she said. "I just want to find out how the government works."

"Well, that's wonderful," I said, and meant it, but I was also envious. How I wished Joel could be so focused and interested in something beyond himself. He was back in school after the suspension and attending all his classes— I'd checked with Phil Potter—but he rarely participated in classroom discussions and his homework was poor. Of course, I knew why. Phil even had a phrase for it: The Caroline Factor. "Every one of those kids under suspicion is having some kind of problem or other. And I've got to tell you, Barbara, that fight between Ben and Joel and those lie detector tests all over again"—his sigh comes loud and clear over the phone receiver—"it doesn't matter that they passed, now they're all skittish."

At first Frances, Dan, and I tried to get the boys to say what the fight was about. Joel wouldn't even respond, while Ben told Frances, "It just happened." And when Frances wondered out loud how a fight that causes one black eye, ten stitches, and numerous bruises *just happens* to two boys who don't do that sort of thing, he said, "It just does." So we reluctantly yielded to Reg's request that Joel and Ben take a second set of lie detector tests. He said that because the boys wouldn't talk, it was hard not to come to negative conclusions, and that another test would allay suspicions. They passed with flying colors, but it doesn't seem to me that anyone's suspicions have been allayed at all. When I expressed this thought to Edgar, he said, "You know how it is, Barbara. Some people think when there's smoke, there has to be a fire."

Sarah's voice in my ear brought me back to reality. ". . . if you'd like to join us?"

"Sorry, Sarah," I said, "could you repeat that?"

She cleared her throat. "The Action Rights Abortion Alliance is planning a protest march in Syracuse at the end of October, and I was wondering if you'd like to join us."

"Are you a member?"

"I joined after the bombing, because I believe women have rights that shouldn't be trampled on."

"Good for you."

Sarah warmed to her words. "Or that other people should tell a woman what she can or can't do with her own body."

"I agree," I said. "Absolutely."

"Women have to have control over their reproductive rights!"

"Oh, yes," I said, smiling at her vehemence, but also wishing I could be as young and as passionate again. Not that I was ever like Sarah. I didn't channel my youthful passions into philosophies or political movements. I was too much a product of my parents to question or challenge authority, and far too busy putting my energies into trying to grow up in the way deemed proper at the time, by finding a husband and anticipating my future career as a wife and mother. My life has taken a certain path, but regret would be too strong a word to describe how I feel about it. Rather, the sensation is a faint sense of loss, the kind of grief I feel when I hear that a young person has died, someone unknown to me but whose life showed vitality and promise. That's the person I lost when I chose Dan and Cassandra, an unknown woman with untapped abilities, my shadow self.

"So you'll go on the march?" Sarah asked.

"Who else is going?"

"Frances Phillips. She said yes right away."

"And your mom?"

"Uh-huh."

"Okay, you can sign me on, too."

"Thanks!"

On the bridge night following Daphne's abortion we don't play bridge at all. First of all the abortion took place two days earlier, and Daphne is cramping and clotting and wants to lie flat with a heating pad on her abdomen. But she didn't want to cancel our bridge night, only the bridge. She insisted we come to her house as scheduled and provide her with moral support. "Matt's small supply of nurturing has run out," she said to me on the phone, "and besides, he agreed to clean the house." So we sit in Daphne's extraordinarily tidy living room, sipping tea and plying her with aspirin, sympathy, and conversation about protest marches, abortions, and sexual experiences.

"Here's what I've learned about abortions," Daphne says, shifting and wincing. "They're not open-heart surgery, but they're not trivial either. You can get up and walk afterward, but it hurts like hell, somewhere between menstrual cramps and childbirth. The only thing good about it is that the alternative is so much worse."

"I had an abortion once," Virginia says, and we look at her in surprise. "Back in the bad old days. I was nineteen and in college. A friend of mine knew a woman doctor who would do it. So it wasn't one of those back-room horror stories, at least I got decent medical care, but I was terrified. But she wanted two hundred dollars, and I had to tell my mother. I thought she'd kill me, but she got the money somehow and covered up for me. But you know something? She never talked about it, she never even asked me how I felt. It was a nonsubject. As far as she was concerned, it never happened. I guess it was too painful for her."

"Mothers are funny," Daphne says.

"But we're mothers," I point out.

We laugh and Daphne remembers travelling to Washington to join a huge rally in support of *Roe* v. *Wade*. "I had to leave Celia with Matt. She was two or so. I had this wonderful weekend, marching and screaming and singing and feeling at one with all my sisters. Then I came home to find Celia had strep throat, Matt hadn't washed a dish, and a dirty diaper was floating around in the upstairs toilet. What a downer."

"Well, I'm glad young women like Sarah are getting involved," I say. "I had this feeling teenage girls think feminism is passé."

Virginia shakes her head. "Sarah doesn't consider herself a feminist. She says she's a humanist, she's interested in everybody's rights—men, women, children, the earth."

"Sarah's going to be someone important some day," I say. "She's going to move mountains."

"And feel a lot of pain," Virginia says. "She suffers more about everything than anybody I know."

"But she's right and I'm proud of her," Frances says. "We can't sit back while pro-lifers bomb clinics. We can't let them turn the clock back on us."

"God," Daphne says, "remember what it was like when your period was late? Remember the Fate Worse Than Death?"

Virginia and I nod, but Frances says, "Actually, I was a virgin when I got married, technically, that is."

Daphne snorts. "I just *loved* those girls in the dorm who claimed they were going to be virgins on their wedding nights so help them God, and you knew they were petting like crazy. When you told them they could still get pregnant if the guy had sperm on his fingers, they went into shock."

"Oh, I was naive," Frances says. "My mother was too uptight to tell me anything about sex."

"But I wonder if we haven't gone too far in the other direction," I say. "There's so much sex everywhere—in the movies and videos and magazines. It seems so blatant. Is there any value to mystery?"

"To privacy, maybe," Virginia says.

"Well, I've got something for you straight from the horse's mouth," Daphne says. "My cousin's twenty-year-old daughter informed her that it's easy to find good sex, but it's hard to find good men."

We sit there in silence, our mugs of tea poised at our mouths.

"I couldn't have said that at twenty," Virginia says.

"Me either," I say, thinking it was the reverse for me. I had found Dan, who was a patient and wonderful man but whose sexual experiences had been limited to fumbling encounters in the backseats of cars. Our first acts of intercourse were not spectacularly successful, particularly from my point of view. But then I wasn't entirely sure how to make them better. I knew how to masturbate myself to orgasm, but I didn't think I had any right to ask a man to do the same things I did to myself. It took several months of experimentation, whispered questions and answers, and the realization that Dan's enthusiasm was genuine for me to tell him exactly what I wanted. At the time I thought how unfortunate it had been that while my mother was so forthcoming about menstruation, she'd been unable to talk about sexual satisfaction. All she'd told me was that when there was love between two people, happiness followed. Now I wonder if it's really any better to have the mechanics down pat, if the emotional context is so thin.

"We're going to have to face the fact," Frances says, "that our children are going to be a lot more sexually active than we ever were."

"Not going to be," Daphne says. "*Are* more. I think even Julian's getting some."

"Julian!" I exclaim. "He's only fourteen."

"Fifteen, as of two weeks ago, and going steady with the Steiner girl."

"But she isn't in high school yet, is she?" Virginia asks.

"She's better developed than I was at eighteen," Daphne says. "When she's over here, I can practically feel the hormones raging." She gasps slightly and presses her hand to her abdomen.

We all lean forward. "Are you okay?" I say.

"Seven point nine on the Richter scale," she says, and gives us a jaunty smile. "Don't worry. I'll survive."

But when Frances and I drive home, our mood is somber. We talk about how pale and thin Daphne is, and how unfair nature is to make women fertile long after they've completed their families and are finished having babies. We talk about Julian and the Steiner girl and agree that early sex will cause changes in the way men treat women and women treat men, although we're not sure exactly what. And we shake our heads about how times have changed and wonder what it all means.

We arrive at my house, and I put my hand on the door handle. "Thanks for the ride," I say.

"No problem," Frances says, but when I've opened the door, she adds, "Have you by any chance noticed how much time Joel spends at Marla Hudson's?"

"I know he goes over there. The pool's a big attraction."

"There's no water in the pool now."

I close the door. "What do you mean?"

"Joel's there a lot, and so is Ben."

I study Frances's face, which, even when frowning, has a beautiful symmetry and color. "Do you think she had something to do with their fight?"

"I don't know."

"Isn't she helping Ben with his writing?"

Frances nods.

"I thought you were pleased about that."

"I was. It's just that . . . oh, maybe I'm just imagining things, except Ben's so different. It doesn't show on the outside. He keeps up his schoolwork, but he's lost any . . . lightness he had. He's moody and stiff. He hardly talks to me at all. He . . ." her voice trails off.

"All the boys under suspicion are having problems. Karen Palmeri told me Bobby wants to drop out of school. Tim Kyle got in trouble shoplifting. And look at Joel." I'm trying to be soothing, but all I've done is make myself feel awful, remembering the argument Dan and Joel had at dinner over an economics paper due the next day, which Joel hadn't started but said he would write that night. Like all such arguments, which are more and more frequent, this one went around and around with Joel becoming increasingly less communicative while Dan grew ever more frustrated. I stepped in when Dan's voice started rising, because I knew how bad he would feel later on. Dan's not accustomed to being angry, but lately he can't help himself, and I understand only too well. "We feel so helpless," I add. "It's awful."

Frances sighs. "I'm sorry. I know I'm not the only one who's suffering. Maybe what I'm doing is looking for a scapegoat—someone to blame for something no one can fix."

"Let's hope that when Molly and Virginia go on *Oprah*, something good will come of it. Some news, something."

"Oh, Barbara, we know that's a crock, don't we?" Frances says, and a sudden despair makes her voice shrill. "All that energy expended on nothing, all that useless, *wasted* hope. When I see Molly, I just want to shake her and say let it go, let it goddamn *go*."

"Frances—"

"But then on the other hand, I know how important that hope is to her. Then I feel terrible, because I'm being so selfish, and at least I have my child safe at home." She pauses. "Except that it doesn't feel safe. I have this sensation of dread inside as if something terrible is going to happen."

I put my hand on her arm. "What could happen?"

"I don't know."

I think of our vacation without Joel at The Rideau Manor, and I say, "It isn't just Caroline. It's the children growing up and changing."

Frances takes a deep breath. "I feel like I've had to be everything to Ben, because Paul lives so far away. I guess I'm finding it hard to handle the fact that he doesn't need me the same way, and that I can't fix things for him anymore."

I have a sudden vision of Ben and Joel heading out to play one snowy day when they were three years old. Both little boys were dressed in heavy sweaters and pants, topped by thick snowsuits (Joel's was red; Ben's blue), hats, mittens, and boots. Frances and I had pulled the hoods of the snowsuits over their toques and wrapped scarves around their necks, which we pulled up in the front to cover their mouths and noses and tied in big knots in the back. There was almost nothing of them visible except their eyes and foreheads. They walked out into the snow, waddling in the manner of drunken sailors and very young children who've been bundled up tight by their mothers against the cold.

I say, "This is going to pass, Frances, and they're going to be okay. They're going to become men and have careers and families, and someday we're going to be sitting in our rocking chairs, remembering that rough year we had back in nineteen ninety."

"We're not going to laugh," Frances says.

"No, but it'll just be a faint memory with all the sharp points and hard edges worn off."

"You're right," Frances says. "I know you're right."

"Everyone grows up."

"Actually, I know a lot of people in arrested adolescent development."

"But do their mothers still take care of them?"

Frances smiles at me. "Not one."

"There. See?"

Frances puts her arm around me and squeezes. "Thanks, Barbara, I needed that."

I hug her back, but I needed it, too. Motherhood is like that day many years ago when I got caught in the waves at Jones Beach. It's hard to keep your footing when you're being battered by changes and events that seem overwhelming. Sometimes you have to fight hard to keep your balance, sometimes you need someone to pull you upright, and sometimes it's all you can do to tread in one place and keep your head above water.

Chapter

3

On the last Tuesday in October, on my day off, Marla phones me early in the morning. "I'm back," she says, "and no more traveling for a while." She's been busy with the house and the film being made of her book *Silver Crescents*. Every once in a while she'd fly down to South Carolina and visit the set where the film was being shot. She explained to me that she had the right to visit but not to interfere, a situation that could have been more frustrating except that, on the whole, she really liked what the director was doing with the script.

"Have they finished shooting?" I ask.

"It's in the can, and I want to celebrate today."

"Today?" I say hesitantly. I got up in the morning with chores and errands heavily on my mind. "I don't know. I've got a lot to do."

"Have you looked outside?"

I've spent the last hour in the basement, performing the seasonal clothing exchange, taking winter clothes out of the quilted bags and putting the summer clothes in. Now I take a good look outside my kitchen window. It's one of those glorious autumn days when the sky is clear, there's no wind, and the leaves of the trees are a brilliant yellow, orange, and russet. On days like these the tree-covered hillsides around Cassandra seem to be covered in sheets of flames.

"We're not going to have too many more days like this," she says.

"No," I say, "but—"

"And I bought one of those sensational-looking picnic baskets from Garibaldi's."

Garibaldi's is a business in Laurel Grove whose picnic baskets are famous throughout central New York. They're the old-fashioned kind, made of heavy wicker, shaped like suitcases, and packed with china, linens, flatware, and goblets. The staff also provides gourmet meals with themes, like Sybaritic Suppers and Lunches for Lovers.

"I've got cold chicken braised with mango," Marla continues, "herbed potato salad, hearts of palm and cherry tomatoes in vinaigrette, and amaretto cheesecake."

"Oh," I say, weakening.

"What's the alternative?"

"Vacuuming, grocery shopping, the hardware store."

"Bobbie, you need a life."

I sigh. "This is true," although I think it's easy for Marla to say. She has a cleaning lady who comes twice a week.

"Close your eyes and picture this," Marla says. "We're sitting on a blanket beside a rock whose surface has been covered by a checkered cloth. Our lunch is spread out on the cloth. The china is cream encircled by a pale green band. There's a crystal bud vase with one yellow rose."

I've closed my eyes, but now I open them. "You're kidding."

"Absolutely not. A crystal bud vase with a yellow rose, sterling knives and forks, goblets rimmed with silver. We sip our wine and nibble on strawberries."

By now I'm smiling. "And no bugs," I say.

"Not at this time of year. Just the sun to warm us and a light breeze to keep us comfortable."

Marla's always had the ability to transport me into another world that's more interesting and magical than my own. When I was younger, she created fantastical places that existed only in our imaginations. At thirteen years old, we made-believe the rec room in her basement was a stage and played at being beautiful dancers or singers; at sixteen, her bedroom became a runway on which we became seductresses, stripping to flashlights and the beat of imaginary music. Now she has the money to create a different kind of fantasy, one where I can step out of my life in Cassandra for a few hours, leave behind the dirty kitchen floor and the three mounds of dirty underwear, shirts, and sheets, and act like one of those gentlewomen in Victorian novels whose leisure is built on class, money, and servants.

"I'm tempted," I say.

"Good," Marla says. "I'll pick you up at twelve."

I didn't ask where the picnic was going to take place, because I didn't really care, but I'm taken aback in an unpleasant way when Marla turns off Highway 240 and onto the road that leads to Misty Lake.

"Misty Lake?" I say.

"It's beautiful this time of year," she says.

"So are Pike Lake and Blue Springs Lake."

"I come here often," she says.

What can I say? It's her picnic, I'm an invited guest, and I lost the right of refusal when I agreed to come. But I don't like the lake, I haven't for years, even though a lot of people in Cassandra think it's the prettiest one around and spend many hours during the summer swimming in it and sunbathing on the rocks. I've always found it uncomfortable, although I didn't always know why. Now as we get out of the car, I understand that I prefer a sandy beach to a pebbly one. And I don't like the narrowness of the beach and the sharp upward angle of the hill behind it. I realize that every time I've been at the lake, I've had the same uneasy feeling that the hill is hovering at my back and that the trees, rocks, and earth will break away and fall on me.

We take the picnic basket and blanket out of the car, and Marla leads me up a pathway that winds from the graveled parking area up into the trees. We're dressed for picnicking, but Marla is a lot more elegant than I am. Her jeans are cut tight and have blue leather pockets, her sweatshirt is white with a handpainted Mexican design in blue and gold, and

she wears turquoise drop earrings and a gold chain necklace.
I'm in my old stretch jeans and a cast-off sweatshirt of Dan's
with the name of his company, LogoDraw, across the chest.
I don't wear any jewelry.

"Here we are," Marla says. "Isn't it nice?"

We've arrived at an open space about halfway up the
hillside that's perfect for a picnic. The ground is flat and
mossy, and there's a wide, flat rock jutting out from the
earth that can serve as a table. We'll be able to sit and eat,
looking down at the lake. The water is calm, a clear, steely
green, shaded by overhanging trees, and we seem to be the
only people for miles. All I hear are birds singing, the rustle
of squirrels, and the sounds Marla makes as she opens the
picnic basket and sets out our lunch. The china is indeed
creamy and edged in pale green, the rose is yellow, and the
glassware has rims of sterling silver.

"How pretty," I say.

"Do you like martinis?" she asks.

"You packed martinis?"

She lifts a small silver shaker. "I even have olives." She
hands me a wide-mouthed goblet.

"Martinis and wine at lunch," I say. "This must be very
California."

"Actually," Marla says, "no one drinks liquor at lunch in
L.A. They don't have to. They're all intoxicated by dreams
of fame and fortune." She pours the martini into my glass,
opens a jar, and adds two olives. Then she opens a shallow
plastic box and offers me rounds of pumpernickel bread
topped with cream cheese, capers, and slices of smoked
salmon.

"Mmmm," I say, nibbling appreciatively. "Is L.A. such an
unreal place?"

She nods. "Built on quicksilver."

"Do you miss it?"

"No."

The martini makes a warm path down my throat. "But
isn't Cassandra boring?"

"Do *you* find it boring?"

"No, but then I haven't lived in California."

"It's good here for me," Marla says. "It's solid."

Then I can't help myself and ask the question that's been burning on my tongue for months. "Is Didi going to come to live here?" And I'm immediately sorry, because the question hangs in the air between us for a long, uncomfortable silence while Marla stares at the lake, and I don't know where to look. *You're too curious, Barbara,* my mother used to tell me, *and you know what curiosity did to the cat.* "Not that it's any of my business," I add quickly.

There's another long pause, and then Marla says, "She was knifed to death in L.A. last year."

I'm so shocked that I don't know what to do or say. The sun doesn't feel warm anymore, and I sit frozen, staring at her, at the way her drop earring brushes her shoulder when she turns her head to look at me. She's very calm. "I'm sorry. I should've told you before."

I take a deep, shaky breath. "No, I'm the one who's sorry," I say. "I'm so, so sorry."

Marla sips her martini and looks back at the lake. "After it happened, I stopped writing. I couldn't stand California anymore. I had nowhere to go, so I came here. And it's helped, even though I couldn't wait to leave Cassandra when I was growing up. Funny, isn't it? How our childhood places turn out to be so important."

But I'm hardly listening to her. I'm imagining Joel dead, bleeding to death like Didi, and I've seen so many tragedies on television I can create the entire scene in seconds: the dark streets, the screams, the sound of running feet, the blood on the pavement, the sirens, the ambulance, the police. Tears fill my eyes. "Oh, Marla," I say, "it must have been terrible."

"It was terrible. It was worse than anything I've ever been through—even Christian's death."

Maybe it's the heat of the martini in my blood, or the shock of Marla's news, or the hideous scene in my mind's eye, but the words break out of me in a furious burst. "I hate this place! I don't know why you come here."

"Yes, you do."

I shake my head.

"Think back to that night."

"Oh, no," I say angrily, "I'm not playing that game with you. The past is over."

"The past lives in the present."

"He's been dead for twenty-five years. For god's sake, let him rest."

"Why?"

"Because there's no point in dredging things up."

"What things?"

Her questions are like small, sharp hooks, the kind Dan uses for fishing. I remember that when I first saw Marla in the airport after all those years, I found something cruel and predatory about her features and fierce intensity. I try to think of a way of turning the conversation in another direction. I'm too afraid to talk about Didi so I wave my hand at the food. "Let's eat. What did you promise? Chicken with mango? Amaretto cheesecake?"

Marla doesn't move. "It was you," she says.

"What?"

"You were with Christian before he got in the car."

I try to stare her down, but I feel a tremor in my hands and realize that if I don't put my martini down, I'm going to spill it. Carefully, I put the glass down on the rock, and then I stand up. "I think we better leave."

Marla looks up at me. "Why?"

Another fish hook snares my skin. I feel the hillside pressing against my back, and a nauseating vertigo hits me. Quickly, I put my hand on the trunk of a tree for balance, but I feel as if the vertigo has made part of my mind slip, leaving a dark space that I never knew existed, a space where Frances planted a seed and suspicions have taken root. Instinctively I go on the attack. "The fight was over you, wasn't it?"

"Fight?" she frowns. "What fight?"

"Between Joel and Ben."

She shrugs.

"You're manipulating those boys."

"I like them."

"You've made Joel want you."

"I can't help how he feels."

"Do you know what's happening to him?" I cry. "Do you have any idea unhappy he is?"

"I had nothing to do with Caroline's disappearance."

"But you've made it worse!"

"He had to grow up sometime, Bobbie. He couldn't be a mama's boy forever."

The trembling has spread from my hands to all of me, and I'm racked with shudders in my legs, my abdomen, my chest. That seed of suspicion has flourished beyond imagining. Tendrils of a dark, horrible idea snake through my mind, entwining with thoughts of Tony Molino, and spreading in seconds until I can think of nothing else. I hold on to a branch of the tree but lean forward and hiss, "Don't you dare sleep with him."

Marla gives me a startled look. "I'm not going to sleep with Joel," she says. "You don't have to worry about that."

"Promise me!"

She takes a sip of her martini.

"Promise me!"

"Bobbie, I don't need Joel. I'm sleeping with Ben."

For a brief second, the flood of relief pushes the vertigo away, but then it's back again, and the hill is falling down onto me, and my mind cracks wider, part of it slipping sideways, sickeningly, revealing another dark place, another horrible vision. I cry out, and Marla stands up quickly.

"Bobbie?"

A larger sound comes out of me, a wail that I hear as if from a very long distance.

"Bobbie! Are you all right?"

I crouch down, put my hands over my face. I'm engulfed in the dark place and crushed by the memories that have been hidden there.

Memory: broad shoulders, dark curly hair, green eyes outlined in dark lashes, jealousy and desire, a wanting so badly that I ached with it and could hardly bear to be near him.

Memory: a moonlit night, laughter in the distance, the crackle of fire, a guitar being strummed erratically. I'm standing under the very same trees that shade me now, and I hear voices raised, arguing, angry, pleading, denying, cursing.

Memory: moving quickly, a shadow among shadows, intercepting him as he came, whispering so he'd know I was there, holding him from leaving, and feeling the muscles in his arm tense under my fingers.

"No!" I say, and stand up so suddenly that Marla backs away. Then I start running, crashing down through the trees, falling and stumbling, nausea pressing its thick hand against the back of my throat.

"Bobbie!"

I hear Marla behind me, but I don't stop running. I can't. If I stop for one second, I'm afraid the rest of the memory will escape from the darkness where it's been concealed for so long. I reach the beach and turn blindly to the left away from the car. I head for the rock where Sandy Arbut jumped that night, fully dressed, into the lake.

"Bobbie!"

But the memory keeps pushing, slipping out past the heavy pounding of my heart and the sharp intake of my breath, and I'm no longer running on the pebbly beach but am standing with my back against a tree. I can feel the roughness of the bark through the thin cotton of my blouse and the scrape of it on my hair as the pressure of Christian's mouth on mine bends my head back. How I wanted that mouth. I've watched it in class, dreamed of it, pressed my lips against my pillow, hated Martha for owning it. I've fantasized about the day Christian would realize I was the one he wanted, me, Bobbie Gardiner, who was not as pretty as Martha Hudson, not as vivacious, but sweet all the same, and just right for him. I wouldn't tease him the way she did. I wouldn't play with his feelings and make him jealous. I would give him all the love that filled my heart and made it swell until I thought it would explode from the pressure.

I played out the same soap opera scenario a thousand times—the day it would hit him that I was the one, the sudden recognition in his eyes, the slow, achingly beautiful smile as he looked at me, the secret meetings, the passion between us, the day we let the world know who we were. I never went so far as to imagine Martha's anger and jealousy, that was too painful and I felt too guilty. But the fantasy was there no matter how hard I tried to like Brian and simulate passion when we petted in the backseat of his car. Poor Brian. I committed falsehoods whenever I was with him, closing my eyes and making believe it was Christian's mouth, Christian's hands, Christian's body.

So what was I thinking that night when I heard Christian coming through the trees and knew how angry and upset he was? When I grabbed him by the arm and pulled him deep into the shadows? When I pulled his head down and kissed him as passionately and fiercely as I knew how, pushing my tongue between his lips and arching my back so my breasts pressed against his chest? I didn't bother to think. It was my wildest fantasies come to life, the moment I'd dreamed about for so long coming true. And it didn't matter that he hadn't had that sudden recognition of my value and importance. It didn't matter that I was just an object on which he could expend his sexual energy and take whatever revenge on Martha that he wanted. Nothing mattered but the feel of his lips, his hand on my breast, the edge of his cheekbone illuminated by the moonlight. It seemed enough to me that he was there and, after his first gasp of disbelief, hot and eager.

That heat—the driving passion of a young male being given his head after months of frustration. Nothing in my experience with boys had prepared me for what was to come. Nothing. Now I start coughing, the vomit rising in my throat. I'm forced to stop and kneel down at the water's edge as salmon, capers, cream cheese, and pumpernickel explode from my throat. I'm crying, too, and my chin is covered with tears and saliva.

Marla kneels down next to me and takes me by the shoulders. "Bobbie, I'm sorry. I only wanted to know the truth. I don't really care what happened."

But I can't stand her voice or her sympathy. I stand up and start running again, leaving her by the water's edge. I'm back in that dark shadowy place under the trees, but I'm no longer standing. We're on the ground now, and I'm naked. My clothes have come off faster than I would have thought believable—my blouse disappeared, my shorts were yanked off, my bra and panties stripped away. I lie in moss, leaves, and earth, and Christian is everywhere, kissing my mouth, feeling my breasts, taking the nipples between his teeth. I don't dare make a sound, even when his fingers touch that very place I've denied Brian for so long. Christian's not naked, but his pants are unzipped and, along with his underpants, have been pulled down below his erection, which juts up against my hip. He makes a deep sound in his throat when my legs fall open and his fingers slide up into me. I, who have never even done that to myself, lie rigidly back as he probes with one finger, two, and then three. I feel myself being roughly stretched and pulled, and tears spring into my eyes. But still I make no sound, because isn't this what I wanted? Isn't this what I asked for?

And then Christian's on me, in me, pushing and causing a sharp pain as he enters, and I understand that I never wanted this. Not his belt buckle grinding into my skin. Not his weight pressing the air out of my chest. Not the brutal, careless pounding that drives me into the earth. I wanted something different, something softer, gentler, caring, but it's too late. I'm crying silently as he ejaculates and grunts, my head bent back, tears flowing back into my hair. For a few minutes, he lies on top of me, breathing hard, his mouth against my tensed throat.

"Bobbie?" he whispers.

I don't answer, I can't, and when he slides out of me, I curl onto my side, pull my knees up, and bury my face in my hands.

"Bobbie, are you okay?" He touches my shoulder so tentatively it could be a butterfly alighting on my skin. "Bobbie?"

I crunch up tighter.

"Shit," he says under his breath. "Goddamn fuck." I hear his fist slam into the tree by my head, another curse, a sound that could be a sob, and the metal screech of a zipper being yanked up. My clothes land across my legs, and then he's gone. His leaving was a cold breeze slithering down my bare back so that I begin to tremble.

Now I've run as far as I can—to the far edge of the rocky ledge that's cantilevered high out over the lake. My chest is heaving from the exertion of running, and I'm still crying, but now I wipe my eyes and look into the water. No one has ever found out how deep the water is under the ledge, only that the shore below it disappears at a steep angle. Generations of teenage boys have tried to dive to the bottom but have come up sputtering and gasping for air, defeated by the depth and the coldness of the water. I don't know why I've come out to the very edge, only that I feel the need to look down into water as deep as I can find as if there will be answers there to how memory can be hidden so cunningly and how a person can be tricked by her own mind. It's obvious that my guilt over Christian's death and betrayal of Marla must have been so painful, so overwhelming that I managed to erase it, wiping it away as if my mind were a slate and sex with Christian had been only a mark made upon it in chalk. What I find so painful now, and so disorienting, is how I could have spent the next twenty-five years in such ignorance.

"It's too cold to swim." Marla stands on the beach near the ledge, and although she's attempting to be lighthearted, I can tell by her voice that she's frightened.

But I don't want her to see what has become of my face, which feels as if it has sagged into a thousand heavy folds, so I face the hillside where the land rises so steeply out of the water that there's no more beach. Bits of land poke out into the lake, jagged rocks, angled trees, and clumps of vegetation. The water, free of the summer algae, is so clear I can see the tops of water weeds swaying beneath the surface of the lake. Something catches my eye, filaments of something swaying along with the weeds that is not weed, twig, or fish. I strain to look deeper, below the glitter of the sun on the surface. And then I figure it out. A strand of red is loosely encircling a tall, green stem, and if I follow it down just a bit, I can see it's attached to a pale, oval disk that floats below.

My scream pierces the air and echoes around the lake, and

then I scream again. Marla runs onto the ledge and out to me, grabbing me by the hand. "Bobbie! What is it?"

My teeth have started chattering, and I can hardly speak. "Over there . . . see it? Over . . . over there."

"Where?"

I clutch her hard, pull her toward me so her head is at the same angle as mine. "In the weeds."

"The weeds," she echoes.

I lift a trembling finger and point. "See?"

"I don't see . . ." I feel her stiffen. "Oh my God."

And then I'm sinking down to the rock, and she's holding me, and I'm crying so hard I think I'll never stop, and she's saying, "It's okay, Bobbie. It's okay. It's going to be all right."

EPILOGUE

THANKSGIVING

It is customary for some of us in Cassandra to spend the Thanksgiving meal together. Different couples host the event in different years, but no one is totally responsible for the meal. The hosts provide the turkey, stuffing, gravy, and cranberry sauce. The rest of us contribute other dishes. Daphne is famous for her sweet potato casserole, which is made with cream, marshmallows, and cornflakes. I usually make a potato scallop according to a recipe handed down by my grandmother to my mother to me. And we all make desserts, because one dessert would be disappointing. But this year, Ben and Joel have convinced Marla that she should combine Thanksgiving with a party to show off her house, her first social event in Cassandra. She's invited Dan and me, Daphne and Matt, Virginia and Raymond, Frances, Brian and Molly, and all the children, and her meal is being cooked, delivered, and served by Rendezvous, the most exclusive caterer in Laurel Grove.

Curiosity, freedom from cooking, and the pleasures of being waited on are so seductive that we don't hesitate to throw tradition aside, even though we firmly believe that store-bought food is never as good as homemade. By five o'clock on the afternoon of November 25, we're gathered at Marla's, admiring her house and being served champagne by two black-suited waiters who glide silently in and out of the kitchen, carrying goblets and hors d'oeuvres on silver trays. We're all dressed for the occasion. The men are in suits, and the women are wearing their Sunday best, although no one can out-elegant Marla, who's wearing diamonds at her ears and neck and a black silk dress with a scoop neck and long, slim skirt whose simplicity is both expensive and stunning. I'm in a red dress shot through with silver and gold threads that I bought the week before at Trottman's in Laurel Grove where the prices can take your breath away. Joel is wearing a new suit, a dark blue worsted with a blue and red tie, and his hair has been slicked back in a style once favored by thirties gangsters. I think he looks incredibly handsome, but when I told him so, he said thanks and added, "But you're my mother." Which is true, but I don't think it prejudices me one way or the other.

Marla's house is beautiful. She's maintained the charm of coves, moldings, and the lovely details of an older home while eliminating the dark corners and inconveniences. We go on a tour with our drinks in our hands and ooh and aah over the ultramodern kitchen and bathrooms, the turret with its curving windows, and the modern glass sculpture that's lit within and cascades down over the staircase. A pale blue-and-rose oriental carpet stretches across the living room floor, and the room is large enough for several conversation areas with rose leather sofas and chairs upholstered in fabric of cream, pale blue, and green. We would be more jealous of this display of wealth and cooler to Marla (Cassandrans don't believe in ostentation), but the story of Didi has made us compassionate. When I told Frances, Daphne, and Virginia, they were horrified, but I could tell they were thinking, with only the slightest smugness, that money can't buy happiness, that's for sure.

When we finish the tour, we sit around the fireplace, enjoying the leaping flames while the wind howls outside and sleet drives against the windows. I think that a stranger standing in the entrance to the living room wouldn't guess from our conversation (we're discussing house renovations) and the occasional laughter that we are fragile, all of us recovering in one way or another from the discovery of Caroline's body in Misty Lake. Of course, it hit Molly and Brian the hardest, particularly Molly, who had held on to her hopes so tenaciously. I don't think Brian ever believed Caroline was still alive. They're here and smiling, but they look exhausted, and Molly's hair, which she stopped dyeing, is now almost white.

The mystery of Caroline's murder didn't even last long enough for the police to start a serious investigation. Three days after her body was pulled out of the lake, Mary Morris's son, Robert, who was a year behind Caroline in school, hung himself from a beam in the attic of his house. He was a thin, quiet boy with a bad complexion, who, as it turns out, no one knew very well, including his mother. The key to who he was in a diary that the police found in his bedroom. It was torn, smudged, and incoherent in places, but the police were able to piece together a sad and horrible story of sexual fantasies that named half-a-dozen girls in Cassandra, dark visions of blood and murder, rambling tracts on Nazis and white supremacy, and an account of Caroline's death complete with a map and crude pictures of knives and guns.

Robert had taken his mother's car that morning (she walked to work), picked up Caroline on her way to school, and driven her to Misty Lake. The diary didn't tell why she got into the car with him, whether she got frightened when she discovered he was driving her someplace else, or if she struggled with him or cried out at any time. According to Reg, the diary listed each event of the murder in a brief sentence beside a small dagger dripping blood. Robert had gotten her out onto the ledge, strangled her with his belt, raped her, filled her jacket with stones, and rolled her and her bookbag off into the water. Then he went home, put the car back in the garage, and biked to school. The records show that Robert wasn't late for school that day but was in his homeroom at the sound of the first bell. Reg also told me that the police figure it must have taken the entire spring and summer for Caroline's clothes to rot sufficiently for the stones to no longer hold the body down. By autumn her body had risen and would have surfaced, if what was left of her pants hadn't snagged on an underwater log.

It was also clear from Robert's diary that he was terrified by the emotions in Cassandra after the discovery of Caroline's body. It shook the whole town, making all of us look with covert and frightened glances at our neighbors as if they were unknown to us. The old fears of a killer loose in Cassandra resurfaced, and gossip had it that the police planned to search every house in town. Many people were horrified that they'd spent the summer swimming, jumping, diving, and having a good time above the place where the body must have been lying. There was a lot of anger and talk of vengeance. There were mutterings about lynchings not being good enough for whoever committed such a heinous crime.

I suppose we should be grateful that Robert spared us the torment of a trial and the rehashing of horrible facts, but his suicide had its own painful repercussions. Mary, who's been divorced from Robert's father for many years (he lives in Rochester), collapsed and had to be hospitalized for several weeks. Her older daughter came back from college to run the dry cleaner's but recently hung a sign on the window that says CLOSED FOR THE SEASON. Friends of Mary say she's going to sell her house and business and move to Florida, where her mother is living. They say she's developed heart palpitations and is so nauseated she can hardly eat. They say she feels she can't hold her head up in Cassandra or look anyone in the eye. I never knew Mary well, but I feel a deep horror whenever I think about what she must feel, that sensation of the earth disappearing beneath her feet and the long fall into the dark depths of despair. I can sympathize with her even as I shy away from her pain. How well do any of us know our children? How well do any of us know our spouses or our friends? How well do we even know ourselves?

What wasn't clear from Robert's diary was whether he'd had anything to do with the graffiti that had been written on the lockers, garage doors, and Ashley Drugs. It isn't mentioned in the diary, and Reg is of the opinion that the vandalism was the work of someone else or a group of persons who would get a sick excitement not from committing murder but from taking advantage of it to create some mayhem. Piggybackers, Reg called them during his news conference on local TV. "Assholes" was what he said in private, adding that if he ever found out who did it, they'd feel the letter of the law, by God, crushing them right into the ground.

By the end of November, one could say that Cassandra, if not normal, was back on an even keel. Phil Potter had closed the school for the week of the two funerals and brought in a host of psychologists and social workers when the school reopened. Deacon's Hardware was also open again, although Brian was only coming in half-time. Virginia told me Molly couldn't bear the job of getting rid of Caroline's things so Brian was doing it. The producer of *Oprah* didn't cancel the show on missing kids, but she was no longer interested in having the Deacons and Silvers on the panel, saying they might do a show in the spring on grieving parents and would contact Molly then. There was also a flurry of publicity, but it died away once the funerals were over and other tragedies took their place on the front pages of the newspapers. I heard gossip that ABC was thinking of a TV movie of the week, but Marla told me it wasn't true. She knew someone who knew someone big in television in New York, and the word was that, despite the twist Sarah had given the story, Caroline's murder wasn't all that interesting or different from the thousands of others around the country that occurred every year.

A waiter whispers in Marla's ear, and she stands up and announces that dinner is served. We file into the dining room where two tables (the grown-up table and the teenage table) have been set with white linen, bone china, sterling silver, and cut-glass goblets. Ben and Joel have appointed themselves assistants, and usher people into their seats. I'm put between Brian and Matt and opposite Virginia while Dan sits at Marla's left near the head of the table. One waiter fills the wineglasses while the other brings in the turkey, already sliced but put back together in its original shape, on a huge platter, and we all applaud. Then as the waiters come back and forth from the kitchen, bearing platters of food, Brian clinks his fork against his glass and stands up.

In the silence, everyone looks at him, and he clears his throat. "Considering this is Thanksgiving, I'd like to give some special thanks today on behalf of Molly and myself. First to our gracious hostess who's made this Thanksgiving a special one for all of us and especially me, who usually has to carve the turkey."

Marla nods, we smile, and Raymond, who is also usually dragooned into carving, says, "Hear, hear."

"Secondly, I want to give thanks to all of you, our friends, who've stood by us during this difficult time in our lives. We know you've been there for us, and we're grateful."

"You would've done it for us," Virginia says, and we murmur our assent.

Brian clears his throat again, and I see that his hands, which are resting on slightly bent fingers spread out on the tablecloth, are trembling slightly. "And thirdly, well, I don't think God would think me ungrateful if I don't thank him today for taking Caroline away from us. But I know He works in ways I'll never understand but must accept to the best of my ability." Molly lifts her napkin to her mouth and holds it there as if she's going to cry. "But Molly and I do want to give special thanks today that our ordeal is over and that, in his mercy, He's seen fit to bring Caroline finally to peace."

Brian sits down abruptly, Matt blows his nose loudly into his napkin, and Frances says, "That was beautiful."

Marla lifts her wineglass and says, "To friends. To Cassandra."

"To friends," we echo. "To Cassandra," and the room fills with the tinkling sound of glass meeting glass.

"And now," Marla adds, "let's eat."

The food is good, and the conversation around the table is livelier than I've ever heard it, but then I think we're not quite ourselves tonight. Brian's speech has made us sentimental, and we hide our feelings by speaking and laughing a little more loudly than we would otherwise. And the elegance of our surroundings and the unusual experience of being waited on in a private home forces us to be a little more sophisticated than we usually are. We strain for conversation that is smarter and wittier than our ordinary evenings when the men often discuss work, sports, or cars and the women talk about children, shopping, and town gossip. Tonight the conversation revolves around a state legislator who's suddenly resigned, and Matt waxes eloquent about kickbacks and corrupt tendering practices. I listen, but I'm also watching Joel, who is talking earnestly to Sarah.

He's still having trouble at school—there's been another failed algebra exam—but Phil tells me that the psychologists say the healing process is a slow one and we have to be patient. Dan finds Joel as prickly as ever, but I think he's slowly emerging from the dark woods he's been inhabiting ever since Caroline disappeared. I sense an easing in him, I think he smiles more frequently. But the strongest evidence is my birthday, which we celebrated quietly with dinner at home—Dan made his only specialties, a variation on Chicken Kiev with swiss cheese and asparagus, and an upside-down pineapple cake that he and Joel decorated with forty-three candles. Joel participated in the meal by helping bake the cake, singing "Happy Birthday," and giving me a kiss (he hasn't kissed me in months) and two gifts. The first was a dark green sweater that I knew Dan had suggested because I'd admired it in a store in Laurel Grove when Dan and I had been shopping. But the second gift was something Joel had picked out himself—a mug decorated with turquoise and yellow flowers and the initials "M.O.M" on one side.

"M.O.M.—Mom," I said. "That's nice."

"Turn it around," Joel said impatiently.

And when I did, I saw that the initials stood for something—"Most Outstanding Mom," which was written in a flowery turquoise script.

"Why, thank you," I said, and tears came into my eyes.

"It's just a mug," Joel said, but that's when he leaned over and kissed me on the cheek.

And then there's Sarah. Joel doesn't seem to go to Marla's anymore, and Virginia's told me that he's come to her house several times and lounged around the living room with Sarah. We're both wondering whether something is developing in that direction. Joel's finally grown tall enough so that he and Sarah can see eye to eye, and Sarah's stopped dyeing her hair and is letting it grow. Also, much to Virginia's relief, she's added colors other than black to her wardrobe. "Nothing too way out," Virginia told us one bridge night. "We're not talking chartreuse here, just the primary colors."

But it may be that Joel and Sarah are just friends, and I think that would be better than a romantic relationship with all its attendant emotions. Joel hasn't had any friends who are girls, and I can't think of a better influence than Sarah with her fierce political passions and constant questioning of the status quo. She wasn't successful at toppling the prom queen and king, and none of us made the abortion rally because of the funerals, but this hasn't stopped her. She's become a vegetarian, joined an environmental watch group and become an avid recycler, causing Virginia and Raymond no end of grief if they fail to adhere to proper guidelines for garbage disposal.

But if my worries for Joel and Sarah are easing, my concern for Ben is not. He continues to excel in school, but Frances finds him more and more distant. I will never tell Frances that he and Marla are lovers, because I couldn't bear to inflict that pain on her, but I also will never believe the relationship is a healthy one. When I talk to Ben, I sense a dark turbulence below his careful reserve as if a volcano were smoldering inside him. I don't talk to Marla about him either. The only thing she will say about Ben is that his soul is older than anyone's she's ever met.

Marla and I spent an evening at her house after Caroline's funeral talking about Christian and drinking until three in the morning. Since I'm not much of a drinker and it doesn't take much to make me tipsy, my three martinis made me so drunk that I was afraid to drive home and had to call Dan, waking him up, and ask him to pick me up. Marla was only slightly less intoxicated than I was, but we both knew the liquor was necessary. It oiled the road to confession and forgiveness, and eased us back into our friendship. We cried so much we used up a box of tissues, but we also laughed a lot too, and more so as the evening went on. Our hilarity reached its greatest and most grotesque height at two-fifteen when we agreed that Christian was not only a lousy lover but an equally lousy driver. We laughed so hard I thought I would die, but we both understood that the blackness of our humor served to put Christian finally to rest.

The evening with Marla has partially helped me come to terms with my shock over the way I had suppressed the past, but I still have a long way to go. Sometimes I feel overwhelmed with tears, and I often lie in Dan's arms at night and cry. Sometimes I'm afraid there are other frightening things hidden in my mind. And sometimes, when I'm walking or working at my desk in the library or standing in front of my sink at home, I have a sudden disoriented feeling, as if the world has shifted. This makes me dizzy and I have to close my eyes until the sensation passes. But knowing about what happened with Christian has also ended certain mysteries in my life—why I threw myself so aggressively into consoling Marla to the point that I almost jeopardized my final exams, why I never wrote to her (other than Christmas cards) or wanted to see her after she left Cassandra, why I tried to turn conversations to a new tack whenever the subject of Christian and that night came up, why I disliked Misty Lake so much, and why my relationship with Eugene in college was so unsatisfactory. He told me I was frigid and cold and should learn how to masturbate. He was right about the latter, but Dan was the beneficiary. I also think Dan's sweetness and gentleness spoke directly to my subconscious, releasing me from the inhibitions that Christian's careless lovemaking had engendered.

We've come to the end of the meal, and people are giving other thanks now, funny ones and silly ones. Marla gives thanks that I've talked her into running for the library board, a job she describes as highbrow/lowbrow, that is, saving literature for the world while slashing unnecessary reading from the budget. The kids throw themselves into giving thanks with fervor. Tracy Deacon gives thanks that her bangs have finally grown out. Julian Feller, who's grown three inches during the summer and is going to be big like Daphne, demonstrates smart-aleckness by thanking his parents for getting it together enough to have had him fourteen years before. I look around the table: at the pool of warm light illuminating the wreckage of our meal; at Frances, who's laughing at something Dan has said to her; at Daphne, who's raised her glass of wine and winks at me over its rim; at all my friends' flushed and smiling faces, and I think these people, these flawed, decent people, are my family—that this is all that I have.

The tears that come so easily to me now threaten to spill over, and I leave the table, murmuring about visiting the amenities. But I don't go to the main-floor bathroom but climb the stairs to the turret room where Marla has created an oasis of peace high among the trees. I need to get away from the sound of the voices and laughter. I need a place to cry where no one will knock on the door or wait outside. The turret room is dark and quiet, except for the sounds of wind, sleet on the windows, and the creaking of branches outside. The only light on in the room is a lamp over Marla's desk. I sit on her bed in the shadows, take a handful of tissues from the box on the night table, and let the tears come. I cry for everything: for Caroline, who was so beautiful; for Marla, who is childless; for Dan and me, who are leaving our youth behind; and for all the Joels who no longer exist, the baby who wiggled into my arms, the little boy who said he was going to marry me when he grew up, the ten-year-old running for all he was worth around the bases during a Little League game. We all lose our children, one way or another, that's what I've come to understand.

I cry my sadness out, knowing it won't be the last time, and then blow my nose and wipe my eyes. My purse is downstairs, and I'll have to get my lipstick and comb and do some repairs before I rejoin the party. I get up, but before I leave the turret, I'm drawn to Marla's desk and the pool of light that illuminates a neat pile of papers beside her computer. I walk over and read:

PROLOGUE

The lake is a dark, gray-green blanket, concealing what lies beneath. Items have dropped off boats and disappeared. Secrets spoken by lovers have fallen to its surface and sunk without trace. In the winter of 1932, a child broke through the ice while trying to cross to the end of the lake on a dare, and his body was never . . .

I shudder and then hear, "Barbara?" I turn and see Dan standing at the top of the stairs, his blond hair gleaming in the light of the chandelier. "Are you okay?"

I walk over, put my arms around his neck, and hug him tightly. I feel the warmth of his body and the solidity of his chest. "I'm fine," I say. "I just needed a few minutes to myself."

KATHRYN

LYNN

DAVIS

ALL

WE HOLD

DEAR

POCKET
B O O K S

Another SUMMER OF L♥VE Trilogy

by Leah Laiman

MAID OF HONOR

THE BRIDESMAID

BRIDE AND GROOM

POCKET BOOKS